THE RIGHT MR. WRONG

emily michel

For Allen.
For a supervillain, you're a pretty nice guy.
I can't wait to see what you do with your life.

AUTHOR'S NOTE

If you don't like spoilers of any kind, skip to Chapter 1. But if you need to know a little to protect your mental health, please read on.

Want to see Ryan's and Elissa's core memories? For free bonus content, other short stories, updates on current and future projects, early looks at covers, excerpts, and review copies, sign up for my Magical Musings Newsletter at

www.EmilyMichelAuthor.com/Newsletter

* * *

This book contains the following elements: profanity, open door sex scenes, alcohol use, difficult parent/adult-child relationships, past cancer diagnosis, hospital visits (unrelated to cancer), and brief mention of a past homophobic incident.

I welcome comments on my website should you find something not mentioned above.

CHAPTER 1
a small request

A crime scene from a B movie—that's what the kitchen looked like, with red sauce, chunks of meat, and wavy noodles everywhere. Tears welled in Elissa's eyes as she wondered what exactly she'd done wrong. The only thing she wanted this New Year's Day was to enjoy the meal she'd prepared with love for her parents and her brother and sister. That was it, a small request of the fates after the worst year she'd ever endured.

She'd spent half the day following her mother's lasagna recipe, the same recipe that had graced the Wrights' table on special occasions for Elissa's entire life. Homemade sauce, premium cheeses, the perfect mix of ground beef and Italian sausage, an offering to whatever god or gods might be watching. Something to guarantee her family better luck in the year to come than in the one past. But the fates deemed it too big a favor, and the remains of the lasagna spread across the kitchen floor, a murder committed on the hopes of her future.

"Elissa, is everything okay?" Her mother poked her head into the kitchen, and her eyes widened as she took in the disaster. "Oh, dear."

Dana's understatement of the year—the lowest of bars, since it was the first day—released the sob that had stuck in Elissa's chest the instant the pan slipped out of the oven mitts. Nothing seemed to go her way lately. This was merely the latest in a long line of misadventures that had started nearly a year ago, with her mother's cancer diagnosis.

Elissa's sobs only grew when her mother pulled her in for a hug. Mom's shushing noises did nothing to soothe Elissa.

They were alone for the moment. Her sister would show whenever it suited her. Dad was out on a walk, but her mom had been too tired to join him. Even now, the dark circles under her eyes sent pangs of guilt through Elissa. Fortunately, her brother was fast asleep. Leo had been the only member of the family to make it to midnight and ring in the New Year last night.

"What happened?" her mother asked when the sobbing finally quieted a few minutes later.

Elissa pulled off the oven mitts and tossed them onto the kitchen counter. She wiped the tears from her cheeks and surveyed the damage.

"It just slipped. I'm sorry, Mom."

"There's nothing to be sorry for. Accidents happen." She rubbed Elissa's back. At least the strength in her hands had returned to normal. "I'll get the dustpan and mop."

"No, I made the mess. I'll clean it up."

"I guess that lesson sunk in deeper than I intended. This is too big. You need an extra pair of hands."

Knowing it would be impossible to convince her mother otherwise, Elissa merely nodded. Her mother went to the utility closet and pulled out the dustpan, the mop, and a bucket. Elissa carefully picked up the remnants of the glass pan. She let out a sigh, grateful her brat of a sister wasn't here to tease her relentlessly, as she always did whenever Elissa made a mistake. Since that rarely happened, Ami never missed an opportunity.

Her mom pulled out her phone.

"Who are you calling?"

"I'm texting your dad so he can go for pizza. It'll be fine, Elissa."

Elissa scooped most of the mess with the dustpan while her

mom went back and forth with her dad for a few minutes. Mom filled the bucket when she was done. She took out the trash and Elissa finished the job. Soon enough, the kitchen was nearly back to its normal, sparkling state.

"Come on. Let me pour you a glass of wine," her mom said with a final swipe of the counters to remove the splattered sauce.

Elissa trudged behind her mother to the festive table, candles lit and light sparkling off their best crystal wine glasses. They were supposed to be celebrating a return to normal after the incredibly crappy year they'd just finished. Perhaps it hadn't gone exactly according to plan, but soon everyone would gather around this table. Together.

That was a good thing, maybe the only good thing to happen in the last year. For a while there, Elissa wasn't sure it would happen.

Mom poured the wine, a little more than what Elissa usually drank and definitely more than the doctor suggested her mother could have.

As if she could read Elissa's mind, her mother said, "Don't start. It's New Year's and an extra-large glass after that mess won't kill me."

"Mom! Don't even joke about it."

Her mother heaved a sigh and ran a hand over her too-short graying hair, newly grown since her last treatment. "I don't know how else to handle it, Lissa. I'm not a crier, and I'm certainly not going to lash out at you for an accident. So, gallows humor it is."

Silence descended as they examined their glasses. On top of her mother's diagnosis, her sister was on academic suspension at the university, her brother had been in the hospital twice in the last year because of his asthma, and Elissa had broken up with her long-term boyfriend. Her father had been the only member of the family not directly touched by their string of bad luck, but he had been run ragged dealing with everyone else's crap.

"Then, to new beginnings." Elissa raised her glass, though

she doubted they'd get what they wanted.

They clinked their glasses and sipped at the red wine.

"I appreciate all the trouble you went through today. You didn't need to." Mom put her glass on the table and rotated it slowly, watching the light play off the wine and the crystal.

Of course Elissa had to go through all the trouble. The mandate her mother had handed her when diagnosed with cancer almost a year ago declared everything should remain as normal as possible.

Her mom's exact words at the family meeting had been, "I don't want anything to change."

As the eldest daughter, "normal" fell primarily on Elissa's shoulders. Ensuring everyone had everything they needed, keeping traditions, updating extended family, even getting the Christmas cards out on time. Things she'd usually helped with but had taken over completely this past year.

And "normal" also meant lasagna for New Year's Day, as it had always been. Her mom was too tired to cook, and Elissa stepped in. She'd asked her useless teenage brother to help, but he'd fallen asleep.

Elissa put down her wine, too. The complex flavors turned to dust in her mouth, and she couldn't swallow. They still had one more hurdle before her father could sound the all-clear. One more follow-up with the oncologist to see if Mom was in remission. Only then would Elissa breathe easy.

"Elissa, now that my chemo is done, you should really consider getting on with your life. I appreciate everything you've done for me, for this family over the last year, but you're twenty-five. It's time for you to live your own life and not worry about us."

Here we go again.

Since her last treatment a few weeks ago, she'd been meddling. When was Elissa going to move out? Had she been on any dates recently? Shouldn't she be looking into getting a newer car?

"Let's see what the doctor has to say, Mom." Elissa wasn't yet ready to trust in her mom's progress. If she did, and the cancer wasn't gone…

"I'm fine. I feel pretty good, actually, and the doctor has always said the chances for remission were high. We caught the cancer early. You need to move on."

"We've talked about this. I want to make sure you're okay before I move out. Anyway, tax season is about to start. I won't have time to find an apartment, let alone move, before April."

Elissa had chosen a practical career in accounting. Most of the year, her hours were normal and manageable. But from February until mid-April, she wouldn't have time to do anything other than work, eat, and sleep.

"Fine. But would you please consider a small request before the IRS ends your social life for three months?"

How could she deny her mother anything? She'd raised three kids—one with a chronic health condition, one with a chronic attitude condition, and one with a chronic tendency for perfectionism—and seemed to have kicked cancer's butt.

"Sure, Mom."

"Go on a date. A friend of mine has a son about your age. He's single. Give it a shot."

Elissa didn't hide her eye roll. Yet another bone of contention between the two was her complete lack of a dating life this past year. She'd stayed in Tucson to take care of her family, and her live-in boyfriend hadn't. Good riddance and a sacrifice she'd make again. Her mom didn't need to worry about her dating life, too, not while waiting for the all-clear from the doc.

Life this past year had consisted of little besides work, chores around the house, toting her brother around town, and Mom's appointments. It wasn't much to brag about, and after all, it was a new year.

New beginnings, right?

"Fine. *One* date, but then you have to lay off. Once you have the all-clear and tax season is over, we can revisit this. Deal?"

"Deal!" Her mom beamed like she'd won an important victory.

Maybe she had.

CHAPTER 2
the cousin group chat

R yan sat with arms crossed on the big, overstuffed leather recliner in the living room, glaring at his father and brother as they waited for his mother to join them. The lack of cars outside when he arrived and the quiet interior had set off alarm bells. His gut insisted he'd walked into a trap, or else the rest of the family, all those aunts, uncles, cousins, second cousins, and great-whatevers, would be here to enjoy the food he smelled cooking in the kitchen.

At the DeMarco clan's annual Christmas brunch, Ryan had politely declined his father's invitation to join them for New Year's dinner. He'd hoped to hook up with the holiday hire before she went back to college in California in two weeks. He should have figured out his parents' plan earlier. The clues had all been there. His parents had each called several times, but he'd never returned those calls. Instead, they'd sent their minion.

His older brother Alex had shown up at the bar where Ryan worked minutes before the New Year's party officially started. Immersed in the chaos of New Year's Eve and with his arms around the holiday hire—what had been her name?—Ryan's stomach plummeted when he caught a glimpse of his brother. His parents weren't going to take no for an answer, apparently.

"What is it?" Ryan asked.

"You need to come for dinner tomorrow, Ry."

"I don't want to come for dinner tomorrow, Alex. I want to sleep and

not deal with the parental bullshit."

"Don't make me do this." Alex pulled out his phone and typed.

"Do what?"

"Invoke the cousin group chat."

Fuck. That was at least a dozen people between his mom's side, his dad's side, and several second cousins, all living in and around Tucson. Best-case scenario, his phone would blow up with messages. Worst-case, they'd all crash the work party and make his night a living hell.

"Fine." He slammed down a heavy beer mug and glared at Alex. "I'll be there. Six?"

"Yeah, six will work. See you then, Ryan."

His mother finally strode in, the tapping of her heels on the terracotta tile silenced by the colorful rug. She made herself comfortable on the couch next to Alex and shared a look with her husband. All eyes turned to Ryan.

"We are concerned about your future, sweetheart." His mother's expression was appropriately grave.

Oh, shit. His mother only called him "sweetheart" when she wanted something from him. Or when he was in serious trouble. Or when they told him his Nonna was dying. The warmth fled his body, leaving his hands cold.

"You graduated over five years ago and are still working as a bartender," his father said. "I know it must be difficult to find a job with a degree in global studies, but have you even considered doing *something* with it?"

Alessandro DeMarco couldn't keep the scorn out of his voice when mentioning Ryan's one shining moment. He had earned his BA in global studies, with honors, thank you very much, but for his father, he may as well had never gone to college. If it wasn't related to the family business, or an obvious career path like pre-med or pre-law, it didn't count. There were plenty of jobs with non-profits and government agencies for someone with his credentials, but he had other ideas.

"No, Dad, I'm just going to blow my trust fund and be a

bartender for the rest of my life."

His words had their desired effect. With his father's reddened face and lowered brows, Ryan was once again in familiar territory. It seemed he'd spent his entire life on the wrong side of this man. Why should his late twenties be any different?

"You need to take this seriously, Ryan," Alex said. "Do you want to work for tips for the rest of your life when you have other alternatives?"

"Better than wasting away in an office all day."

The answer was quick and hot, laced with a venom he hadn't expected of himself. It was an old wound, an old argument. Ryan had never wanted to be part of the real estate empire his grandfather had started and his father had brought to fruition. Half the reason he worked as a bartender was it pissed off his father to have a DeMarco working for tips. The other half was he'd rather spend his time in more creative pursuits.

"You don't leave me a choice, Ryan." Alessandro's voice was sharp and firm, the no-nonsense press of his lips sending Ryan right back to his teenage years. "Your grandmother may have tolerated your attitude, but I won't. As of next month, you will no longer be receiving your allowance from the trust fund."

"But—"

His father held up a hand, and Ryan shut his mouth with a click of his teeth. "The trust fund allows the trustee to release the remainder of your portion to you on your thirtieth birthday. Prove you can get your life in order before then, or I will redistribute your share to the other beneficiaries."

That was over two years. Ryan stood with his hands fisted at his side. "You can't do that!"

His father remained seated, calm as though he'd merely doled out mundane family news. This wasn't his cousin dumping her boyfriend. This was his entire future. He had plans for the money. Important plans.

"I talked to my lawyer. I can, in fact, do that. All decisions regarding the trust fund are in my hands now that your grandmother is gone. And as you have yet to show any ambition or talent or desire to be a grown man, I've decided you won't receive the money until you can prove otherwise."

Ryan could try to fight this, but it would require the money he no longer had access to. He opened his mouth to protest again but closed it. His father had won this round.

Alessandro rose and stalked out of the room, leaving Ryan simmering in his anger. They sat in silence until the door to the office slammed shut.

"Mom…" Ryan turned to her with his best puppy-dog-eyed look, but her face hardened before any further words fell out of his mouth.

"Enough, sweetheart. It wasn't supposed to happen like this, but you had to push his buttons. You've managed to avoid any resemblance of adult responsibility thanks to your grandmother. She's gone now, and your father is in charge of the family."

Her words were a knife in the gut. Ryan itched to shout at her, tell her he wasn't stupid. Nonna was dead, but he still couldn't get out those words. He knew it in his head, but the idea hadn't burrowed into his heart. Until today. Today reminded him of how much his grandmother had truly meant to him. She had been the only person in his entire family, including his aunts and uncles and all those cousins, who'd understood him. Nonna was gone, and his father now had the ultimate authority over everyone's future, including his.

"We only want what's best for you." His mother's tone softened and became her usual conciliatory alto attempting to smooth over whatever damage his father had inflicted. She reached out a hand Ryan did not take.

"If you need a real job," his brother said, "Val is leaving soon. We could use an office manager who is at least familiar with the family."

"I have a job." Ryan wished he could keep the snide tone out of his voice. It made him sound like a petulant teenager, but he was beyond pissed off.

What his family didn't know was how lucrative bartending could be, especially at a busy, high-end restaurant. And though he didn't plan to bartend for the rest of his life, it was more flexible and more fun than anything the family business could offer. His family wouldn't understand—they were doers, not creators.

Ryan needed his trust fund allowance. Though it wasn't enough to live on, it had financed his years of research and the equipment needed to turn his dream into a reality. He was a script away from seeing the fruits of his labor of love.

"Think it over." His mother rose from the couch to head to the kitchen. "And you know where to find us."

Once again, his mother failed him. Instead of backing him, of trying to support him, she took his father's side. Every damn time. And if it wasn't his father's side, she took his brother's.

"I don't get it, Ry," his brother said once their mother left. "Everyone enjoys working for DeMarco Properties. It's a good company."

"If I'd wanted to join the family business, I wouldn't have majored in global studies. Real estate was never interesting to me, and I want more from life besides buying, selling, or renting property."

Running DeMarco Property Management someday was Alex's dream, not Ryan's.

"Then do *something* with your degree. Show Dad you're not going to waste your life."

"That's impossible. The only way he's ever going to accept me as a grown-ass adult is if I work for him. And there will be a blizzard in Tucson before that ever happens."

Ryan rose from his chair, and it rocked back and forth for a moment. The clicks and squeaks spoke volumes in the quiet between brothers.

"Would it really be so bad?" Alex asked, his voice even.

"Yeah, it would."

Little by little, it would eat at him until nothing was left of his soul. Ryan stormed into the foyer where his motorcycle helmet stared at him from the entry table. He grabbed it and headed for the front door.

"Wait!" His brother's voice echoed in the tiled entry.

Ryan hesitated, fingers on the door handle. He could storm out, ignoring Alex and possibly causing an irreparable rift. He'd never have to worry about pleasing his parents again or competing with his older brother. Those activities had never gotten him anywhere, anyway. But a small voice in his subconscious, which sounded suspiciously like his Nonna, reminded him family was important and shouldn't lightly be tossed to the side. Ryan turned around.

"I'm not staying for dinner."

Alex held up his hands in surrender. "I didn't think you would after that conversation."

"Why did you drag me here?"

"I didn't know they were going to ambush you before we ate. I would've told them it was a very bad idea. You get hangry." A grin softened the words.

Ryan couldn't help himself and grinned back.

"Listen, you don't want to work for Dad, fine." Alex leaned against the table where Ryan's helmet had rested a moment earlier. "But I have a proposition for you."

More alarm bells rang through his head. Alex's propositions rarely turned out well for anyone other than Alex.

"Spit it out."

"Mom keeps trying to set me up with the daughter of a friend. What if you call her instead?"

"Why not you? What's wrong with her?"

"Do you even know how many of these dates Mom has tried

to con me into? Listen, dude, you'd be doing me a favor and throwing them a bone at the same time. Date someone you know they'd approve, instead of the women I know you pick just to piss them off. If you do it, I'll owe you, and they'll see you're trying."

A favor from Alex was an excellent thing to have in his back pocket, and what was one date? Hell, maybe he'd even like her. Probably not. He'd been surrounded by the daughters of his mother's friends for most of his life. He refused to date any of them since they didn't want a casual hookup but a chance at the DeMarco fortune, or better yet, at his older brother. What choice did he have? Ryan nodded in defeat.

"Great! I'll send the number."

Ryan turned to the door and opened it.

"Hey, Happy New Year!" Alex's words seemed sincere.

"Happy New Year," he muttered before stepping out into the chilly desert evening and pulling on his helmet.

The city lights sparkled in the valley below the Catalina Foothills, the last breath of the holidays coming to a close. He straddled his bike and started it, the engine rumbling beneath him.

What could go wrong with one date?

CHAPTER 3
sparkling wine goes with everything

For the first time since before Christmas, Elissa had the TV all to herself. Wrapped in a fuzzy blanket, she reveled in the quiet. Her brother was out with friends for the last Friday of winter break, making up for his lousy excuse for a New Year's Eve. Her mom felt the best she had in a while, so Dad swept her away for a date night before their appointment with the oncologist next week.

Elissa looked forward to the quiet, but fate had other ideas.

Footsteps crunched on the gravel path leading to her parents' front door and a familiar, rhythmic knock sounded before a tall woman with curly black hair and snappy brown eyes barged in like she'd been doing the last twenty years.

"Happy New Year!" Jules's smile was as big as her personality: warm, caring, mischievous. She'd been Elissa's friend since kindergarten, as opposite as it was possible to be and still be best friends.

Jules plopped down on the couch beside Elissa, setting down a bottle of sparkling wine on the coffee table with a loud thunk. She pulled Elissa into one of her famous hugs, the ones that made you feel loved and part of whatever ridiculousness Jules planned next. As much as she'd been looking forward to some alone time, she never turned down a chance to be with her bestie.

"Happy New Year," Elissa said as they both settled into the soft cushions of the worn, but oh-so-comfortable couch.

"What is my favorite nerd doing by herself on the first Friday of a new year?"

"I *was* enjoying it." Elissa found the grin growing on her own face. Jules was the only person she could tease like this. Her BFF was the one bright spot in what had been a soul-sucking year with little to smile about.

"Well, now you can enjoy it even more because I'm here. I won't let you waste your night watching"—Jules looked at the TV for a minute to figure out exactly what Elissa was watching—"another *Lord of the Rings* marathon."

"*Lord of the Rings* is comfort TV."

"Lady, you don't need comfort TV. You need comfort dick."

Jules waggled her eyebrows at Elissa. It had been an ongoing discussion for the last few months once Jules had decided an appropriate interval had passed for her to grieve her relationship with Victor. Between her best friend and her mother, the pressure was on to re-enter the dating game.

"Have anyone in mind?" By the grace of God, Elissa kept a straight face.

Jules narrowed her eyes and studied her before her smile returned. She ruffled Elissa's hair before pulling her in for a side hug.

"You're messing with me."

"Guilty as charged. What brings you to my parents' couch on a Friday?"

"I knew you'd be here. Where else would I find my favorite nerd?"

"Not a nerd."

"Uh-huh. Tell that to Gandalf on the *Enterprise*."

"Gandalf isn't on—"

"Yeah, I know. Nerd."

Jules bounced up, her never-ending energy propelling her to the kitchen where she grabbed a couple of wineglasses and some cookies from the cookie jar. She nestled onto the couch and poured the wine for both of them.

"Cheers."

The glasses clinked in a satisfactory way. Elissa took a cookie from the napkin before sipping the bubbly. The bubbles fizzed on her tongue, releasing the sweet scent of the surprisingly dry wine.

"Are you sure this goes with cookies?" Elissa examined the chocolate chip cookie in her hand.

"Sparkling wine goes with everything, dahling."

Jules would know. She worked at a high-end restaurant her parents only went to for their anniversary. Elissa took a bite of the cookie. As usual, Jules was right. She gave her friend a wide smile.

"You can say it. I don't hear it often enough." Jules waggled her eyebrows.

"You are right, Jules. Sparkling wine goes with everything. Dahling."

Jules pulled down the blanket on the back of the couch and wrapped herself in it. The two friends settled into a comforting routine they'd repeated so many times it was second nature. The only difference now was the wine. It used to be milk or juice, then they'd upgraded to soda and tea. When the movie ended, Jules turned to Elissa.

"How was your New Year's Eve?"

Elissa opened her mouth to answer, but her friend interrupted before she could.

"No, let me guess. Your parents crashed before the ball went down in Times Square, you fell asleep on the couch trying to keep Leo company, and the poor kid had no one to ring in the year with."

Jules hit it on the head. It had been a spectacularly boring New Year, the worst ever. Elissa vowed next year he would have a proper New Year's party.

"You know me so well."

"Ah, lady, what am I going to do with you?"

"It's been a rough year, Jules. I wasn't in the mood for a party."

"But things are better?"

"Mom's got an appointment next week, so we'll see."

The past year was filled with *we'll sees*, and Elissa was tired of holding her breath, waiting for the worst. She was ready to move on, she really was, as soon as her mom got the all-clear. And tax season was over. Couldn't forget that. So April. She'd be ready in April.

"You can't always be waiting for the bad. You gotta get out there and find the good."

"But as soon as something good happens, the bad follows."

"Lissa…"

Jules pulled her in for a hug. They'd had dozens of arguments over the decades about tempting fate, about the wheel of fortune constantly spinning out bad things, sometimes terrible things, right after the good. Arguing further was useless.

"You brought the wine, so let me clean up," Elissa said as she pulled back from the hug. Jules rubbed her hair and planted a kiss on her forehead.

"Fine, but one of these days, I'm gonna convince you that you're wrong."

Elissa unwrapped herself from her blanket and cleared the coffee table of their glasses and the napkin now holding only crumbs. As she walked into the kitchen, her phone vibrated on the now-empty coffee table.

Quick as a cat, Jules grabbed it. "Ooh, who could it be? I thought I was your only friend."

Rolling her eyes, Elissa put the glasses in the sink and tossed the napkin into the trash. If she tried grabbing her phone from Jules, her friend's long arms would have no problem keeping the device well out of her reach. It was probably her mom or Leo, anyway, telling her they'd be late. Jules would return it quicker if she didn't fuss. Elissa washed the glasses and walked into the living room.

Her suspicions high—Jules had been awfully quiet—she tiptoed behind the couch, looking over her friend's shoulder. As usual, she was unable to get the jump on Jules, who promptly turned the phone over so Elissa couldn't see what she'd been up to.

"Whatcha doing?" Elissa asked in a singsong voice, sitting on the couch.

"Nothing." Jules handed the phone over, a remarkably innocent look on her face. Too innocent. And the corner of her mouth twitched, despite her friend's stubborn desire to look as though she hadn't been doing anything to Elissa's phone.

"Jules…"

"If you didn't want me to have access to your phone, you would've chosen a better passcode than my birthday." Jules lost her battle with the impish grin. Elissa was in trouble. Jules had done *something* Elissa wouldn't be happy about.

She unlocked her phone to discover a brief exchange of texts, beginning with one from an unknown number.

> Unknown: Hi this is Ryan. I've heard so
> much about you. Hope its ok I texted

Ryan? Did she know a Ryan? Oh wait, her mom mentioned earlier today she'd given Elissa's number to her friend's son so they could arrange a date. This must be him.

And Jules, being Jules, had run with it. She'd answered for Elissa, knowing if she'd left it up to her friend, the poor guy would be waiting a while for a reply. Elissa had a tendency to overthink everything. She even had a shirt to prove it.

> E: Hi, Ryan. I've heard so much about you, too.
> Glad you messaged me.

The little thinking bubble appeared.

"So, who's Ryan?"

"None of your business." Elissa's face heated, and she tried to keep the phone facing away from Jules.

"I don't think I've seen your face so red since you got sunburned after falling asleep next to the pool senior year. You know you're going to tell me, eventually. Why not get it over with now?"

The phone buzzed in her hand, and before she could stop Jules, her friend grabbed it from her. She stood and held the phone high over her head, keeping it out of Elissa's reach.

"Give me my phone, Jules." Trying to reclaim it would be an exercise in futility.

"What, so you can go to your room, alone and unhappy? Not happening, lady. It's about time you put yourself first." Jules tapped, hit send, then handed the phone to her. "There. You're committed now. Tell me what's going on."

"I hate you."

"No you don't." Her friend settled back down on the couch and lifted her wineglass. Elissa read the messages.

> Unknown: I don't mind getting to know you over text but would you be up for meeting in person?
>
> E: Yes, that would be lovely.

Elissa had been half afraid Jules would send something inappropriate as she had many times in the past, but this was a nice, basic exchange of information. And Jules had written the texts like Elissa would have, all the punctuation in the right place. Just because it was informal writing didn't mean she could simply forget proper English grammar. They'd been texting each other for the last decade, so Jules knew better than anyone how much of a grammar snob Elissa could be.

"Ryan is the son of one of Mom's friends. I told her she could set me up on a date before tax season. She didn't waste any time." Elissa gave in to the inevitable. Jules was right—she would find out one way or another.

"I've got your back, Lissa. What better way to start the new year? A new guy in your life after the rat-bastard."

Yep, inappropriate. But appreciated.

The phone buzzed once more.

Unknown: Anytime, anyplace. LMK

Now what did she say? Elissa had never been particularly adept at flirting, and her attempts over text were even worse. She handed the phone to Jules.

"I can't, Jules. What if I totally geek out on him? What if I use the wrong emoji?"

"Fine. What do you want me to say?"

"Just pretend you're me, but..." She waved her hands around wildly. "But less cringe."

Jules's fingers flew over the screen. After a short pause to read what she'd written, her friend hit send and gave the phone back.

E: Would you like to meet for drinks on Tuesday after work?

"See, it's not that hard," Jules said with a smile. "I even added him to your contacts."

Her friend was right, it wasn't that hard, but she was out of practice.

R: Sounds perfect. When and where?

It had worked. Something so simple had worked. She answered for herself, like a goddamned adult. Ooh, did she owe the Wright Family swear jar if she only thought the swear word? It went to their next family fun night, so might as well. There was the new bowling alley and arcade opening.

E: Sandpiper, 5:30.

R: Great, see you Tuesday

"Thank you," she said, actually meaning it.

"Anytime, lady. If my love life is non-existent, at least I can help with yours. Now, can we watch that one scene with the dude with the pointy ears again? The actor who was in *Pirates of the Caribbean.*"

"Anything for you, Jules."

Watching Orlando Bloom dressed as an elf was far from some sort of hardship. Jules poured more sparkling wine, and they snuggled together under the blanket. Grown-up grape juice with her bestie was the perfect Friday night for Elissa.

CHAPTER 4
two sonorans

A whirlwind of inspiration struck Ryan Sunday around lunch. After suffering weeks of writer's block, he jumped on this opportunity and grabbed all the books, his laptop, and his noise cancelling headphones and set up shop on the kitchen table where there was plenty of space to spread out. Several hours later, a tap on his shoulder startled Ryan. With noise-canceling headphones on, he'd missed Iz returning from their errands.

"Jesus, Iz."

"Sorry, Ry. Didn't mean to scare you." Something was off. His usually chill friend and roommate—because who else would put up with a spoiled rich kid—had a crease in their forehead and their voice was leaden. "Your brother's been texting. It might be important."

Ryan took the phone from their outstretched hand, handling it like a rattler. He didn't want to see what his brother had texted him, but it likely had to do with the phone number from three nights ago. Or maybe his dad had changed his mind. Yeah, and if pigs could fly...

"Only one way to find out, Ryan," Iz said, reading him like a book. They'd been friends since kindergarten, and Iz had been one of the two people who'd always had his back. Since his grandmother was gone, it was just Iz now.

"Yeah, but..."

"And yet, you're still staring at that thing like it's going to bite you. I guarantee it won't."

"I know."

Iz rubbed at the crease between their eyes. "Ry, not tonight. Just fucking see what your brother wants."

"Okay, Iz, thanks." He unlocked the phone as Iz trudged to the living room with a tired wave. As soon as he was done here, he'd have a conversation with them. He hated when Iz's mood dipped. His friend was the furthest from a whiny bitch as was possible to be, but this listlessness was worse.

Ryan straightened the papers strewn all over the table, put them next to the books with multicolored sticky notes stacked in haphazard piles, careful not to knock over his collection of beer and soda cans. He glanced over the messages. His brother had been texting him for the last thirty minutes.

> A: Hey, how did it go?

> A: You there?

> A: When's the date?

> A: Do I need to call her?

And more of the same. Ryan replied, if only to get his brother off his back.

> R: Tuesday 5:30 Sandpiper.

There, that should satisfy Mr. Stick-up-his-ass. Now to see what was wrong with his friend.

While Ryan handled Alex, Iz had changed from the bright outfit earlier into jeans, a plain T-shirt, and tennis shoes. The makeup was gone, too. Without them, Iz looked the same as they'd been in high school, round face, nearly black hair a smidge below their chin, dark brown eyes with a touch of sadness in them. The only clue Iz wasn't that person anymore was the red polish on their nails.

Ryan snuck up behind them. "Boo!"

"For fuck's sake," Iz said as Ryan laughed.

"C'mon, time for a break. I've been working on the damned podcast all afternoon, and I'm taking you out for dinner." He kept his tone light. Ryan was more than happy to pay. He owed Iz so much, but his friend wasn't the type to demand it. "Gotta spend the trust fund while we can."

Iz's lips twitched, some of their sparkle returning. "That's right, let the DeMarco fortune pay for our Sonoran dogs."

Sonoran dogs? Damn, Iz only ate Sonoran dogs on bad days.

"You're a cheap date." Hell, Ryan could afford the Sonoran dogs on his earnings as a bartender. Of course, they might be in for more of these cheap meals in the next several months if his father followed through and he couldn't find a way to balance the budget.

"You know it!" A ghost of a smile tipped up Iz's lips.

"Fine, but you're driving."

"Like I'd get on that death trap with you. Grab your wallet."

Ryan did and met Iz in the parking lot.

"What's up?" Ryan asked as Iz drove to their favorite food truck about a mile away. While Mama O's had the best, this was closer and almost as tasty.

Iz sighed and was quiet for a moment.

"It was a rough day. I didn't feel like dealing with anyone else's bullshit tonight. I just want my damned Sonoran dog."

"Okay. Wanna talk about it?"

Iz had come out as non-binary their sophomore year in college. Their outward expressions of gender changed too. Gone were the tees they'd both lived in when not in school uniforms. In their place, bold-patterned feminine shirts and lots of glitter and rhinestones. Iz tried makeup, too, often getting help from mutual friends.

It took about a second for Ryan to get on board. The doubt in Iz's eyes almost broke Ryan's heart. After an initial moment of confusion, the little pieces throughout their lives suddenly fell into place. It made sense, all of it. Ryan had smiled at his friend, and neither had looked back.

"Nah. I'll be fine, but a quiet night will help." Iz tapped their fingers against the steering wheel in rhythm to the music. The city lights flashed by, and traffic was light.

"One quiet night, coming right up."

"So…what did your brother want?"

It was Ryan's turn to sigh.

"That bad?"

"Yes…no. Alex said he'd owe me a favor if I went out with this woman Mom has been trying to convince him to date. He thought they'd see it as a…what do they call it?"

"A sign of good faith?"

"Yeah, that."

"Do you think it'll work, or will she become one more number in your contacts you never call?"

"It's worth a date to find out, I guess." The last time he'd dated someone pre-approved by his family, she'd been more interested in their contacts than in him. He hadn't repeated the experience in years, instead amassing an impressive list of one-night stands and short flings.

"I don't envy you. I mean, my family ain't perfect, but the level of control your dad has…That shit is messed up."

"You don't need to tell me."

"And I'm too afraid to tell your dad."

They both laughed. Alessandro DeMarco only tolerated Iz. It had been that way forever. Few people were good enough to be in the inner DeMarco circle. Once it was apparent Iz wasn't going anywhere, it became not worth fighting about. Besides, Ryan was only the spare, not the heir. Alex's connections were much more important.

His father may have never understood their friendship, but there was a lot about his younger son he didn't know. If he'd bothered to show up more, he'd know Iz had always been in Ryan's cheering section. And his grades wouldn't have been half as good if his friend hadn't been proactively arranging study groups among their friends.

"Do you think your aunt will give me more hours?" Ryan asked as they pulled into the abandoned lot their favorite food truck occupied on Sundays, Wednesdays, and Fridays from noon to eight p.m.

Iz's grandparents had built their own restaurant empire, starting with the original Mama O's Tacos shop. Now Mama O's was only beaten by Eegee's for the number of shops spread around Tucson, and the Ochoas owned two more upscale restaurants, Los Vaqueros Steakhouse, and Nopalitos, specializing in Sonoran-style food. Ryan usually bartended at Nopalitos but had been around long enough he was a solid emergency sub at the steakhouse. Iz worked for their parents, doing all the marketing material. They would eventually strike out on their own, but for now the experience Iz earned while working for the family business was invaluable.

"I don't know. We have a great set of bartenders right now. But wasn't the idea to cut back so you had more time to work on your podcast?"

The podcast Ryan had been planning for the past couple of years. He could monetize it, turn it into his primary source of income. But seed money would help a fuckton.

"It was, but I need to prove to them I can make it without the trust fund. Only then will I have access to said trust fund."

"Isn't that circular logic?" They got out of the car, Ryan followed, and the doors slammed shut. "I mean, if you don't need the money, then you can have the money?"

"Welcome to my world." Ryan kicked at the rocks in the sand as they walked to the line, sending a few skittering under the truck.

"Rich people are weird."

"Your family is rich, too."

"Yeah, but we're not used to it yet, so it doesn't count. Why doesn't your dad say what he means? Come work for me, and you can have whatever you want. Don't and fuck you."

"Can I help you?" the cashier asked when it was their turn, shutting Iz up for the moment.

"Hey, we'll have two Sonorans, an order of fries, and two Mexicokes." Ryan pulled out his wallet.

A couple minutes later, they sat down at a picnic bench under a pop-up canopy and waited for their number to be called. Ryan regretted not grabbing his favorite hoodie. He was used to the typical warm desert nights, but January was chilly once the sun went down. At least the stars shone brightly, even among the buildings of Midtown.

"I don't get it." Iz shook their head. "Why don't you tell your dad what your plan is?"

Ryan glared at his friend. He could hear his father's response. "He'd be happier with me as a bartender. At least that's real work. Podcasting, that's a hobby, especially a podcast about food."

"But it's not. You have to write, record, edit, market. Those are all valuable skills."

"I know that, and you know that, but Alessandro DeMarco has a narrow definition of gainful employment. Podcasting is not on the list." No matter if it was his son's dream or not.

"Would working for your father be so awful? Just long enough for him to release your trust fund to you. Then you could do whatever the hell you wanted. I wish I had that option."

The reality check hit Ryan in the gut, leaving him breathless for a moment. Iz's family didn't have the generational capital Ryan's grandfather had mortgaged to amass the fortune his descendants currently enjoyed. Everything the Ochoas had, they had earned through hard work, luck, and Abuelo Ochoa's preternatural business skill.

How bad could it be for Ryan to work for his family's business for a couple of years? At thirty, he would have more than enough capital to provide a substantial cushion, no matter what he ended up doing for the rest of his life. Could he swallow his pride for two and a half years in order to live the rest of his life in comfort and freedom? Or would it kill every last creative brain cell?

Their order was ready, and Ryan collected the paper trays.

"Maybe you're right," he said as he returned, setting the food on the table. Iz smiled sadly. "But maybe I can get away with dating the socialite Mom keeps trying to inflict on Alex and presenting my business plan."

"But Ry, don't you need to have a plan before you can present it?" Iz laughed. They knew the plan was mostly in Ryan's head and had more in common with a fever dream than a business document.

"One step at a time, Iz. Please, God, one step at a time." Ryan smiled to take the bleak note out of his voice, and it might have worked. Maybe.

CHAPTER 5
excellent taste

E lissa sat in her dilapidated old car, fiddling with her phone and thinking about anything other than what waited for her inside the restaurant. She needed a new car, but with so many memories attached to old Bertha, she had a hard time letting go. It had been her dad's car all through middle and high school. She'd learned to drive with Bertha. There was still a stain in the backseat where her sister had spilled a strawberry Eegee's slushy. Tucked in the driver's cupholder was a Lego minifig, a gift from her brother when her dad had passed along the car. He'd insisted she needed a copilot.

She turned off the phone and put it into her plain, black clutch, but still couldn't force herself out of the car, enjoying the gentle warmth of the desert sun that usually tried to kill her. Elissa hadn't been on a date since her mom's diagnosis. Life had been great in the weeks before Dana had made the phone call that began the whole mess of last year. Elissa's live-in boyfriend had received a job offer in Denver, and she planned to tell her family she would be moving with him.

Her first instinct had been a nice Sunday dinner conversation informing them of her decision and timeline, but her mother invited her over for a random Taco Tuesday night and broke the bad news. The prognosis was good, but all Elissa heard was her mom had cancer. As soon as dinner was over, she went straight home and told Victor Denver was off the table for her, at least for now.

She hadn't asked him to postpone his move. The job offer was too perfect to put off for a girlfriend, but she had expected some support, an attempt to make the long-distance thing work. After all, they'd been together for three years, living together for one. Instead, as the tears dripped down her face, he said he was tired of coming in second to her family and to move her stuff out of his apartment by the end of the month. She'd been dumped when she needed his comfort the most. So she moved in with her parents, another small jab that made the previous year the worst ever.

Enough procrastinating.

Elissa took a deep breath and finally opened the car door, the cool January breeze causing goosebumps. She could do this for her mother. And maybe she'd do it for herself. She deserved the possibility of love, didn't she? Even if this date was a disaster, it would get her out there, and when tax season was over, she could try again.

She resisted the temptation to check her phone again, having promised Jules she would leave it off tonight. She could practically hear her friend rolling her eyes in exasperation as she read the text at lunch.

> J: For God's sake Lissa! It's drinks. What r the chances anyone needs u for the time it takes to drink a glass of wine and talk to a dude?

Jules had a point. The chances were slim anything would blow up in the next hour, but with everything that had happened over the last year, she still felt uneasy about leaving her phone off. Elissa locked the car door, not entirely sure why she bothered. It wasn't as though anyone would steal the clunker, but old habits die hard. She gave herself a mental kick in the pants to stop procrastinating and squared her shoulders.

Plastering a smile on her face, she entered the restaurant with as much confidence as she could muster.

Jules stood behind the reception stand, and Elissa's smile grew genuine as she locked eyes with her friend. She'd almost forgotten Jules would be here. It was, after all, why she'd chosen now and here. Relief flowed through her, and her edges softened. Jules would support her, come hell or high water. No matter what happened, she'd be fine.

"Hey, lady!" Jules came out from behind the podium and pulled her in for a quick hug. She whispered in Elissa's ear. "Glad you didn't bail. Your mom has excellent taste. Look in the corner."

A man lounged at the corner table, his arms stretched out and fingers drumming on the padding along the back of the bench that lined the length of the wall. Muscles rippled under his tight T-shirt and artfully tousled dark brown hair softened his clean-shaven, strong-jawed face. His face was relaxed but blank as his gaze aimlessly roamed the room. Jules was right. Dana Wright had excellent taste.

When his gaze lit upon her, his attention changed from disinterested boredom to laser focus in an instant. A half smile fixed itself on his lips.

Jules gave her a small push toward him before hightailing it behind the podium. "I'll put your drink order in."

As Elissa approached, she couldn't help but notice how his light tawny skin glowed golden in the dim light of the bar. He stood and held out his hand in greeting, his smile now relaxed. Her date was about average height. Relief filled her. She was a couple inches over five feet, and tall men tended to overwhelm her. His eyes were warm and soft brown, like a broken-in leather chair, and a spark lit their depths as she took his hand firmly in hers.

"Hi. Are you Ryan?" A genuine smile brightened her words, surprising her.

"I am." He hesitated, and his smile faltered for an instant. He cleared his throat and rubbed the back of his neck. "You must be…"

After a long pause, it dawned on her. He didn't remember her name. Son of a—nope, this man was not going to cost her a dollar to the swear jar. The glow surrounding them faded, the magic of the moment gone. The bonehead couldn't even remember her name.

"Elissa." Her tone dulled, and the good vibes from a moment before disappeared.

He turned up the wattage on his charming smile, one she was certain had dazzled many women before her. Perhaps it was meant to ease her mind about him forgetting her name. Maybe it was his default setting.

"I'm sorry, my phone died, and I'm bad about remembering stuff without it. It's nice to meet you, Elissa."

Or he was just clueless enough to think if he turned on the charm, she'd forgive any misstep. She almost did. He *was* pretty.

Elissa sat in the chair across from him, hiding her irritation with a little sigh. It was the first date, and he had apologized. But he'd also lumped her in with "stuff." She'd promised her mother, so she'd sit here and survive this date. Sometimes first impressions were wrong.

Ryan had a deep and rumbly voice, and he smelled incredible. Even surrounded by the strong scents of a restaurant, she could pick out lemon, something woodsy, and…motor oil? She held tight to her smile. If she kept at it, maybe she'd convince herself she was having a good time.

She didn't know why she was being so touchy. Yeah, he'd forgotten her name, but they hadn't met before. Was she taking her doubts about dating out on this stranger? Or had the past year soured her on the potential for her happiness in general?

"So, Elissa, what would you like to drink?" Ryan played with the napkin under his own drink, a dark golden beer.

"Oh, Jules is already on it." She glanced at the bar. Yep, Jules was speaking with the bartender.

"You come here a lot?"

"Jules is my best friend, and since I haven't been out on a date in a while, I wanted to play it safe."

"That's smart. Never can be too safe. I've told my cousins to always make sure someone knows where they are if they're out on a date with a stranger."

Okay, that was kinda sweet, looking out for his cousins. She'd cut him some slack for not remembering her name. Not everyone had Elissa's nearly perfect recall for names and faces, and first dates were full of missteps and awkward questions.

Don't rush to judgment, Elissa. He hasn't done anything wrong. Yet.

Ryan looked at a loss for what to say next, opening and closing his mouth a couple times, as if he was quickly discarding any idea coming into his head. While they were stuck in awkward mode, the bartender finally came over, bringing her a glass of rosé.

"Anything else I can get for you right now?" she asked.

"I'm fine. Elissa?"

She appreciated he didn't assume. "The wine is perfect for now, thanks."

They lapsed into uncomfortable silence again. She'd almost forgotten how much she hated this part of dating. What questions could she pose that wouldn't seem trite, cliché, or boring? He saved her from launching the opening salvo. Ryan leaned forward, his attention focused on her in a way that made her think of the interview she'd gone through to be hired for her current job. He folded his hands on the table, in the same manner Victor often had when they discussed touchy subjects, like moving to Denver.

"Tell me about yourself." His tone struck the Victor chord, too. The humdrum ordinariness of it all, as though bored with the world. As though it was her job to amuse him.

Elissa folded her arms across her chest and leaned back in her chair, as far as she could in the limited space. Irritation fought with disappointment. How dare he approach this like some sort of work, like she was a candidate for him to accept or reject.

"This is a date, not a job interview."

"You think dating me would be a job?" The corners of his lips twitched before he could hide his amusement.

"Possibly." Most guys were a job of one sort or another. Victor had needed constant reassurance he was important to her, and still he'd left. The rest of her pre-Victor boyfriends had wanted her to play dumb. She'd refused, and here she was. "How would I know with a question like that?"

"How about, if you don't want to be here, why didn't you call the whole thing off?"

"Even if I had, wasn't your phone dead? Then I would have been the girl who stood up the guy at the bar."

"Touché." His eyes were still focused on her face and caught the light in a way that belied the overall impression he was bored or couldn't care less. They glinted with…something. Humor? More likely irritation. This was not off to a strong start if they were already irritating the hell out of each other. "But why are you here, Elissa?"

Elissa uncrossed her arms and forced herself to relax. She'd promised her mother she'd give this a chance. It wasn't his fault his opening reminded her of Victor. There were only so many ways a first date could go. Instead of being willfully annoying, she answered his question.

"Likely the same reason as you, I guess. I love my mother."

He chuckled and turned his beer on the little napkin. "So not exactly the same reason. I just want mine off my back."

"I wouldn't mind that either, but when your mom has cancer, you don't say no."

He paled and the amusement left his voice. "Oh shit,

seriously? I'm sorry."

Elissa winced. She hadn't meant to play the cancer card. She didn't need his pity, but something about him had her filters off. For some reason, he brought out the self she kept buried under her perfectionism and optimism. The one who was a little cynical, a little bitter at the hand fate had dealt her.

"No, my bad. I didn't mean to... doesn't matter. She finished her treatments a little while ago and we're waiting for test results. Her doctors have been optimistic, so I guess so am I."

"It does matter. I hope the results are what you want."

And those words made him different from Victor. She let go of the bitterness of her last relationship and leaned into the possibility before her.

"Thanks. I do too, but..."

"But what?"

"You'll think I'm a conspiracy theorist."

His smile returned, softening his eyes. "I promise I won't think you're a conspiracy theorist. Unless you go off about the moon landing being a hoax."

"No, that was absolutely real. At least, that's what JFK and Elvis told me at the last Conspiracies Anonymous meeting."

He laughed outright, a full-throated, panty-melting laugh. Heat spread through her body and settled between her thighs. Holy sh—shirt.

"I think we're going to get along just fine, Elissa." He raised his beer and toasted her.

She smiled over the rim of her glass and returned the gesture before taking another sip of the slightly sweet wine. Maybe he was right. A rocky start was no reason to bail early. And it would be a fun story, someday.

"So what is your conspiracy theory?" he asked after a moment.

"Whenever something good happens, bad luck seems to find

me. I'm always waiting for the other shoe to drop, because it always does."

"Hmm, I wouldn't say that's a conspiracy theory. More like…Elissa's Law."

"*Elissa's* Law?"

"Yeah, Murphy's Law, but happening to a beautiful woman."

The flush ran up her chest and her neck, then settled on her cheeks. They burned with the compliment. She wasn't usually this affected when men complimented her looks.

"That's not real."

"Could be." He grinned. "Okay, now a boring question, because I have to know. What do you do for a living?"

"*That's* what you're going with for a follow-up?"

"Listen, I have theories about you, and I have to know if they're right."

"Theories? Like what?" She absently ran her finger along the rim of her wineglass.

"Answer my question, and maybe I'll tell you."

"*Maybe* you'll tell me?"

"Depends if I'm right or not."

She sipped the wine, considering carefully. She liked how he challenged her, liked the mischievous glint in his eyes. Liked how his smile lit her up.

"I'm an accountant. I earned my CPA over a year ago and work for a great firm that does a lot of work with local businesses."

He blinked at her slowly, and his dark lashes stayed closed for an instant longer than needed. Elissa knew what had to be going through his head. It was the same thing that went through almost everyone's mind when she told them what she did for a living. She was too pretty to be a numbers nerd. The little flame of hope flickered and smoked, dying a little.

"What?" She didn't let him speak once he opened his eyes.

"Don't think a woman can handle numbers?"

Ryan gave her a lazy smile. "No, that's not what I was thinking. You could give me a chance to tell you what I *do* think. I'll be honest with you."

Honesty. She liked it. Some said she was far too honest, and she often had to remind herself to sugarcoat the truth. "Fine. What do you think?"

"I think you have to be pretty smart to be a CPA so soon."

Dammit, he complimented her brain. She'd learned to brush off compliments on her looks, but a thrill shimmied along her spine whenever someone mentioned how smart she was. It was the only way anyone could manipulate her. Tell her she was intelligent, and she was mere putty in their hands.

The flame of hope roared to life, crackling with fresh fuel and warming her from head to toe. She attempted to cover her delight by asking the same question.

"What do you do?"

His lips cocked into a wry smile before he answered. "Seriously?"

Of course, seriously. All she knew about him was his name and the fact their mothers knew each other.

"You said you'd be honest with me."

"True, but you didn't like that question. Why don't we play a game and you guess? I don't want this to be too easy."

His warm brown eyes still sparked with whatever emotion he wasn't sharing with her. Probably annoyance, but the way he'd smiled at her earlier threw some doubt into the mix.

"I hate guessing games." Elissa's arms seemed to cross her chest of their own accord, and her face flushed with frustration.

"Then you'll never find out."

Ryan was definitely teasing her. She'd show him.

"Fine!" Elissa inspected him from head to toe and thought back to how he smelled and the contours of his hand in hers. A wicked grin spread on her lips as she noticed his pupils dilate in reaction to her examination. "Mechanic."

His eyebrows rose in surprise. "What makes you think that?"

"You smell like motor oil."

Ryan looked down at his shirt and jeans and over to his black leather jacket, folded on the seat next to him. He picked it up and sniffed at it.

"I don't smell anything."

Elissa shrugged smugly. "Olfactory fatigue. If it's around all the time, you stop smelling it."

He grinned and took a gulp of beer. "Big words. I like it. Not a mechanic, but I work on my bike myself whenever possible. Two more guesses."

"You never stipulated there would only be three guesses."

"I don't want to be here all night."

"You think it would take that long?"

He raised his eyebrows and allowed a devilish smile to lift the corners of his mouth.

"Ugh, fine," she said.

Elissa stared at him, only allowing herself to become mildly distracted by his eyes, still sparkling with an unknown emotion. He was amused, but there was something else. They'd only just met, yet she was almost sure he would invite her to his place if she gave him the smallest sign she was interested.

"Shoe sales." Elissa wanted to see what he'd do when she gave him an obviously wrong answer.

Unfortunately, she'd said this as he'd taken a sip of his beer. He choked and coughed. No one could simultaneously swallow and laugh. It was a miracle she didn't get sprayed by beer. She pushed over an extra napkin and sat back in her chair, a triumphant grin on her face. He wasn't angry at her suggestion, so perhaps he wasn't as arrogant as she first assumed.

Once his breathing was under control, Ryan chuckled. "Nope. Strike two."

Elissa studied him, *really* studied him. From the tips of his motorcycle boots to the top of his head. Everything was high quality, if plain. And nobody got their hair perfect by accident. Ryan had some money but spent it sparingly on items that were important to him. The boots, his hair, his bike. Those form-fitting jeans. She tapped her finger against her lips.

"What happens if I guess right?" she asked.

"I'll buy you another drink and tell you my theory."

"If I don't want another drink?"

"Raincheck."

This time, she knew. Those sparks in his eyes weren't merely laughter or annoyance. He was attracted to her, too. Little butterflies stirred in her stomach, reminding her the feeling was mutual. But one foot in front of another. She wasn't going home with him, not today, at least.

Elissa tucked an errant strand of her boring brown hair behind an ear, took a sip of her wine, and smiled at him. She had his number.

CHAPTER 6
nefarious purposes

Ryan honest-to-god liked this woman. She called him on his usual bullshit, perfectly willing to walk away, and wasn't at all impressed by his family. Or his money, apparently. Her intelligence and wit had his brain screaming for more, and her body...dear God. He clenched his hands into fists to keep from touching her.

He waited for her final guess. Anticipation swirled through his body, his heart raced, and his skin tingled. Her eyes, blue as a lake on a hot summer day, narrowed.

"Remember, I don't like games." A damned cute frown creased the skin between Elissa's eyebrows. "Even when I win, I end up losing."

"But you were playing along so nicely." He couldn't keep himself from teasing her, flashing a panty-melting smile.

After arranging this date, he'd asked himself what the hell had made him agree to it. He'd known the answer to that, too, and hated the shallowness of it. Half-a-million dollars would motivate anyone agree to a date, even when he was certain she'd only be doing it for his family name and the connections it could give her. Like all the other women from his mother's social circle. But when his doom waltzed through the door and turned out to be pretty, petite, and smart, he knew she could be the cherry on top of his semi-charmed life.

"What if you don't appreciate my guess?" She sipped her

rosé.

"I have thick skin, I don't need you to sugarcoat the truth."

At first, he'd been afraid she had no personality. She was dressed professionally, in a black pencil skirt and a light gray sweater which hugged her curvaceous figure. Her brown hair hit her dainty chin in soft waves, a typical conservative bob. But then he'd noticed her shoes. Ballet flats, sure, but painted with bright red flowers. A splash of color and whimsy in an otherwise corporate outfit. There was more to this woman than a first glance would ever reveal. And he'd been proven right.

"Fine, but you can't say I didn't warn you."

Ryan swished his hand through the air, indicating she should continue. He'd already made up his mind to ask for another date. She was pleasant to look at, had a brain in her pretty head, and would make his parents happy. With any luck, she'd like him for himself and not just his connections.

She might make you happy, too, if you let her.

"You're not what you seem." Her words were crisp, analytical, as he'd expect from an accountant. "You want everyone to believe you're ordinary, like them, but you're not. Maybe you've even bought into the fantasy, but you can't hide the arrogance coming from money gives. So, I don't believe you do anything for a living. At least, nothing that contributes to society the way you could."

His lips thinned, and his fingers drummed on the table. She was so close, and the last bit hurt. Sure, slinging cocktails, pouring beer, and helping with inventory wouldn't change the world, but it was honest work. It didn't matter it was far from what he could be achieving, as his parents always pointed out. He planned on turning those experiences into something more, something new, something *his*. Before he could respond, defend his life choices—why he felt the need would forever remain a mystery, though—she apologized.

"Sorry. I said I'd be honest, but I know sometimes I go too

far." She fiddled with her clutch and refused to make eye contact. "So why don't we say goodbye and put a mark in the bad dates column?"

But it hadn't been a bad date. Yeah, forgetting her name hadn't been his finest moment. He'd only remembered he had a date this evening twenty minutes before he was supposed to meet her. His phone was dead, and he had no time to charge it. All he could remember was it began with an L sound. And his brain had gone totally blank when faced with those cute little freckles dotting her nose under her intense gaze. He could lose himself there for hours, days, years, if she let him. No, not a bad date at all.

"I said I wanted the truth, and you gave it. But you need to give me a chance to respond and don't assume I'm angry with the truth. I'll never be angry with the truth from you."

Hurt, sure. He liked her, and her words stung. But they'd known each other for less than thirty minutes. Surely he could change her mind. He still had the DeMarco charm, after all.

A blush spread over her cheeks, setting the sparse freckles into stark relief. She fiddled with her clutch some more.

"I'm sorry, I didn't mean..."

He slid his fingers around the hand grasping the clutch and squeezed gently. "We're good, Elissa. Just getting to know each other. It doesn't have to be perfect."

"You don't know me at all."

"I'd like to. You're the ideal woman for me to date. Stable job, attractive but not so beautiful you'd be a distraction, polite to a fault, well-educated, you dress like the accountant you are, and don't have any unfortunate piercings or visible tattoos. The exact opposite of every woman I've dated the last decade. My parents will be thrilled I bought you a drink."

Her luscious pink lips thinned. She wasn't taking this as intended. Shit.

"I mean, I know I'm not my brother, but I think we get along well enough to…"

"Enough to what, Ryan?" A shadow crossed her face and she pulled her hand out of his light grip. "I-I should go."

"No, wait a second."

He needed her to stay, needed her to say yes to another date. He hadn't enjoyed himself this much in a while, and the thought of her leaving, let alone leaving while pissed off at him, made him desperate.

A wild idea popped into his head. Absolutely wild. He couldn't. He wouldn't.

She pushed her chair away from the table. Time was up. His ADHD bypassed his better angels, and the words tore through his filters like rampaging javelinas.

"What I'm saying is you'll do just fine. I'll take you out a few times, take you to a family function or two, and my mother will stop hounding me to date in my league. You'll have a good time, network with my family—they'll adore you, by the way—and their extensive business contacts, then we can call it quits." This had to work. Few people would turn down easy access to the DeMarco family. The plan would give her a chance to appreciate him for who *he* was, and he could work with that. "They'll give me hell for dumping you, keeping all those juicy connections ripe for the picking. You'll be set for several years, and I'll show them I'm trying. Sounds like a win-win to me. You in?"

Elissa's face changed from pink to red, and those blue eyes of hers narrowed. Her mouth opened and shut once or twice before she got any words out.

"Am I…in? Am I in? In for what? Some scam on your family? A good time that's going exactly nowhere? In for being used for your nefarious purposes?"

"Nefarious purposes?" He ran his hand through his hair and sipped on his beer. It was too late to take the words back. He had to count on the legendary DeMarco charm to persuade her to go along. One date with this woman only left him hungry for more. "I'm not trying to do anything other than get my family to mind their own business about my love life. But yeah, seems about right. So, what do you think?"

The knuckles on the hand wrapped around her wine glass faded to white, and for a moment, he was afraid the glass would shatter. She set it down on the table and slowly unwound her fingers, placing her hands on the edge of the table.

"What do I think?" Her voice went husky instead of high. "You want to buy my presence with the promise of connections?"

"No, well, maybe, I guess." *Yeah, real smooth.* This was not going well. In fact, he could smell the faint odor of dumpster fire brewing. "It sounds like we could both use a break from our mothers' matchmaking. This is about the pleasure of your company at a few events. Sex would be entirely optional."

Oh my god, had those words left his mouth? Don't bring up sex when someone talks about buying anything. Jesus, this was a complete shitshow. So much for the DeMarco charm.

"Sex. Is. Optional," she whispered, not meeting his gaze. "Good to know."

Elissa licked her lips and turned her sharp eyes to him. Anger simmered in their depths. He'd lost. He'd offered everything he had, and she wanted nothing to do with it. With him.

"I think you need to leave now." Her voice was no longer soft or confused. In fact, it drew the gazes of several others nearby, including her friend.

"I thought you liked honesty." He held tight to this last straw, but it wouldn't hold.

"There's honesty, and then there's…you. You need to look at yourself in the mirror and ask, 'Am I the asshole?' If the answer isn't yes, you need to keep doing it until you figure out where this conversation went off the rails."

His hopes, which had been growing ever since she walked

into the bar, crashed and burned.

"You're right. This was a mistake."

He grabbed his black leather jacket and pulled his wallet out of the inside pocket. Ryan tossed down enough cash to cover their two drinks and a generous tip. He snatched his motorcycle helmet from where it had been resting at his feet, strode to the door without another word, and stepped into the cooling twilight of a January evening.

Jamming the helmet on his head, he stalked over to his bike. Ryan took a deep breath before starting it. He'd fucked that up about as well as anyone could have. Stupid ADHD. No filters between his brain and his mouth. And she hadn't bought into his bullshit. Part of him was relieved. Not many would turn down the chance to make nice with the DeMarcos, even if it meant using him to do so. He'd seriously misjudged her.

The other part of him was more disappointed than he'd ever admit out loud.

He'd spent so many years dating women he knew would piss off his parents, he'd forgotten they weren't his type. They'd been hookups he'd found on the dating apps, with the occasional friend willing to play along. The sex had been enjoyable, usually, and the commitment nonexistent.

He'd hoped to find the same tonight, but instead Elissa had walked through the door. She'd looked the part, but he doubted no-commitment sex was in her wheelhouse, let alone pulling a fast one over on his family. And something about her had Ryan wanting more.

CHAPTER 7
an offer i could refuse

Elissa watched, smug, as Ryan grabbed his jacket and stormed out of the restaurant. Had he expected he could smolder at her and she'd just take his hand and fake out his family? Dude didn't know who he was messing with. Good riddance.

She sighed. He was so hot, though. Besides the arrogance, she wouldn't have minded spending a bit more time with him. After all, he'd pegged her brain as her best asset right off the bat and hadn't minded her honesty. Not to mention his eyes. She could get lost in those eyes if she let herself.

A tap on her shoulder brought her out of her reverie. Jules stood in front of her, her brows drawn down in concern.

"What happened?"

"He had an offer I could refuse. He didn't take rejection kindly." Elissa shook her head, still in shock.

Her friend looked down at the money on the table. "Well, at least he paid for the drinks. I'll cash you out. Stay as long as you want, lady."

Elissa contemplated her half-empty glass of rosé while Jules cleared away the beer glass. Another small sigh escaped her lips. Her anger over how the date had ended hid her disappointment. For a moment, she'd thought they had a connection, that he found her amusing or attractive. Something.

Now that the date was officially over, she gave in to the

inevitable. Elissa pulled out her phone and turned it on. Her eyes widened as she caught a notification from a minute after she must've turned the darn thing off.

> R: Family emergency. My sister called her oldest may have a broken arm and she needs someone to watch the other 2. Call or text and we can reschedule

What? What! If Ryan was babysitting his niblings, who had she been on a date with?!

Had he lied about his name, trying to coax some woman, any woman, to play along with his scheme? A chill shivered down her spine and her hand shook. What would have happened if she'd said yes, like an itty-bitty part of her buried deep, deep down wished?

"Son of a bitch!"

"Guess you owe the Wright family swear jar," Jules said from behind her, laughter dancing in her voice.

"I don't know. I think even Mom will let me have that one." Even the one where she called him an asshole, because the truth was appreciated in the Wright household. Somewhere along the way, Elissa had internalized her mother's great idea to keep Ami from swearing a blue streak in high school. "Take a look."

She shoved her phone at Jules and took a sip of her wine, trying to calm her racing heart. It sorta worked. Or the wine made her see the humor in the situation. Because how, in the twenty-first century, do people end up on a date with the whole wrong person? No wonder he couldn't remember her name. *She* wasn't the right date.

"You had a date with the wrong Ryan?" People glanced over, and Jules lowered her voice. "How the fuck is that possible?"

Elissa pointed an accusatory finger, trying to keep the smile off her face. It wasn't funny. It wasn't. "*You* told me to turn off my phone!"

"I have a God-awful dating life. Why would you listen to me?"

"At least you have a dating life. I haven't dated anyone since Victor."

"I know, lady." Jules squeezed her shoulder. "Stick around for a bit, and I'll see you out. Make sure the asshole isn't lurking in the shadows."

"Thanks, Jules. You're the best."

"Better believe it!"

An hour later, Jules took a short break and walked Elissa to her car. Stewing in her anger, she was home before she realized it.

"How was your date?" her mom asked as Elissa walked down the hall.

"I don't want to talk about it," she mumbled, desperately longing for nothing more than to crawl into bed and pretend this whole evening had never happened. That way, she would never have to admit she was as disappointed as she was angry.

"Come on, it couldn't have been that bad. I've met Ryan. He seems very nice."

"I said I don't want to talk about it." She sounded a lot like her sister Ami, and heat spread across her cheeks.

"Oh. Okay, sweetie."

The regret in her mother's voice stopped Elissa dead in her tracks outside her bedroom door. It wasn't long ago her mom hadn't been well enough for Elissa to pour her heart out to her, and she'd missed those moments. A lot. She turned around, slunk into the room, and plopped onto the sofa.

"I'm sorry, Mom. It was a rough night."

"Tell me about it."

Elissa told her the whole story. Her mother was trying hard not to laugh. Elissa had been on a date with a complete stranger. The guy could've been a serial killer. But the way he'd looked at her sparked a smoldering fire in her.

"Then I told him to look at himself in the mirror and ask if he was the…" Elissa caught herself before what she'd actually said slipped out. "Um, the jerk."

Dana lost the battle with her sense of the absurd. Her peals of laughter rang through the house, drawing her father out of his office and her brother out of his room. Throwing a disgusted look at her mom, Elissa stalked out of the living room, leaving her mother to explain to the rest of her family her embarrassing evening. She stomped down the hall, yanked open her bedroom door, and threw herself on her bed. Elissa screamed into her pillow.

This was bad. She'd made a connection with a jerk while a nice guy, who only ditched her because his nibling may have broken an arm, had politely informed her he couldn't show. What did that say about her? And why hadn't she felt something was off?

His eyes. They sparked with intelligence. And those full lips, always turned up at the corners as though he found the whole world amusing. His hair falling softly over one eye, only to be pushed back into place by a firm hand. His deep voice had a rumble to it that reminded her of the purr from the chubby tuxedo cat Jules had when they were kids. Only an hour with him, and the worst ending to a date she'd ever had, and she was all sorts of bothered.

"Nuts!" she said to no one in particular. She could only hope she'd left him in as much a state as she now found herself.

Okay, it was funny. A little. Or she was having a nervous reaction to a bad situation. Elissa pulled out her phone and decided she'd put Jerk-Ryan out of her mind by texting Nice-guy Ryan. She didn't need any more jerks in her life, not even ones as drool-worthy as this one had been.

E: Thank you for letting me know. I'm sorry to

> hear about your sister's kid. I hope everything
> is OK. Would you like to reschedule? Maybe
> Thursday or next Tuesday?

She should postpone this new dating endeavor. Her mom hadn't gotten the all-clear from her doctor yet, and Elissa had little time to spare between work and helping her family. Tax season was around the corner, and she still lived with her parents. The whole idea of facing the twenty-something-and-single dating scene filled her with existential dread.

No, fear and dread had controlled her life last year. This year needed to be different. She wouldn't postpone the date with Nice-Ryan. He'd made the effort to contact her, and she promised her mother to go on a date with him. She hit send.

She might have a lot of frogs to kiss before she found the one who turned into a prince. Wasn't it better to start the kissing now? She couldn't let her perfectionist tendencies interfere with a happily ever after.

Elissa readied for bed, checking her phone again before plugging it in for the night. She had a reply from Nice-Ryan.

> R: Tuesday sounds great. Same place and
> time?

Elissa refused to repeat tonight in the exact same place, even if Jules would be there to hold her hand after. She shot off a suggestion to Nice-Ryan. He confirmed a moment later, and Elissa made an event in her calendar.

She snuggled into bed, pulling the covers up to her ears. Yes, the best way to get the jerk with the beautiful eyes out of her mind was to go on a nice, normal date with a nice, normal guy. They would receive positive news from Mom's doctor, and she could finally enter the world of adulting for real. It was the perfect moment to manifest what she wanted from the universe, and some instinct told her it would be a good year.

CHAPTER 8
tell me i'm right. and pretty.

Ryan zigzagged through the end of rush hour traffic to his apartment. He pulled into the apartment parking lot and tucked his motorcycle under the carport next to Iz's battered old Civic. The thing looked like a piece of shit, but it ran like a dream and had a kick-ass sound system. Iz wouldn't have it any other way.

He unlocked the door and called out, "Hello?"

No answer. Resigning himself to an empty apartment, Ryan plugged in his dead phone and made a sandwich. He took his sandwich to the living room and turned on the TV, but he didn't really watch the show. A pair of lake-blue eyes and smiling pink lips occupied most of the retail space in his head. It would be easier to forget her if her brains and honesty hadn't also left a lasting impression. It had been a long time since he'd enjoyed a date so much, the ending notwithstanding.

He should call her and apologize. Tell her he was an idiot. Explain the situation better. No, the only part she'd buy was the idiot bit.

The small voice in the back of his head, which oddly sounded more like Elissa's today, told him he'd been an asshole tonight, but it might be worth a shot. Their mothers were friends—he'd likely be running into her again sooner or later. More than that, it was the right thing to do. Iz would say the same thing, after calling him a dickhead first.

Ryan pushed aside the huge DeMarco ego he'd inherited from his father, heaved himself off the couch, and grabbed his phone from the kitchen. His lock screen informed him he had three texts. One was from Alex, and two were from someone named Laurel. The name was familiar, but he couldn't put a face to it. Why was she in his contacts? He clicked on the first of her messages received around five, when he'd realized his phone was dead.

> L: So sorry I have to work late. Another time?

Wait, what? He reread the first message, then read the second.

> L: I'm free Thursday. Can we meet closer to my work?

And the text from Alex, about a half hour ago.

> A: How did it go with Laurel?

Had he been on a date with a complete stranger? No fucking way. What were the chances of this? Ryan bet Elissa could've told him the odds. He called his brother.

"Who is this?" Alex said.

"It's Ryan, asshole."

"You can't possibly be my brother. My brother never calls when a text will do."

"What does Laurel look like?" He opened the fridge and stared at the contents as if they held the answer.

"What do you mean, what does she look like? You just saw her."

"She didn't show, and my phone died."

"Well, that's going to make the next charity event super awkward. Laurel's the party planner."

"Just tell me what she looks like. Please, Alex." Ryan shut

the fridge door and thunked his forehead against it, bracing himself for the bad news.

"Yeah, okay." His brother paused. "She's an inch or two shorter than you—"

"I'm gonna stop you there."

His stomach dropped. Elissa was barely taller than Nonna had been. If Laurel was almost as tall as he was, he'd fucked up. He'd been on a date with the wrong woman. There was no way he was telling his brother. That would lead to their cousins finding out. And their parents and aunts and uncles. It would become a funny story they'd tell at every opportunity to embarrass him, from now until eternity. Shit.

"Why? What's going on?"

Ryan trudged to the living room and collapsed onto the couch.

"It doesn't matter. I don't know why I let you talk me into it in the first place. Dad would never let me off the hook just for dating someone Mom approves."

"It was always a long shot, Ryan, but you seemed adamant you didn't want to work for him. I tried to give you something you could do that was more…palatable."

"I appreciate that, but now what am I gonna do?"

"Are you sure you won't work for him?" Alex switched from brotherly concern to chief operations officer. "The company keeps him busy. Even if you took over for Val, you still wouldn't see him often. The pay is similar to your bartending gig and you get benefits. And if you hate it, quit once Dad releases your trust fund."

Ryan had taken on the bartending job five years ago to help Iz's family when they'd been shorthanded after opening their latest restaurant. Back then, he had no idea what he'd wanted to do with his degree in global studies. Now he did, but it would be ten times harder and take twice as long to build his career as a food podcaster without the money from his trust.

"Let me think about it." Ryan shoved his free hand through his hair, tugging tight and letting the pain ground him.

"Okay, but don't take too long. Val needs to leave in the next few weeks. House hunting, packing, all that shit."

"Thanks for the heads-up, Alex. Talk to you soon."

He had no way of contacting Elissa. If he walked into the Sandpiper without apologizing, her friend would likely have his balls. He'd gotten on the wrong side of a few other best friends of the many girls he'd dated and barely lived to regret it.

There was one thing he could do to redeem himself. Ryan flopped on the couch and texted Laurel.

R: I'm an asshole. You don't want to date me.

At least he saved some poor woman from having to deal with his bullshit. In fact…

Ryan spent the next ten minutes going through his contacts and deleting at least a dozen of those other poor women he'd wronged. God, he was an asshole. He tossed the phone onto the coffee table, threw his arm over his eyes, and allowed himself to wallow in self-pity.

He had a decision to make. A part of him longed to tell his father to go to hell and take his money with him. Cut his ties with the DeMarco fortune and sink or swim on his own merits. The less stupid part of him knew he was incredibly privileged to have access to generational wealth, and he'd be a fool to throw it away. Could he give the next two years and change to the family business and still live with himself at age thirty?

Ryan had no fucking clue.

The person he could trust to talk this through was Iz, but they had totally different schedules. Ryan worked nights mostly, sometimes afternoons, while Iz generally kept business hours. And they had a boyfriend, which meant dates and sleepovers. He had to wait until they were in the same room at the same time and he had enough bandwidth to handle a conversation

Ryan was pretty sure would hurt his feelings.

He went to bed, haunted by the hurt in Elissa's eyes. If he could have it to do over, he'd keep his damned mouth shut.

It was after close in the small hours of Friday morning before the stars aligned.

"Shh, Teo's asleep," Iz said from the kitchen as Ryan shut and locked the door behind him. They pulled out two beers. "Want one?"

"God, yes. Why are you up?"

"You've been trying to talk to me for a couple days. Couldn't sleep, so figured now was good."

"What did I ever do to deserve you as a friend?"

Ryan slid onto a chair next to their little four-person table. Iz slid the can of Barrio Blonde across as they sat. Ryan popped the top and took a glug.

"Called my third-grade bully 'poopy pants.'"

Ryan chuckled. He'd caught hell from his parents, but the fuck if he was going to let some snot-nosed bully push around his best friend. Fucker was lucky the teacher intervened before Ryan's fist landed in his gut. Ryan would have called expulsion a fair trade.

"So, what's up, Ry?"

"I fucked up."

"Not the first time."

"Yeah, but this was a doozy."

He told Iz all about the failed date. Told them about the choice in front of him.

"I mean, you work for *my* family." Iz polished off their beer.

"Yeah, but they like me. I've never been anything other than a disappointment to my parents. Every time I try to stand out, I get a pat on the head before they turn their attention back to

Alex."

"You used to work summers for your grandfather. What would be so different now?"

Ryan had, indeed, worked summers for DeMarco Property Management. It was part of the deal. Work summers starting at sixteen until college graduation. The idea was to work in a different department each summer to learn the business as a whole, but also to discover what department would be a good fit. Alex and his cousins had all played along. Hell, they'd even seemed to enjoy it. Alex was now their father's right hand. Two of his cousins managed large apartment complexes. One had an entry-level position in the marketing department. Another studied accounting at the U. And the last was in his junior year of high school and already looking forward to working in the summer.

The first summer after he'd turned sixteen, Ryan had worked on a maintenance crew and enjoyed it. Every day carried a new set of problems to fix, and he was all over the city. One day it would be painting a unit for a new tenant, the next would be fixing a leak, the next would be pool maintenance.

But the following summer they put him in the office working in accounting with his aunt. Ryan hated numbers, loathed them. He had nightmares during the school year where he was faced with nonsense numbers chasing him through bewildering landscapes covered in graph paper. He skipped out and joined the maintenance crews. His grandfather's face had never been so red as when he had finally caught on to Ryan's little scheme.

His Nonna had argued his case, and his grandfather had allowed him to continue working maintenance that summer. He was dead by the next summer, and Ryan's father had enough crap to deal with afterward. Ryan was allowed to resume his duties in the maintenance division, and his dad had seemed to forget about him.

"I don't know, and I don't want to find out. But if I want my trust fund, I have to play nice."

"It's future security for a couple years' work. A lot of people would kill for that kind of money."

Ryan ran a hand through his hair. "I know, first-world problems."

"Doesn't mean they're not real. Do you have a business plan yet? If you gave your dad a hint what the money would be used for, would he lay off?"

"He'd think it was a waste of time."

Any activity not about profit was viewed as a waste of time and resources. He needed the trust fund money to help him grow his audience and monetize his creative endeavor. Ryan was sure, with a little patience, TLC, and being able to supplement his bartending job with his trust fund, he could eventually podcast full time.

"How do you know if you won't try?"

"Stop making sense, Iz. You're supposed to be my friend and tell me I'm right. And pretty."

He finished his beer as Iz laughed at him

"You are pretty, and you're not exactly wrong," they said after catching their breath. "But you're not exactly right, either. Adulting sucks, and this has to be your decision. The way I see it is that, yes, you'd have to trade a job you like for one you don't. A flexible job for a nine-to-five. But after two years, you can tell that job to suck it and do whatever your shriveled heart desires for the rest of your life. It might be worth it."

"You're right." Of course Iz was right. They had an annoying habit of usually being right.

Ryan was smart and reasonably responsible with money. Over the next two years, he'd save every penny possible, and with his trust fund, he wouldn't have to worry about monetizing his podcast for a while. He could indulge his creative streak for the first time in his life and focus on creating the best podcast possible. Buying, selling, leasing, and maintaining properties wouldn't make him happy, but it would allow him to do what did make him happy. Just delayed.

"So, have you made up your mind?" Iz stretched and yawned. Time to settle this so they both could sleep.

"Yes."

"And?"

"I'll talk to my dad first thing Monday."

"Good boy."

"I hate you."

"No, you don't. Goodnight, Ryan."

"Night, Iz. And thanks."

Iz winked as they went back to their bedroom. Ryan grabbed another beer and turned on the TV. It was a *Lord of the Rings* kind of night.

CHAPTER 9
sister hugs

E lissa paced restlessly from the kitchen to the picture window in the living room. Her boss had been sweet and given her a couple hours off so she could be at home when her parents returned from the doctor. Today was the day their fortunes changed. For better or for worse.

Elissa didn't know which she preferred—no, that wasn't right. She wanted her mother to be okay. But if she *was* okay, something else might go wrong. Life had taught her it likely would. What and when were the only questions left.

A car door slammed outside, announcing Leo was home from school. With the cost of the cancer treatments, they hadn't been able to afford another car or the insurance premiums, and Mom usually took him to and from school since it was on her route to work. He got a ride from a friend today.

"Is it them?" Ami called from the living room, nose in her phone.

"No, it's Leo."

Elissa pounced as soon as Leo walked in, pulling him in for a hug.

"Ugh." He stiffened in her arms. "Sister hugs."

"Don't worry, dumbass." Ami slid her phone into her pocket. "I won't hug your stinky teenage self."

"Thanks, Ami. You're the best."

Elissa released him, and her younger siblings did their stupid handshake, a confusing dance of fists and fingers that ended in a butt-bump.

"You two are weird," she said with an eye roll as she walked to the kitchen.

She poured water for them both, sliding the glasses over the kitchen island. Leo dumped his backpack onto a bar stool and chugged the water. Ami toyed with hers absently.

Elissa was nearly a carbon copy of their mom, sharing the same short and curvy build and blue eyes. So much so, her dad still joked she was an immaculate conception clone. Ami and Leo were both blond, built more like their dad, slender and several inches taller than Elissa. Ami's eyes were hazel, as were Dad's, but Leo had blue eyes like Elissa, though his were a couple shades lighter. And he had Dad's dimpled chin.

Elissa broke the heavy silence. "It's going to be okay."

"You don't know that," Ami snapped at her.

"Ames…" Leo slung an arm around her shoulders.

The creak of the old garage door, which had needed to be replaced for at least two years, drew all three sets of eyes to the entry off the kitchen. The air grew still with anticipation.

Peter Wright opened the door with a smile on his face she hadn't seen since the love of his life had been diagnosed.

Relief flooded through her, and Elissa took a breath that seemed deeper and more cleansing than any before this moment. Her mom was going to be okay. Everything was going to be okay. Oh please, let everything be okay.

Dana walked in carrying a bag from their favorite Chinese restaurant and a bottle of bubbly. Because, after all, sparkling wine goes with everything.

As soon as their mom dropped the food on the dining room table, the three kids wrapped her in a group hug, all their bickering forgotten in the pure, unadulterated joy of this moment.

Her father's arms wrapped around her, around all of them,

completing the moment. They stood like a big Wright ball of love, for who knew how long.

"Is that moo shu?" Leo muttered finally.

Trust the teenage boy to crack first.

"Of course," Mom said, half laugh and half sob.

"Good, I'm hungry."

Dad ruffled his hair and the hug broke. Mom took a step to the kitchen, but Elissa put a hand on her arm.

"We've got it, Mom. Leo, plates and forks."

"I'll take chopsticks," Ami called.

"And chopsticks. Ami, you pop the wine and I'll get the glasses."

"Oh, don't fuss, Lissa." Her mom waved a dismissal.

"You know she wouldn't have it any other way, Mom." Ami pulled the foil off the bottle.

Elissa shook her head as she pulled out the champagne flutes from the cabinet. Unlike at New Year's, she didn't have to blow out the dust from a year of disuse.

Leo returned, carrying paper plates and utensils. Ami worked the cork out of the bottle with a quiet *pop*.

"What about me?" he asked, a grin on his face. He knew he wasn't getting any wine, but it was becoming a family joke.

"You know where the soda is, young man," her mom said. "You're only seventeen."

Seventeen. And a junior in high school. With a driver's license. Going on dates. With girls. A kid with a mom who would now make it to graduation. And weddings and the birth of grandbabies, if anyone decided to have those. Elissa brushed the tears away. They'd all have a chance to do those things with their mom around. The prognosis may have been good, but there was always the possibility the odds would not be with them.

Ami hovered the bottle over the last empty glass, her brows raised.

"Maybe this once, Dana." Their dad sat in the chair at the

far end.

Leo practiced his best puppy-dog eyes and folded his hands in front of him in supplication.

"Please? Just a tiny bit?"

"Ugh, fine." Mom turned her sharp eyes on Ami. "If it's over half full, you're on dish duty at the next four Sunday dinners."

"I got this. Don't worry."

Ami poured the perfect under-half-full glass, and everyone took their places at the table.

Dad raised his glass. "To my beautiful wife."

Everyone clinked their glasses and sipped, then passed around the containers of Chinese food.

"Are you gonna keep the whole story to yourselves?" Ami demanded when plates were full.

"Not much to tell," Mom said. "Bloodwork came back with all markers exactly where the doctor wanted them. I'm in remission. I have to go in for testing every few months for another year or so. After that, I can drop to once a year. We can resume normal activities."

"That's it?" Leo asked around a bite of food. Teenage boys could be so gross.

"Yes," Dad said.

"Boring."

"Yeah. Isn't that something?" He leaned over and kissed Dana on the cheek.

He wasn't wrong. This past year had been far too exciting. With the cancer treatments, Elissa moving in after her breakup with Victor, Ami's academic and other issues at the university, and Leo's two trips to the hospital for pneumonia and bronchitis. Boring sounded darn good, a nice change of pace.

Leo rolled his eyes, and an impish grin spread over his face.

"Hey, Ami, did you hear about Elissa's date?"

The blood drained from Elissa's face. She loved Ami, truly, but they had a more antagonistic relationship. Her sister knew every one of her buttons and pressed them as often and as hard as she could. Elissa couldn't do much about it except try to disengage. Someday, though, stuff would get real and Ami wouldn't know what hit her.

"Oh? Spill the tea." Ami tapped her fingers together in front of her face like a supervillain from a movie.

"It was a disaster! Like, epic."

"Really?" She nudged Elissa with her elbow. "Was he ugly?"

"No." Elissa took a gulp of her wine. She was going to need it.

"Poor?"

"No!"

"Then why don't you want his babies, Lissa?" Ami's voice was all saccharine sweet.

"Stop teasing your sister," Dad said, as he had at nearly every family dinner for the past ten years.

"I wouldn't have to tease her if she'd tell me sh—stuff."

"It's fine, Dad. I met the wrong guy," Elissa answered, refusing to meet her sister's gaze. She twirled some lo mein on her fork. "Not just wrong for me, but the wrong guy. I found out later the guy I was supposed to meet couldn't make it."

"You went on a blind date with a total stranger? The unpredictable disappointment box has already been filled. Stay in your own!"

"You are not a disappointment, Ami," their mother said.

Ami waved away her words, laser focused on Elissa. She was much more interested in getting the details of this sub-Reddit worthy disaster of a date.

"The guy I met expected different things from a relationship. I called Nice-Ryan, and we rescheduled to Tuesday. A funny story to tell someday."

She still didn't find it funny, especially since Jerk-Ryan still insisted on giving her erotic dreams every night. It would stop, she was sure, once she met Nice-Ryan. She would request a picture this time, and she wouldn't turn off her phone until he walked into the restaurant.

"Nice-Ryan?" Ami asked, a cat-who-ate-the-canary grin on her face.

Elissa hadn't met to let that slip.

"The other guy's name was Ryan, too," she mumbled.

"So what do you call him? Not-quite-right-Ryan? Wrong-Ryan? Creep-Ryan?"

"Shut up. It's not my fault. He said his name was Ryan and seemed pleasant enough until the end."

"What? Did he say lewd things to you? Whisper in your ear, tell you what he'd do to you in the bedroom? You could use some lewdness in your life," Ami teased.

Elissa's face heated.

"Ami..." Mom said, and their dad cleared his throat.

Ami closed her mouth with a click of the teeth. Her cheeks reddened. She'd forgotten their parents were in the room. Ami always itched to push the envelope, but she usually waited until the two of them were alone.

"Sorry," her sister mumbled. "So why did Nice-Ryan stand you up?"

"Family emergency."

"You two will be the perfect match. Before long, Mom will have those grandchildren she refuses to acknowledge she wants."

"I am too young to be a grandmother," Mom protested, but there was a hint of a blush on her cheeks.

"You'd be the most beautiful grandmother in the room." Dad intertwined their fingers and gazed adoringly at her.

"Eww," Leo said.

"Yeah, I'm with stinky boy. Eww," Ami chimed in, doing a fist bump with Leo.

"Oh, Elissa, on the way back from the doctor's, your mom and I talked about a getaway to celebrate the good news. Will you be around to stay with Leo sometime in the next month?"

"I don't need anyone to stay with me. I'm almost eighteen," Leo said.

"In nine months," Dad reminded him.

"If she can't, I can." Ami took a long sip of her wine.

"No!" their parents said in unison.

"I'm hurt, truly hurt." No actual hurt on her face, Ami winked at Leo and plastered a pout on her lips. Her parents missed it in their shock. "You don't think I'm capable of watching my baby brother? You left both of us with Elissa when she was only eighteen, and now you don't want to leave the twenty-one-year-old in charge?"

"Ami, the one time we left you alone because you insisted you could handle it, we came back to find Elissa cleaning all the trash from the party you threw. She's the responsible one."

"And I'm the eternal fuckup, never able to live up to Miss Perfect, Elissa Wright, who never does anything wrong."

"Swear jar, Ami," Mom said automatically.

Now her sister looked hurt. Ami made mistakes, and Elissa envied her sister that ability. Because Elissa never could make mistakes. The stakes were too high. If *she* messed up, the carefully scaffolded world her parents built around this family, built around Leo, would come tumbling down. So Elissa became the reliable one, the one you called in a crisis, the one who always did the right thing and put family first.

Sometimes, she hated being the reliable one.

"Yeah, of course I'll do it. I live here, after all."

She hoped her offer would distract them from dredging up more of Ami's poor choices.

"And you don't have a social life, except for Jules," Leo said. "She'll just hang out here and raid the liquor cabinet."

True. But also… "Hey!"

Ami dropped her chopsticks with a loud clatter. "And there's Elissa, coming to the rescue. I don't need you to rescue me anymore. I'm a big girl now. I'm done. No swear jar. I don't live here anymore."

She pushed her chair back.

"How about we forget the swear jar today?" Their dad covered Mom's hand and sent a pleading glance at Ami. "We have a lot to celebrate."

Ami froze, and all three kids looked at their mom.

"Yeah." A tremulous smile formed on Dana's lips. "We can forget the swear jar today. Please stay, Ami."

Leo opened his mouth, about to let some four-letter word drop to test the waters.

Elissa kicked him in the shin. "Don't even think about it."

"Think about what?" He looked all to innocent.

"Yeah, don't push it, doofus." Ami ruffled his hair, and the tension left the room.

After dinner, Elissa cleared the table, then dashed off a quick note to Jules, letting her know Dana would be fine.

She chuckled as a screen full of happy emojis greeted the news.

CHAPTER 10
beg for a job

Ryan's alarm woke him at six on Monday morning. He almost threw his phone across the room before he remembered why he'd set it so early. It was time to go begging. Today was going to suck.

What did one wear to beg for a job? A suit, of course. He pulled a wrinkled navy suit out of his closet and hung it in the bathroom to steam while he showered. He didn't even own an iron. Steam poured out of the shower, and Ryan stepped over the edge of the tub and washed.

He still wasn't sure selling out to his corporate overlord family would be worth it. But if he wanted access to his trust fund, this was his last chance. His attempts to convince a sophisticated woman to play girlfriend had failed, and not only was he not ready to explain his grand plan, but he wasn't even sure he had one. A podcast and associated YouTube channel dedicated to the intersection of history, food, and culture were unlikely to inspire any confidence from his father. Even with a handful of completed scripts and a solid business plan, he'd think it was a waste of time, as he had the school plays, creative writing, and photography in high school. Ryan had excelled in those subjects, and had actual fun, but it wasn't good enough for his father.

Shower thoughts. Sometimes he had strokes of genius, sometimes he overthought the only viable decision on the table.

Sometimes, he imagined a curvy woman with lake-blue eyes was in the shower with him, her pretty pink lips—

Enough.

He toweled off and dressed in a white shirt, a red and blue striped tie, and his navy suit. He looked at himself in the tiny mirror in his bathroom. A wrinkled mess stared back, uncomfortable in his own skin. Ryan yanked off the tie, tossed the jacket on the bed, and dug through his closet for his best pair of jeans. He pulled out a button-down short-sleeved shirt with a geometric pattern he liked. In a few minutes, he was eating toast in the kitchen and staring at the pile of research books. His fingers itched to pull out his laptop and work on the script. Now, when he needed to leave in a few minutes, did the ideas start flowing.

Mateo came out of Iz's room as Ryan shoved his arms into his leather jacket.

"Dude, where you going?" his best friend's boyfriend said with a wide yawn.

"Job begging," Ryan replied.

"Good luck."

Iz poked their head out at this exchange.

"Gonna see you at Nopalitos later?" they asked.

"Depends, Iz. I hope so."

"Tell Alex hi from me."

Ryan grabbed his helmet and keys and headed out the door. It was only a fifteen-minute drive to the offices of DeMarco Property Management. He parked his bike under the solar panels that covered most of the lot. His dad's Mercedes was already there, as was his brother's Buick. Since he was a few minutes early, and the door wouldn't be unlocked yet, he took a moment to gather his thoughts.

His dad would be pleased his power play had worked. Ryan hoped he'd be able to work maintenance, the only thing about property management he enjoyed. Hell, he'd even been able to help his current landlord, who'd taken a bit off his rent when he'd been available to help other tenants with urgent or emergency maintenance problems.

The click of the door unlocking brought him back to the present.

"Ryan?" A woman about his age opened the door. Valerie, the office manager who would soon be moving.

"Hi, Val."

"Come on in. You should've knocked."

"Nah, I needed a moment. Alex says you're moving soon?"

Val had been with the company since it had become apparent Ryan wanted nothing to do with it, six months after he'd graduated from the U.

"Yeah. Ben got a great offer in Phoenix. We close on the house there next week, and the movers come in three weeks, the Saturday after my last day."

He stepped inside and the door closed behind him. The lights were on, but Val seemed to be the only person here. Most of the employees came in around eight. Tuesdays and Thursdays, DPM was open until seven at night to help accommodate people who worked typical business hours. The office manager usually came in early. His dad's schedule varied, but Alex was usually in during normal operating hours.

Most of the employees worked in an open office, each with their own cubicle, but there were several offices on the perimeter. His dad and brother each had one, CEO and Chief Operating Officer respectively. His two aunts had their own offices as well. Annetta was the bookkeeper and Gisella was in charge of marketing.

"You here to see your father?" Val settled into her seat at the reception desk.

Ryan sighed. It was his last chance to walk out of here, find work somewhere else, convince Iz's family to give him more hours. But unless he worked in a similar field, his dad wouldn't relent until Ryan had a job he approved of. Bartending, podcasting, and living off the trust fund didn't qualify.

"Yes."

"Head on back. I'll let him know you're coming." She picked up the phone as he trudged toward his father's office.

Before he could knock on his father's door, it opened to reveal his brother's slightly taller, slimmer frame. Alex took after their mother in this, as well as with his lighter brown hair and hazel eyes. But in his approach to life and business, he was their dad's twin. Ryan, on the other hand, looked almost exactly like their dad, but his personality was unique in the family. His grandmother had once told him he was a pearl in the middle of gold coins. Then she gave him a cookie.

"Hi, Ryan. Come on in," Alex said with a professional smile.

His brother clapped him on the back as he moved into the office. His dad stood as Ryan entered and held out a hand. He took it and gave it the firm shake Alessandro had taught him at age ten.

"Ryan. We weren't expecting you." His dad sat down. Alex took a chair in front of the desk, but Ryan remained standing. "What do you need?"

Fair. Except for planned family events, Ryan usually only ever talked to his father when he needed something from him or when his mother passed the phone on their weekly calls.

He steeled himself.

"I've been thinking a lot about your ultimatum at New Year's," Ryan said. "I graduated five years ago, and I can see from your perspective where I haven't accomplished much. My goals are different than the rest of the family, and in order to reach those goals, I need access to my trust fund."

"If you're trying to argue your way out of working for the family business—" his father said.

"I'm not. Please, just hear me out. Working for the family will give me much less time to devote to my own goals. I'd like

70

to negotiate a limit after which I'll be able to pursue my own ambitions without you holding the trust fund over my head like a g—like a sword."

He caught himself in time to not profane God in front of his father. That would've lost him the argument.

Alessandro DeMarco tented his fingers and pressed his lips together, age-old signs he was seriously considering the deal on the table. After a moment, he made eye contact with his younger son.

"You turn thirty in a little over two years," he said. "You give that time to this company, and if you decide to pursue your own goals after, the trust fund will be yours, free and clear, but not a penny until then."

"Great." Ryan had successfully negotiated with his father, a feat he'd rarely accomplished in his almost twenty-eight years on earth. A minor miracle. Maybe a major miracle. "I'd like—"

His dad held up a finger. Ryan swallowed what he'd been about to say.

"Since you worked every summer in maintenance, you will use the next two years to rotate between departments. Not accounting," his father said as Ryan opened his mouth to object. "It was a disaster then, and it would be a disaster now. But marketing, sales, acquisitions, and here in the office."

Ryan nodded. It was a reasonable requirement.

"As I noted, Val is leaving us, so I'll have you start as office manager. I haven't interviewed anyone I liked yet. It's an effective way for you to get to know everyone and, of course, how the office and the company runs as a whole."

"I'll need to give the Ochoas my two-weeks' notice. I'll know which weekday shifts I can get covered by the end of the day."

Two of the shifts were the next two Saturdays, so he could work those. One shift was tomorrow night, and he'd volunteered to take it from the usual bartender so she could go to a concert. It was too late for anyone else to cover, but the rest should be easy. The other bartenders all owed him favors.

"It's just a bartending job," his father said.

"It's *my* job, with my best friend's family. I'm not leaving them holding the bag, and I refuse to throw away a lifetime of friendship over any job." Ryan tried to keep the anger out of his voice, but from his brother's face, he hadn't been successful.

Alessandro's eyes narrowed, and he pressed his lips together. "Fine. Can you be here first thing tomorrow to train with Val?"

"Yes, but I have a shift I have to work tomorrow night, so I can only work until three." And going in to the restaurant from four until close was going to suck ass, but there wasn't much he could do about it now.

His dad gave him a sharp nod, acknowledging the facts while not being happy about them at all. It's not like Ryan was thrilled with the whole arrangement, either. They'd have to make the best of the situation. Alessandro rose and held out his hand again. Ryan took it.

"Bring your paperwork tomorrow and a shirt and tie. I know you enjoy getting under my skin with how you dress, but you'll be the first person someone sees when they walk through our door. First impressions matter." His father returned to his work, effectively dismissing his younger son.

That last bit was all too true, as Ryan had discovered to his detriment during his absolute clusterfuck of a date last week.

"Fine. See you tomorrow." Ryan left. Anything further at this point would be fruitless. His brother followed him out of the office and closed the door behind them.

"Should I check the forecast?" Alex grinned and waved his phone around.

"What?"

"You said there'd be a blizzard in Tucson before you worked for Dad—"

Ryan punched Alex's shoulder.

"Ow!" Alex rubbed the spot and chuckled.

"I did some thinking."

"Ah, you mean Iz talked some sense into you."

"Fuck you." He hated that his brother knew him so well. "But yes, Iz pointed out that with access to the trust fund, I won't have to work for a long while after I'm done here. I'll finally be able to give my project my full attention."

"You're being so cagey about this project, Ry. Want to fill me in?"

"Nope, you'll get all judgy, or worse, try to help. When I have a prototype and a business plan, I promise you'll be one of the first to hear it."

"Only so I can play Dad." Alex's hazel eyes twinkled.

"God, yes. That way I can throw together counterarguments for when he tries to tear the whole thing apart." Ryan snorted a laugh, and his brother joined him. His dad was a tough negotiator and a great businessman. If his plan could pass Alessandro DeMarco's tests, he'd be fine.

"So, I'll see you in the morning?"

"Looks like."

They bro-hugged, part handshake, part hug, part dominance display. Alex went to his office and closed the door, and Ryan walked to the reception area.

"It seems I have an apprentice," Val said with a grin as he walked to her desk.

"Yes, ma'am." Ryan returned the grin. "See you in the morning."

Ryan snagged his helmet from where he'd left it and strode into the clear mid-morning sunshine. He took a deep breath, appreciating his last day of freedom.

CHAPTER 11
a prayer to saint eligius

B efore Elissa got out of the car on Tuesday evening, she checked her phone for the thousandth time. No messages.

Well, none from her date. About thirty from Jules. Mostly to hype her up, but the last few were bordering on begging for details as soon as Elissa said goodnight.

She'd exchanged photos with Nice-Ryan over the weekend, and the sandy-blond subject of the picture she'd doubled-checked stood right in front of the restaurant, five minutes early. Shorter than average, nerdy but in a cute way, with thick-rimmed glasses framing his light brown eyes. He was exactly her type. Her mom had done good.

"Hi, Ryan." Elissa hurried over to him.

"Elissa, it's such a pleasure to finally meet you."

His handshake was firm and brief, businesslike. His smile was friendly and he kept his gaze on her face. He gave off nice vibes.

"You, too. I've never been here before, but my friend says Nopalitos serves the best margaritas in the city."

"That's a high bar. After you." Nice-Ryan held open the door and led her straight to the bar area, finding the lone table available. "This okay, or would you rather sit at the bar?"

"This is fine." Her short legs made the tall bar stools a bit uncomfortable. This Ryan was waving all kinds of green flags. She relaxed a bit more and tucked a stray strand of hair behind her ear.

"Be right with you!" called a voice muffled by the din.

"It's busy for a Tuesday," Ryan said.

Elissa glanced at the TVs above the bar. "Basketball game on."

"Oh, sorry, I don't follow sports much."

"Me either, for the most part, but Wildcats basketball is the one exception, if only because my parents and brother won't shut up about it."

"Ah, gotcha. My sister and I were raised by a single mom. She didn't have a lot of time for things like sports, so I was the odd man out."

Someone cleared their throat above them.

She looked up, only to freeze as she recognized the man in front of her. Jerk-Ryan. What the hell was he doing here? More importantly, how was she going to explain his presence to the very nice, very normal guy sitting across from her? She drew in a deep breath, uncertain if she was preparing to yell at the jerk or defend her bad luck.

"Welcome to Nopalitos. What can I get you folks?"

Heat rushed to her cheeks. His voice featured in several NSFW dreams this past week, dreams let left her wanting, needing, and gasping. It was even more sensual in real life, and he looked even better than she remembered.

She vaguely noticed Nice-Ryan ordering.

Jerk-Ryan worked here? Here? With those expensive clothes and his arrogant attitude? As a server, a bartender?

The jerk scribbled on a notepad as Ryan ordered, gave them a bland server's smile, and returned to the bar. Her gaze dropped to his tight butt as he walked away, but just for a second. She let out the breath she'd been holding and turned her attention to her actual date. Not the jerk. The nice guy.

C'mon, Elissa, get a grip.

She shook her head to clear the cobwebs, and her heart rate

dipped back to the normal range.

"So, Elissa, my mom says you're an accountant. What company?"

"JMS Accounting."

"Oh, I've heard of them. Well regarded."

"Do you work in accounting?" Her mother would totally set her up with another numbers nerd. Odds were he was in finance or banking, possibly an accountant himself. Elissa liked numbers, excelled at numbers, but often found her fellow accountants a bit…well, boring. There was a stereotype for a reason.

"Adjacent, I guess. I'm a loan officer for a mortgage company."

Bingo! She hated that she was right. She hated even more that she'd made a game out of this. She should do better.

"What do you do in your off hours?" she asked. *Workout, hang with his bros at some fancy-pants bar, or read literature,* her brain filled in before he could answer.

Shut up, she told it. *He's nice.*

"I hit the gym and run, and I read. Mostly mid-century American literature. What about you?"

Two out of three wasn't bad. *No, bad Elissa. This is not a game.*

He could be holding something back. If she was that boring and predictable, she would. She chose her next statement with all the care of grabbing a knife from a disorganized knife drawer.

"I swim and hike, and I like funny books." She watched him closely. Even more important than someone's own preferences for how they spend their free time was their reaction to someone else's choices.

His eyes swept along her arms, looking at the proof she worked out as she mentioned her favorite ways to exercise, but otherwise was unfazed. But when she mentioned she read commercial fiction, and funny fiction at that, he rolled his eyes ever so subtly. Mid-century literature was all well and good, but he didn't have to yuck her yum. This discussion was depressing.

And, as loath as she was to admit it, she missed the banter she'd enjoyed last week with Jerk-Ryan. It may have ended poorly, but she'd had fun until his untoward offer.

"Who's your favorite author?" she asked.

Maybe he'd surprise her. Maybe it wouldn't be Hemingway, or Updike, or Orwell. All great writers, but everyone knew them. Maybe he'd pick someone she'd never heard of, and she could add a new book to her never-ending to be read pile.

"Hemingway."

Nope. She kept her polite smile plastered on.

"But I also like Kerouac. How about you?"

Better. Not an author she would have guessed from him.

"Oh, Douglas Adams is my all-time favorite." She could see the wheels turning in his head. "*Hitchhiker's Guide to the Galaxy.* Don't panic and always bring your towel."

Her polite smile faded when nothing replaced the confusion. Oh well. They didn't have to enjoy the same things to have an interesting conversation. Besides, it would give her a chance to tell someone new about her favorite things. Certainly better than being arm candy for an obnoxious jerk.

"Here you go. Two house margaritas, frozen, no salt." Jerk-Ryan's voice startled her out of her reverie. Speak of the devil. "Anything else I can get for you?"

Again with the bland, customer-service smile. But did his gaze keep sliding to her? No, she was imagining things. Either he'd forgotten about her, or he was trying not to be an asshole. She'd take the blessing and call it a win.

"No, thank you," Elissa murmured.

"Thanks, man," Nice-Ryan said.

Jerk-Ryan returned to the bar, and Elissa tore her attention away. Something about the man drew her eye, made her want to watch him. But it was unfair to the man at the table with her, who'd been nothing but polite.

"Cheers," he said.

"Cheers."

They clinked glasses, and Elissa took a sip of her margarita. She much preferred her margaritas on the rocks with salt. But this was uncommonly delightful for frozen, a nice balance of lime, sugar, and tequila. Top shelf tequila. And was that a touch of Tajin? Tasty.

"So you like sci-fi?" Nice-Ryan's voice pulled her back to their previous convo.

"Only the funny stuff. Scalzi is also a favorite. You said you run. Do you do races or just for exercise?"

"Treadmill at the gym. Lets me customize my workout."

As Nice-Ryan went all rhapsodic about the fantastic equipment at his gym, her attention wandered to the other Ryan. The way he moved through the crowd, the smile on his face as he greeted customers, the occasional laugh carrying over the noise of a busy restaurant. What was wrong with her? Pining over some dude who didn't even acknowledge her existence. She was better than this.

But every time she tried to pay attention, her eyes glazed over. She gave encouraging nods, asked a few follow-up questions, but Nice-Ryan seemed more than happy to talk about himself, while the handsome, mysterious jerk kept invading her thoughts as he'd done for the past week. Her brain wanted nothing more to do with Jerk-Ryan, but she needed to have a serious conversation with the rest of her body.

When he distracted himself with his almost empty glass, she glanced at her watch. Forty-five minutes! It seemed like hours.

"Do you have somewhere else you need to be?" he asked, catching her checking her watch.

Dang it!

"Yes, actually." She decided to play the family card since he had last time. "I promised to bring home dinner for my kid brother tonight. My parents are out with friends, and if I don't bring him food, he'll play video games until they get home."

Elissa opened her clutch and pulled out a credit card.

"No. I'll pick up the drinks. Family comes first. I had a nice time, Elissa."

Crap. She'd hoped he'd been as bored as her. Apparently, her politeness had passed for interest, and he hadn't even noticed she'd been a bad date. Elissa was at a loss for how to let him down easy. She needed Jules's advice. Instead, she stuck out her hand.

"Thank you for a lovely evening, Ryan."

Another face popped into her mind as she said the name. A leaner face, framed with dark hair, and brown eyes that did uncomfortable things to her female anatomy. Damn.

"I'd like to do this again."

Double damn. And add two dollars to the swear jar. The way she was going, they'd have family fun night before the end of the quarter. She really, really needed to talk to Jules. But she had an ace up her sleeve.

"Sure, but tax season is around the corner, so I need to check my calendar. I'll text you in a couple days." Maybe she would try again. She owed him a better date far, far away from hot guys who kept distracting her.

Nice-Ryan signaled to the object of her distraction, and Elissa left before she had to confront him again. The sun was down and the chill had her rubbing her arms as she walked to her car in the well-lit parking lot. She texted Leo as soon as she shut the door.

E: I'm getting sandwiches. Want one?

L: Yes date bad?

E: Ugh.

L: U didn't want 2 lie so ur bringing me dinner

E: Why do you insist on using abbreviations?

Autofill is there for a reason.

L: Ur old

Elissa sent an emoji with the tongue sticking out.

E: Do you want a sandwich or not?

He sent back the drooling emoji, which Elissa took to mean yes. Teenagers were weird. There was a Baggins between here and home, and he loved their jalapeño popper grilled cheese. She placed her order via the app, choosing the Thanksgiving dinner sandwich.

Motion outside caught her eye. Nice-Ryan—no, too boring to be nice—Beige-Flag-Ryan strode out of the restaurant. She was supposed to be in a hurry, so she ducked down and hoped he didn't look around for her. A few minutes later, a car pulled out.

Cautiously, she sat up and looked out the window to see a Prius turning right out of the parking lot. Sighing in relief, she sent a reply to Jules's earlier text.

E: Date sucked. Details later.

She stuck the key in the ignition and turned.

The engine gave a tired whine, the lights flashed, and nothing.

Dammit.

Elissa turned the key again, sending a prayer to Saint Eligius, the patron of mechanics. And to hedge her bets, Saint Jude. She hoped Bertha wasn't a lost cause just yet, but the car was old enough to drive itself now. No luck. *Grrr-grrr-grrr* went poor Bertha's engine.

She bent forward until her forehead touched the steering wheel. Could anything else go wrong tonight?

CHAPTER 12
the least i could do

R yan watched the sway of Elissa's generous hips as she left the restaurant. Fuck him, this was the last thing he'd needed tonight. Faced with his most recent mistake appearing at his workplace, he'd tried to pretend he'd never seen her before in his life. He enjoyed her expression when he refused to acknowledge their previous acquaintance, somewhere between disappointment, annoyance, and surprise.

Her date waved at him, and Ryan hurried over. Mr. Nerd, in his shirt and tie and hair straight out of 1950s Hollywood, smiled cooly at him.

"Ready for the check?" Ryan asked.

"Just put it on this." He handed over a credit card.

Ryan waited half a beat. Most people added a please or thank you, but he guessed the douche was used to being waited on. Admittedly, so was he, but his Nonna drilled in good manners no matter what. He was excellent at remembering with retail and food workers, but sometimes forgot himself when dealing with assholes, returning their own energy.

"Of course. Be right back."

Ryan walked behind the bar to run the card. As he slid it through the machine, he noticed the dude's name was Ryan, too. No wonder Elissa had believed he was there to meet her. Same name, a set-up date, and he'd forgotten who he was supposed to meet. It had been a recipe for disaster. Well, at least this Ryan seemed suited to her. Neither had raised their voice, nor had anyone left in a huff. Tonight appeared to be going better than last Tuesday.

Receipt in hand, he sauntered over with his best customer service smile on his face.

"Thanks so much for coming in tonight. Have a great evening."

"Hey, I have a question," the other Ryan said, stopping him before he could go check on the rest of his customers.

"Sure."

"Do you think the date went well?"

"I've seen a lot worse."

The other dude smiled, turning his attention to the receipt. "I thought it went well, too! Have a great night."

Poor clueless nerd. He'd been honest. As a bartender, he'd seen good dates, bad dates, and a few ugly ones, too. That had been mediocre at best, and it had probably been his fault.

After she recognized him, he tried to play it cool, but his attention kept straying in her direction. And every time he glanced over at their table, she was looking at him.

Nerdy guy yammered on, but her focus hadn't been on him. When she would realize she'd been spotted, pink would tinge her cheeks, and she'd turn to her date. The first time it happened, Ryan assumed she was still working on accepting the fact he'd showed up again in her life so soon. The second time, he assumed they needed something, but their drinks were only half empty, and the chip basket was still full.

The third time he caught her watching him, he gave her a slow smile, putting as much sex into it as possible. He was a DeMarco—there was a lot of sex in his smile. Her cheeks went from pink to red, and he winked at her before she jerked her attention back to the other guy.

And now she was gone, and he'd lost another chance with her. Admittedly, it was a snowball's chance in the middle of an

Arizona June, but still a chance.

He slid behind the bar. The crowd was big but manageable, and he could use some fresh air. He turned to the other bartender.

"Hey you good for a few minutes? Could use a short break."

"Sure, Ry."

Ryan walked out the rear exit, past the dumpster, to a small metal bistro table with a few chairs. He sat down and looked into the clear sky, the stars bright despite being in a city. One of the things he loved about Tucson—skies dark enough to appreciate the show Mother Nature put on every night.

Why was he so bothered by Elissa being here? She'd told him to fuck off. Nicely, but her meaning was crystal clear. Once a woman told him to go, he went and never looked back. But here she was, her eyes just as blue, her smile just as engaging as the one haunting his dreams. But those eyes and that smile weren't meant for him. He'd fucked up.

That was it. It had been a decade since he'd so royally borked a first date. Hell, most women were more than happy to forgive him once they learned his last name. He'd never even gotten that far with Elissa. His pride was injured, another piece of evidence he was an asshole.

He wasn't alone with his thoughts for long. Celeste, Iz's aunt, walked out, sneaking a smoke break. Iz kept telling her to quit. So did he, but Celeste never listened.

"Who's the girl, mijo?" She took a long drag on her cigarette.

"No one, Celeste."

She chuckled knowingly. "You were watching her while she was here. It was a little creepy, to be honest, like you were stalking her."

"I'm not stalking her. She came to *my* bar."

"So, why were you watching her?"

"Ugh, I don't wanna talk about it."

Celeste took another drag on her cigarette and offered it to him. After he declined, she tossed it on the ground and twisted it out with her foot. She patted his shoulder.

"You're a good man, Ryan DeMarco, and you're a kind friend to our Iz."

Ryan groaned again as Celeste walked back inside. He wasn't a good man. He was a rich asshole who liked pissing off his parents and having a new woman on his arm every few weeks. Which, to be honest, was because he liked pissing off his parents.

Ryan took a deep breath of the cool evening air, trying not to smell the typical pungent odors behind a restaurant. An unmistakable grinding of an engine refusing to catch drew his attention around the side of the building. A car door slammed, and a strained voice broke the quiet of the evening.

"Bertha, baby, come on. Don't do this to me."

He knew that voice, but what was she still doing here? Slowly, so as not to spook her, he approached. Elissa stood in front of her car, a battered old BMW, with the hood raised. She shined the flashlight on her phone into the engine compartment, but from the look on her face—pursed lips twisted to the side and a lovely furrow in her brow—she had no clue what she was doing.

"Can I help you?" He kept his voice smooth and quiet.

It wasn't good enough. She jumped and almost hit her head on the hood, then stepped back from him. Ryan held up his hand as the light tried to blind him.

"No, thank you. I'll call AAA." Her voice was prim with a slight tremble.

"You sure? It would only take a minute for me to take a look."

"Do you even know what you're looking for? You said you only worked on your own motorcycle."

His mouth tried to twitch into a smile at her bitchy tone and the fact she'd remembered that detail about him, but he schooled it back into neutrality.

"I have an idea or two. I've learned my way around engines." Iz's dad had taught him in high school, and Ryan loved tinkering.

"I'm not some damsel in distress for you to rescue."

"Never said you were. A lot of guys are clueless about engines, as much as we like to pretend otherwise. Plus, it's kinda the least I could do after our date." He owed her so much more than a quick look at her engine.

She arched an eyebrow at him. Oh dear God, she was fucking adorable when she tried to look disapproving. But instead of giving her his panty-dropping smile, he tried to look chagrinned. It was hard—those muscles hadn't gotten a workout lately. Perhaps he was letting his ego grow a bit too much.

"Yes, it is." Her tone softened, and she gestured broadly at the engine compartment, a game show girl revealing a prize.

Ryan had his own phone out and shined the light over the engine. Everything looked in order. In fact, for a car over a decade old, things were in great shape.

"Your battery's probably dead. We keep a jump starter in the office. Come inside with me while I find it. You don't need to be out here alone in the dark. The guy you were with should've stayed."

She cleared her throat and stared at her feet, which were clad in Vans painted in an impressionistic style. "Um, he didn't know I was still here."

"Elissa, did you hide from your date?"

"Oh, so you remember my name this time?"

He let the fact she didn't answer his question slide. "You're hard to forget. And there was no way I could forget your name when I didn't even know it in the first place."

"Okay, fair." Her lips twitched as she almost smiled.

"Let's go inside."

Ryan walked toward the back door, staying in front of Elissa so she wouldn't get freaked out by having an unknown man walk behind her. But close enough in case anyone was lurking. Anyone besides him, that is.

He held the door open and Elissa slipped inside.

"Second door on the right," he said.

He followed her down the hall, and she waited on the far side of the office door. He ducked inside, found the jump starter, and was out in under thirty seconds.

"Is this your office?" she asked, all traces of, admittedly deserved, bitchiness gone, replaced by simple curiosity. He could work with curiosity.

"Oh no, I'm just a bartender."

"No such thing." She smiled for real.

"Thank you for your vote of confidence." God, what he wouldn't do to earn more of her smiles. "My best friend's parents own this place, and everyone knows where the jump starter is. Food service workers rarely have super-reliable, late-model vehicles. And some of our customers occasionally need a jump. It's handy to have. Surprised you don't have one with an older car."

She bit her lip. As cute as she looked with an eyebrow raised, she looked drop-dead gorgeous biting her lip. All he wished to do was kiss her until she forgot why she was biting it.

He turned and walked down the hall and out the door instead. No kissing the damsel in distress. Especially after suggesting she'd make satisfactory arm candy. Not until he properly apologized.

"I did." She chuckled wryly. "My sister borrowed it."

"I need to have a talk with your sister."

"Everyone needs to have a talk with my sister. Ami is the wild child in the family."

The exact type of woman he usually pursued. But he had no interest in her sister. Elissa had captured his attention, his fantasies, and he desperately wanted her to be safe.

"Get on in and turn the key when I tell you."

He attached the jump starter and gave the word. The Beemer's engine turned over like a dream. He unhooked the cables and closed the hood with a solid thunk.

Elissa rolled down the window. "Thank you."

"Like I said, it's the least I could do. I owe you an apology, Elissa. I'm sorry for suggesting you'd only be good for impressing my parents. You deserve a whole hell of a lot better from any man. There's no excuse, but I'm used to people wanting to be around me so they can meet my family. I didn't want you to leave, so I offered the thing most people wouldn't turn down. I misjudged you and insulted you, and for that I am truly, deeply sorry."

She tapped her fingers on the steering wheel. "One question."

"Anything."

"Is your name actually Ryan?"

"Yeah, it is. Strange world, isn't it?"

The genuine, delight-filled smile only reinforced his opinion. He'd do anything to see it again.

"Well, Ryan, it was nice meeting you. The real you, this time."

"Goodnight, Elissa. Drive safe."

She wiggled her fingers at him, rolled up her window, and inched away. Only after she turned onto the street did Ryan register he'd forgotten to shoot his shot and ask for her number.

CHAPTER 13
i'll get the rum

E lissa kicked at Jules's door at half past five the next night bearing grinders, ranch fries, and two pina colada Eegee's, big enough for two drinks each.

The door opened and Jules snatched the slushies out of her hand. "I'll get the rum."

Thank God. After last night, she needed nothing more than to get drunk off her butt with her best friend.

Elissa deposited the bag of food on the coffee table as Jules pulled out two stemless wineglasses and a bottle of dark rum. She poured an unhealthy shot into each glass and spooned the frozen pineapple-coconut mixture over it.

Boxes were pushed against the wall next to the door, and there was no sign of Jules's roommate. Elissa sat on the couch and pulled out the sandwiches and the box of fries, snagging a couple as Jules stirred.

A moment later, Jules handed over an icy glass of alcoholic goodness before plopping next to Elissa.

"So, how was the date? Did you at least meet the right person?"

"I'm never going to live that down, am I?" Elissa said in mock despair as she kicked off her shoes.

"Nope, not if I have anything to say about it. And I do, cuz I'm your BFF! Cheers, lady."

They clinked glasses and sipped. Only way to enjoy Eegee's

once she passed the legal drinking age.

"Ugh, don't remind me. Why are you my BFF again?"

"Because…you need someone to reach the stuff from the top shelf for you, and since you don't have a man in your life right now, that's me!"

Elissa nudged Jules's shoulder with her own and giggled.

"So…?" Jules wagged a ranch-drenched fry at her as she settled into the comfortably worn couch.

"You first. What's going on with the boxes?"

"That's why I told you to come over. Ashley got offered a fellowship in Australia. I'm gonna need a new roomie, and with your mom doing better, you might be ready to move out."

Elissa opened and closed her mouth a few times. She'd been resigned to waiting until April or May before seriously considering a move, but now this opportunity dropped in her lap to have her BFF be her roomie, too. The stars had aligned and fate had finally broken her way.

"When?" she finally managed.

"Ash is packing the U-Haul on Friday, taking the stuff she wants to keep to her dad in Albuquerque. Told her she could leave her bed and furniture here if she doesn't want to lug and store that shit. Bet you can get it for a steal. But *only* if you tell me what happened last night!"

"Why mention it now? Why didn't you offer as soon as you found out?" She did not wish to be a pity roomie.

"I knew you wouldn't even think about it until your mom got the all-clear. I can swing the rent by myself for a bit, so I was gonna give it a month or two. But your mom's gonna be fine, and you can move before tax season swings into full gear. Whaddya say? Roomies?"

"I'm in!"

"Excellent." Jules held out her glass again, and they clinked them together even more enthusiastically, if that was possible. "Now, spill. And if you ever hold out on me as a roomie, you'll have to worry about waking up with a handlebar mustache drawn in Sharpie."

"I don't know…I might have the jawline to pull it off."

"Didn't say it was going on your face."

They fell into giggling while they sipped their drinks and ate their dinner.

"So, seriously, how was the date?" Jules rose to refresh their drinks.

"Oh, it was interesting."

"Interesting good, or interesting bad?"

"Both." Elissa took a large bite of her grinder to give herself a moment to think.

"Don't think I didn't see what you did there." Jules returned with two more pina coladas. "I can wait, you know. I'm amazeballs at waiting."

"No you're not," she said around a mouthful of sandwich.

"No, I'm not, so you better spill before I force it out of you. It couldn't have been that bad."

Elissa held up a finger as she swallowed the food and washed it down with pina colada.

"Worse."

"What? Was he some sort of perv?"

"No, but the guy from the other night worked there."

Jules's mouth dropped open. Elissa put her finger under her jaw and pushed it closed.

"You're shittin' me!"

"Nope. He's a bartender." Elissa pulled the blanket from the back of the couch over her lap. The cold drink was giving her the shivers. Or maybe it was her brush with the handsome man from her dreams last night.

"Fuck. What happened?"

"Nothing. He was perfectly polite, pretended he didn't know me."

"Bastard."

"What else was he supposed to do? Explain to my new date that he impersonated him and made an indecent proposal?"

"Fine, he gets a pass. That would be beyond awkward." Jules sipped her drink. "But I gotta know, is his name actually Ryan?"

"Yep."

"What are the fucking odds?"

"We must've known at least five Ryans at school, Jules. It's not an uncommon name."

She waved away Elissa's rational explanation. "What about Nice-Ryan? How was he?"

Elissa didn't know how to answer. She'd been so distracted by the other Ryan, she hadn't paid much attention to the Ryan she was supposed to be on a date with. Guilt ate her up inside.

"He was nice, I guess. I don't know. I didn't expect to go on a date and run into someone else I'd dated."

Her friend cracked a smile. "Well, now you can join the club. What did you tell him at the end?"

"I told him thanks for a lovely evening and left it at that. Decided in the car Mr. Beige Flag would be a better name for him. You have to help me come up with something to tell him so he knows I'm not interested. In fact, if I have to have another conversation with him, I might pull out my hair. The dude went on for fifteen minutes about his gym."

"So no sparks?"

"Not with *Beige-Flag*-Ryan." Elissa grinned wickedly—she'd never had two men interested in her at once. She kinda liked it.

"No, don't tell me—"

"Bertha did as Bertha does, and Jerk-Ryan came to my rescue. He even apologized."

Jules widened her eyes. "And what did you say?"

"I said it was nice to finally meet the real him."

"Oh, please tell me you got his number." Her friend folded her hands in prayer. "Please, please, please. My love life is a tragedy and I need to live vicariously through someone right now."

Her face fell as the blood drained away. She *hadn't* asked for his number. What was wrong with her?

"By the look on your face, the answer is no." Jules sighed melodramatically. "I guess we're both doomed."

"To being doomed with your BFF." Elissa raised her drink.

"Fuckin' A."

CHAPTER 14
2 years, 3 months, 8 days to go

Another Monday morning. Another alarm going off at six. Another drive into the office. Another pot of coffee started. Another day of following in his brother's footsteps. God, he hated this.

Only two years, three months, and eight days to go, Ryan reminded himself as he poured two cups of coffee. It had been two weeks of hell, getting up so early after years of working the evening shift. Many nights had him in bed at two, only for his fucking alarm going off a measly four hours later. He hadn't touched the script for his podcast in two weeks.

"Thanks, Ryan," Val said when he came out of the break room and joined her at her desk. "You're looking better rested. Get all your shifts at Nopalitos covered?"

"Yep, I'm all yours this week." He smiled and took a sip of the coffee.

Iz had covered his Thursday shift so Ryan could sleep and stop pissing off his dad, and Saturday had been his last night at Nopalitos. His friend never understood how much satisfaction he got from pushing his father's buttons. Probably because Iz had a much better relationship with their parents, even after coming out.

"I gave you all the basics the last two weeks, so I'll let you lead and step in if needed. I'm glad you'll be here Thursday. That's the first of the month, when rent is due, so I'll go over what you need to do."

Yay. And maybe he wouldn't run away screaming from the drudgery of it all.

"And we have the initial meeting with our accounting firm today. Tax season is coming up, and the accountant will be working with your aunt and you to gather all the required paperwork, so you need to pay attention during the meeting."

Even more good news. Numbers. God, he hated numbers, too. What the hell had he been thinking?

Long term. Two years of this and he'd have access to his trust fund. If he had access to his trust fund, he wouldn't have to worry about money when he finally got his podcast up and running. He'd be able to take the risks he needed to generate income from what he truly enjoyed doing. A couple of years of pulling in a reasonable salary while securing his access to his trust fund was worth it, even if he had to keep reminding himself of that fact. And keep the caffeine flowing so he didn't die of ADHD-induced boredom.

"When is the meeting?" he asked.

"After lunch. It will take most of the afternoon. I'll sit in so I can go over any questions you have after."

"Thanks, Val. You're really making this transition easy."

"Of course. I love working here. It was hard to quit, but the job in Phoenix was a big step up for Ben. Your dad already found a job for me close to our new house with a friend of his from one of the associations he belongs to."

"I'm glad he was able to help you." Ryan wished his father would extend him the same grace and courtesy he did for his employees. But DeMarcos were held to a higher standard than pretty much anyone else, and Ryan had Alex. The bar was high, and he always came up short. The next two years could help him come to terms with his thorny relationship with his dad.

The morning passed quickly. He impressed Val with his understanding of the procedures she'd taught him, and she only had to correct one of the forms he filled out. With the sun shining brightly in the late-January sky, he decided to eat lunch at the park down the street and returned promptly at twelve thirty, in plenty of time before the meeting with the accountants.

A few minutes before one, the bell on the door tinkled as it opened to reveal a statuesque woman with short, steel-gray hair dressed impeccably in a navy pantsuit with a pink blouse. She removed her sunglasses as she walked in and approached the reception desk. Ryan stood to greet her.

"Good afternoon, how may I help you?" See, he could be a solid employee.

"Hello. My name is Karina Jansen. I have an appointment with Annetta Herrera and Valerie Mullins."

"It's a pleasure to meet you, Ms. Jansen." Ryan extended his hand, which she shook with a firmness his father would be pleased with. "Ryan DeMarco. I'll be taking over for Val when she leaves. I look forward to working with you."

"Ah, the wayward son," Ms. Jansen said. "I'm glad Alessandro was finally able to convince you to work here. He was worried about you. I'm sorry Val is leaving."

"Karina!" Val's voice rang out behind him as she came out of the break room. "It's so good to see you."

"Young Mr. DeMarco informs me you're leaving?" the older woman said.

"Ben got a great job offer..."

Ryan tuned them out and busied himself with straightening the desk. Someone from the marketing department would cover the phone and any walk-ins while they were in the meeting. Wayward son, huh? Good to know what others thought of him because of his father. Another reason he didn't want to work here. Too many expectations. At Nopalitos, as long as the drinks were first-rate and on time, no one gave a shit whether he was wayward or not.

The tinkling bell brought his attention to the door as Val and

Ms. Jansen were heading to the meeting room.

A short figure stood in the doorway, the bright sunlight behind her highlighting her wavy brown hair and putting her luscious curves into stark relief. As she took off her own sunglasses, lake-blue eyes set off by her blue blouse glanced around the room. Holy shit. *Elissa.* He would never forget her name again, or those eyes. They'd met him every night in his dreams since the debacle of a date. And twice as often since their run-in at Nopalitos. The things he'd imagined her doing...

Fate had brought them back together. Not once, but twice now, and if she was doing the company's taxes, they'd be working together for a couple months. He had to find some way to capitalize on this bit of luck. He'd regret it for the rest of his life if he didn't at least try.

Her blue eyes passed right by him, found Karina, and she stepped into the building. Then she stopped dead and her head twisted toward him, her mouth dropping open in surprise, the perfect cartoon double take. Ryan gave her his best *professional* smile. No room for the bedroom eyes and wicked grin he usually served to women he found attractive. Not now that he was the face of DeMarco Properties. But damn, was he tempted.

"Hello, Elissa." He walked around his desk. "Can I help you?"

CHAPTER 15
do you two know each other?

E lissa had ridden with Karina to the meeting at DeMarco Property Management, their first big client of the tax season. Elissa's phone rang as Karina locked the car door.

"It's from Henry and Associates. I left a message the other day," Elissa said.

"Okay. I'll head in so we're not late. Join us when you're done."

It didn't take long, moving their appointment tomorrow from 9:30 a.m. to 10:00. Elissa updated the group calendar and walked in the door. A little bell announced her arrival, and she looked around for Karina. A few chairs lined the walls of the small entrance area and a reception desk sat directly in front of her, with a man in a light blue dress shirt and dark blue tie standing behind it. Ah, there, to the left was Karina, talking with another woman.

Wait. The man was familiar. The way he stood, the smile on his face. Her eyes found him again and, although she stifled a gasp, her jaw dropped. Jerk-Ryan. It wasn't possible, but there he was with a friendly smile on his face, only a few feet separating them. She closed her mouth and blinked, allowing her eyes to remain closed for a second. How had she not recognized him?

Because the last time you saw him, it was in a bar.

Elissa opened her eyes. She hadn't expected to see Jerk-Ryan in her client's reception area. That would be ridiculous.

No, he wasn't Jerk-Ryan, not anymore. He'd been kind and helpful in the parking lot at Nopalitos. He'd apologized. *Not-a-jerk-Ryan?* No, just Ryan.

Stop overthinking. Easier said than done.

He was so close she could smell the scent of motor oil and lemons she'd caught a whiff of at the Sandpiper three weeks ago. Had it been so long? Maybe because his face kept making guest appearances in her dreams. His hands and those lips…did things to her. Things that had a blush inching up her neck merely from thinking about them.

His mouth moved, and she caught the tail end of what he said. She took a step back, trying to put emotional distance between them as much as physical distance.

"No, thank you. I'm here with Karina." Elissa was unfailingly polite. It had served her well but felt *wrong* with Ryan.

"Oh, do you two know each other?" Karina asked, turning around.

The young woman next to her glanced between her and Just-Ryan, and a small grin turned up her lips. Elissa almost shouted it was nothing like that. But she was afraid she was only lying to herself.

"We've run into each other a time or two, here and there," Ryan said, saving her. "Here, let me show you to the meeting room."

She brought up the end of the procession and caught herself watching his butt as he led the way. As good as he'd looked on their disastrous date, as good as he'd looked as a knight in shining armor, she liked this professional look even better. Something about a man in a tie. Ryan held open the door, and Elissa walked within inches of him. As much as her brain told her this was a professional meeting, and she was a professional and should act like one, her body sizzled with heat as she passed him, so close she could touch him and claim it was an accident. Her face warmed again, and she turned away before he could see her reaction.

What were the chances they'd be thrown into the same place at the same time three times now? Her brain tried to calculate the odds but stopped as an older woman rose from her place at the head of the table and greeted Karina warmly. She was here for business, not pleasure. It didn't matter what the odds were, but it was weird how fate kept weaving their paths together. Could the universe be telling her something?

"How are you, Annetta?" Karina wrapped the other woman's hand with her own.

"I'm doing very well. Who is this?" Annetta examined Elissa from head to toe, pausing for a moment on her shoes of the day, Elissa's favorites, with her namesake butterflies painted across the toes in a rich golden brown on the black ballet flats. Her dad's passion, and all three of the Wright children were named after moths and butterflies. Her parents were strange—her father for picking the names and her mother for letting him.

"This is Elissa Wright. I'm planning on retiring in the next few years, so Elissa will be shadowing me, getting to know our clients on a more personal level, so she can take over when I do."

"It's a pleasure, Ms. Herrera." Elissa held out her hand, and the other woman shook it.

"Call me Annetta. Sit, please."

Karina sat next to Annetta and Elissa chose the chair next to her mentor. Valerie sat down across from them, but Ryan still stood at the door.

"Can I get anyone anything? Water? Coffee?" he asked.

He, too, was acting professionally and didn't seem to be affected by her presence here. *No fair.* She couldn't stop her gaze from finding him, couldn't stop herself from wanting to be near him.

"Coffee would be lovely," Karina said.

"Make that two, baby." Annetta replied.

"Aunt Annetta, you promised to keep it professional." But

Ryan's eyes twinkled and he smiled. God, he looked fantastic when he smiled.

Bad Elissa.

"Sorry, make that two, *Ryan*," Annetta corrected herself.

"Water, please," Elissa said in a small voice. He nodded and left, allowing the door to close with a quiet click.

Holy crap, he was the boss's son. Karina had briefed her on the structure of DeMarco Property Management but only mentioned one son, Alexander. No wonder Ryan believed she might wish to take advantage of his family contacts. The DeMarcos were a Tucson fixture, appearing at all the charitable events, sponsoring a gallery at the art museum, and Elissa was pretty sure there was a scholarship to the U.

A moment later, the door opened, and two men entered. The first was an older version of Ryan, most likely Alessandro DeMarco. The other bore little resemblance to Mr. DeMarco, but he reminded her of Ryan. Probably the smile, though it didn't compel her to throw her morals out the window and drop her panties.

"Karina! Good to see you again," the older man said as he approached her mentor.

"Alessandro!" Karina stood and shook the man's hand before turning to the younger one. "Alex. It's great to see both of you. I'd like to introduce Elissa Wright. She'll be taking over for me when I retire, so she'll be my shadow for the next couple years."

"Elissa, welcome to DeMarco Property Management." Mr. DeMarco offered his hand.

"Thank you." She took it. Firm grip, brief shake, all business.

"Ms. Wright, it's a pleasure to meet you." The younger DeMarco held out his hand, too.

Alex DeMarco was tall and lithe and completely corporate. Short, immaculately styled light brown hair, suit, tie, expensive shoes, and an even more expensive watch. His pupils dilated as he tried to keep his hazel eyes focused on her face, but they'd dart down for a split second every once in a while as he checked her out. At least he was trying not to be obvious about it, and he wasn't leering, merely looking. But unlike with his brother, she was not at all tempted to return the favor.

"Thanks. I'm happy to be here. I've heard great things about your business."

His hand was warm and soft and held hers exactly the right duration to seem friendly but professional.

"Excellent. I look forward to working with you."

Alex pulled out her chair, laying the charm on thick. Too thick. If she showed the slightest interest, Alex would jump at the chance to ask her out. But Elissa wasn't interested. Not only was he the chief operating officer, and thus posed a potential conflict of interest, he wasn't her type. He was too tall and too perfect, almost artificially so. After Victor, she'd sworn never to date a man who was too perfect again. It was hard enough to satisfy her own expectations, let alone those of a perfect man.

"We won't hold you up," the elder DeMarco said to Karina. "I just wanted to say hello. I know we'll be meeting several times before this is done. Have you met Ryan yet?"

"Yes. You'll have to tell me what you did to lure him in. The last time we talked, you seemed to think he'd never come around."

"It's a good story," Alex said, but shut his mouth when his father shot him a disapproving look.

Excellent timing, since the subject of their discussion walked back into the room.

CHAPTER 16
confirm my hypothesis

R yan was proud of himself. He'd been polite and hadn't even allowed his eyes to roam her body. Instead, he counted the freckles on her nose and traced the outline of her delicate mouth with his eyes. He was becoming a professional after two weeks. Then he realized what he'd just thought about himself and mentally slapped his forehead. *Dumbass, this isn't what you want.*

Carefully balancing the tray of beverages, Ryan opened the door to the conference room and stopped dead in the doorway. All eyes turned to him, but it was all he could do to avoid dropping the damned tray and rushing over to where his brother hovered over Elissa. What the hell he was going to do once he got there was a mystery. Fight his brother over a woman who wanted, rightly, nothing to do with him? Ryan placed the tray at the far end of the table and took the water to her first. At least he could put some distance between them.

"Excuse me, Alex." He would not allow the strange brew of emotions seething inside him to show.

Alex took two steps back, and those emotions went from almost boiling over to a slow simmer. He placed the water to her right and gave her a quick grin. When her eyes met his, he could've sworn a hint of relief flashed as Elissa began to return the smile before she recognized who it was, exactly, she was smiling at. Ryan stepped away.

God, she smelled fan-fucking-tastic. A soft, powdery scent had lingered in the air around her and activated some part of his unconscious mind. Heat headed straight to his groin, and he turned to prepare the coffee before anyone noticed. Focusing on the minutiae of his job, he carried the tray over to his aunt and Karina Jansen. Ryan set the cups in front of the two women and left the sugar and cream on the tray, which he placed between them. He took his seat next to Val and grabbed a pen and a pad of paper from the middle of the table, ready to begin.

Alex had stayed those two steps away from Elissa, and Ryan forced himself to pay attention to the conversation. He wouldn't compete with his brother for a woman. He couldn't, anyway. Whenever given a choice, they always went for the sophisticated heir apparent.

"Don't hesitate to call if I can help in any way," his dad said. "I know we'll be meeting once you have a draft, but I'm available whenever you need."

"Thank you, Alessandro. Alex, it was good to see you." Karina shook his dad's hand again.

"It was nice to meet you both," Elissa said in her pleasant, professional voice. It was not the same voice she'd used with him. She'd been passionate, though irate. He missed that Elissa.

His dad murmured something polite, but Alex took a step toward Elissa. Ryan's arms tensed and his legs inched him away from the table before he could stop them. His brain flooded with all kinds of neurochemicals that made him itch to hit his brother. He forced himself to sip the water he'd brought instead. This was getting ridiculous.

"Karina, Elissa, a true pleasure." Alex shook Karina's hand with professional ease. But when he shook Elissa's hand, he enclosed it in both of his. The primitive part of Ryan's brain didn't like it one bit. He glared at Alex as his brother crossed the room.

Alex clapped him on the shoulder. "Good luck, Ryan." He

exited with a wink.

Good fucking riddance, but why in the hell did his brother *wink* at him.

"Let's get down to business," his aunt said once the door had closed behind Alex.

As they discussed the upcoming tax season, Ryan relaxed into his role. He took detailed notes of all the forms and files he'd need to hand over, looking to Val for clarification when necessary. His eyes roamed over to Elissa from time to time, but she was furiously taking notes, too. In different colored pens with a variety of highlighters arrayed in front of her. She switched between them efficiently, hardly breaking pace with the conversation. Fuck, he was attracted to a nerd.

Ryan's handwriting worsened as he futilely tried to keep pace, but paying attention to the conversation was difficult enough with his ADHD. He'd figure out what he wrote later.

An hour passed, and he suppressed a sigh of relief when Karina called for a break. He finished writing and looked up to see Elissa's gaze slide away from him. He looked down at his notepad and quashed the smile trying to force its way onto his lips. Ryan cleared his throat, put down his pen, and stretched his arms, lacing his fingers together. Annetta smiled at him as she rose and excused herself.

"Coffee in the same place as usual?" Karina stood and stretched.

Val nodded, and Karina left, carrying the coffee mug with her.

"Do either of you need anything?" Val rose, too. They both shook their heads in the negative. "I'll go check at reception, make sure nothing's come up. You're doing great, Ryan, so you can start without me when Annetta and Karina return."

Val exited the room, leaving the door open. Ryan felt Elissa *not* looking at him. Her gaze seemed to float everywhere in the room, but when it came around to him, it would suddenly dart to anywhere else. He plastered a polite smile on his face, hiding the wide grin he wished he could give her, and leaned back in his chair.

"I never got to tell you how much I liked your shoes at the Sandpiper," he said, trying to break the awkward silence. Those eyes finally locked onto his face, widening in surprise, and pink tinged her cheeks at his compliment. "Where did you find them?"

The pink in her cheeks turned to red.

"I made them," she mumbled.

It was his turn to be surprised. But he shouldn't have been. He'd noticed her appearance was at odds with the passion he detected under her calm exterior, much like a strong current in a wide river. A current that would drag him under if he let it, and fuck, he was tempted to let it.

"Are you wearing them today?"

She shook her head and tucked an errant strand of hair behind her ear. A tiny pearl earring caught the overhead light, its pale pink hue matching the color of her cheeks. The corners of her lips twitched before she could force them into a serious line.

He pushed all the way back from the table and tried to look under it to see for himself. The angle was all wrong.

"What are you doing?"

"I want to see what your shoes look like today."

"Why?" Elissa narrowed her eyes at him, brows drawn down in an adorable frown. Could this woman do anything that wasn't adorable?

"To confirm my hypothesis."

"And what is your hypothesis?" Her tone was suspicious.

"That you're wearing a full-body mask. That under the cool, calm accountant persona is a passionate artist just dying for someone to ask her about her shoes." He graced her with the full DeMarco smile no woman had ever been able to turn down.

He'd seen his grandfather, his father, and his brother use it countless times. So had he, but rarely for such a simple request. Usually, his goal was much more carnal.

"I *am* an accountant. It's not a persona."

"But are you also an artist?" His words were gentle. He genuinely wanted to know.

"It's a craft, not an art."

"Bullsh—baloney. There's not much difference, but if you're going to get all technical, let's call it creative."

She stared at him for a moment, evaluating him. Coming to a conclusion, she pushed away from the table, crossed one leg over the other, and pulled off a shoe. Elissa tossed it to him over the table, and he caught it, still surprised his challenge had worked. Dragging his gaze from her, he examined the shoe in hand.

It was a simple ballet flat, but instead of the Van Gogh-style sunflowers, the background colors bled into each other yet still gave the impression of green leaves. Painted on top, in clear lines, was a white butterfly with golden stripes. The effect was nearly photorealistic with the subject in crystal-clear detail and the background out of focus. *Beautiful.*

"Thank you," she said.

Shit, he must've said it out loud. He looked up and his heart stopped. She was biting her lip, and the simple gesture sent a shock straight to his cock. Damn, she was going to be the death of him.

The silence stretched, and she held out a hand.

"Can I have my shoe?"

The little imp on his shoulder got the better of him. "I don't know. What will happen if I don't give it back?"

She couldn't stop the smile from curving her pink lips. "I'm a good shot. I'll throw the other one."

"And then I'll have both."

"Oh, you think so?"

Elissa rose out of the chair and limped around the table, only one shoe on. The look on her face, half exasperation, half playful, all flirtation, left him sitting in his own chair still as a statue. By the time he'd thought to move, she was standing in front of him, hands on her hips. He couldn't help himself. His eyes traveled down her body, tracing the curves of her breasts, the flare of her hips, her shapely legs, and her cute little foot, toes painted a pink to match her earrings.

He returned his eyes to her face. Her cheeks were flushed, her blue eyes sparkled like the summer lake they reminded him of, and her full lips curled into an authentic smile. All he wanted to do was look at her, possibly forever.

Elissa licked her lips, and his gaze traced the movement of her tongue.

"Mr. DeMarco, may I please have my shoe?" Elissa asked breathlessly, and for a solid second, Ryan was tempted to kiss her until she could only ask questions breathlessly. Or no questions at all.

Voices in the hall brought him to his senses.

"Of course," he said, a tad breathless himself.

Their fingers brushed as he handed back her shoe, sending an electric charge up his arm. He tried not to examine them for scorch marks as she dropped the shoe to the floor and slipped her foot into it. As the voices moved closer, she walked around the table and settled herself onto the chair. Ryan cleared his throat and scooted his chair back to the table.

They studiously avoided looking at each other for the rest of the afternoon.

Chapter 17
maybe five

I t had been both the shortest and longest afternoon of her entire life.

As 4:30 rolled around, Elissa found herself utterly exhausted. At first, she'd been able to ignore Ryan. They'd both been focusing on their jobs, taking notes, asking the occasional question. She'd caught herself staring at the man once or twice but tore her eyes away before he'd looked up. She'd hoped it would be easy. Then Karina had called for a break.

And he'd challenged her. Called her out on the costume she put on every day. Called attention to the one piece of her wardrobe hardly anyone ever noticed. Surprised he saw through her so easily, she'd flirted with him. He wasn't living down to her expectations. His teasing was gentle, and he seemed to appreciate her craft. She'd been two heartbeats away from saying or doing something she might regret, like giving him her phone number, when the voices of their bosses in the hall had brought them both back to reality.

His presence loomed like the heat of the desert sun in the summer, inescapable and overpowering. Her attention wandered, all too frequently drawn to the man sitting across from her. Their eyes locked a time or two, and both quickly returned their focus to the task at hand, but the blood rose in her cheeks.

By the end of the session, her notes were a disaster, her pens and highlighters in disarray, and she found herself tired and frustrated in a way she'd never felt before. She didn't know if God took pity on her, but as she was about to request a short break, Annetta Herrera clapped her hands together.

"Well, I think that covers what we need for now. Ryan and Val will pull the paperwork this week and have it ready for you early next week. Anything else you need from us right now?"

Karina thanked her for her time, and Annetta left with Ryan on her heels. Elissa packed up her notes and pens and highlighters, as well as the summary from last tax year.

"Take your time, Elissa," her boss said. "I'm going to see if Alessandro is available. I have to know how he brought his younger son into the fold. Ryan DeMarco has been a thorn in his side for a decade now. Wait for me in the reception area."

Karina strode out, leaving Elissa alone with her thoughts. Three interactions with the man. One decidedly dreadful, but until his indecent proposal, she'd been enjoying herself. He'd been chivalrous two weeks ago in the parking lot of Nopalitos, and he'd genuinely apologized. Today, he'd been fun and flirty, but hadn't invaded her personal space as his brother had. He was smart and sexy as hell. *Heck. Sexy as heck.*

The way his warm, brown eyes followed her, the way they'd traced her body during the first break, didn't make her feel ogled. They made her feel seen and appreciated. Working with him over the next few months was going to be problematic on many levels. It was an ethical gray area, and she wasn't sure she could keep her emotions—or her hormones—at bay.

A soft knock brought her head up as she was sliding the last of the papers away. Ryan leaned against the doorjamb, hands in his pockets and a small grin on his lips.

"Need any help?"

"Your timing is impeccable." She gestured to the empty table.

"You have no idea." His voice dipped lower, sending her

thoughts gliding down to the recesses of her mind where she stored all the lascivious ideas she kept hidden from view.

She bit her lip, and his gaze zeroed in on the small gesture. If he kept looking at her like that, those lascivious ideas would surface, and then what would happen? Her entire body tingled at the suggestion, from her toes to her nose to other, more intimate parts.

"I'm fine, thanks." Elissa hitched her bag over her shoulder.

"You sure? I can at least see you out."

She was tempted, oh was she tempted to spend a few more minutes in his presence. But the next few months were going to be hard enough. No need to add fuel to the fire. She walked to the door.

"I have to wait for Karina. We drove together."

"Good, I don't want you in that POS more than you have to be."

"Bertha is not a"—even using an initialism still felt like breaking the no swearing rule, so she lowered her voice—"POS."

He leaned in close, and his breath tickled the hair around her ear. "Whatever you say, Elissa."

Oh dear God, her name on his lips sent a shot of lust straight to her core. And sent every single reply right out of her head. She froze for a moment, trying to come up with something to say. He chuckled as the moment grew longer.

"Please, lead the way." Her voice was not nearly as strong as it should be. Ryan stole her breath away.

On legs wobblier than she'd ever admit, especially to this man, she followed him to the front. He ducked behind the front desk and grabbed his leather jacket from a hook on the side and the helmet from underneath.

"Have a good evening," he said as he walked by.

"You too," she whispered, and he smirked as he wiggled his fingers at her, letting the door close behind him.

She heaved a sigh of relief as she collapsed onto a chair, fanning herself. Was she even going to survive working with the man for the next two months? A few minutes later, Karina walked up to her.

"Ready?"

Elissa retrieved her bag and followed her mentor out the door. She settled into the passenger seat and noticed Ryan leaning against a motorcycle a couple of parking spaces over, texting on his phone, helmet on the seat. His unruly hair covered one eye, and his tie was gone, the top buttons of his shirt undone under the unzipped leather jacket he wore. As if he could feel her eyes on him, he looked up, and their gazes met. Heat pulsed through her body. Karina started the car and pulled out of the parking spot. Ryan gave her a sexy wink as they passed him. She turned her head, her cheeks flushing. It was going to be fucking hell until tax season was over.

And she owed a dollar to the swear jar at home. Maybe five.

Forty-five minutes later, she walked into the apartment she now shared with Jules and made a beeline for the fridge. She grabbed a bottle of pre-mixed margarita, then filled a glass with some ice. She plopped on the couch and poured enough to cover the ice, leaving the bottle on the coffee table.

There were still many boxes littered around from when she moved in on Saturday, but as she'd been living with her parents, she didn't bring much. Only some books, some old Blu-rays, her clothes, craft supplies, and bedding. A few of her favorite glasses and mugs. The books, movies, and craft supplies would have to wait until she got more storage, thus they were still in the boxes.

She was halfway through her first drink and an old episode of *Parks and Recreation* when Jules walked in. She'd worked the day shift today and took in the scene.

"That is the best idea I've seen all fucking day. Lemme find a glass."

Jules kicked off her shoes—one flew past Elissa's head before thunking against the wall—and grabbed a glass and ice. She filled the glass to the brim, carefully sat next to Elissa, and took a long pull.

"Oh, yeah, that's the stuff. So, lady, I know why I'm drinking, but this isn't exactly typical Lissa behavior. What's up?"

"You'll never guess who was at one of my appointments today!"

"Bill Gates? No, um, Chris Evans? Um—"

"Jerk-Ryan!" She felt bad for calling him that, though. Yeah, he'd had a jerky moment with her but hadn't been anything other than a nice, attractive guy since.

Jules smiled around the lip of her glass. "Oh, that's three. Can't fight the rule of three. You run into the same hot dude three times, and fate is trying to tell you something very, very specific. You gotta go out with this guy."

"I do not."

"Yeah, you do. The universe is calling, and if you don't answer, I won't be responsible for the shitshow about to descend on your life."

"How do you know he isn't the you-know-what-show?"

Jules shrugged and took another drink. "Could be. But then he's a shitshow the universe knows you need."

"I don't have his number."

"But you know his name, right? Know where he works?"

Elissa nodded.

"Easy-peasy-lemon-squeezy. You can find him again, ask for his number, and demand his fine ass take you out."

"Not easy-peasy…ethics…jerk!" Elissa ran out of words for the second time that day. She was saved from having to explain her word salad by her mom's ringtone sounding from her bag.

"You could let it go to voicemail. We're having an important discussion here," Jules said with a laugh.

Elissa ignored her and answered.

"Hi, Mom."

"Hi, sweetie. What do you want stocked for when you stay with Leo next week? I'm picking up groceries on Thursday."

"Why are you asking today? It's Monday."

"In case you didn't know. You have plenty of time to think this over and let me know by Wednesday. You have a tendency to overthink things."

Tendency was a bit of an understatement.

"Okay, yeah. I'll text you if I think of anything specific, but I'm good with what you typically have on hand. And I can shop, too."

"I know, but you're doing us a huge favor. It's the least we can do."

"I'm happy to do it. You and Dad deserve a break."

"So we'll see you at dinner on Sunday?"

"Yep."

"Love you."

"Love you, too, Mom."

The call ended, and she slid the phone onto the charging pad by the front door before returning to the kitchen.

"How's Dana?" Jules asked. It was still weird to hear her friend call her mother by her first name. It was Mrs. Wright until Jules turned eighteen.

"Excited about the trip."

"Excellent. I can invite Aidan over while you're gone."

"Who's Aidan?"

"Dude I've been sexting."

"Oh, is that what those noises were last night? I thought you were watching porn. You could invite Aidan over when I'm here."

"Yeah, but loud, kinky sex is easier when your roomie is gone. Want some more?" Jules held up the bottle of margaritas.

"Yes, please."

Wish I could have loud, kinky sex. But no, it would be just her and her vibrator for the foreseeable future. It had been getting a workout lately, with Not-a-Jerk-Ryan making all too frequent cameos in her fantasies.

She went to close her bag and noticed a piece of paper folded in half. She didn't remember putting any paper in her bag. Elissa pulled it out and opened it.

Ryan DeMarco 555-8995

Her heart stopped. The man had slipped his phone number in her bag. Now what?

"Whatcha got there, Lissa?" Jules said over her shoulder.

Elissa jumped. "When did you get sneaky?"

"Easy when you didn't hear me call your name three times."

Her friend snatched the paper out of her hand, replacing it with her margarita.

"Is this Jerk-Ryan?" A huge smile planted itself firmly on Jules's lips. "You really need a better nickname for him. So...what are you gonna do about this?"

Elissa stared at the paper like she would a diamondback curled under the patio furniture.

"I don't know."

"How about this? I will put it on the fridge while you overthink this to death. And when you finally break down and realize the universe is flashing a huge ole Bat Signal at you, you call the dude. Or text."

"But—"

"And if you don't, I'll do it for you. I sure as shit do not want to get on the universe's bad side. You have two weeks. Now, I'm going to see if Aidan is online so we can have phone sex again." Jules took her half-finished margarita to her bedroom.

Fuck. And now she definitely owed five dollars to the swear jar.

CHAPTER 18
a stupid amount of satisfaction

E lissa didn't call that night. Ryan tried not to be disappointed. She didn't call the next day either. Or the next.

He resigned himself to not hearing from her. At least not personally. They'd be working together, and this was a signal as clear as the night sky around the Mount Graham Observatory. Elissa didn't want to date him. He couldn't blame her, he'd fucked up big time. He was disappointed, but he'd deal.

Finally, Friday rolled around. Taking the lead on all the office manager crap kept him on his toes, and pulling together all the files the accountants needed familiarized him with the filing systems. It went quicker than Ryan expected.

"It's like you planned this, Val," he said as she looked over the files he'd pulled.

"No, Mr. DeMarco, I'd never be that sneaky." A wide grin spread over her face.

The office had opened an hour ago, and someone was covering the front desk while Val ensured Ryan hadn't missed anything. It was her last day, and his dad was treating the whole office to lunch.

"Looks like everything is here. Why don't you call Karina and let her know it's ready?"

Val loaded the files into banker's boxes, which she'd labeled with the company's name, date, and general description of the contents. Ryan walked up front, letting the young woman from marketing return to her own job. He found the accounting firm's number and dialed.

"JMS Accounting," a male voice answered. "How may I help you?"

"Karina Jansen, please," Ryan said.

"I'm sorry, she is out of the office today. I can transfer you to her associate, Elissa Wright."

Ryan's heartbeat quickened at the mention of her name, and his mouth was suddenly dry. Licking his lips, he croaked out, "That's fine."

Soft hold music played for a moment while he willed his heart to slow down and took a sip out of the water bottle on Val's desk. No, his desk, now. What would Elissa think when she recognized who it was? Would she bring up that he'd slipped his number into her bag? Would she hate him, think him creepy? And why, for fuck's sake, was he at all worried about any of this?

"Elissa Wright." Her voice sent a shiver along his spine.

His words stuck halfway up his throat. All that came out was a weird creak. Great, now she would think him a heavy-breathing creep.

"Hello?"

Ryan cleared his throat and tried again, but his voice was rough and barely audible.

"Hello, Elissa."

"Hi," she said, all business. "How can I help you?"

He cleared his throat again, and his voice came out normal.

"This is Ryan DeMarco, over at DeMarco Property Management. The files Ms. Jansen needs are ready."

It was her turn to clear her throat. The sound of it gave him a stupid amount of satisfaction.

"Yes, um, yes, thanks. When can I pick them up?"

Now, he wanted to say. Instead, he said, "When would be convenient for you? We'll be closed this afternoon for Val's going away party, but later this morning or early next week will be fine."

"Let me check my calendar." A long pause. "Will Monday afternoon work?"

"That will be fine. Any particular time?"

"I'll head over after lunch, so one o'clock?"

"I'll be here. Have a nice weekend, Elissa."

"Thank you. You, too, Ryan."

A current rushed straight to a part of his anatomy that had no right to be so excited during the workday. He ended the call, chugged down half of his water, and counted to ten slowly. If her voice over the phone could do this to him, what the fuck was going to happen when he saw her in person on Monday afternoon?

For a moment, he allowed himself to hope she hadn't seen the number, and that was why she hadn't called. Ridiculous, but she seemed just as thrown by him as he was by her. Perhaps, given their need to work together, he could convince her to see things his way. Convince her to agree to another date, a real one where he acted like himself, and not some rich, entitled asshole.

He busied himself with typical DPM tasks for the rest of the morning, and before he knew it, Alex collected him for the farewell luncheon.

"Come on, Ry, it's raining. I'll give you a lift," Alex said.

Ryan glanced out the window, the first time all morning. It was, in fact, raining. A gentle rain that sometimes hit in the winter. It wouldn't last long, and if it did, Alex could drop him at home and he'd talk Iz into helping him retrieve his bike tomorrow.

"Why are you being nice?"

"I'm allowed to be nice to my little brother."

"Sure, yeah, but this is twice in, like, a month. Who are you trying to impress?"

Alex chuckled, but there was an edge to it. "No one. So…

do you want a ride or are you gonna be an asshole?"

"Both, duh."

This time, Alex's laugh was genuine. "There's the asshat I know and love. Grab your shit and let's go. Don't wanna be late."

They drove to Val's party at her favorite bar and grill, letting Alex's classic rock playlist fill the silence. He didn't miss the usual awkwardness.

Burgers, beers, and cake filled their bellies, toasts were proposed, and speeches—short, thank fuck—were given. The rain did not let up, so Alex dropped him at his complex. Ryan watched the taillights of the Buick fade before heading to the second-floor apartment he'd shared with Iz since they both graduated college.

The neighborhood might be a little sketchy—just a little, though, since in five years, only two packages had been stolen— but the rent was reasonable and the square footage was twenty-five percent larger than most comparable places. He knew the landlord through his father, and she was a decent person. Even if there was a family discount at a DeMarco property, he preferred to keep as much distance between himself and the family business, until now.

He unlocked the door and tossed his helmet on the table next to the door and his jacket over a nearby chair.

"Iz?"

No answer. He had the place to himself.

After working in a busy office all week, it felt remarkably quiet. He grabbed a beer from the fridge, flipped on the TV, found a *Transformers* movie, and fell asleep before the first smash-em-up fight.

The door slammed, jolting him out of his doze. Beer sloshed out of the can.

"Dammit, you made me spill my beer," he mumbled.

"Dude, were you asleep? At six on a Friday?" Iz laughed,

tossing their keys on the table next to Ryan's helmet.

"Did you suddenly age fifty years?" Mateo placed take-out containers on the kitchen counter. Dinner.

Ryan hadn't thought further than getting home and resting. Planning anything for dinner seemed like a lot. Hell, thinking more than thirty seconds into the future seemed like a lot.

"Yep. Corporate America—sucks the life right out of you."

"Come here, Ry. Have some food and tell us about your day so we can laugh at you."

"Best idea I've heard all day." Except for Elissa's upcoming visit on Monday.

Iz pulled out plates while Mateo opened the containers from their favorite Thai place. The savory sweet smell of spicy coconut and lemongrass filled the living area, and despite having eaten well a few hours before, his stomach grumbled loudly. Ryan snatched beers from the fridge and before long, all three were stuffing their faces.

"So, you gonna work on your script this weekend?" Iz asked after wolfing down three spring rolls.

"I want to, I really do, but this job is taking everything I have." As expected, dammit. "I don't think I have it in me this weekend."

"My cousin is writing a novel." Teo snagged the dumpling Ryan was a second too slow to grab. He grinned widely as he popped the delicious nugget into his mouth. *Bastard.* "She says it's hard working a nine-to-five and finding time for being creative."

Ryan hadn't worried about it much before. He'd loved working at Nopalitos, loved working for Iz's family. Sure, some days had been hard, but mostly he'd left work as energized as when he researched or tried to draft a script. But now, his energy was gone at the end of a day. All he wanted was to sleep away the weekend. Starting ASAP.

"How does she do it?"

Teo shrugged. "Sometimes she doesn't. She's been working on this book for at least six months, and I have no idea if it's even close to being done. But she told me she sets aside a little time every week and sets achievable goals so she's always moving forward."

"Yeah, I guess I could try that."

Iz snorted. "The day Ryan DeMarco sets an achievable goal is the day I will let him take me for a ride on his stupid motorcycle."

"She's not stupid."

Iz had a point, though. He was a "go big or go home" kind of goal setter, but it rarely worked out great for him. It left him frustrated and discouraged, and he usually dropped whatever it was. Or scrambled at the last minute to complete something and was disappointed in the final product.

"No, she's not," Teo jumped in before Iz's teasing could get under Ryan's skin. "And neither are you, but your ADHD brain means you gotta chunk it down, man. Small, quick goals will likely work best for you."

"You should listen to my brilliant clinical social worker boyfriend who works with neurodivergent kids all day." Iz waved their chopsticks around wildly.

"Yeah, I should. Doesn't mean I will."

"Ass." But Iz said it with a wink.

Teo had a point, but breaking down his big ideas was as difficult as meeting his unreasonable goals. Maybe someday he'd have the time and patience for it. Or he'd find a therapist who could help him with that shit. But not today.

They finished dinner, then the movie, and Ryan turned in embarrassingly early. It wasn't even nine. But as tired as he was, Ryan found himself staring at the stain on the ceiling that looked strangely like a hippopotamus. Whenever he closed his eyes, Elissa's face, scent, and voice filled the void.

His cock hardened. Dammit, he did not need to have sexy

thoughts about someone who didn't want him, especially when he was going to work with her over the next few months. If he tried to take care of this the usual way, he wasn't sure he'd be able to look her in the eyes on Monday afternoon.

Fuck. He threw off the covers, stumbled to the bathroom, and took the coldest shower of his life.

It didn't help. Instead, all he could think of was her voice on the phone, husky with some secret emotion. God, he hoped it was desire.

He squeezed his cock, trying to relieve the pressure. As the cold water pelted his back, he imagined his hand was hers, and she was in the shower with him, water streaming down her pale skin and trickling between her breasts.

His dick hardened in his hand, not the direction he wanted this to go. But it was a harmless fantasy. He stroked, faster, harder, all the while imagining her lips, her hands, her skin, her scent, the little sounds she might make. It took an embarrassingly short time for him to shoot his load against the tile.

Ryan thunked his head against the wall and turned up the temperature. Monday was going to be hell.

CHAPTER 19
it's just pizza

Elissa pulled into her parents' driveway on Sunday evening. They were leaving for the conference first thing in the morning, so she would be taking Leo to school. Hopefully, Jules and whatever boy toy she found available would appreciate the alone time.

She knocked on the door, but when no one answered, she walked in. Loud voices echoed down the hall, coming from the kitchen. Elissa left her suitcase in the entry and headed toward the yelling.

"When were you going to tell us you dropped out of community college, Ami?" her mom shouted.

Oh, snap.

"I'm done, Mom," Ami shouted right back. "I hate school. Hate it. I can't get it right. Can't you just let me do my own thing?"

"Your own thing?"

Elissa resisted the urge to cover her ears as her mother's voice rose in pitch.

"Dana." Her dad's softer voice stopped her mother as Elissa walked into the kitchen.

"Don't you always do your own thing?" Elissa meant it to be a joke, but the way Ami's eyes sparked with anger told her it hadn't been received that way.

"I don't need your shit, too, Lissa. Why do you think I got

here early? Mom and Dad are bad enough." Her sister's cheeks were red with anger.

"Ami!" Mom snapped. "Swear jar, now!"

"Fuck that, Mom. I'm an adult, now. I can make my own *fucking* decisions, I have my own *fucking* job, my own *fucking* car, and my own *fucking* apartment, and I can fucking swear if I want to. Don't need this bullshit anymore. I dropped before the deadline, and you have your money. If you can talk to me like an adult, call me. Otherwise, I'm done."

Ami wiped away the tears dripping down her face with a ferocity that drove Elissa to hug the wall as her sister stomped by, leaving the kitchen deathly quiet. The front door slammed. Elissa looked between her parents and the door, tempted to chase after her sister and smooth things over, but Ami was in no mood to listen to anyone.

Elissa looked from one parent to the other. Her dad's shoulders slumped, and her mother turned away, trying to stifle the sobs rising from deep within her.

"Don't worry, Mom, she'll calm down and call you tomorrow to apologize."

Ami always did. Her sister's anger ran hot but fast. Ami had a heart of gold, but she also had a habit of choosing something easy or fun over what most people with common sense would choose. But Elissa admired her little sister. She was brave in a way Elissa never could be, and that was part of the friction in their relationship. Elissa was firmly in oldest daughter role, Leo was the baby, leaving Ami to her own devices. A small part of Elissa was jealous.

"Elissa, why don't you go check on Leo?" Her dad wrapped his arms around her mom.

She left them standing in the kitchen and went to her brother's room. Her mother's sobs tore through the house as she rapped softly on Leo's door.

"Come in," he called.

Elissa slipped in, closing the door behind her with a quiet snick.

"Hey, Elissa." Leo sat on his bed, book in hand, headphones on. "Is it over?"

"Yep."

He took off the headphones. "Well?"

Elissa sighed and sat down on the bed next to him.

"Ami stormed out, Mom's crying, and Dad looked...heartbroken."

"I told her it was a bad idea not to mention it before the money was returned."

"You *knew*?"

"Duh." He rolled his eyes. "We talk when you're not around. In fact, we talk a lot when you're not around, since you'll go running to Mom and Dad with this stuff."

She opened her mouth to protest but gave it a second thought. Fair. If she'd known Ami had dropped out of community college, she would've blabbed to their parents. She'd sworn not to tell them what she knew about Ami's suspension from the U last year, and guilt filled Elissa every time it was brought up. It was the one thing she'd ever kept from her parents, and she tried to keep it the only thing. Their parents would be more understanding if they knew the whole story, but Ami had begged to be the one to tell them in her own time.

"Now what?" he asked when she didn't say anything.

"I don't know, Leo the Lion. Wait, I guess."

He'd made a noise of protest when she'd called him by his childhood nickname but leaned against her. She hugged him, and they sat there quietly for a few minutes. It had been a rough year. Things had been looking up, but baggage from the past kept intruding on the present. She'd give Ami a day or two to calm down before talking to her. Like an adult. Her sister wasn't wrong—she deserved to be treated with more respect.

When the silence got to her, Elissa asked, "What are you

reading?"

Leo picked up the book, a ragged old Discworld book.

"That's a good one." In fact, it was her favorite, but she wouldn't tell Leo that. Let the kid figure it out on his own.

"I know."

A firm knock brought their attention to the door. Dad opened it.

"We're ordering pizza tonight," he said. "Any requests?"

"Pepperoni," Leo piped up.

Their dad waved their hand in dismissal and his lips twitched, banishing his grim expression. "Yeah, figured. Elissa?"

"Whatever you want is fine." She gave him a quick grin.

"Sure. Give us about twenty minutes?" At their nods, he closed the door, and his footsteps faded down the hall.

"Why do you do that?" Leo asked.

"Do what?"

"Never seem to have an opinion. I know you love ham and pineapple"—he grimaced at her audacity—"but you never, ever ask for it. You go along with what everyone else wants. And no one else *ever* wants ham and pineapple, weirdo."

Did she? She tried to think of the last time she spoke up when orders were being taken and drew a blank.

"I order it when I'm alone. It's just pizza. No big deal."

"I dunno, everyone else has an opinion. Why don't you?"

Why didn't she? Well, mostly because everyone else was so much louder, with more pressing needs. Leo ate the most pizza, so first choice should be his. Mom could barely eat after some of her chemo treatments, and if she craved anything, it got ordered. Ami was loud and got pouty if she didn't get what she wanted. And Dad usually placed the order. Elissa's opinion wasn't sought often, and when she had one, it felt selfish to put her wants first.

Look at her, getting all introspective over pizza.

"I don't care all that much," she said.

"Liar."

"I do not lie."

"Okay, fine. Delusional."

"Can we change the subject?"

"Fine." Leo rolled his eyes theatrically. "What's new, Lissa?"

"Tax season."

She grinned wickedly when her brother groaned in response. Leo hated math, loved English class, and wrote whenever he could.

"No, it's really good. With my CPA, I'm shadowing Karina so I can take over her accounts when she retires. I got to meet some big clients this week." Not to mention a sexy office manager. The mere thought of him sent blood rushing to her cheeks and other parts of her body that would be embarrassing to explain to her little brother. "How's school? It's weird I don't know, but I don't get the daily grunt reports at dinner."

"I don't grunt."

"Yeah, you do." She shoved his shoulder, but when he tried to lick her hand, she snatched it back.

He laughed like a cartoon villain before answering. "I still suck at math, but I'm doing fine at everything else."

"You know you can ask me for help."

"I'm passing with a C, but math is boring."

It was the same argument they always had. It was the same argument Leo had with Dad. Elissa let it drop.

They chatted for a bit longer about the upcoming school play, where Leo had a small role. Another soft knock stopped the conversation, and their mom opened the door. Her eyes were puffy and her nose was red, but she gave them a fleeting grin.

"Pizza should be here soon. Why don't you come out and get your drinks while I find the paper plates?"

Before long, they were all seated at the dining room table, sipping their drinks, with hot cheesy goodness piled in the middle.

After a few bites, Mom cleared her throat. "So, Elissa, how

was your week?"

Elissa told them pretty much what she'd told Leo.

"Oh, and you know the guy I had a blind date with, the one from the Sandpiper that turned out to be the wrong guy?" she said.

"What did you call him? Jerk-Ryan?" Her dad gestured with the pizza in his hand, almost losing a pepperoni.

"Yeah." Though the other guy had turned out to be Beige-Flag-Ryan and—oh, she'd left him on read for too long. Oh no. She and Jules had gotten a little sloppy, and though she'd planned on having her friend talk her through letting the dude down gently, the idea had exited her head as quickly as his presence had exited her life.

"If he's a jerk, why are you bringing him up?" her mom asked.

"Well, he works for a company Karina and I are preparing taxes for, and he might be less of a jerk than I assumed." A small smiled forced itself onto her lips.

"So, you might see him again?" Her mom brightened, hoping Elissa might be interested in a guy for the first time in a year.

"I'll have to. He has the files I need."

She wouldn't mention it to her family, but she was looking forward to picking up the files tomorrow afternoon. The hottie behind the desk had become a bit of an obsession for her. At least three times a day since Monday, she had pulled out her phone and typed out a text. Then deleted it.

"Well, that's nice," her dad said.

Nice had nothing to do with it. The erotic dreams featuring him right after their "date" had faded, and she'd thought she was in the clear, until she had arrived at DeMarco Property Management. Now, they were back even more frequently than before, and she'd had to recharge her vibrator's batteries twice this past week. She didn't need the chaos Ryan would bring into her life. Did she?

CHAPTER 20
the black sheep

Half of Ryan looked forward to going to work. That half wanted to see Elissa so bad it would be embarrassing if he admitted it to anyone. That half was downright panting at the idea of collecting even more spank bank material for his imagination.

The other half of Ryan was as nervous as the first time he ever asked out a girl in eighth grade. Sweaty palms, racing heart, and a cock that wouldn't behave no matter how many times he jerked off in the shower.

Maybe she had merely missed the phone number he'd dropped into her bag when she wasn't looking. Or she had chosen not to call. Which would be worse?

The morning flew by as he fielded questions, answered the phones, and went over Val's checklist. It wasn't a difficult job, but it demanded attention to detail and prompt replies, two things he'd struggled with all his life. His ADHD brain could focus when it wanted. Unfortunately, property management details did not give enough happy brain chemicals to make it easy in this case. Ryan was more than ready for lunch when it rolled around. He'd brought a sandwich today, unwilling to take any chance of missing Elissa's visit, and ate it on the bench in front of the office. The sun warmed his face and his soul.

February was one of his favorite months. Between the generally excellent weather for riding and the Tucson Rodeo, it flew by. But this year, who knew?

Sandwich long gone, he lounged on the bench, waiting for his afternoon visitor. A familiar sedan pulled in and parked in a visitor spot. His heart raced in anticipation, only to be rewarded when the door opened and Elissa's petite figure stepped out of the vehicle. Today, she wore a black skirt with a gauzy overlay. Although the gauzy part came to mid-calf, the opaque skirt was a few inches above her knees, giving him the impression that the half-hidden skin was something scandalous, something he wasn't supposed to see. Scattered across the fabric, blue polka-dots perfectly matched her royal blue, sleeveless V-neck shirt, which hinted at the swell of her breasts.

Ryan suppressed the urge to whistle in appreciation. Instead, he refocused his attention on her car. Anything to quell the hunger her presence sparked. He glanced around—no one else was nearby—and adjusted his hardening cock.

Focus on the car, asshole, not the woman.

In the dark parking lot of Nopalitos, he'd paid little attention to anything other than the battery. The BMW with faded dark blue paint had to be at least fifteen years old. Accountants made decent money, but she may have had to take out loans, making an old, mostly reliable vehicle a better fit. It seemed to be in good shape otherwise, and he heard no concerning squeals as it drove past. In his examination of her car, his gaze inadvertently landed on the trunk as she bent over to retrieve something from it. Her round ass had him hard again, goddammit.

He adjusted himself again, but the movement drew her attention to him. A smile twitched up the corners of her lips, and she shifted so the swell of her breasts became full-on cleavage. He got a clear view of her black lace bra and suppressed a groan as he rose off the bench.

Think boring thoughts. Math, basketball stats, inventory lists.

Finally certain he wouldn't embarrass himself, he

approached her and waved. Her sparkling eyes were even more blue today, mirroring the color of her shirt.

"Need any help?" he asked as she pulled out a folding cart.

"No, I'm fine."

Ryan fought the desire to offer his hand in greeting, afraid what his reaction to even this simple, everyday touch would be.

"Okay. I'll show you to the file room."

He turned around and led her to the building, holding the door open for her and her little cart. Elissa paused in the reception area while he passed her.

"Ms. Wright is here for the files. I'll be back as soon as I help her," he told his cousin, who manned the phones during his lunch break.

She looked over at Elissa and a knowing grin spread over her face. This would not be good for him.

"Sure thing, Ryan, but leave the door open at least three inches." Her eyes darted between Ryan and Elissa, and she waggled her eyebrows suggestively at her older cousin.

"Trinity, we're not teenagers anymore. I'm helping Ms. Wright with the file boxes Val and I put together last week."

"Sure you are, cuz. Sure."

"Whatever." He led her through the open office and into the hall. Trinity's soft laugh followed them. He glanced back. "Do you work with your family, Ms. Wright?"

The color had risen in her cheeks again, painting them a lovely pink. Her skin was so responsive. He'd love…*Nope, keep your brain out of the gutter.*

"Oh, God, no," Elissa said with a chuckle. "Don't get me wrong, I love my brother and sister and my parents, but we'd be at each other's throats if we had to work together."

Her smile returned. He needed it to stay.

"Then count yourself lucky." He gave her the full DeMarco smile. "This way."

He continued past the break room and to the file room

where he'd spent a good chunk of last week. The boxes were on a table right next to the door, which Ryan left open. More than three inches.

"This is everything?"

"As far as I know. If anything is missing, I'm only a phone call away."

He kept the smile plastered on his face. Now wasn't a bad time to find out if she was ignoring him or just hadn't seen the phone number. Half the office was at lunch, and the hall was empty. He grabbed the first box and placed it on the cart.

"I'm sorry—"

"About that phone—"

They spoke at the same time. Her eyes widened and her cheeks turned an even deeper shade of pink, highlighting her freckles. Fuck him. He loved this look for her.

"Please, ladies first," he said gruffly.

"What makes you think I'm a lady?" She was downright red now.

He wasn't gonna touch that with a ten-foot pole. "Fine, I'll go first. I'm sorry I gave you my number unsolicited. I felt a connection during the break and didn't want to lose the chance to talk to you again. I'll keep this professional whether you call or not. Promise."

She wouldn't meet his eyes. Shit. Oh well, win some, lose some.

"I tried," she said in a quiet voice. She cleared her throat and finally met his gaze. "I must have deleted ten messages in the last week. I-I have this little tendency to overthink things, and, well, it was turned up to eleven this week."

Oh. A small spark of hope took root in his soul.

"I get it. My problem is the exact opposite. ADHD usually has me leaping, then looking. One of the reasons why I said what I said at the Sandpiper. Most of the time, I live to regret my mistakes."

"So far, you've lived to regret all your mistakes, I think."

"True."

She laughed and leaned back against the filing cabinet she stood next to and looked him up and down.

"Okay, I have a question I've been dying to ask. You don't have to tell me, but who, exactly, were you expecting to meet that day? You'd obviously forgotten her name."

"Someone my mother was trying to set up with my brother. He wanted Mom off his case, and I wanted to do anything to appease my parents other than work here, so I agreed to take her out."

"Did you try again?"

"No. I texted and said she didn't want to date an asshole like me."

She tapped a finger on her lips as her smile widened. "Do you know how I described you to my friend?"

He shook his head.

"Jerk-Ryan."

Not as bad as he expected. Most of the women he knew would've called him something much worse. Asshole or fuckwit were perennial favorites.

"But my friend called you something NSFW."

Ah. There you go.

"I wanted to call and apologize that night," he said. "But…"

"You realized you'd been on the wrong date."

He nodded. Elissa pressed her lips together and twisted them to the side in an effort to think through her options. It was damn cute.

"Okay, I'll accept your apology," she said after a moment. "But on two conditions."

Ryan couldn't keep the smile from creeping up. "Name them."

"First, why did you want to avoid working here?"

"I'm the black sheep. Zero interest in the family business.

My dad thinks I'm wasting my life and told me he'd cut me off from the trust fund my grandparents set up if I didn't clean up my act. Working here was one way, but I thought if I could bring home someone more to their liking, I could get them off my back."

"So, you asking me to be arm candy was a compliment?"

"No, it was a dick move. I don't always think through the consequences. What's the second condition?"

"Take me on another date."

CHAPTER 21
tall order

T he words came out without a conscious choice. Elissa had planned on asking him to take the boxes to her car. They looked heavy. His arm muscles had flexed with the strain of lifting them under the snug-fitting dress shirt he wore, driving every sane thought out of her mind.

The heat rose in her cheeks again. She'd never asked a man out before. Where the hell had this come from? What the fuck was she thinking? *Swear jar.*

Elissa kept her eyes on Not-Actually-a-Jerk Ryan. The brilliant smile he'd worn while escorting her to the file room returned, sending her heart into palpitations. Warmth settled places that hadn't received attention from a man in some time. This could be a wonderful thing. It could also blow up in her face.

"Done!" he said before she could take her words back.

Ryan lifted the second box, muscles flexing once again. She caught her breath as though she'd been running. He placed it gently on top of the other box, and when he rose, he was standing a few inches away, a knowing smirk on his lips. She ached to close the distance between them and kiss his smirk into oblivion. He smelled enticing, looked enticing. For a heartbeat, she considered dropping caution like a hot potato, but he stepped away.

"Let's get these loaded, and then I'll collect on that

condition." He turned toward the door.

She held the front door open for him as he wheeled her cart to her car. Elissa popped the trunk. She couldn't keep her eyes off him, how his body moved with ease as he lifted the heavy boxes, how his butt looked as he loaded them, and how his carefully styled hair fell over one eye. She startled when he closed the trunk and turned to her, his smirk back. Dammit.

Another dollar to the swear jar. She might not be a permanent resident of her parents' home anymore, but she was staying there right now. She'd count tonight and make suggestions for family fun night.

"Thank you," she mumbled, frantically suppressing the instinct to fan her heated face.

"Are you free Thursday?" Ryan leaned against her car.

"Yes." The word was out before she could stop it, even though she hadn't checked her calendar, even though she hadn't given a single thought about her darn calendar. She might regret it later, but this man made her giddy, disregarding all her usual precautions.

"Great! I know the perfect place. Give me your number, and I'll text you the address. How does five work?"

"Five thirty," she countered before giving him her phone number. It was tax season. The days of getting out early were gone until April.

"Five thirty," he agreed. Her phone dinged. "There. You have my number now, and I swear this place has the best Sonoran dogs in Tucson."

"That's a tall order. What if I'm not impressed?"

"You will be. I guarantee it."

"I'm gonna hold you to it."

He took a few steps away from her car, hands stuck firmly in his pockets as though trying not to touch her. She got in the driver's seat.

"Goodbye, Elissa."

She liked the sound of her name from his lips. Too much. She shut the car door.

"I'll see you Thursday, Ryan."

Ryan's gaze lingered on her for a moment as she started the engine before he returned to the office. Elissa watched him the entire way. Once the front door closed, she leaned her forehead onto her steering wheel.

"What am I doing?"

There was no answer either from herself or any divine presence that wanted to make itself known. To be fair, she never knew what she was doing in these situations. A mutual friend had introduced her to Victor in college. It had been years since she'd had to negotiate a date.

Yet she'd worn the sexiest office-appropriate outfit in her closet. With her only black bra. She'd known she'd be here today, known she'd see Ryan, and had dressed appropriately.

She drove straight to JMS Accounting, unloaded the boxes, and wheeled them to the secure storage room. It was emptier than it had been her first year working here. More and more of their clients were switching to digital only, but DeMarco Property Management still insisted on a paper trail. She doubted it would last much longer. Alex DeMarco seemed ready to transition to the easier digital paperwork. But if they'd already done it, she wouldn't have found Ryan. Thank heaven for technophobes.

Elissa went to her office, checked her voicemail and email, and kept herself reasonably busy the rest of the afternoon. In the back of her mind, though, a niggling thought kept trying to come to the forefront. She was ethically obligated to avoid conflicts of interest. Would dating a new office manager who had nothing to do with the documents in her possession, other than pulling them for her, be a conflict? She was the junior member of this team, mostly organizing the files, prepping documents, and arranging meetings. He was not the company bookkeeper. It was a gray area, and Elissa was a rule follower. She hated gray areas.

But this gray area had Ryan in it. And she liked Ryan. A lot. Even given their less-than-stellar start.

See where the next date goes, then talk to Karina. That's what mentors are for.

She couldn't ignore her conscience when it made this much sense. The date could flop even worse than with Mr. Beige-Flag, and this point would be moot. No need to bring it up until she established how a date went when they were one hundred percent honest with each other.

A few minutes after five, she shut down her computer and drove to her parents' house. Leo was in the kitchen, rummaging through the cupboards. He turned to her with a granola bar in one hand and a bag of chips in the other.

"Give me a few minutes and I'll throw the casserole Mom left in the oven," she said.

"Can I still have these?"

"Go for it. I'm not your mother."

He laughed as he took his snacks to his room like the teen goblin boy he was.

She preheated the oven and texted Jules.

> E: I have a date.

> J: What????? With a boy?????

> E: No, with an alien. Yes, with a boy.

> J: Who??? Please tell me not the dweeb from last week

> E: Not the dweeb from last week.

> J: Thank fucking god so who?

> E: The other Ryan.

> J: Lissa!!!!!! OMG I never thought you'd do

it!!!!! He's yummy I'm so happy

        E: Easy on the exclamation points, lady.

J: AYFKM????? You have a date!!!!!!! I will use all the !!!!!!! I want bitch

        E: Love you.

J: LYT

Elissa threw in the casserole and changed into her pj's. She glanced at the clock when she came out. A shiver of anticipation ran down her spine. Only seventy-one hours until her date.

CHAPTER 22
is this seat taken?

R yan had been this close to kissing Elissa in that damn file
room. When she'd demanded a date, his heart had soared.
His thoughts had whirled, and he'd barely been able to add her
number to his contacts. He'd also forgotten the name of any
place to meet her except Mama O's. He would deal with the
fallout of meeting her at the OG taco shop started by Iz's
grandparents. Half the staff knew him, and the Ochoas were
always popping in.

Whistling, Ryan walked into the office.

"Well, that's new." Trinity sat behind *his* desk. "Could it be
our Ryan actually enjoys working here? Or perhaps the new
accountant is the reason for his cheery disposition this fine
afternoon?"

"Shut up," he said, with no hostility. His mood was too good.

As he came around the desk, his cousin rose with a broad
smile.

"Oh, that's not gonna work on me, cousin of mine. I have a
bit of juicy gossip the rest of the family might be interested in
hearing about."

He turned his darkest glare on her. She took a half step back
before remembering he was all bluff. He would never hurt any
of his cousins, but he wasn't above some blackmail now and
then. Unfortunately, Trin was far too ladylike for him to have
any dirt on her. Or at least too talented at hiding her unladylike

activities.

"What do you want?" Ryan asked instead.

She tented her fingers in front of her chest and tapped them together, her brows drawn down in consideration.

"Hmmm...bartend my next party."

He rolled his eyes. Her friends threw themselves at him, and she was always trying to fix him up with one of them. But his love life wasn't anyone's business but his own, especially concerning Elissa. She was special.

"Only if everyone is over twenty-one." His tone left no room for argument. When she opened her mouth to protest anyway, he gave her a look their grandfather had mastered. "I'm serious, Trinity. If I have any doubts, I will card, and if they're under twenty-one, I'm taking all the liquor and leaving."

Ryan didn't mind risks but getting caught serving to a bunch of underage partiers was not something he wanted on his record.

"Fine." She pouted in a way he was sure usually got her exactly what she wanted, but he'd been immune since that pout had convinced him to give her a candy bar right before going on a ride at the county fair. He grimaced at the memory of being covered in a seven-year-old's puke. "I guess Joey can't come. He'll be so disappointed."

Damn straight, her brother would be disappointed. He was still in high school and had no reason to be around a bunch of drunk twenty-somethings.

"When is the party?"

"Rodeo weekend. Think of some fun specialty cocktails to serve and send me the ingredients. I'll buy everything. You just need to help me set up and serve. Then I'll pretend you didn't have a big boner for the hot little accountant."

"Jesus, can you be any more vulgar?"

"Of course I can, but I don't want to offend your tender sensibilities."

She nearly skipped to her desk, leaving him to shake his head in frustration. She'd always pushed boundaries.

The next few days dragged like nothing he'd experienced before. Every request seemed to be designed to take him away from thoughts of Elissa. Each night, he suffered through cold showers that didn't work, and he'd be embarrassed to admit how much X-rated exercise his hand was getting.

When the clock hit five on Thursday, he was out of the office so fast he left skid marks under his desk. He nearly toppled over his motorcycle when he pulled into the parking lot of Mama O's Tacos, home of the best Sonoran hot dogs, period.

He took a deep breath before heading in, his eyes glued to his phone, hoping Elissa hadn't canceled.

"Ryan!" a voice called out from behind. He turned to see Celeste, Iz's aunt. She folded him into a warm hug. "It's so good to see you. What are you doing here?"

His mother had never been big on PDA, and her body was sharp angles. Celeste was round and soft, and only his Nonna had ever given better hugs. Now that she was gone, Iz's aunt was the closest he had. He returned the hug.

Ryan made sure no one else was around and said in a low voice, "I'm meeting a date."

Celeste lowered her own voice in a conspiratorial whisper. "Ooh. Do I know her?"

"You know the woman from a few weeks ago?"

"The one you stared at all night and gave a jump start?" At his nod, she continued with a mischievous grin. "Was it just her car you jumped?"

"Celeste!" He closed his eyes and rubbed his temples. Iz's family wasn't shy about these things.

"I'm kidding. Does Iz know?"

"No, not yet, but I suspect that will change as soon as you get home."

She *tsked*. "My lips are sealed, mijo, and I am insulted you think I would tell Iz about your secret date."

Desperately, Ryan tried to change the subject. "What are you doing here?"

Celeste managed Nopalitos and rarely ventured to the other restaurants in the Ochoa brand.

"Manager here is new and needs help with some of the paperwork, so I volunteered."

"You're good people, Celeste."

"Thanks, but someone's gotta do it, and I'm the nicest."

They walked into the small restaurant. Most people ordered take out, but some liked to sit and eat here. He scanned the room, from the order counter to the salsa bar to the handful of high-top tables and a few booths. His gaze halted on a figure sitting at a high-top. He'd been dreaming of those curves all week. Her brown hair hit the collar of her light blue Oxford shirt tucked into a pair of gray slacks. The roundness of her ass filled the bar stool perfectly, and her feet dangled, one shoe hanging off her toes. They were his favorites, painted with golden-brown butterflies.

"Looks like I'm late." Ryan waved at the table and gave the older woman a half smile.

"You let me know if you need rescuing." Celeste disappeared into the back with a wave.

Ryan strolled to the table and leaned in close enough to smell her powdery perfume.

"Is this seat taken?" he asked, his voice low and raspy. God, why did merely being in her presence do this to him?

Elissa jumped and turned to look at him. Delight soon replaced the alarm his stealthy approach had generated. Those blue eyes twinkled, and her perfect pink bow of a mouth curled into a generous smile, her white teeth flashing in the multicolored lights strung across the ceiling.

"Ryan! Hi!" She slipped her phone into her purse and seemed genuinely pleased to see him. He could get used to that.

"Hello, Elissa. Have you ordered?"

"Just water."

"Let's head to the counter."

But as they approached, the server clearing a table turned around and squealed when she recognized him.

"Ryan!" Becca dropped the tray of trash on a table and threw herself at him.

He'd talked Iz's dad into hiring their old friend from high school for a few shifts when she needed a second job. They'd dated a few times in high school but quickly realized they were better friends.

"Becs, how are you?"

She released him quickly and cleared the discarded trash.

"Same old, same old. It's been ages."

He rolled his eyes at her exaggeration. "Three weeks."

"Well, when I'm used to seeing you at least once a week, three weeks is ages. What brings you in?"

Ryan glanced at Elissa. She had a strained smile on her face and some of the twinkle had gone out of her eyes. Crap, did she think he had a thing for Becca? He'd nip any misconception she had in the bud.

"I invited Elissa out for the best Sonoran dogs in Tucson."

"So, no pressure, then?" Becca laughed.

He ignored her for a moment and focused on Elissa. "Becca and I are friends from way back when. I helped her find the job here."

The tightness at the corners of her lips eased.

"Helped." Becca shook her head. "I guess it helps when your best friend is the owner's kid."

"Well, yeah."

"Are the Sonoran dogs here really that good?" Elissa asked Becca. "We used to get tacos from the one near our house, but I've never tried the dogs."

"I wouldn't know—I'm a vegetarian! But this doofus raves about them all the time."

"I might be a little biased. I've been eating here since I was old enough to drive myself." His parents would never lower themselves to eat at a simple taco joint. Nopalitos, sure. Los Vaqueros, every chance they got. But not Mama O's. Pity. They were missing out.

"Let's put your money where your mouth is." Elissa grabbed him by the hand.

His mind slipped right into the gutter. He knew exactly where he wanted his mouth, and money had nothing to do with it.

CHAPTER 23
swearing at a copier

A jolt of desire shot through her as soon as her fingers touched his, creating an ache deep in her core. An ache she'd never felt before, an ache she knew in her heart could only be soothed by one person.

They placed their order and returned to the table with a beer for him, a limonada for her, and a number on a stick. Ryan stuck the number into the condiment tray as he sat next to her. Elissa's skin prickled as his arm grazed hers.

"How was your day?" he asked.

She surprised herself with disappointment at his nice, normal question. Their last conversations had been so much more interesting, even when they'd been discussing the stupid files. This one was so…prosaic.

As she opened her mouth to respond politely with an equally boring answer, he spoke up.

"That was weak sauce. I don't care how your day was. What I meant to ask was, did you miss me?"

He gave her his thousand-watt smile, which she couldn't help returning.

"You're supposed to care how my day was," she shot back, needling him.

"Why? You'll just say 'fine.' We don't know each other well enough for you to tell me about the client who made you want to tear your hair out, or how you swore at the copier when you had to change the toner, or—"

Elissa laughed, full-throated and genuine. The only other person who could make her laugh like that was Jules. She took it as a promising sign, another thing to like about him.

"So, *did* you miss me?" Ryan asked again.

She tried so hard to give him a stern look, matching her mother's expression when she'd caught one of them, usually *not* her, misbehaving. She failed. Instead, Elissa pressed her lips together and shook her head.

"I don't believe you," he said. "I'm utterly missable."

Becca brought over their hot dogs, interrupting her train of thought.

"Here you go. Enjoy."

Elissa would later swear the woman winked, even odds if it was at her or Ryan.

"Dig in." He lifted the bacon-wrapped hot dog loaded with beans, tomatoes, onions, and all sorts of condiments and took a huge bite.

While he kept his smoldering eyes on her lips, Elissa followed suit. Half the toppings slipped out onto the plate, but wow, it was so yummy. The pinto beans were well seasoned, the right amount of mayo, and the pico de gallo—oh, that was some of the best she'd ever had.

He washed down his mouthful with some beer. "Good, huh?"

"You promised me the best Sonoran dog in Tucson. I have to say, you're a man of your word."

"See? I'm not a jerk, usually. Just that one time."

Elissa snorted in derision. He probably had been a jerk many times in his life, but a few moments of jerkiness did not mean he was fundamentally a jerk.

"Okay, more than once. But I swear, I normally don't insult beautiful, intelligent women by suggesting their only duty is to act as arm candy for privileged assholes."

"Fine. I will no longer refer to you as Jerk-Ryan. Especially since the other Ryan I was supposed to meet turned out to be one giant beige flag."

"Why, thank you, Your Majesty."

She huffed out an exaggerated, exasperated sigh, but softened it with a curl of her lips. "Would you believe I didn't have time to miss anybody this week? Not even someone as missable as you."

His smiled widened when she called him missable, but didn't tease her about it.

"Tax season that bad already?"

"No, but my parents are out of town, so I'm staying with my younger brother."

"How much younger?"

"He's seventeen, a junior in high school."

"Ah. No one ever trusted me enough to be responsible for a younger family member."

Deadpan, she said, "Gee, I don't know why."

He nudged her shoulder with his own while laughing. Heat coiled through her from the point of contact. He might as well have slid his hand under her shirt, with the way her body reacted, like there weren't two layers of fabric between them.

Elissa snuck a glance in his direction, wondering if he felt even a part of what she did. Ryan held himself stock-still, a look of shock on his face, but only for an instant. He forced himself to relax. She could see it in the slow easing of tension in his shoulders and in the return of the smile that did weird things to her insides. Before he noticed her watching, she refocused her attention to her drink, swirling the straw around the ice.

"I don't swear." She tried easing him back into the conversation. Elissa wasn't sure what to do with the knowledge that he felt the same spark, so she changed the subject to something safe.

He cleared his throat, but his voice was the low rumble of his greeting. "What?"

"Earlier, you said I might've spent my day swearing at the copier. I don't swear. At least, not usually."

He cleared his throat again and took a sip of his beer.

"Ah, a goody two-shoes." His voice returned to its clear tenor. She didn't know which she liked more. This voice was musical, one she would never tire of hearing. But when he rumbled, ooh, it was liquid warmth stroking her core.

"No. Well, yeah. Mostly. I was the oldest, my baby brother was sick, and my younger sister was—is—entropy incarnate. I tried not to be a problem. When Ami entered her cursing like a sailor phase in middle school, my mom instituted a swear jar, and I internalized it. Besides, we use the money for a family fun night, you know, go to the movies or bowling. Things have to be going to heck in a handbasket for me to use anything above a PG rating."

"Sounds like a challenge." Impish delight sparked in his warm brown eyes.

"NO!" she said with a bark of laughter. "It wasn't a challenge. I was just...sharing something personal. It's your turn."

"I'll take it under advisement." He grinned, and she knew he wasn't going to let it go. Ryan would push her boundaries. Let him try. Her sister had been pushing since the day she was born. "I, on the other hand, spent a good part of my afternoon swearing at a copier."

"That wasn't personal."

"It got pretty personal with the copier. I mean, I called its mother a bitch, then accused it of fucking her."

The sip of limonada she'd taken almost came out her nose. Instead, she went into a coughing fit. Ryan placed a hand on her back and patted gently. Warmth radiated from his touch, and heat rose in her cheeks as tears leaked from her eyes. Once she got her breathing under control, she took another sip.

"I'm sorry, Elissa. I didn't mean—" His face was pale with shock, all traces of humor gone.

"No, no, it was funny, but I need to clean up. I'll be right back." She gave him her best smile as she hopped down from the barstool and went to the ladies' room.

Looking in the mirror, Elissa was surprised the worst effect of the incident was smeared mascara. She took a paper towel and dabbed at her eyes, wiping away the mess, and gave herself a stern glare.

What the hell are you doing?

Her reflection had no defense. Elissa had expected she'd meet some nice guy who wouldn't sweep her off her feet but would be patient enough to develop a deep and abiding relationship. She wasn't a woman who got swept off her feet. She'd made sure she was sensible enough to not expect sweeping. And yet...

Not only was he sexy as hell, but he was smart, with humor lacing even his sharpest comment. She couldn't stop thinking about him, even when she'd believed he was an entitled jerk. And he was, sometimes. Everyone had bad days, but she hadn't seen a whiff of that guy since the first time they met.

"Oh, fudge nuts."

She was falling for him. Elissa wasn't a risk-taker. It was what made her a skilled accountant. She conserved resources and was careful about who she let in her life. Ryan threw her for a loop. Every cell in her body yearned for him, even those brain cells she was so proud of. But a small voice in the far corners of her mind screamed caution. She couldn't predict what would happen, and it would end her if her heart broke.

Elissa was getting ahead of herself. It was just hot dogs. She straightened her shirt, washed her hands, and returned to the table.

CHAPTER 24
want me to ask her out for you?

Ryan couldn't keep himself from staring after Elissa as she walked to the ladies' room. He hadn't meant to cause her to choke. He was trying to disguise his nervousness with humor. Ryan hadn't been nervous around a woman since he was seventeen. He knew exactly how they'd react, especially when they learned who his family was.

Elissa was like no other woman he'd met. His usual charm never seemed to make a dent, but when he was authentically himself, she opened up. She didn't care who his family was. She only seemed to care how he treated others.

"Hey, man!" a familiar voice said from the opposite direction of his stare. "I didn't know you'd be here tonight."

Iz clapped a hand to his shoulder. Shit, what were they doing here? They usually stuck closer to home. He tore his gaze away from where Elissa had disappeared. Iz had gone all out tonight. Their golden-brown skin was highlighted with sparkly powder on the cheekbones and gold eyeshadow. Short, black hair with an off-center red streak complemented the red silk shirt Iz wore. And their nails were painted like a ladybug—red with black dots.

"Hi, Iz. Got a hot date?"

"How could you tell?" They laughed as they took the seat to Ryan's right. "Don't you remember? I said I was coming here to catch the game."

Now that Iz mentioned it, he vaguely recalled a conversation in the last couple of days discussing this fact. *Son of a bitch.* There went his plan to charm the pants off the lovely accountant.

"Where's Mateo?" He resigned himself to an interrupted date.

"He'll be here soon," Iz said. "Teo is on call, and someone called about forty-five minutes ago."

The two of them were good together. Iz was kinder and more patient with Mateo around, with Ryan and with their family. Iz didn't have a mean bone in their body, but Teo had taught them to slow down and appreciate people more. And Teo had come out of his shell, more confident and less defensive when meeting new people.

Iz's love could do that. While most of the DeMarco family were short on praise and long on criticism for his accomplishments, Iz had his back. They had encouraged his creative pursuits, usually sitting right next to Ryan's Nonna. Always in the audience at the school plays, applauding his attempts at photography, giving constructive feedback on his writing. Ryan didn't know where he'd be without Iz and Nonna. No, he did know. He would be the first-class asshole he'd come off as during his first date with Elissa.

Movement down the hallway drew his attention—Elissa. Out of the corner of his eye, he watched as Iz's glance followed his. A smile twitched up the corner of his friend's mouth as they leaned toward Ryan.

"She's pretty. Want me to ask her out for you?"

An old joke from middle school, when an unsure thirteen-year-old Ryan had begged his best friend to ask out the prettiest girl in their class for him. It had gone about as well as any adult could have predicted. The young lady in question had giggled and walked away, leaving a heartbroken Ryan in her wake, and an amused Iz. Who never let him forget it.

"Nope. I think I've got it handled." Ryan suppressed a grin as Elissa approached and took the seat to his left. Iz's eyes widened in surprise, and their mouth hung open.

"Elissa, this is my BFF, Iz Ochoa."

"BFF? Seriously, are you a teenage girl?" Iz's tone was teasing and a wide grin creased their face.

"I've known you since kindergarten. What else would you call us?"

Sitting right next to her, Ryan took in the way Elissa's eyes crinkled when she had a smile on her face. And the hint of a dimple in her right cheek had him yearning to kiss it.

"Childhood friend? Sib from another parental unit? Hell, I'd take the simple roommate."

Ryan held his breath. Since Iz and Mateo began dating two years ago, Ryan hadn't had enough interest in any particular woman to worry about how she felt about his non-binary best friend and their pansexual significant other. Hell, he didn't think he'd introduced more than one or two of them to the couple. But he cared now. As much as Elissa intrigued him, teased him, kindled a fire deep down, if she had a problem with Iz and Teo, he'd walk away and never give her another thought.

Her eyes were wider than before, and her mouth fell open a little, but when Iz stuck out a hand, she took it.

"Nice to meet you, Iz," she said, her voice soft.

"Elissa. I know that name... Oh, you're the mystery date!"

The flush rose in Ryan's cheeks. He elbowed his friend.

"Ow. Stop it, Ryan. I wasn't gonna say anything else."

"Then there's something else to tell?" Elissa raised her eyebrows, but the twinkle never left her eyes. She was teasing him in more ways than one.

"BFF to BFF confidentiality, miss," Iz said in mock seriousness. "Strictly protected. Will take it to my grave."

She laughed, a musical sound that eased his mind. "Well, I don't want anyone to get into legal trouble."

"Who's the hottie?" another familiar voice asked from the other side of Iz. Mateo had finally arrived.

He was dressed in slacks and a green button down short-sleeve shirt that complemented his medium brown skin—professional enough for a therapist, casual enough to avoid too much authority around the teens he often worked with. He wore his tight curls on the longer side.

"That's Ryan, sweetie," Iz said.

After planting a kiss on Iz's cheek, he looked straight at Elissa.

"We all know Ryan's a hottie, hon. I was talking about the cutie next to him." Mateo rounded the trio and took a seat on the other side of Elissa, sticking out a hand. "Hello, I'm Teo."

Elissa's fingers brushed Ryan's arm and little electric sparks traveled straight to his brain and down to his cock. Goosebumps rose on his flesh, and a small part of him was jealous of the contact Teo currently had with her, even though it was a simple, quick handshake.

"It's nice to meet you, Teo, I'm Elissa."

"Ooh, the infamous missed opportunity." Teo's full lips turned up at the corners.

"Teo," Ryan warned.

"Sweetie, I've already explained to Elissa that conversation is under BFF seal," Iz said with a grin.

"Which apparently doesn't extend to significant others," Ryan muttered irritably.

"What, are you two teenage girls?" Teo asked.

"That's already been covered, too." Iz chuckled.

Elissa had remained quiet during their discussion but hadn't taken her eyes off Iz. The tension rose in his friend as they noticed, too.

"You look like a lady with a question." Iz's voice was strained and their body stiff.

"Oh, sorry, didn't mean to stare." Elissa's cheeks flushed. "Where did you get that highlighter? It is absolutely gorgeous."

All the tension left Iz's body and a wide smile bloomed on

their face as Iz touched their cheek.

"Isn't it? I found it on Insta and fell in love with it."

Ryan's own muscles relaxed as Elissa and Iz exchanged makeup recommendations. A poke at his right arm drew his attention to Mateo.

"I like her. Iz has been dying to tell someone about that damn highlighter. She couldn't have asked a better question. How the fuck did you find her?"

"I'm starting to think divine intervention, to be honest."

"Here, give me your phone, and I'll find it for you," Iz was saying.

Elissa pulled out her phone and went to unlock it. The color drained out of her face.

"Oh, oh crap. I'm sorry, I have to go." Her voice quavered as she gathered her clutch and keys and hopped off the bar stool. The keys rattled as her hands shook.

Ryan stood and wrapped his arm around her shoulders. "What's wrong?"

"It's my brother." Tears welled in her eyes, and he could barely make out her words. "He's having an asthma attack, and his meds aren't working. I gotta go."

"You're in no condition to drive. Give me the keys."

"No, I-I couldn't. That's nice, but—"

"Elissa, you shouldn't be driving," Teo said in his therapist voice. "It's okay to accept help."

Elissa's gaze darted from Teo to Ryan, and she swayed as she tried to decide. Ryan wrapped a hand around the one holding the keys and smiled reassuringly. Some of her panic fled, and she let go of the keys.

"Thank you." She stared into his eyes for a heartbeat.

"Anytime, beautiful. Lead the way."

She straightened her spine and unlocked. Her voice was firm, now, all traces of vulnerability gone. "Leo, I'm on my way. Breathe with me. In, two, three…"

CHAPTER 25
it's what i live for

E lissa gave Ryan her parents' address and left her phone on the entire way home. They pulled into the driveway twenty minutes after she'd seen Leo's text.

"You can come in and wait. I should be—"

"I've got you, Elissa. Go take care of your brother. I'll keep the car running and get you to the hospital if you need me."

If she wasn't so scared about Leo, the warm, gooey feeling his words sent careening through her brain would warrant further investigation. But she was, so she smiled wanly before running into the house. Leo sat in the recliner in the living room, hands folded on top of his head. She heard the wheezing as soon as the door slammed behind her.

"What did you take?" she asked.

He pointed at the coffee table where an array of medications sat in a jumble. Elissa sorted through them.

"How many puffs of albuterol?"

Leo held up two fingers.

"When?"

"Thirty minutes." His voice was soft, and he had to catch his breath after uttering those two words.

"We're going to the hospital." If the albuterol hadn't helped in thirty minutes, he needed more than what was available at the house.

He shook his head at her.

"There's no use in arguing with me. I'm the responsible one, and I say we're going to the hospital. Get some shoes on and gather your meds."

Elissa hurried to the kitchen to grab a gallon-sized zipper bag to hold his medications and was back before Leo had both shoes on. While he tossed his meds in the bag, she walked to her room, rummaged in her suitcase for the power of attorney she had for his medical treatment, and in five minutes, they were out the door.

She opened Bertha's rear door. Leo glanced from Ryan in the driver's seat to her.

"Leo, Ryan. Ryan has graciously offered to drive us to the hospital."

"I thought...you said...he was...a jerk?" Leo slid into the seat and buckled in, but the faintest smile curved his lips.

"I may have been wrong."

Ryan chuckled. "Nice to meet you, Leo. Wish it was under better circumstances."

Leo waved briefly, then put his hands on his head to open his lungs as much as possible. He breathed in through his nose and out through his mouth. Elissa got into the passenger seat and told Ryan which emergency room to go to. From long experience, she knew which one took her parents' insurance.

As Ryan pulled into the parking lot, she turned to her brother.

"Do you need a wheelchair?"

He shook his head. Leo sounded a little better, but he was still wheezing. Ryan parked and helped Leo out, walking behind her brother without making it look like he was there to catch him. He sat next to Leo as Elissa explained what was going on to the intake clerk. She took the forms she needed to fill out and sat next to her brother. He leaned into her, resting his head on her shoulder. It couldn't have been comfortable as she was so much shorter. A wave of nostalgia washed over her. It had been years since he'd leaned on her like this. Nostalgia was quickly replaced by worry. Leo must be feeling terrible if he was resorting to the tricks of his childhood for comfort.

"I think we're good for now, Ryan. I, um—"

"I'll call Iz or use a rideshare. Don't worry about me, I can take care of myself." He held out her keys but closed his fingers around hers as she tried to take them. "Are you sure you'll be okay to drive home?"

Irritation flashed through her, but his expression was merely concerned. Concern for her well-being, concern for her brother. It had been a long, long time since someone cared. Everyone in her life assumed she had everything handled.

"I'll use an Uber if I'm not."

"Or you can call me. I don't live far."

Teo's words came back to her. *It's okay to accept help.*

"I'll keep that in mind."

He stood. "Text me when you get home, okay? Feel better soon, Leo."

"Thank you. Really. And…you're not a jerk." Not at all.

Ryan smiled and left, and Elissa returned her attention to the paperwork.

"I saw…you," Leo said.

"Saw me what?" She was distracted as she tried to fill out all this nonsense.

"Looking at his butt."

Elissa snorted. She had been for a second. She completed the paperwork in record time, and a nurse called them about fifteen minutes later. After taking his vitals and asking a few questions, the nurse left.

With every pained breath Leo took, she kicked herself. Elissa had been out enjoying life while her brother got sick. He'd only called after trying everything else. Leo hated being the sick kid, always had. He fought it with every fiber of his being now that he was a teenager. And tonight, she hadn't been there when he needed her.

"Why haven't you called Mom and Dad?" He paused every couple words to catch his breath.

This was bad, real bad. Elissa hadn't seen him this bad since she'd started college. She should call her parents, but the guilt over leaving him to his own devices for an extra hour stayed her hand. There wasn't anything they could do right now, anyway. By the time they made the drive home from the conference, this would be resolved.

Elissa shrugged, and Leo gave her a knowing smile.

"Don't want...to tell them...you fucked up?"

"Swear jar."

He stuck out his tongue at her, drawing her attention to the blue tint to his lips and his pale face. The doctor better get here soon or she'd make a fuss.

"Okay, I won't enforce it today," she said, relenting in the face of his illness.

Leo leaned against her again. The silence in the room while they waited was broken by his wheezes and the crinkle of the paper cover on the exam table. Before long, a woman's voice called out on the other side of the curtain.

"May I come in?"

"Yes," Elissa said.

The curtain twitched back and a tall, dark-haired woman stepped in. Her coat and badge labeled her as a doctor, but she barely looked as old as Elissa.

"Hi, I'm Doctor Ruiz. Can I have your name and date of birth?"

Leo obliged, sucking in air in between words.

"Thank you, Leo." The doctor turned to Elissa. "And you are?"

"I'm Elissa Wright, his sister. Our parents are out of town. I have a power of attorney so I can make decisions for my brother in their absence. I gave a copy to the intake clerk."

"That's fine. Thank you. Now, why don't you tell me what's going on?"

Elissa opened her mouth to tell the doctor what happened, but she held up a hand.

"I need to hear from your brother. If he forgets anything, you can fill in the blanks later."

Elissa closed her mouth and tried not to let the hurt show. Leo shot her a look of triumph before turning his attention to the doctor. In halting sentences, pausing frequently to catch his breath, her brother described his evening before Elissa rode to the rescue. He'd been feeling blah all afternoon, but the walk home from his friend's house had done him in. The friend had dogs, which Leo was allergic to. He drank some water, took an allergy pill, and lay down for a nap. When he woke, he was wheezing and used his albuterol, and when it didn't work, he'd called her.

"Is there anything you'd like to add?" the doctor asked her.

Elissa shook her head, and from her bag, she pulled out the medications Leo took regularly.

"Our mom usually has a list of all his current meds, but I forgot to ask for it before she left. Here's what he usually takes."

"Thank you. I'm ordering a stronger broncho-dilator." The doctor made some notes on the computer by the bedside. "We'll see how you respond, Leo, and go from there. In the meantime, I'll take a look at these medications and see where you might want to make some modifications until you can see your regular doctor, okay?"

Leo nodded, and the young doctor left, toting the medications with her. A few minutes later, a respiratory therapist and a nurse came in with a nebulizer and began the treatment. Fifteen minutes after that, Leo's lips were a nice pink, and his face was no longer deathly pale. The tension left Elissa's shoulders.

"You look good," she said. "You know, for a hobbit."

He chuckled, but didn't engage in their usual banter as the respiratory therapist took away the equipment, and the doctor returned for an assessment. After a brief examination, she hung the stethoscope around her neck and smiled at Leo.

"Your lungs sound much better, and I like the color in your cheeks. I'll sign the discharge papers, but you need to go see your primary care provider as soon as possible for a follow-up. I would mention to them you haven't been taking your long-term control meds."

Elissa snapped her head around and glared at her brother. She opened her mouth to read him the riot act but stopped when she took in his posture. Leo hung his head, his shoulders hunched, his hands clasped in his lap.

"Perhaps this discussion can wait until your brother gets some rest?" the doctor suggested, handing over the bag of medications.

"Yeah, that's a great idea." Elissa shoved the meds in her bag.

"Do either of you have any questions for me?"

Leo shook his head. Elissa said, "No, but thank you, Doctor."

"Okay. Leo, plenty of rest and fluids. No school tomorrow. And see your PCP."

Buzzing off the adrenaline for the night, Elissa was fine driving, hyperalert though there was almost zero traffic. It was nearly midnight when they finally returned home, and Elissa tucked her brother into bed.

"If you wake up and feel bad, come get me."

"Yes, Mom."

She smoothed his hair back but resisted the urge to plant a kiss on his forehead.

As she was shutting the door behind her, he said quietly, "Thanks, Liss."

"It's what I live for."

Elissa dropped on the bed in her old room and stared at the ceiling. The adrenaline had worn off, and the sluggish aftereffects had her struggling to put more than two words together, let alone to summon the courage to call her parents. The important thing was Leo was fine. He was a stupid teenager who hadn't been taking the medicine he was supposed to, but he was fine. That's what she'd concentrate on when she called her parents. In the morning.

For a second, as she closed her eyes, she thought about texting Ryan and letting him know she was okay. But before she could pull out her phone, she was sound asleep.

CHAPTER 26
not my girl

S leep eluded Ryan. He resisted the urge to text or call Elissa to find out how her brother was doing. If things were bad, she wouldn't appreciate the interruption. But he couldn't stop thinking and worrying about her.

Ryan watched a movie, then another. When movies didn't help, he binged half a season of *Brooklyn 99*. He kept his phone beside him, hoping she'd contact him to let him know how things went. When the sun rose and she hadn't, he pretended that wasn't what he'd expected. After all, they'd only been on two dates, and had only a handful of interactions.

"You look like shit," Iz said when they emerged from their room at something resembling a normal hour. His friend poured a cup of coffee. "Refill?"

"No, thanks. That's the second pot. I'm good."

"Jesus, Ryan. That's a lot of caffeine, even for you. You gonna be okay?"

"Yeah, I'll be fine. I'll crash as soon as I get home tonight."

The last was a real downer. He'd been hoping to work on his podcast script, but working all day, every day, limited the time he could dedicate to his passion project. After spending all night worrying about Elissa and her brother, he needed sleep more than he needed to work on some stupid podcast. No matter how much he wished otherwise.

"Whatever you say, man. Want me to give you a ride in? I'm

sure you can convince one of your cousins or your brother to bring you home."

Sounded like a great idea. He didn't need to be riding his motorcycle when he was this tired. Tired bikers were dead bikers.

"Thanks, Iz. Let me get ready."

While Iz drove, Ryan sent a quick text to check in with Elissa.

R: I hope everything is ok

Ryan promised himself he wouldn't check his phone incessantly. If her night was anything like his, she might still be asleep. And if things were worse, she might be too busy to be the emotional support human for a worried date. Before he could silence it and tuck it into his pocket, the phone dinged at him.

E: OMG, I'm so sorry. I crashed last night
before I could text you. Leo is a lot better
and he's still asleep.

Of course she texted in complete sentences. Ryan smiled to himself as relief flowed through him like a cool shower after a hot day. He liked that. He liked her.

R: No worries figured something like that

E: Called my parents at 6 and they're
coming home today. Leo hasn't been
taking his meds, so there will be lots of
yelling. He's home from school and I'll be
home from work this morning.

R: Good. I was—

Ryan deleted what he was going to write. He had been worried, but it wasn't his style to worry about the women in his life, with the rare exception of a cousin. He didn't need to clue in this woman about how much she'd already got under his skin.

"Your girl okay?" Iz asked as they pulled into the parking lot.

"Not my girl."

"She should be. I saw how you looked at her last night."

"Just because I find her attractive does not mean she's 'my girl.'"

"You sure?"

No, he wasn't sure. He liked the idea, more than he'd care to admit, but they'd only been on two dates, one of which would likely win a contest for worst date ever. How would having a girlfriend affect his ultimate goal? He needed to survive the next two years so he could work on his true calling instead of wasting time with the family business. Ryan had been busting his ass trying to find the primary and secondary sources he needed to make his work as rigorous as possible. He'd been listening to a wide variety of podcasts to figure out how those creators put their shows together. He was almost there. Only a script stood between him and his first episode. And a catchy name, of course.

Ryan exited the car without answering Iz. He waved as the car drove off before dragging himself to the front door. Locking the door behind him, he tossed his keys and phone on the reception desk on his way to the break room. He started the coffee and shot off a quick response to Elissa.

> R: If you get bored I take lunch at 12 and get off at 4:30.

> E: Thank you again. You really were my knight in shining armor last night. Sorry I was in distress.

> R: Everyone needs help sometimes. Don't apologize that it was your turn

She responded with an upside-down smiley face. He had no

idea how to take it, but he smiled. He did that a fuckton around this woman.

He sighed and headed to his desk. His Aunt Annetta stood outside the door, digging in her purse for her keys. Ryan opened the door for her, leaving it unlocked.

"Grazie, Ryan."

"You're here early."

The other employees, as well as his other aunt, his father, and his brother, would all be here in the next thirty minutes.

"Yes. I have an early meeting across town, and I forgot a file I need. I'll be in and out."

"Anything I can help with?"

"Aren't you sweet? Where was this Ryan the last five years?"

Aunt Annetta was mostly teasing, but Ryan hadn't spent a lot of time with his family outside of the frequent gatherings. One didn't simply walk away from the DeMarco family. Especially when one still wanted access to one's trust fund. Maybe he was getting too pretentious using all these "ones."

"I've never wanted to be part of the family business."

"But you want your money." She frowned at him as they walked into the main office space and Ryan flipped on the lights.

"Yes, but only because it will allow me to follow my own path. Don't get me wrong, Auntie, I'm very grateful for everything the DeMarco money has given me, including my education. But I don't give a shit about real estate. I find it incredibly boring, and numbers hurt my head. From everything I've seen the last few weeks, this is a great place to work, but it's not for me. I'm playing my dad's game, until he's satisfied I've done my duty to the family. Then I'll go make my mark on the world."

Annetta patted his arm. "If you say so, Ryan, but I'm not sure how you'll do that with a degree in global studies. I mean, it could be worse, but what kind of job did you think you could find?"

His aunt headed to her office. A good thing—he didn't want her to see the impish grin forming on his face. Would she be surprised to find out that's exactly why he'd picked it? He'd been shocked when he found he loved it. No more forcing himself to study enough to earn Bs and Cs. Except for the general studies classes required by the university, he found the courses stimulating, and it had no longer been a struggle to earn As. He never knew he had it in him, but apparently he'd just needed something he wanted to learn.

While his degree seemed impractical to his family, understanding history, politics, and how different countries interacted with all the new technology had become incredibly relevant for the world they all lived in. The Ochoas had needed a bartender around the time of his graduation, and he discovered the breadth and depth of the Tucson foodie world. After all, it was a UNESCO City of Gastronomy. And it all clicked. How food currently moved around the world, how the import and export of food had drastically changed the course of human history.

The kernel of the idea of his podcast formed about two years ago. He liked bartending, truly, but it lacked some of the intellectual stimulation he never realized he needed until college. He'd been reading a bunch of random history books, listening to podcasts, then he took a trip with his cousin Trinity to Europe and it came together. His job gave him the freedom to chase his passion and his trust fund the cash to buy the books and the equipment he needed. His collection of food-related history books was wild, and he'd been playing with recording equipment and researching best business practices. He'd finally been ready to write the pilot episode when his father insisted on this bargain.

Ryan sat at his desk for a few minutes until someone else walked through the door, one of the non-relatives working here. He went back, got another cup of coffee, and assumed his station, guarding the entrance to DeMarco Property

Management.

Another cog in the machine. He still had two more years and some change left of this before he would have the freedom to do as he saw fit again. At least he still had Iz and Teo in his life. And Elissa…well, if working here gave him more time with her, he could live with that.

CHAPTER 27
go easy on the dingus

Dana and Peter Wright arrived home a little before lunch, intent on teaching their youngest child a valuable lesson. The expression they wore had often been pointed at Ami and Leo, but rarely at Elissa. Today looked like a rare day.

"What happened?" Mom asked. "Why weren't you here?"

"I met a friend after work. Leo's seventeen, old enough to manage his own treatment."

"But he wasn't. How did you let this happen in only four days? I'd expect this of Ami, but you, Elissa, you're better than this."

"It's not her fault!" Leo said from his perch on the barstool.

"Leo, honey…" It was never good when their mom used "honey."

"You need to take your meds," her father said. "And last night is a perfect example of why. If you don't take your long-term medications, you will have attacks."

Her brother's face shut down. He'd already tuned them out, and their parents might as well be talking to a wall. Elissa intervened, though her gut roiled at standing up to her parents.

"He knows all this. Telling him again won't motivate him to take his meds."

She instantly regretted it. Her mother's laser gaze focused right on her, her color high. The fear she must've been marinating in all morning came pouring out in anger.

"*You* were supposed to look out for him," she said.

Leo stood and moved between the two women. "They're my meds. I chose not to take them. Elissa couldn't make me. You can't make me. I hate how you watch me take them each night, like I can't be trusted."

"Well, obviously…" their dad said.

Like prairie dogs following a potential predator, three heads turned toward him, irritation plain on three faces. Peter held up his hands and backed away.

"I wanted to see what would happen if I didn't take the medications for a bit. I've been so much better, maybe I could go without. I was wrong, but Elissa was there to bail me out."

Weird having Leo defend her. But she appreciated it, more than she'd ever tell him. She rarely defended herself.

"She shouldn't have to," Mom said. "That's the point. You have to take your medications, and if you won't do it on your own, I'll be there to observe."

"Mom—" Elissa tried to intercede for her brother. This wouldn't end well.

"Enough, Elissa. This is between us and your brother. Why don't you go to work? Thank your boss for us, please."

Leo's blue eyes pleaded for her to stay.

"I'll go, but go easy on the dingus, okay? He's a teenager and they're supposed to push boundaries."

"We don't need you to tell us how to raise a teenager. This isn't our first rodeo!"

"Dana," her dad said. "She's not wrong. Elissa was the easy one, but this is how normal teenagers act. Leo has learned an important lesson, and we'll talk to him, but calmly."

"But—"

"You're scared and it's coming out as anger, love. Take a breath, and we'll sort this out."

Her mom looked like she'd argue for a moment, but she stalked over to the fridge and poured herself a glass of water.

"I think we're good, Lissa. Thank you. You did well." Her dad hugged her.

"Yeah, thanks. But did you have to call me a dingus?" Leo said, but he let her hug him.

"Yes, because you were. I still love you." And she planted a kiss on his cheek.

"Ugh, sister germs!" He made a show of wiping off his cheek as she grabbed her purse.

"You'll probably be grounded, but I'll take you out for lunch on your next day off, K?"

He gave her a thumbs up and she left.

They had all spent so much effort over the last seventeen years making sure Leo was okay, from the day he was born five weeks early to his first diagnosis to today. Now that he was old enough to manage his asthma on his own, they were all having a hard time letting go. Her parents could try to hover over him, but it would only push him away. She didn't envy her brother.

Elissa wandered into the office after lunch. She stopped by Karina's desk.

"Thanks, Karina," she said.

"No problem, Elissa. How's your brother?"

"Okay. He wasn't taking his meds. Mom and Dad are trying to convince him not to do it again. Loudly."

"It's rough being a teen with a chronic illness. My oldest has diabetes, and she went through something similar at that age. He should outgrow it."

"I hope you're right," Elissa said. Because the alternative was horrible.

"You could use a quiet day. Why don't you go through the files from our clients? I'll send you checklists for each, and you can ensure we have everything we need. I want to start with the DeMarco account next week. They're long-time clients and have a lot of different subsidiaries to sort through."

That sounded exactly like her speed today. After the

adrenaline rush of last night, coupled with the lack of sleep, she needed an easy job, but one that would keep her busy enough to avoid the messy emotions until she had a moment to deal with them. Elissa stopped in the office kitchen to grab a cup of tea on her way to her desk. It was almost an afternoon for coffee, but after the wild ride she'd had last night, she refused to risk the caffeine overload.

She printed off the checklists and went to their file room. In her precise fashion, she attached the appropriate checklist to each box of papers she'd spent the week collecting from some of their largest accounts. Once that was accomplished, she pulled over the DeMarco boxes and went through it.

It was a long process. Every time she read the name DeMarco, she couldn't help her thoughts turning to Ryan, with his brown eyes crinkled in laughter from yesterday. How his hair kept flopping over one eye. The way his shirt stretched across his well-defined shoulders. The heat rose as she focused on his physical attributes. She tried distracting herself with the checklist in front of her. A simple task to match the name of the document in the box with the name on the list. Except today it wasn't simple. Her brain couldn't seem to handle anything requiring thought.

She went through the boxes twice and still couldn't find all the documents. Was she not seeing them, or had the documents been omitted? Or was something else going on? A headache formed at the back of her skull.

None of the people she'd met at DPM had seemed the sort to hide anything on purpose. So, where were the documents? Karina wanted to get started, Elissa wanted to get started, and the godforsaken paperwork wasn't where it was supposed to be.

Elissa rubbed her temples, closed her eyes, and counted to ten. Occam's Razor. The simplest explanation was the most likely explanation. In the chaos of a long-time employee leaving an inexperienced replacement in charge of the project, some documents had been forgotten or misplaced.

Or she simply wasn't seeing them in the box because she was so fucking tired.

Dammit. Swear jar.

She put the box to the side and worked through a few others. None of those had missing documents.

Just before five, Karina poked her head in.

"How's it going?"

Elissa waved a hand at the boxes. "I've gone through about half of them. Most of those are fine, but I can't find some of the paperwork for the DeMarco account. I don't know if I'm not seeing it, or it's not there."

"It can wait until Monday. Go home and rest this weekend and try again on Monday. If the papers aren't there, I'm sure they're at the DPM office. Give the cute new office manager a call if you still can't find them."

She winked and the heat rose up Elissa's chest.

"You noticed?"

"That he's cute, yes. That you couldn't keep your eyes off him? What do the kids say these days? Also yes. It's fine, it doesn't hurt to look. But if anything else happens, let me know so we can handle things professionally. Have a good weekend, Elissa."

"Thanks, Karina. You too."

How many dates counted as "anything else"? She'd need to talk to Karina soon, but after she rested and thought about what to say.

Elissa stayed a little late to finish the box in front of her. This one was fine, too. Well, no use worrying about it until Monday. Elissa locked the file room, checked the messages on her desk phone, made a couple of notes for next week, and left by 5:30.

She walked into her apartment, and Jules enveloped her in a hug.

"Hey, bitty babe. How's Leo?"

And Elissa broke. Sobs too big for her petite body came pouring from her, along with a healthy dose of tears and snot. Jules shushed her and wrangled the two of them over to the couch, grabbing a box of tissues along the way. She had no idea how her friend managed it.

When she calmed, Elissa finally told Jules everything that had happened with Leo. She'd been so busy holding it together for her brother, her parents, and her work she'd forgotten to let it out. Trust Jules to be the first to remind her.

"That sucks." Her friend summed up in two words exactly how Elissa felt.

"Stupid teenage boy."

"You know it. Let's order an insane amount of pizza and watch a movie that requires exactly zero brain cells. *Pitch Perfect* or *Easy A?*"

Chapter 28
three drafts

R yan had set his alarm for eight on Saturday morning. He woke at noon.

"Fuck!"

Iz and Teo were in Phoenix for a cousin's wedding, and he'd been excited to devote an entire weekend to writing his script, hoping he could finally wrangle this thing. But the sleepless night on Thursday had undone all the work of adjusting his sleep patterns to working a day job, instead of nights at a busy restaurant. Another reason he'd resisted working at the family company—he was naturally a night owl, and showing up anywhere before ten had been damned near impossible.

Now the whole weekend he'd set aside was down to only a day and a half.

He rolled out of bed and stumbled to the kitchen. The pod went into the Keurig, the bread went into the toaster, and he went into the bathroom. After using the facilities and splashing water on his face, he returned to the kitchen to an overflowing mug and burnt toast.

"Fuck!"

Ryan cleaned up and tried again. More success. He collapsed onto the couch and turned on a basketball game. When halftime rolled around, he was finally awake enough to start on his draft. First, a shower.

Six hours later, three drafts sat in the trash, and he was half-tempted to take the lot of them to the community grill and burn them. They'd make better kindling for grilling burgers than they would a podcast. He sat at the kitchen table, his notebook open and his head down, surrounded by his piles of research material. His process was as organized as it was going to be, but obviously it wasn't enough. Nothing was.

Time to see if a little alcohol might get him over whatever was holding him back. He poured himself a gin and tonic and plopped on his chair. But before he could start draft number four, his phone dinged.

Don't look, don't look, don't look.

He looked. God-fucking-dammit. But a smile snuck out when he noticed who it was from. Elissa.

E: Whatcha doing?

Before he could think twice, he responded.

R: Drinking and trying to write. You?

He held his breath. What would an accountant who seemed to have her entire life in order think about an overprivileged asshole whose day job was office manager for his family's real estate empire trying to write?

E: Drinking and watching Friends marathon whatcha writing

Wait, where was the punctuation?

R: Elissa Wright, are you drunk texting me

He finished his drink and watched the thinking bubble pulse.

E: Maaaayybeeee 😶

Ryan chuckled at her attempt to flirt via text. Obviously not something she did often, if ever.

E: Tell me what you're writing and I'll tell
you what I'm drinking.

R: A script. Your turn

E: A script for what?

Oh, he needed another drink for this discussion. But first...

R: Answer me and I'll tell you

E: No fun

He grabbed the gin and bottle of tonic and poured another,
adding two lime wedges.

R: I'm plenty of fun but you have to live up to
your end of the deal

E: Fine pina colada eegee with rum

He sent a bunch of laughing emojis.

E: We out of wine

E: *We're

Ah, she was sobering up a bit.

R: I am working on a script for a podcast I'm
trying to start. Stupid thing kicks my ass every
time

He sat on the couch, abandoning his passion project for now.
He'd tried today, he really had, and still...nothing. Maybe the
inner voice that sounded awfully close to his dad's was right—
this was a waste of time. No one would listen to some dude
yammer on about food and history and booze, and he was foolish
to believe he'd be successful.

E: I'm sure you'll make it behave what's it
about?

R: History of food and how the production and trade have changed the world in both good ways and bad. I majored in global studies and minored in history then worked as a bartender. Loved working in the food industry and wanted to do something with everything I learned.

E: sounds amazing I'd totally listen to that. But why a podcast and not a book?

R: I tried a book but my ADHD is a bitch when it comes to focusing for too long on one thing. This story is so big, spanning the course of human civilization. I needed a platform that would allow me to tell the whole story. No one is doing anything like it.

E: Soooo why are you working for your dad

Money. It was the answer to everything in life. He could've searched for another job or requested for more shifts at Nopalitos. Learned to manage with what he earned, like almost everyone else. The money from his trust fund had already bought him a first-rate setup. He had a high-end laptop, an excellent microphone, quality headphones, and great editing software.

If he failed, he'd need a cushion, and the temptation to have more—more time, more freedom, both bought with the trust fund—had him agreeing to work for his father. But had he not showed up at DeMarco Property Management when he did, he may never have reconnected with Elissa Wright. And that would've been a damned shame.

R: Blackmail sort of

E: ????

R: I have a trust fund. My dad now controls it.
He won't let me have access to it unless I work
for the family business for the next 2 years

E: That sucks

R: Yeah but I'm trying to put together a
business plan to convince him this podcast
can be monetized. Maybe he'll back off

The thinking bubble appeared and stayed for a long, long time.

E: I helped a couple of friends work
through the finance stuff for their
business plans in college. Want me to
look at what you have?

He hadn't been fishing for help. Just trying to explain to the girl he was...what? Dating? Attracted to? Simping for? All of the above, to be honest. Ryan wished her to know he was more than an office manager for his father's property management company. He had plans for his future and wasn't always an entitled asshole.

R: That would be great! You sure it's not too
much to ask?

E: I wouldn't offer if I couldn't handle it.
Let's meet on Thursday and you show me
what you have.

Her punctuation was back with its usual precision. Guess he'd sobered her right up.

Where to meet? They'd only been on half of an official date. Inviting her here would be creepy. And suggesting her place would be even creepier.

> R: Himmel Library as soon as you're off work?
> They're open to 7 on Thursdays.

> E: Perfect. I'll see you then. OMG is it
> midnight already?

> R: Afraid of turning into a pumpkin?

> E: You're lucky I still have thumbs 😄.

> Goodnight Ryan.

Ryan chuckled. He had never dated anyone with Elissa's sense of humor before.

> R: Goodnight Elissa

He resisted the temptation to add any sort of cute emoji, as much as he wanted to. Iz would tease him horribly the next time they got into his messages and saw smileys or, god forbid, heart eyes. Jesus.

It was late, and if he had any hope of writing tomorrow, he should go to bed. He polished off his drink and turned in.

But Sunday was only a little better for productivity than Saturday had been, and two more drafts landed in the trash before the handle on the front door jangled around four. Iz and Mateo walked in carrying grocery bags.

"Can we get a hand, dude?" Iz asked.

Ryan gave up his fruitless attempt at writing for the weekend and helped unload the groceries. Once everything was put away, Iz and Teo started on Sunday dinner. Soon, rich scents wafted through the air, and Ryan's appetite awakened as he cleared his mess so they could eat at the table.

"That smells fucking amazing," he said.

Teo stood in front of the stove, stirring something in the Dutch oven while Iz chopped lettuce and vegetables for a salad.

"Jambalaya, like my grandma used to make," Teo said. "Can you pull out some beer?"

Ryan hurried to the small fridge stocked with beer they kept in the living room, a leftover from his dorm days with Iz. He pulled out three Barrio Rojos and grabbed the forks and napkins his friend had placed on the counter. Ryan made quick work on setting the table, and soon the three of them sat down for dinner, the fragrant scent of onions, peppers, and spices making him drool.

Mateo brought over the salad and a plate for Ryan, with Iz right behind carrying two more plates. The flavors burst on his tongue, the spiciness a counterpoint to the rich flavors of the rice and sausage.

"Kudos to your grandma, Teo," he said around a mouthful.

A pained looked crossed Teo's face, which he attempted to cover with a smile an instant later.

"I'll pass them along the next time I talk to her."

The smile was more a grimace, and it never reached his eyes. Ryan didn't press the issue. He could ask Iz later.

"So, has the infamous script finally triumphed over the intrepid writer?" Iz changed the subject.

Ryan purposely took another bite in order to avoid answering the question for a minute.

"Want to join me in freeing its remains from this mortal coil?" he shot back. "I've got charcoal and lighter fluid."

Iz smiled at him. "Can't be that bad, sweetie."

"Oh, it's not bad, Iz. It's fucking awful."

Mateo choked on his beer and was subjected to the ministrations of both Iz and Ryan. After a moment, he held up his hands in surrender.

"Enough. I'm not dying today."

Iz lifted Teo's hand and gave the back a quick kiss before returning their attention to Ryan.

"What's wrong with it?" they asked.

Ryan sighed. What wasn't wrong with it? "It's boring, for one. I sound like Mr. Butler from freshman English. People will tune out and unsubscribe."

"You're a good storyteller, Ryan," Iz said. "Write it like you were telling me the story. Actually, don't write it. Let's sit down after dinner, and you tell me the story. We'll record it, and you can transcribe it."

"Fan-fucking-tastic!" Performing was easier to Ryan than writing, and if he did as Iz suggested, he might end up with a rough draft by the end of the night.

"I've been known to have a bright idea on occasion." This time, Iz's smile was genuine, lighting up their face. "But only if you do the dishes."

"You've got yourself a deal."

Chapter 29
left side of bitchy

Monday morning fully ruined the high Elissa had been riding since drunk texting Ryan on Saturday night. She almost slept through her alarm, spilled coffee on herself, and, once she'd changed, her damned car wouldn't start. Her mood was on the left side of bitchy and was quickly approaching Wicked Witch of the West.

She caught a ride share into work, arriving a few minutes late. After apologizing profusely to Karina, Elissa locked herself in the file room to finish the task she'd begun Friday afternoon. By lunch, she'd verified all documents were present for all their clients, except for DeMarco Property Management. She saved DPM for last and planned on tackling the boxes on a full stomach.

Elissa took her lunch outside, finding a sunny bench. She stretched out her legs and rolled her head around, trying to loosen muscles stiff after a morning hunched over boxes of paperwork. The sunlight and fresh air revived her, and she closed her eyes to listen to the birds in the nearby trees.

"Elissa?" a familiar voice broke the spell.

Who had the gall to bother her when it was obvious she didn't want to be bothered? Ryan stood in front of her, blocking the sun. But not the Ryan she'd been lusting after. No, it was Beige-Flag Ryan, glorious in his genial blandness.

The Ryan she kept forgetting to call. The Ryan she needed

to let down easy. Oh dear.

"Hi, Ryan."

"Hi, Elissa. I was starting to worry you'd dropped off the face of the earth. You never called."

"I'm so sorry. Things have been…" What had things been? Pretty good, actually. She had moved out of her parents' house, had a new man in her life who made her tingle in all kinds of places, and her mom was healthy. A small alarm bell sounded in the back of her mind. "Busy. Very busy. Is that why you're here? Checking up on me?"

"I have an appointment to drop off my tax paperwork at your firm. I asked around, and JMS Accounting received great word of mouth. I didn't think you'd mind."

She didn't, but it seemed weird. Out of all the firms, most of them well-regarded, he'd chosen hers. Elissa shrugged it off.

"No, I don't mind. I'm on lunch break right now, but if you want to chat after, I'll be right here."

"That would be nice." He turned and walked to her office, looking at her as he opened the door. When he made eye contact, his gaze quickly skittered to the interior.

Elissa pulled out her sandwich and fruit and enjoyed her lunch alfresco, ignoring the alarm that counting her blessings had sounded. By the time she brushed the crumbs off her blouse, Mr. Beige Flag was walking toward her. She still had fifteen minutes left before she needed to return to work, so she was stuck talking to the guy until she could politely excuse herself.

He sat down on the far side of the bench, giving her plenty of space. What tension had built as Elissa anticipated this conversation eased, if only a little.

"How have you been?" As an opening gambit, it was unimaginative, but not everyone could ask if a seat was taken in just the right kind of voice to send shivers down her spine.

"Busy, of course. Taxes are due in two months. Right now, most of our clients are businesses, but individuals will start trickling in."

"Do you handle business or individual clients?"

"Mostly business, but a few individuals. We try to finish the businesses early so we have time to do individual returns."

"You don't have much time for a personal life right now, I bet, or else I think I would have heard back from you."

Elissa cringed. It was more than fair to call her out.

"I'm sorry. I should've called. I moved out of my parents' house, and tax season…" And then the other Ryan had entered the picture, and any hope for this nice but boring man had evaporated like a puddle after a monsoon storm. She had no excuse, other than avoiding the confrontation. Confrontation was not her jam.

He waved it off. "I get it. You're busy. After April?"

He looked so hopeful, but it was best to burst his bubble now.

"You're a nice guy, Ryan, but I don't think it's in the cards for us."

Anger flashed across his face so quickly that if Elissa had blinked, she would've missed it. His hands clenched at his sides, and a strained smile found its way to his lips.

"Well, excuse me for thinking we'd connected. Sorry I was wrong. Have a nice life, Elissa." He stood and hurried away, and the tension left her body with a long whoosh.

She'd dodged a bullet with him.

Elissa pushed into the building. If he came by again and sought her out, she'd let Karina know. Her boss would have her back.

She spent the afternoon concentrating on the DeMarco box. She'd been so tired when she'd gone through the contents on Friday, she hoped she'd merely made a mistake. Hours later, after going through every single damn—swear jar!—piece of paper, she knew she'd missed nothing. A few papers they needed simply weren't there.

Glancing at her watch, Elissa still had thirty minutes before close of business. Just enough time to call over to the DPM office so someone—hopefully not Ryan, she hated confrontation—could pull the files. She stopped by Karina's office to let her know what was going on before picking up the phone on her own desk.

"DeMarco Property Management," a cheerful, feminine voice answered.

A part of her was deeply disappointed, another part greatly relieved. Ryan DeMarco had gotten under her skin in a remarkably short time.

"Hi, this is Elissa Wright with JMS Accounting. We seem to be missing paperwork. I was hoping to speak with Annetta or Ryan about stopping by tomorrow."

"They have both left for the day. I'll take a message, though."

Elissa left her name and number and ended the call.

Karina paused by her desk on her way out the door a few minutes later. It was still early enough in the season most of the staff could leave at a normal time. In a couple of weeks, that would change.

"Were you able to talk to anyone at DPM?" her mentor asked.

Elissa shook her head.

"Stop by before you come in tomorrow. I'd like to start ASAP. There have been some changes with the death of Giorgina DeMarco last year. It might complicate matters enough to cause a headache or two."

"I will. Have a good night."

"You, too."

She watched Karina leave and stared at her phone. She hated mixing business with pleasure, and she hadn't been lying earlier. Despite making a date to go over Ryan's business plan Thursday night, she had no time for extracurriculars at the moment. She barely had time for curriculars. This entire enterprise was ill-conceived and would likely lead to heartache.

Can you live with the heartache of never trying?
She texted him anyway.

> E: Hate to bother you after hours, but
> we're missing some files. I'll be stopping
> by first thing to look for them.

He texted back right away.

> R: Yeah no problem. Do you have a list? Do you
> need to meet tonight?

She smiled. Though he could be trying to still get on her good side, something told her he'd offer the same to anyone. Maybe she was delulu, but she'd misjudged him on their first meeting.

> E: Tomorrow is fine.

> R: cu then

With a fluttering heart at the thought of seeing him twice this week, Elissa placed the list of missing files in her bag. She checked messages again before turning off her computer for the night. Ami had agreed to pick her up after work and look at old Bertha. It was going to be a long night, but tomorrow morning was looking bright.

CHAPTER 30
quite the mouth

For the first time in weeks, Ryan looked forward to work. Not the work itself, of course, but who he would see today.

He pulled into the parking lot a half hour early and her ancient Beemer was already parked in a visitor spot. A smile planted itself on his face as he removed his helmet and hurried to the doors.

Elissa stood next to them, staring down at her phone, but looked up as he approached. A flush painted her cheeks the perfect shade of pink, highlighting her freckles, and she grinned at him as she tucked a strand of hair behind her ear.

"Good morning"—he stopped himself from calling her beautiful by the skin of his teeth—"Ms. Wright."

"Good morning, Mr. DeMarco." Her voice was husky. *He* did that to her.

Ryan unlocked the door and held it open. Elissa walked through and stopped at the reception desk. He locked the door behind him. Nobody without a key would arrive for another twenty minutes. He dropped his stuff at his desk.

"I didn't expect you so early. Can I get five minutes to start the coffee before we pull what's missing?"

"Sure. Sorry, I guess I take 'first thing' pretty literally. I can wait here if—"

"It's just coffee. And I'm glad you're here. Come on."

She followed as he led the way. Elissa's subtle perfume

wafted over to him, invading his personal space and filling his thoughts with things that didn't belong in the workplace. He tried taking a deep breath to clear his head, but it only further suffused his senses with her. Shit, this wasn't working.

"Did I thank you for being so understanding and helpful on Thursday?" she asked as he loaded grounds and water into the machine.

"I believe you called me your 'knight in shining armor,' but I could be misremembering."

"Ah, yes, now that you mention it, I do recall saying something to that effect. It shouldn't have happened, though. Leo's old enough to take his medicine without anyone making him."

"Trust me, I know from experience. Teenage boys are stupid. They resent anything they have to do and will gladly suffer any consequences. The more my parents pushed me to get good grades, the fewer homework assignments I turned in."

"Seriously? Why?"

"I hated they didn't trust me. I wanted to be different. Hell, I still don't know all the reasons why. I was stupid. Once I got to college and they were no longer breathing down my neck to get things done, when I was doing what *I* wanted, I did fine."

"Makes sense. I was terrified to disappoint mine. They had their hands full with Leo being sick and Ami being a brat. I tried hard not to be a problem."

"I can see that."

Elissa's spine straightened, and a cloud flowed over her open expression. He'd said the wrong thing. Shit.

"Sorry, I didn't mean to insult you. Let's find these files."

The file room was at the far end of the hall, and Elissa followed in silence.

"I'm not insulted," she said quietly as he unlocked the door. "It's just…I kinda wish I had screwed up once in a while. I feel like I missed out."

"Maybe you did. But I missed out on lots of things after getting grounded for my screwups, so we're even. You got a list of what we forgot?"

They entered the file room, and he turned to find her holding out a piece of paper. He took it with a smile, one she returned.

"Silly of you to assume I wouldn't."

"I did not assume, I was being polite."

"Sure you were."

She sat in a familiar shabby desk chair someone had recently tucked next to the door. It squeaked as she twisted this way and that. He turned away before she could see his smile widen.

Ryan read over the list. "I don't remember these on the original list. It may take me a few minutes."

"No worries—it must've been confusing getting this stuff ready while also learning everything you could from Val."

"Yeah, and I was tired. I'd been covering a couple of Saturday shifts at Nopalitos, too, so this is my fault." He waved the paper in her general direction before finding the first filing cabinet.

"These things happen." She spun in the chair again, and it squeaked. Why was the sound so familiar? "Hey, your friend Iz…"

Ryan steeled himself. There were often lots of questions about Iz. His own family bombarded him when Iz was finally comfortable coming out more broadly. He didn't know how Mateo handled it, but the questions always made him doubt the integrity of others. He thought she'd handled Iz's appearance Thursday night well, but maybe she disguised her prejudices.

"I didn't get a chance to ask before I left. What are their pronouns?"

The tension left his body so quickly he almost slumped on the floor.

"They/them." Ryan clutched the first file tightly. "Iz uses

gender neutral pronouns. How did you know?"

"I'm trying to be a better ally and educate myself. I would've asked Iz, but Leo called."

Squeak, squeak, squeak.

Oh, oh no. Now he remembered why the chair was so familiar. It had been his grandmother's, and it had a nasty habit of—

Before he could warn her, the arm of the chair fell off and Elissa tumbled out, knocking into the file room door. It slammed shut. With his keys on the outside. Fuck.

"Are you okay?" He rushed over. Whether they were trapped in the file room was less important than if Elissa had been hurt.

Her face was bright red, but she rose to her feet and brushed off her skirt.

"Nothing hurt but my ego. *That* was embarrassing."

She pulled on the handle, but the door wouldn't open. She pulled again more forcefully.

"I think we're stuck," he said. "My keys were still in the lock."

Elissa beat at the door. Wham, wham, wham. Pause. Wham, wham, wham.

Ryan walked up behind her and placed his hand over hers, stopping them mid-wham. "Stop."

She whirled around and lifted her hands to his chest, her small fists curled as though she would soon pummel him the way she had the door.

The color drained from her face, and for a second, Ryan was certain she was going to faint. He slid in next to her, wrapping an arm around her waist so he could catch her if she did. He led her to a much more reliable chair on the other side of the file room.

"Put your head between your knees."

She looked up with wide eyes before she did as he said. Ryan kneeled in front of her, holding her hands and rubbing slow, soothing circles with his thumbs.

"What's wrong, Elissa?"

Elissa took a few deep breaths before answering. "I don't do well when I think things are out of my control. Being locked in a room I can't get out of sets me off. It's not claustrophobia, exactly. If the door hadn't been locked, I would've been fine."

"Control freak. Cool."

She sat up straight and pulled her hands away.

"I am not—"

"A joke. A bad one."

She glared at him.

"Sorry." He gave her his best puppy dog eyes and sweetest smile. "I did mention I'm an asshole, right?"

Her expression softened as he stood and gave her some space.

"How come you aren't freaked out?"

"My whole childhood was planned for me. The instant I had any say in what I did, I let chaos reign. I go with the flow. Plans have a way of unravelling, anyway, and I like not knowing what comes next. As your knight in shining armor who specializes in chaos, what can I do to help?"

"Get me out?" Her gaze darted to the door.

"Sure, I'll try, but no one else is due in for a few minutes." Ryan knocked on the door. "Hey, anyone out there?"

He tried twice more, but nobody came to investigate. Looking at Elissa, with her wild eyes and too-pale face, he knew they couldn't just wait patiently. He kneeled in front of her again and took her hand. She let him.

"How about a distraction instead? You can help me find these files. We'll try again after."

He glanced at his watch. Seven thirty-two. In ten to twenty minutes, several people would arrive, including his aunt, who was usually in by seven forty-five. Nearly everyone else would be in by eight.

"Okay."

"You need the list?" he asked.

"No, I have it memorized. Show me where to look."

He set her in front of the first filing cabinet while he worked next to her, pulling some documents for a small apartment complex near the air force base. Ryan kept glancing over at her. Her color was returning to normal, and the panic had left her eyes, but she still looked shaky. Maybe something else to distract her.

"Are we still on for Thursday night?"

"Yes, absolutely." She said it so forcefully, it was as if she was trying to convince herself as well as him.

"Need anything from me?"

"Whatever you have so far. See where you are and then we can plan."

"Plans are for pussies."

"Well, it's a good thing I have one of those."

He snapped to attention, whipping his head around to find her pretending to ignore his reaction. But a tiny crease in her lips gave her away. At least her anxiety had lessened.

"For someone who doesn't swear, you have quite the mouth on you, Elissa Wright." He pulled the last file on his list.

"You have no idea."

"Care to show me?"

Ryan was teasing. Mostly teasing, trying to distract her. He'd swear on a stack of bibles he'd meant nothing by it. But before he could blink, Elissa Wright had grabbed his tie and pulled him down until her lips were a hairsbreadth from his.

"Yes."

Elissa closed the minuscule distance between them and pressed her lips to his. Dropping the file, he placed a hand lightly on her waist and drew her body closer as the heat of the kiss flooded his system.

Chapter 31
at least there was cake

She was kissing Ryan DeMarco. She was *kissing* Ryan DeMarco.

Her anxiety disappeared as she lost herself in this moment that had been teasing her dreams for weeks now. His kindness had overwhelmed her judgment, and she couldn't fight the need to kiss him any longer.

He still tasted of his minty toothpaste, and the citrusy scent that seemed to cling to him filled the small room. His hand rose to cup her cheek as she opened for him. His tongue darted out to flick against her lower lip.

With a moan, Elissa released her grip on his tie and tangled her hands into the hair at his nape, holding him even closer. She nipped at his retreating tongue, and Ryan's other hand drifted up to hold her still. He plunged his tongue into her mouth, and she sucked on it.

As far as distractions, this was beyond anything she'd experienced before. Consumed by the need to be close to him, to drink him in, to press against him, she wanted nothing more than to ditch all propriety and do something she refused to regret.

"Elissa," he groaned, breaking the kiss. He ran his thumbs along her cheekbones. "We shouldn't—"

She stood on tiptoes and kissed him again. He seemed to lose his train of thought as their tongues tangled and his hands wandered down her body. With practiced ease, he spun them so her back was to the filing cabinet and pressed his hands against the cool metal next to her shoulders.

A handle dug into her spine, but she didn't care. Barely even noticed. For this brief, shining moment, her world centered on his lips, his taste, his scent, the roughness of his hands, and the softness of his hair.

Voices in the hall dragged her back to reality. She was kissing Ryan *DeMarco*, in the file room of DeMarco Property Management. What was she thinking?

A jangling sound brought Ryan's head up, eyes round. Elissa took a step away, so the person opening the door wouldn't immediately see her, straightening her clothes and patting her hair into place. He took three steps to the side and jerked open a cabinet drawer as the door to the file room opened.

"Hey, Ryan. Did you get locked in?" A woman about Elissa's age took a step in. His cousin, if she recalled correctly. Her gaze found Elissa and her eyes went round. "Elissa, right? What are you doing here?"

"Yeah, Trinity. Elissa stopped by for some missing paperwork."

"Guess it's a good thing I went to break room first. Are you okay?"

"Um, yes, yeah," Elissa stammered, hoping against hope her face wasn't beet red. "Just found the last file, anyway. I'll gather the rest. We'll start work on your taxes later today."

Elissa took the few steps to the table and picked up the files.

"Okay." Trinity didn't look convinced. She pulled the keys out and tossed them at her cousin, who snatched them out of the air. Then she left, the door still wide open.

Elissa concentrated on putting the files into her bag, his warm presence at her back.

"It can't happen again," she said. "It's unprofessional. I can't be making out with a client in the office."

"Not a client," he murmured, his breath hot on her neck.

"Close enough."

"If you're sure." He ran a finger down her spine, and shivers of desire coursed through her.

"I'm sure." She was sure she wanted him even more now.

He stepped back, and she missed him. He was right there, but she missed his touch, his breath, his scent.

"Did I just fuck up getting help on my business plan?"

He was a temptation she wasn't sure she could handle. But he was a temptation she couldn't turn down, either. The mere idea of spending an hour or two with him in the library filled her with more joy than a day filled with numbers that all added up the first time. More joy than a cold margarita on a hot summer day. More joy than Christmas morning. She was a freaking goner.

A conversation with Karina was in order, and soon.

"No, of course not. Thursday, right after work at Himmel Library?"

Heat flashed in his eyes, letting her know developing a business plan was not the only thing on the table. "I'll see you out, then."

He followed her out the door, down the hall, and held the front door open. She had to pass within inches of him, and her skin knew it. Heat flowed over her, through her, and she panted like she'd run a mile.

"Goodbye, Elissa," he said. "I'll see you Thursday."

Her brain painted an image of him, shirtless in the file room, and the flush bloomed on her cheeks.

"Goodbye, Ryan," she managed before she ran to her car.

His chuckle followed her all the way. She unlocked old Bertha and climbed in, glancing at the building. He still stood there, watching. Elissa started the car and drove away. Half a block later, she pulled into a grocery store parking lot.

"Oh, fuck." She rested her head on the steering wheel.

Worth the dollar she now owed the swear jar.

Elissa counted to ten, then did it again, before she finished driving to the office. She waved to the receptionist as she walked carefully, slowly, not at all flustered, to her cubicle.

All of her carefully curated experiences were not helping her cope with the chaos Ryan brought into her life. In her three years working for JMS Accounting, she'd never been tempted to ogle a client or one of their employees, let alone carry on an affair.

She tried all morning to put him out of her mind, but every time the DeMarco name appeared on her spreadsheets, she was right back in the file room, kissing him like her life depended on it. Maybe someday the DeMarco name would lose the emotional meaning. Perhaps instead of a handsome, chiseled face with soft, brown eyes, the name would become a series of inputs. Income, expenses, profit, loss. Today was not that day.

Karina popped in before lunch.

"Did you find the missing DeMarco files?"

Elissa startled. She had managed not to think of Ryan for about five minutes, dealing with the files from Saguaro Glen Apartments. No mention of the DeMarco name and good, clean figures. Then her boss had to ruin it.

"Yes." She pointed at them in a neat pile on the corner of her desk. "As you said, left behind with all the chaos of training a new office manager. I'm through some of the smaller properties already."

"Excellent! Let me know if anything comes up with them. Otherwise, give me a report when you're done and we'll go from there."

Karina was gone before Elissa could formulate her explanation about kissing the office manager. It could wait. Probably. But not much longer.

She opened the shared calendar. Karina's schedule was booked the next couple days, but Friday was clear. Elissa would have plenty of time to figure out what to say. If she was going to be a problem, she'd also offer a few possible solutions. Though she didn't want to give up working on a high profile account like DPM, this was the ethical thing to do.

That decided, she found her focus and thoughts of Ryan faded deep into the background. She couldn't work twenty-four seven, though. Eventually, she had to go home. Her old junker groaned a bit when she started it, but she backed up fine. Before she knew it, Elissa pulled into her spot at the apartment complex.

She dragged herself into her apartment on the second floor and opened a bottle of pink wine. With bubbles, thank you very much. It was a bubbles kind of day. There might even be a bubble bath later. Jules was working late, and she'd have plenty of alone time.

She put together a girl dinner of crackers, cheese, and ice cream to go with the sparkling wine. Flopping on the couch, she grabbed the remote and flipped through the streaming services for a few minutes before settling on *Parks and Recreation* for the thousandth time.

Elissa watched two episodes, cleaned up, and drew a bath. The tension in her shoulders was driving her to distraction. She pulled out her favorite rose-scented bubble bath, poured another helping of bubbly into an acrylic cup, and climbed into the tub.

And couldn't get the kiss out of her mind. Or Ryan's firm body pressed to hers. Or his taste as his tongue expertly riled her up and left her wanting oh so much more.

Her free hand drifted over her bubble-coated breasts, teasing her nipple. She placed her empty cup down on the bathroom floor and dipped her other hand into the water. She rubbed gentle circles around her clit, and her back arched at the sensation.

What would it feel like with Ryan's calloused hands? What would he murmur in her ear? What would his lips—

The front door slammed.

"Hey lady!" Jules shouted.

The mood popped like a bubble. Elissa stopped her sexy times.

"In the bathroom!"

Dammit. It was just getting good.

"I brought dessert," Jules said from outside the door. "The pastry chef made a fantastic berry cake tonight and there were leftovers."

At least there was cake.

CHAPTER 32
fine and professional

R yan was a ball of nervous energy Thursday morning. He couldn't get their kiss out of his head, and he'd spent the past two nights imagining her lips on other parts of his body. Desire simmered under his skin and sidetracked his brain at the most inopportune moments.

The day was quiet, leaving Ryan to his own devices a little more than was good at the moment. Without the constant stream of phone calls, meetings, and other nonsense, his mind kept drifting to that kiss. Her lips had been soft and hot, and she'd tasted of coffee and powdered sugar. And the way her breasts had pressed into his chest—

He adjusted himself surreptitiously under his desk. He had to stop thinking about her. Ryan checked the clock on the desk. Close enough to lunchtime, thank fuck. He called over to the marketing department, and they sent someone to watch the phones while he ate and tried to push Elissa out of his head until he finally got to see her in person again.

Unfortunately, Trin was in the break room. Since she'd discovered Elissa with him in the file room, he'd been avoiding her, but it was a challenge. Lunch out Tuesday, took his sandwich to the park yesterday, kept trying to find things to do whenever he spotted her out of the corner of his eye.

Her eyes glinted and a mischievous grin spread over her face. "Ryan kissed a girl and he liked it."

Dammit, he thought he'd gotten away with it. But Trinity was smart, and it wasn't like he and Elissa had been terribly subtle. He was grateful they were the only two in the break room. His cousin would've said the same whether or not they'd been alone.

"Shut up." He grabbed his lunch out of the fridge and popped the leftovers Iz had brought from Nopalitos in the microwave.

Trin sidled up next to him and whispered, "Should I inform HR you're sexually harassing an outside contractor?"

"Don't fucking joke about it! Dad would have my head."

"I was kidding the other day, but now I'm dead serious. You shouldn't be kissing women in the file room, Ryan," she said, all teasing gone. "You're smarter than that."

This, this was what he needed to hear to pry any thoughts of kissing Elissa again from his head. Ryan rubbed his hand down his face and collapsed into a chair.

"I know. I didn't plan to. As much as you all have me pegged as irresponsible and immature, I know better than to kiss someone who doesn't want me to. And I didn't, but that's no excuse."

God, he'd nearly lost all reason as soon as their lips met. He would never admit it to Trinity, but if she hadn't opened the door, he wasn't sure how far they would have carried it. Elissa Wright lit a fire in him that was nearly impossible to extinguish.

"Don't let it happen again, Ry. And don't let any of the bosses find out. Mom would have your balls, and Uncle Sandro would have your head."

If he was lucky, Aunt Annetta and his dad would make it quick. If he was unlucky, they'd draw out the torture.

He pasted a brash smile on. "When was the last time they found out about something I didn't want them to?"

She shrugged and stole a bite off his plate. He resisted the temptation to stab her with the fork.

"When I was out too late at junior prom. I promise, no more filing with the hot accountant." Ryan held up his right hand like he was swearing on a bible.

"You better not. Your father prides himself on the treatment of women here. It's one of the reasons I enjoy working for him."

She stole another bite and left him to his thoughts. Slouched in the chair, Ryan closed his eyes. What had he been thinking? He knew the answer. He hadn't been. As usual, he'd been reacting, letting the circumstances dictate his actions. Even though Elissa had started it, he still shouldn't have kissed her. Not here. It was unprofessional, it could be misinterpreted, and he was better than that.

Except when it came to her, he wasn't. He didn't care if it was unprofessional or misinterpreted. Nothing was better than kissing Elissa. A part of him insisted he call off their library date. The other part gave that voice an ass-kicking, tied it up with duct tape, and shoved it into a deep, dark hole. He was fucked.

He'd spent most of his adult life avoiding long-term relationships. The few he'd tried had ended poorly, usually because the woman had only wanted him for his money and connections. Since his last significant other had spent a family vacation flirting with Alex, he'd sworn off serious girlfriends. He dated sporadically and enjoyed short-term flings, mostly with women who had no idea who his family was. He kept it that way, which had a tendency to end the relationship. It wasn't that he didn't wish to introduce his flings to his family. It was that they'd dump him for greener pastures as soon as he did.

But now, he faced a woman who not only knew who his family was but exactly how much they were worth and didn't seem to give a rat's ass. He couldn't get her out of his head. More than that, he almost didn't care if she tried to use him for his money.

Ryan ate the rest of his lunch without tasting anything. A pity, the food at Nopalitos was usually exceptional, but he might as well have been eating sawdust. He guzzled down a soda for an afternoon caffeine burst and returned to his desk to plug away at paperwork.

Between his cousin's words and his memory of Elissa's kiss, his attention was shot. He'd barely managed not to fuck up a simple greeting on the phone every damn time it had rung. As 4:30 approached, he became antsier, bouncing his leg, tapping his fingers, and swiveling his chair.

The minute Trinity approached to take over the late shift, he was out of there with barely a wave. He grabbed his helmet and rushed through traffic. He shouldn't be so nervous.

It wasn't even a real date. They were going to work on his business plan. In the library. There was no place he'd be able to kiss her since even the private rooms had glass walls. Everything would be just fine. Fine and professional. He could do this.

The branch they'd chosen was a bit of a ride for him, but he made it by five after five. Cars were leaving like rats from a ship. Ryan parked and walked to the doors.

Shit.

He'd misread which days they were open late. Wednesday, not Thursday. Exhausted, he dropped on the bench and pulled out his phone to text Elissa. Maybe she hadn't left work yet and he could save her the trip. This was for the best, at least until they had a conversation about what was and wasn't professional.

Ryan shot off the text and waited for her reply. He didn't wait long. A couple of minutes later, her car pulled into the parking lot. He walked toward it as she parked. She rolled down her window and killed the engine.

"Hi, Elissa."

"Hey, you texted. What's up?"

"I got the days wrong. They closed at five today. It seems I keep owing you apologies."

She waved it away, a forgiving smile on her face. Would she forgive him if he kissed her again, right here, right now?

Professional, asshole.

"Um, we could go to a different library. Or a restaurant." She tapped her fingers on the steering wheel.

Or my place. He quashed the idea before the words could escape into the real world. His place would be a horrible idea. Iz had a late shift tonight at the steakhouse, covering for the manager who had a family emergency. Ryan didn't need the temptation. She wanted to keep their relationship professional, and he would oblige.

"There's a couple of restaurants in the strip mall down the street," Ryan suggested.

Elissa's face hid whatever she was thinking, a blank canvas behind which he could only guess what was going on, but he could've sworn her cheeks were a bit pinker than they had been a moment ago. She took a deep breath and strung her words together so quickly it took his brain a moment to decipher what she said.

"I don't live far. We could go to my apartment."

He stood there like a dumbass for a moment longer than he should have.

"I'm sorry, forget it." Elissa ducked her head and bit her lip. "That's a terrible idea, isn't it?"

"No! No, it's a great idea." Maybe she was offering because she had a roommate. God, he hoped she did. Wait, no, he hoped she didn't. Elissa had him as spun out as a load of laundry. "Give me your address, and I'll grab some takeout on the way over."

Ryan didn't know how strong his grip on his phone was until she tried to take it from his hands. He made himself let go. After she put in her address, she handed it back. Her cheeks were red now. Perhaps she didn't want to keep it professional after all.

"I'll see you soon." She started her car, and Ryan realized he'd forgotten an important question.

"I forgot to ask," he said before she could roll up the window. "What do you want?"

She smiled, a beautiful smile that showed her dimple and made her eyes sparkle in the evening light. "I'm not picky. Whatever is fine."

Ryan watched her drive off, then headed over to his motorcycle. Was this a test? A woman he'd dated a couple of years ago had loved to test him. She'd expected him to be some sort of fucking mind reader. Or was Elissa a woman who sacrificed her wants in favor of whatever person she was dating, like his mother? Everything he'd learned about women over the last decade made him distrust this seemingly simple request, but everything he'd learned about Elissa told him to take what she'd said at face value.

Only one way to find out. He put on his helmet and headed to the Thai place he knew on this side of the city.

CHAPTER 33
that's a big word

Holy cow, holy shit!

What had she done? The words had just popped out of her mouth, her mental filter loaded with holes the size of semitrucks. Why? Why would her brain do this to her? She treated it well. She ate healthy, got plenty of exercise and rest. Why would it betray her now?

Elissa parked Bertha at a ridiculous angle and ran up the stairs. Jules's stuff was everywhere—five blankets on the couch, dirty dishes on the coffee table, dirty clothes piled next to the door, and clean clothes in a basket next to the TV.

"Crap!"

It was going to be one of those nights. She dropped her bag on the end table, pulled out a twenty, and added it to the small collection in a jar on the kitchen table. Jules teased her, saying Elissa was a goddamned adult and didn't need a swear jar. But some habits were hard to break, and she would treat Jules to a night out when it was full.

She grabbed the piles and chucked them into her BFF's room but kept the dirty and clean clothes separate. She was panicked, not a jerk.

She gathered the dishes and put them in the dishwasher, cleared the kitchen table of mail and Jule's spare bag, and looked for any incriminating evidence. Evidence of what, she had no clue. That other men had been here recently? Jules had frequent guests, but they rarely stayed the night. At most, they'd leave a shirt or a sock.

Knock, knock, knock.

Just in time. She ran a hand over her hair, trying not to look like she'd spent the last twenty minutes running around the apartment trying to clean. Elissa smiled and opened the door.

"Hey, come in."

Ryan held a bag of what looked and smelled like Asian food in one hand and a motorcycle helmet in the other. He placed his helmet on the floor next to the door and moved toward the kitchen.

"Hope you like Thai." He put the bag on the kitchen table and pulled out the containers.

"I'm not picky. As long as there's no octopus or lima beans, I'll eat it."

"Well, that's a damn shame." An impish grin brightened his eyes and drew her gaze to his full lips. "It's stir-fried octopus with lima beans."

"Good thing I have leftover pizza in the fridge." She returned his grin with one of her own. "Want a beer?"

"Yeah, sounds great."

She grabbed two from the fridge and some plates and silverware. From the smells emanating from the containers, he had not ordered anything resembling octopus and lima beans. She pulled a container toward her. Rice. He opened another, and she leaned over. Pad Thai. Yum. The last container had red curry chicken, and he'd picked up some spring rolls, too.

"This looks delish. I haven't had Thai in a while."

They filled their plates, and Ryan lifted his can of beer.

"Cheers."

They bumped the cans together and ate in silence for a few bites before Elissa said what was on her mind.

"Thanks for coming here. Writing a business plan in a noisy restaurant isn't exactly conducive to productivity."

"Uh-huh. Conducive. That's a big word."

Dang it. She had a tendency to use big words when nervous. Elissa bit her lip.

He grabbed another spring roll and dipped it into the sweet chili sauce. "I'm kidding. Sorry, growing up in a big family, we tease each other relentlessly. I forget not everyone grows up the same way."

She grinned in relief. "Yeah, it was mostly the five of us. My grandparents and aunts and uncles and cousins all live out of state."

"You seemed to want to meet somewhere public, so I was a little surprised you invited me over."

Elissa pressed her lips together. She was naturally cautious but found herself torn when it came to Ryan DeMarco. She wanted to be alone with him so desperately it was better to meet in public. Yet, somehow, they were here, at her apartment, all alone.

"I did, but, I don't know, you didn't push."

"Well, thank you for trusting me. And thank you for offering to help. Iz's expertise is in restaurants. They've gone over my business plan, but I still have a lot of questions."

"Show me what you got, Mr. DeMarco."

Ryan pulled a few pages out of his backpack. Handing them to Elissa, he didn't meet her eyes. Instead, he focused his attention on the food in front of him. She read it over.

It wasn't bad. There were holes, some pretty big ones, but this was a solid draft. She put the last page aside and turned toward Ryan.

"Want another beer?"

He finally met her eyes. "Yes. Thank you."

Elissa grabbed another beer from the fridge for him, and a half-empty bottle of white she and Jules had opened a couple days ago. She poured herself a glass and carried both drinks over to the table.

"So, what do you think?" Ryan was apparently unable to contain himself any longer. His face was pale in his nervousness, his foot bouncing against the ground, and his fingers tapping an intricate rhythm on her table.

"It's a solid start," she said. "The plan lacked specific financial info, which I expected since you asked for my help in that area. The only real weakness I could see at this stage is the market research. I won't be able to narrow the focus of the money bit until we can at least make some assumptions about your market."

"I've run into some trouble there. Iz can tell you exactly who eats at their family's restaurants. I can find some general information about who listens to podcasts, but who would listen to an in-depth food history podcast? I don't know, and I don't know where to find out, either."

"Let's get comfortable. I have a few suggestions that should help."

Ryan grabbed his half-finished beer from the table and headed to the couch. Elissa swallowed the rest of her wine in a long gulp before refilling the glass. As much as she wanted to sit next to him—who was she kidding—as much as she wanted to sit on his lap, she made herself comfortable at the other end of the couch, tucking her legs underneath her. Serious conversation first.

"So, do you want the good news first, or the bad?" she asked.

"Bad."

"I've done a little research into podcasting in the last few days. The market is getting saturated, so marketing will be key. Which means…"

"I need to do the market research. So, what's the good news?"

Elissa sipped her wine. How would he take the news? Would he even see it as good given his relationship with his family?

"Spit it out," he said when she hesitated.

"Unlike a lot of other start-up podcasters, you have resources. You can pay for the market research, and you can afford ads."

"But the podcast will take longer to be profitable." He tapped his fingers against the can, a nervous habit she found endearing. He was always in motion. A function of his ADHD, but she came from a more sedate family. Plenty of downtime for reading and watching TV and playing board games. She found his energy refreshing.

"Yeah, exactly. I thought you said you weren't good at this."

"I'm not, but I'm not stupid, either. More money upfront means it takes longer to recoup the costs."

"By resources, I don't only mean money, though. You have family who—"

"No." He took a long swig.

"Your dad is a successful businessman, your brother seems to be following in his footsteps. Your aunt is a marketing expert, and you have cousins who might be willing to help. Why not use their expertise?"

"I need to be successful without their help."

"Why? Isn't that what family is for?"

Ryan set the can down on the table and leaned forward.

"Maybe that's how things work in your family, but in mine, the company *is* the family. If your dream doesn't advance the company's bottom line, you need a better dream. If what you're good at falls outside their sphere of influence, it doesn't count. If you can't be the absolute best at everything you attempt, don't expect any accolades. I've lived so long being told that what I want to do, what I'm good at, isn't enough, that I'm not really part of this family because I don't want to be part of the company. This podcast is my dream. I want to create something unique, something that uses the skills I've honed to support myself."

Oh... The tears welled in her eyes as she fought breaking

down entirely. He deserved better. He deserved his dreams.

Before she registered what he was doing, he'd scooted over to her side of the couch and wiped the tears away with his thumb.

"Don't cry for me, Elissa," he murmured. "I grew up luckier than so many others, every need taken care of. The only thing I ever wanted that I never got was my parents' approval. I can live with that."

"It's not fair," she breathed.

"I gave up on fair a while ago. Few things in life are truly fair, Elissa."

"They should be." Elissa regarded Ryan for a moment before she turned her attention to the table and the mess of dishes and containers strewn over it. "I'm gonna clean up while I think of a compelling reason for you to go to your family."

She rose from the couch and cleared the table. But Elissa didn't think about reasons Ryan should go to his family for help. Instead, she thought about how his face lit up when he talked about his podcast. She thought about how *she* could help him. She thought about her future at JMS Accounting and what a relationship with a client's employee who was also a close relative would mean.

What they were doing here, now, was a bad idea. At least until she talked to Karina, they needed to put a pause on whatever this was. She turned around after placing the dishes in the sink, determined to tell him so, only to be met with his broad, muscled chest. The words caught in her throat, and she lifted a hand, half in surprise and half to close the distance between them. She was drawn to him and had to fight her instinct to touch him.

Bad idea.

Clenching her hand into a fist, she forced it down. Elissa looked up when he didn't step away, the heat from his body warming hers. Gone were the traces of humor that had made his eyes sparkle and had turned up his lips. In its stead, what she found mirrored the wildfire of desire sweeping through her soul. Her back was against the kitchen sink, and she had nowhere to run, nor did she wish to. She longed to lose herself in the fire crackling between them. She longed to kiss him again, run her hands under his shirt and touch his skin, strip off her own clothes to experience his hands upon her.

She was tired of never asking for what she wanted.

"Fuck it," she murmured. She'd already paid her twenty dollars, so why not? "Kiss me."

He didn't wait for her to ask again.

Ryan's lips met hers, and a shock wave traveled through Elissa, starting at the point they touched and radiating all the way to her toes. Heat followed in its wake, and she melted against him. He wrapped his arms around her, the only thing holding her up.

Regaining her senses, she ran her hands over his back, the muscles below his shirt firm and rippling with restrained power. Elissa parted her lips, and his tongue traced their contours. Shivers raced along her spine as he ran his hands down her arms, interlacing their fingers. Ryan broke the kiss.

"Like that?" His voice was barely audible, harsh with desire.

"More," she said, surprised at her own audacity, surprised at her own hunger.

Elissa tried to pull her hands away. They itched to undo the buttons on his shirt and run along his skin. Ryan held tight.

"I thought you wanted to keep this professional." The corners of his mouth twitched.

Oh, God, what was she doing? She'd always prided herself on her professionalism, yet here she was, in a compromising position with the son of her firm's biggest client. This was stupid, and Elissa didn't do stupid. Except...

"I did." She bit her lip, grappling with the storm of emotions swirling in her. "I do. At the office."

"We're not at the office." He kept a firm grasp on her hands and smiled wolfishly. His smile melted the last of her reservations. Admittedly, they'd been holding on by the thinnest thread.

"I know."

"I should go." Ryan made no move to leave.

"No!" The idea of him leaving sent waves of dismay through the turmoil already spinning through her. "I don't want you to leave."

"What *do* you want, Elissa?" His voice was soft, his eyes gentle.

When was the last time anyone had cared what she wanted? Her parents had assumed they knew, had pushed her toward a lucrative career. Ami and Leo, like most younger siblings, had no regard at all for her feelings. She was either a partner in crime or an obstacle. Even Karina expected her to take on all her clients when she retired.

"I don't know," she replied after a long pause. "No one's asked me that in a long time."

"Then I should go until you do."

He released her hands. An icy chill replaced the heat of his touch, and an ache settled deep within her.

"Please don't go." Warm tears trailed down her cool cheek.

His hand cupped her cheek, wiping the tears once again. What was it about this man that brought on the waterworks? She hadn't cried this much since her mom's diagnosis.

Ryan placed gentle kisses down her face, tracing the path of her tears. When his lips met hers once more, she tasted the salt of her own tears in their kiss. He kissed her, long and slow, so thoroughly she lost track of time. Their tongues brushed against each other before he delved deeper into her mouth. He kissed her until her momentary turmoil melted away.

Desire, red hot, replaced it and drew her hands to his buttons. What she desired now was his bare skin under her fingertips. She yearned to explore his body, and God, she yearned for him to explore hers. The mere idea of his lips somewhere else on her body sent a jolt of pleasure through her.

Ryan drew away as Elissa worked the first button free, stilling her hands with his own.

"You don't have to do this," he said in a husky voice.

She looked into his eyes, their soft brown now aflame. His breathing was quick and harsh, and his heart raced beneath her hands. Elissa finally knew what she wanted. She wanted him, wanted to touch him and to be touched by him. Ryan seemed determined to stop her even though his kiss told her he wanted her just as badly. She pulled her hands away, and he let them go, a fleeting shadow of disappointment crossing his face.

Elissa unbuttoned her own shirt, first one button, then a second, exposing the swell of her breasts. Ryan's sharp inhale brought her gaze to his. His pupils dilated, and she dropped her eyes again, the passion she'd glimpsed almost too much. Almost.

"I *want* to do this." She undid the third button, exposing the edge of her plain beige bra. "I want you to stay."

He tried to grasp her hands again, but she easily freed herself from his feeble attempt.

"I can stay without…this." Ryan made a half-hearted gesture toward her. She undid a fourth button, and he groaned. "But…professional…"

When it became obvious he was unable to complete the sentence, she pulled her shirt out of her slacks and undid one more button.

"Screw professional," Elissa said.

Ryan grabbed her hands, bringing them to his lips. He kissed her knuckles before releasing them. She worked on his second button as his own fingers undid the last button. Elissa held her breath as his hands encircled her waist for a moment. They were gentle and softer than she'd expected. His thumbs moved in slow circles on either side of her navel. The sensation kindled a blaze deep in her core. She'd never felt this kind of passion before, as though at any moment she'd burst into flames and be glad of it. He brushed his hands up her body as she worked another button on his shirt. She'd exposed a deep V of his bronzed skin, the sparse dark hair arrayed evenly over the well-muscled chest. Elissa traced the edge of the shirt, and he shivered. Ryan's hands now rested on her shoulders. With a quick movement, her shirt fell off, sliding down her arms. She broke her contact with his skin to toss it aside.

"Oh, God." He leaned in to kiss her again.

"No." She placed a finger over his soft lips. "I want your skin against mine."

In a hurried frenzy, she undid the rest of his buttons, yanking his shirttails out of his pants. As soon as she undid the last button, he shrugged out of his shirt and dropped it. Pulling her in to maximize the skin-to-skin contact, he covered her mouth with his own. Their groans resonated, vibrating deep in her chest.

Ryan was as solid as she'd assumed, but feeling the muscles move without a shirt to cover their definition was pure bliss. She couldn't keep her hands still. They flitted over every inch of his exposed skin. When they brushed against the waistband of his pants, she wanted—no, needed—more. She moved her hands to the front and worked on the belt buckle. The tiny clink of the metal seemed to bring Ryan back to reality.

"Elissa." He pulled away from her.

Unconsciously, she reached for him, desperate to touch him. His hands engulfed hers, stilling them. She breathed, quickly, heavily, unsure if she was getting enough oxygen, but not caring if it meant kissing him, touching him.

"Elissa." Ryan's voice dragged her from an edge she'd almost fallen over.

"Ryan." She liked the taste of his name on her lips. She smiled at him, but he didn't return it.

"I don't want you to get in trouble."

There he went again, pulling back when it was getting

interesting.

"I won't."

"How do you know?"

She didn't know. She didn't care. For once in her life, she was willing to take what she wanted and damn the consequences. She freed her hands from the cage of his and framed his face.

"Do you want me, Ryan DeMarco?" Elissa asked, no teasing in her voice or in her face.

"Oh, God, more than anything."

"Then why do you keep stopping this?"

Ryan didn't respond for a long moment. He traced the contours of her face with his fingertips. He brushed his thumb over her lips before settling his hands on her waist.

"You've been in my dreams for so long," he whispered. "I need to know I'm not dreaming this, not pushing you to do something you don't want."

Her heart stopped for a long moment. She'd been in his dreams. He'd been in hers. Elissa leaned in, so close his skin almost touched hers again.

"I want this. If I didn't, you'd know." Her words caused goosebumps to form on his arms.

"Also, I don't have a condom." His voice was sheepish.

"Now that I can solve."

Elissa threaded her fingers into his and pulled him off the couch. She dragged him down the hall and into her bedroom. Pulling him close, she brushed a fleeting kiss to his cheek and pushed him onto her bed.

"Light the candle. I'll be right back."

Before she could second-guess herself, she darted into her friend's room and went straight for the condom stash in the bedside table. Elissa grabbed a handful, not even counting. Jules would forgive her. Hell, Jules would happily throw her a party.

CHAPTER 34
one serious entanglement

C aught in her spell, Ryan did as he was told and lit the candle. The soft vanilla scent mixed with Elissa's powdery fragrance. He wanted her more than he'd ever admit even to himself.

She returned before he could second-guess his decision to stay, flushed and breathless and clutching a handful of condoms. A primal instinct told him he could have her, have all of her, if he just reached out, if he just had the courage to ask.

He allowed a grin to tease at the corner of his lips as he glanced at the hand holding the condoms. "Seems a bit ambitious."

Her face went from pink to red as she followed his gaze. "I could count them, if you want."

Ryan rose from the bed and snagged an arm around her waist. He pulled her tight as he took the condoms from her. Without looking, he tossed them toward the nightstand. At least one hit its target.

"I think we'll manage."

And he kissed her. She tasted of white wine and Thai spices and peanuts. His hand slid into her curls, and they wrapped their silky tendrils around his fingers. He could spend all night just kissing her. His cock hardened, objecting to the idea. Well, maybe not all night.

She kissed him back, her fingers trailing up his chest,

lingering in the dark curls. He let go for a moment to shut the door behind her.

"When does your roommate get back?" He tugged her tight against him, reveling in her silken skin as his hands inched closer and closer to the bra closure.

"Midnight, at the earliest."

"Mmm, good." With a deft flick, he undid her bra.

Elissa gasped. Oh, he loved that little noise. He brushed his lips against hers but quickly moved on to her jaw. Another kiss on her ear. A trail, feather-light, down her neck.

One hand brushed a bra strap down her arm, then repeated the motion on the other side. He put enough distance between them for her undergarment to drop to the floor. Ryan took her mouth again, and her soft breasts pressed into his chest.

His hands trailed along her spine, and she shivered beneath his touch.

"Please," she whispered against his lips.

He silenced her with another deep kiss, teasing her tongue with his as one hand drifted to those luscious breasts. His fingers grazed her nipple, and she gasped again. He swallowed the sound.

"Please what?"

"I don't know. Just, please?"

He trailed kisses down her neck, down her chest. She panted, her hands clutching his hair and tugging in a deliciously sexy way.

"Use your words."

He brushed his thumb over a nipple once, twice, a third time.

"Fuck me. Please, fuck me."

He drew the nipple into his mouth and sucked while his hand teased and tweaked her other nipple. She'd been dropping curses all night, here and there. He loved that he caused her to lose control. And he couldn't wait for her to shatter under his touch. Watching her come undone was going to be the highlight of his life.

The moans coming out of her pink mouth were enough to harden his cock almost painfully. He stroked her nipple with his tongue as his hands moved down her sides and found the button and zipper of her slacks.

With a quick flick, he had them open.

"It will be your pleasure." He pushed her over onto the bed.

She bounced, first with a gasp, then a giggle. Ryan undid his pants and pushed them down. She canted herself up on her elbows and watched as he quickly tugged off his socks. She stared at the tent under his boxer-briefs and bit her lip. With her distracted, he grabbed her pants legs and yanked them right off.

Elissa squealed delightfully, but they quickly turned to gasps as he trailed kisses up her legs. His fingers drifted behind, and goosebumps rose in their wake. As he approached the apex of her thighs, the kisses stopped, and he licked and nibbled. She clutched the covers tight.

"Hands on me, Elissa."

Her eyes were glassy with desire, but she released the comforter and clutched at his hair again.

"Better. Tell me if you want me to stop."

"I don't want you to stop."

"You might change your mind."

"I won't."

Ryan traced his tongue next to the leg hem of her panties. Beige to match the bra, but with lace detailing that made them sweet and sexy. She squirmed delightfully at his attention. His finger traced the other leg hem, dipped under, and found her wet and ready.

"All this for me?"

He glanced at her. The flush painted her tits pink and crept up her neck.

"Yes," she breathed.

His finger brushed over the curls and folds, finding her clit. He gave one slow, circular rub before withdrawing. She whimpered in protest. He didn't give her time to do anything else, though. He grasped her panties and pulled them off. Ryan knelt on the ground and pulled her to the edge of the bed, hooking her legs over his shoulders.

"I want you to come on my face." He placed a kiss on the inside of her thigh.

She shuddered. "But what about you?"

"I can wait. There's plenty of time, and you seem to be under the impression I won't thoroughly enjoy myself. So, what do you say?"

"Please."

"Good girl."

She started to chuckle, but it turned into a sensuous moan as his lips found her clit and sucked. Her hands curled into his hair, holding him in place.

His tongue circled her clit, over and over, then he slipped a finger into her. Her muscles clenched briefly. She was close, so close. And she tasted divine. He rubbed his cock through his underwear and squeezed, hoping to relieve the pressure enough so he wouldn't come before he was inside her.

It worked, for now.

He hooked his finger and found that spot while sucking hard on her clit. She exploded, moaning his name. God, the most beautiful sound he'd ever heard. He wanted more. He wanted it all. Every word, every breath, every climax.

Ryan wiped his mouth with his hand before lying next to her. He kissed her slowly while his hand traced lazy circles on her belly.

"Mmm, that was amazing," she murmured when he finally broke the kiss.

"Yes, it was. Want more?"

Her fingers tapped down his chest, following the trail of hair lower and lower. She brushed against his hardened length through the cloth of his underwear.

"Is this the more?"

"If you want."

"I want. Please."

"Then you shall have."

She hooked her fingers in the waistband and tugged, and Ryan helped. He kicked the underwear off the bed. Her hand wrapped around him and stroked. A moan escaped his lips, and Elissa smiled down at him.

Her thumb brushed the tip, wiping away the drop of pre-cum. She brought it to her mouth and licked it off. No one should look that sexy. The urge to pin her down and bury himself in her hot depths almost won. Instead, he reached over her and grabbed a condom, gently sucking a nipple into his mouth on his way.

"Are you ready for me, Elissa?"

She didn't answer with words, but she cupped his face and kissed him madly, deeply.

Ryan tore the package and rolled the condom over his cock. He nudged her thighs aside and positioned himself at her entrance. With tight, controlled movement, he pressed into her. Slowly, first just the tip. Then a little more. Her pussy took him easily. He pulled out.

She groaned in frustration and locked her legs around his waist.

"Stop teasing." She arched her hips, taking even more of him.

He lost control and buried himself.

She sighed his name, like a prayer—no, a blessing. Fuck. He was a goner.

His fingers found her clit and rubbed as his thrusts grew erratic. It didn't take long for her to shatter around him, and he joined her as her pussy clenched his cock tight. God, he saw stars.

He collapsed on his elbows above her and kissed her again, slow and deep.

"Let me clean up. I'll be right back. Don't move."

She smiled sleepily at him as he slipped out of the room. The bathroom was directly across the hall, and it was still far from midnight. He dropped the condom in the trash and splashed some water on his face. When he returned, she was half asleep on top of the covers.

Ryan pulled back the sheets and tucked her under them before crawling in next to her. Elissa curled into him, her head on his chest. Ryan tucked an arm behind his head and ran his other hand through her hair. She sighed, her breath drifting across his chest. A contented smile pulled on the corners of his mouth as he contemplated the ceiling of her bedroom.

A buzzing noise coming from somewhere in the vicinity of his pants woke him an hour or two later. Ryan carefully extricated himself from Elissa's warm presence. She settled onto her other side as he pulled his phone out of his pants pocket.

Iz. Shit. He hadn't expected to stay for so long, and they were calling to check on him, like the good friend and worrywart they were. With haste and a sprinkling of stealth, Ryan pulled on his underwear and pants and left the bedroom. He called Iz.

"Hey, dude. Where are you?" his friend asked.

"Ummm," Ryan said, stalling. "At a friend's. Sorry I forgot to let you know I'd be late."

"He's fine, Teo, at some woman's place." Iz didn't bother to muffle their voice as they spoke to their significant other. So Teo had initiated this round of mother-henning. Ryan liked Teo, he really did, but Iz was perfectly capable of ruining his night all on their own.

"I didn't say it was a woman."

"I'm the only friend you'd be out so late with unless you were getting laid, so, by process of elimination…"

"Ha, ha. I'll be home soon."

"Nah, don't worry about it. Spend the night. Just placating Teo. Have a good one."

The line went dead, and Ryan stared at the phone. Shit, what was he doing? He didn't spend the night, but he doubted Elissa had ever not spent the night with someone. He didn't do entanglements, and Elissa was one serious entanglement.

He flopped down on the couch, fingering the silk shirt she'd left on the pillow. God, when she'd stripped this off, he'd known he was wrecked. He brought the shirt to his face and breathed in her scent from it. Powdery, faintly floral, it went straight to wherever sex memories were stored, and he desired her as much as ever. Ryan tossed the shirt on the couch and rose in time to see a tall, thin woman with dark hair come in the door.

She took one look at him, half undressed, and grabbed the baseball bat next to the door he hadn't noticed earlier.

"Who the fuck are you, and what the fuck are you doing in my home?" she growled at him, taking a step away from the door. This must be the roommate.

He held up his hands, his phone still in his left, and used a soft voice. "I'm Elissa's friend. She's asleep, and I needed to take a call."

"If you were the kind of friend she'd be sleeping with, I would've known about you. I'm going to call the police." Jules pulled a phone from her pocket.

Great, the last thing he needed was to deal with the police. He'd been working so hard to convince his father he was playing ball, turning his life around. This could ruin everything.

"My name's Ryan DeMarco," he said. "I don't know if Elissa has mentioned me, but we know each other from work. Go wake her up if you don't believe me."

Her thumb hesitated over the phone screen. "Jerk-Ryan?"

He gave her the DeMarco megawatt smile. "None other."

Jules put away the phone but kept the bat up. "Are you leaving?"

Ryan glanced down at the shirt he still held, then at the bat. "Do I need to?"

"That depends. Elissa isn't a one-night stand kind of girl. If you're not planning on sticking around, it might be for the best. I'll tell her you said goodbye."

"You're very protective."

She bounced the bat against her shoulder, never taking her eyes off him. "She's my best friend, and no one else watches out for her. I've got her back."

"I'm glad she has someone like you."

"So, are you staying, or are you gonna run?"

Excellent question. His instincts should've kicked in by now, and he should be hightailing it home. But the image of a peacefully sleeping Elissa drew him right back to her bedroom, and all he wished to do was crawl in and sleep next to her.

"I think I'm gonna stick around."

"Okay. Break her heart and I will find you and hand your balls to you on a silver fucking platter."

"Understood. Does it buy me any points if I say I'd want you to?"

She returned the bat to its place next to the door, the slightest smile on her face.

"One or two. Goodnight, jerk face."

He gave Jules a sarcastic salute and rushed out of there. The woman was scary in her devotion.

Ryan ditched his pants and tossed the shirt over the chair in the corner. He crawled under the covers. Elissa murmured unintelligibly in her sleep and snuggled closer. He kissed the top of her head.

As he fell asleep, a stray thought lodged itself in the back of his mind. Maybe it was time for him to entangle himself.

CHAPTER 35
squishy gray area

E lissa woke in the small hours of the morning, the sky still dark through the sheer curtains in her bedroom. The silence of the room pressed in on her in a way she hadn't experienced before. Something was different. She hadn't gone to bed alone. Her hand drifted to the other side of the bed, only to find cool sheets. Ryan was gone.

Why had he left without saying goodbye? She understood why all the others had left, eventually. Their biggest complaint had always been she'd never been truly present for them. At least, that's what it had boiled down to. Her family came first, pulling her attention from many a budding relationship, and she never had been able to articulate what she wanted, leaving both her and her lover dissatisfied. Her unavailability had irritated Victor to no end. Perhaps she should've paid attention to that red flag long before he'd left her.

She stared at the ceiling and fought the tears welling in her eyes. Last night had been a genuine connection. But she'd been with Ryan last night, all in. Nothing in the world had existed outside the two of them. Maybe he hadn't felt the same. He'd gotten exactly what he'd wanted from her and bolted.

Elissa pushed whatever these emotions were down deep. Obviously, last night had meant more to her than to Ryan. It was time to put her big girl panties on and come to grips with real life.

The door opened, and Ryan crept in.

"Hey, sorry, I didn't mean to wake you."

"I thought you left." Her voice warbled pathetically and more tears dripped down her face. She wiped them away and a tentative smile curled the corners of her mouth.

He sat on the edge of her bed and grabbed a tissue from the box on the nightstand. "I didn't mean to make you cry. I gotta leave in a few, but I made coffee and was going to snuggle you awake."

"It's not your fault." She dabbed the tissue at the tears, more embarrassed than anything now. "It's just…you wouldn't be the first to walk away without saying goodbye."

"I swear to you, Elissa, I will never leave without saying goodbye. Okay?"

"Okay."

He kissed her forehead. "Coffee should be ready. I have a few minutes to join you, but then I really have to go home to shower and change. Showing up to work in yesterday's clothes is bad enough when you aren't related to at least half your coworkers."

Elissa clenched her teeth and sucked in a breath. "Yeah, I can't even imagine."

Ryan laughed. "Come on, gorgeous. Let's get you caffeinated and on with your day."

She followed him to the kitchen and the coffeepot beeped.

"How do you take it?" She grabbed two mugs from the cabinet as he sat at the kitchen table.

"Black."

She poured the coffee, added a generous amount of creamer to her mug, and sat across from him. Ryan took his mug and sipped. Elissa savored her one cup of coffee for the day, sipping as she waited for the caffeine rush to kick in. The silence stretched for a minute until Ryan's hand covered hers.

"You okay? What was going on?"

"I have a slight tendency to overthink things. I assumed you left and I was trying to figure out where I went wrong."

"Ah, yes, the overthinker. A perfect counterbalance to the underthinker, which would be me, by the way, who should have let you know I had to leave early."

She gently tapped his shin with her toes. "We were a bit…distracted…last night."

"Oh, distracted doesn't even begin to cover it, I hope."

"True." And she giggled. God, last night had been mind-blowing.

Ryan took out his phone. "I wish I could *distract* you again, but if I don't leave right the fuck now, I'm going to be super late."

"And when your dad's your boss, it super sucks."

He smiled as he rose. "You got it, gorgeous."

Ryan bent down and tenderly kissed her, a soft, sleepy kiss that left her wanting more. Much, much more.

"You don't play fair," she said when he finally broke off.

"Never. Call you tonight?"

"You better."

He winked, then grabbed his helmet and bag. "Have a lovely day, Elissa."

The door closed softly behind him. She couldn't keep the silly grin off her face or the image of him naked out of her mind.

She put the mug in the sink, put some bread in the toaster, and poured a glass of cranberry juice. The sound of a motorcycle starting in the quiet morning only widened her grin. The toast popped and she sat at the table, only to notice the small pile of papers at the far end. Crap, Ryan's business plan. She'd return it next time.

Next time. She liked the sound of that.

Besides, she could run through some of this market research, refine her numbers. He had the bones of something interesting. With a little fine tuning and some marketing help, this could be a solid career.

Later. First, work. She rushed through her morning routine and was out the door quickly enough not to be late. Best to get the next few hours over with. Elissa steeled herself for an unpleasant conversation. She needed to tell Karina she couldn't work on the DeMarco account any longer. Her mentor may have given her tacit permission to flirt with the cute office manager, and a couple of dates might be excusable. Sleeping with a client was not. Karina wouldn't be happy, but she could work with another junior CPA on this account. Elissa could escape this with only a little embarrassment.

She set her bag and jacket down and went to find Karina. Oddly, the older woman wasn't in her office. Maybe she'd had an outside appointment she'd forgotten to tell Elissa about. Or was simply running late. Elissa settled into her normal morning routine, checking email and voicemail.

A soft cough drew her attention. Mr. Samuels stood at the entrance to her cubicle, sadness making his features even more droopy than usual.

"Elissa," he said in his quiet way.

"Yes, Mr. Samuels?"

"Karina's father died yesterday. Real sudden. Stroke."

"Oh. Oh no!" Elissa's stomach sank. Karina's mother had been ailing for years, but her father still seemed… Wait, if her dad was gone, who was going to take care of her mom?

"I told Karina I would let everyone here know so she didn't have to make so many calls. She's heading to Ohio tomorrow. Today is packing and calling family. She'll likely be out a few weeks. Not only with the funeral arrangements but with her mother's care."

"I understand. I'll send her a text in a day or two. Need me to brief whoever is taking over her accounts? I can do it today."

A small smile creased Mr. Samuels's face. "No need to brief. Karina assures me you are more than capable of handling her cases until she gets back. Said you could even file everything and clear her desk if this takes longer than she's expecting. I'm in one hundred percent agreement. Her clients are familiar with you, and you won't have to waste time briefing anyone. Any new clients will be assigned to other accountants. Since Karina had some of our largest accounts, I'll be overseeing your work, but I have no doubts you're the best person for the job. The load will be heavy. Get whatever help you need. Any questions?"

Pride bloomed in her chest. Karina, her mentor, felt she had this covered. It was the highest praise she'd ever received. Even better than the *summa cum laude* on her diploma from the University of Arizona. And then...

Ryan. She should tell Mr. Samuels about Ryan. The mere idea sent her heart racing and her palms sweating. He was older than her dad, had kids her age. How in the hell could she tell him she was dating an employee of one of their clients? She could see how that conversation would go.

"Gee, Mr. Samuels, I'd love to, and I can with most accounts. But the super important DeMarco account? See, I fucked the owner's son and..."

She must owe another twenty to the swear jar by now. It was Friday, and this would throw the office into chaos for a couple days. She could take the weekend to think—overthink—and devise a plan, and in the meantime, she would avoid the DeMarco account like the plague.

"Everything alright there, Elissa?" Mr. Samuels's voice broke through her spiral.

"Oh yes, sorry. Just thinking about what to tackle first."

Yes, Monday would do.

"Okay. I'm available any time. Do not hesitate to call, text, or email when questions or concerns arise. Let's give Karina a few days before doing more than offering condolences, but she said she'll be bored silly after the funeral."

"Thank you, Mr. Samuels, for your confidence. I won't let you or Karina down." A few days, yes, they'd know more by then, and possibly Karina would return by the end of next week.

She really, really didn't want to have this conversation with a sixty-year-old man. Would it hurt anything to put it off for a few more days?

"I know, Elissa. It's why I chose you for the job. I'm going to unlock her office so you can access anything you need from there. While you see what you can find, I'll call our clients and inform them of the situation."

Elissa nodded and watched her boss's boss walk away. She took a moment to gather herself, deal with the information, and send up a short prayer for Karina and her family. She snagged her bag and walked to Karina's office. The door was cracked open. Pushing it wider, Elissa entered, set her bag down in a chair, and collapsed in the other. It didn't feel right to sit in her mentor's chair.

As usual, Karina's desk was clear. Like most other industries, the vast majority of their work was done digitally. Paper copies were mere backups, hedges against technology that could delete a day's work with a simple keystroke. The boxes from their clients were stored in a secure file room. Via their shared file system, Elissa had access to the ongoing audits, tax returns, and other documents.

She glanced over the large desk calendar Karina had filled out. Although everything went into the shared calendar app, Karina was old school, wanting or needing a physical reminder as well as a ping from her phone. Elissa checked today's date. For the morning, her boss had written "DeMarco" in big, red letters. The afternoon was blocked off for another client in green. That's right, they'd planned on reviewing the DeMarco paperwork this morning, and the other client's after lunch. They were going to hunker down and knock out most of the DeMarco Property Management tax return next week, which would give them plenty of time to see if any other information was missing or if they had any questions. Another few days, and they could audit themselves and draft some recommendations for next year.

Shit, shit, shit.

Elissa placed her head down on the desk. Three more bucks in the swear jar. She should march right into Mr. Samuel's office and recuse herself from this account. But she couldn't, not when everyone needed her. With Karina out of the picture for the foreseeable future, anyone else would have to start over. She'd have to put this thing with Ryan on pause until after Karina returned.

Dashing away tears, she fished her cell phone out of her purse and stared at it.

This is the right thing to do.

Elissa *always* did the right thing. She prioritized her family and her work. She didn't lie, she didn't cheat. She didn't sleep with clients' employees. Or sons, as the case may be.

She didn't put mind-blowing sex above her professional ethics. She was already in a squishy gray area, which made her queasy.

All these thoughts were delaying the inevitable. She had to let him know it was a one and done. Elissa prided herself on her integrity. A clean break right now would alleviate some of her anxiety.

She took a deep breath and composed her text. And deleted it. Tried again. Deleted it again.

It's not like it was the greatest sex she'd ever had.

She forced herself to write out the break-up text. Her finger hovered over the send button.

Okay, it was exactly like it was the greatest sex she'd ever had.

Elissa couldn't do it, not via text. That was far beyond shitty, and Ryan deserved better. She'd do it the next time she saw him. She deleted the last text. Tonight, when he called, she'd tell him what happened and talk to him like the adult she was.

Goddammit.

CHAPTER 36
running late, son?

Ryan rushed through the early morning streets of Tucson. He should be sluggish, but he wasn't. In fact, just the opposite. Ryan DeMarco felt like he could take on the world—fuck, take on his father—and come out on top. Being around Elissa recharged him.

He downed another cup of coffee and took a barely warm shower. His cock kept waking up and missing Elissa. He'd have to remedy that at her earliest convenience. Half-tempted to ask Iz for a ride in—their office was a few blocks away from DPM—Ryan glanced at the clock as he grabbed his bag. He was only a couple minutes behind schedule. Maybe no one would notice.

His luck didn't hold. Though his father rarely arrived before Ryan, today he pulled in as Ryan was dismounting his bike. Well, fuck. Even though he'd been on time or early every damn day for the past month, his father would have something to say about him arriving five minutes late, though no one else was here yet.

Ryan didn't need his dad's bullshit this morning. He pretended not to see his father getting out of his car and hurried inside. He didn't even bother dropping his bag at his desk and went straight to the break room to hide, hoping his dad would follow his own routine.

No luck there, either. Alessandro DeMarco poked his head into the break room, no glint of good humor to be found on his craggy face.

"There you are. Running late, son?"

"Just a bit."

"Out late?"

Ryan didn't know if his father was merely curious or conducting an investigation. He kept his attention on making the coffee while he answered.

"Yes."

He pulled deep on his childhood experiences. Short, definitive answers were best. It gave his father less leverage to pull more information from him.

"You have responsibilities now, Ryan. You shouldn't be out with one of your floozies on a work night."

Big breath in, let it out slowly while counting to three.

Don't let him hear the sigh, or he'll read me the riot act. And, for the love of God, don't tell him to mind his own business.

He couldn't let the slight to Elissa go, though there was no way in fucking hell he was going to tell his father he was banging the hot accountant.

"I understand your concern, but she's not a floozy. It was only the once, Dad. I'll survive." He switched the coffee pot on.

A grunt greeted his words, and Ryan rolled his eyes but not before ensuring his father couldn't see him.

"I've heard that before, and if I recall, she used you for your money, and when she realized you weren't getting your inheritance for another ten years, she dropped you like ASU fumbled the ball last season."

It was true—he'd been used for his money and connections before. Elissa wasn't like that, not at all.

"This one is different."

"We'll see. When do we meet her?"

Never.

"We've been on, like, three dates. I'll let you know."

"I hope she was worth it," Alessandro grumbled as he

withdrew and walked down the hall to his office.

Ryan wasn't sure if he was meant to hear, and he wouldn't have answered his father, anyway. But God yes, Elissa had been worth it. Not just the sex, though that had been beyond fantastic. For a guy who prided himself on his ability with words, they seemed to fail him whenever he thought of Elissa. The night had approached perfection. A quiet meal for two, sharing his life's work with her, even though he'd only known her for a little while.

While the coffee finished brewing, he shuffled to the front door to unlock it for the day. His cousin waited outside, tapping her stilettos against the sidewalk.

"Sorry, running a couple minutes late."

"It's fine, Ryan. I was only out there for a minute."

"So why the toe tapping?"

"I'm worried your dad would find out." She shot him an impish grin.

"Too late."

The color drained from her face. "Oh, fuck me, I was kidding. No wonder you look like shit."

"Thanks. That's helpful. Anyway, he didn't yell at me."

"Your dad didn't yell at you when you were late? What, did aliens switch him out with someone more reasonable?"

The door shut behind them. "I'm just grateful he didn't. If the aliens want the original version, they're welcome to it."

She hit him in the shoulder, a gentle tap to remind him to watch his mouth around here.

"Will you watch the door for a minute while I grab a cup of coffee?" he asked.

She readily agreed, and he hurried back. He had no time to worry about his dad's behavior or to think of Elissa. Well, except for when the phones stopped ringing. Or at lunch. Or on his third coffee break in the afternoon. The day passed slowly, but suddenly, the clock read four thirty, and he couldn't wait to be home and talk to her.

He texted her as soon as he walked in the door.

R: You home yet?

He grabbed some leftovers and a beer out of the fridge and checked his phone. Nothing. Well, it wasn't five yet, she may still be working. Or she could be driving. Talking and driving was risky. He could be patient.

He turned on the TV and found a basketball game.

Okay, who was he kidding? He was not a patient man. But he didn't have a choice. A half dozen texts right now would simply annoy the crap out of her. While Elissa was just as beautiful when annoyed as any other time, he'd prefer not to do that after last night. Not yet, at least.

He ate and drank his beer and yelled at the TV a couple times.

Still no response.

His stomach dropped. Had she changed her mind? It was almost six. Surely she was home by now.

He decided another text was warranted.

R: How bout now?

He stared at the damn phone. No three dots, no response.

Had his father been right? Was she a floozy who had been looking to use him for money and connections and his rockin' bod? After last night, she knew he didn't have the money to run his podcast yet, let alone treat his girl to the luxuries he was brought up with. Maybe she fucked him, decided it was a momentary lapse in judgment, and was waiting to let him down easy. He wouldn't blame her, but he needed something from her, not this silence.

Teo walked in. Apparently, his roommate sucked, and he'd been spending more and more time here lately, even when Iz wasn't here. Ryan didn't mind, he liked Teo. When the lease ran out on this apartment, they could look at getting a bigger place.

"What's up, man? You look like someone wrecked your bike and pissed in your helmet." Teo tossed the keys on the table and went to the fridge for a beer.

"That's a lovely image, dude. Waiting to hear from Elissa. Trying not to come off too needy or demanding, but damn, I've been left on read for over an hour." Ryan hadn't been this nervous about an unreturned text since high school.

Teo clicked his tongue. "Ooh, that's rough. I feel for ya, really. A whole hour. The audacity of the woman."

"Yeah, fucker. Laugh it up."

"Seriously, man, a little chill will go a long way. You both were up late, you saw her this morning, and didn't you say she's an accountant?" At Ryan's nod, Teo continued. "It's her busy season. Give her some time to breathe. She'll text when she's ready."

"But what if she doesn't?" That was the real heart of the matter. What if she didn't want him after all? God, the idea had his toes numb and his brain screaming obscenities at the vagaries of fate.

"Then that will tell you exactly what you need to know. It will suck balls, but you'll know."

"Don't sugarcoat it, man. I can take it."

"Shut up, asshole. Hey, any more of the barbecue pork?"

"Iz made a fuckton."

"They love to take care of us with food, don't they?"

"God love them."

Teo pulled the pork out of the fridge, made a plate, and stuck it in the microwave.

"Any progress on the script?" Teo asked as the food went round and round.

Ryan blew out a breath. He wished he'd had time, but honestly, he hadn't yet. He was too tired at the end of the day, and after last night…

"No, but the recording is there. I just need to sit my ass in a chair and transcribe it."

His phone dinged. About fucking time.

"I'll let you get that," Teo said with a smile.

Ryan returned his attention to his phone and read the text from Elissa.

> E: Sorry, sorry. I fell asleep at my desk.

Part of him felt guilty for tiring her out so much she fell asleep at work. The other half of him was preening with satisfaction. Jesus, even the most enlightened men still had stupid alpha male bullshit going on when it came to sex. Ryan put on his supportive boyfriend hat and told the alpha to go back to sleep. He wasn't needed here.

> R: No I'm sorry. I shouldn't have kept you up last night. Did you drool on any tax returns?

> E: Fortunately not.

> R: You want me to call?

The thought bubble popped up. And stayed a while. Oh, this couldn't be good.

> E: Can we talk this weekend? Karina had a family emergency. Her boss called Annetta today. Until Karina gets back, I'm in charge of her clients. I spent all day making sure I knew exactly where everyone stood and prioritizing the work. I'm going to be so, so busy for the next few weeks, maybe even until Tax Day.

Not good, but not bad, at least not for him. Karina, absolutely, and Elissa's life was going to suck. But he was Supportive Boyfriend tonight, so he had this.

R: I gotchu. We'll talk this weekend. I'll call Saturday, late enough so you can sleep in. Whatever you need Elissa.

E: Thanks. You're amazing. Goodnight.

Ryan sent the winking kissy face. Too cute, but Elissa sent back the face surrounded by hearts, so message received.

Relief flooded him. Of course it had been something out of her control. Of course. But the niggling doubt his father planted this morning wouldn't go away.

CHAPTER 37
that's a shame

When Ryan called on Saturday, Elissa meant to tell him. Just a temporary pause on things until she talked to Mr. Samuels. A day or two, max.

But he'd been so happy to talk to her. Wanted to know everything about her new duties. She couldn't bring herself to tell him anything to ruin his mood.

Fine, this was fine. She'd walk into Mr. Samuels's office first thing on Monday and have him assign DeMarco Property Management to someone else. She didn't have to tell him about her entire relationship with Ryan, merely hit the main points and recuse herself and apologize for not mentioning it before. Blame the shock of the moment, or…something.

Mr. Samuels, I'm sorry, but I met this great guy and he works at DPM. Bailey would be the perfect fit for the account.

Mr. Samuels, the DeMarco account needs to go to someone else. I'd rather date the office manager than handle the taxes for the company.

Mr. Samuels, how did you meet your husband? Because, funny story…

Option one, definitely.

Elissa put on her big girl britches and faced Mr. Samuels in his office at eight thirty Monday morning.

"Hi, Elissa. Ready for the big leagues?"

"Um, yes, about that—"

The phone rang, and he held up a finger. "Can this wait?"

"Sure, I'll check in a bit later." Elissa slunk back to her office.

Later didn't happen that day. Too many files, too many calls, too many doubts. It was fine. This was fine. She could tell Mr. Samuels tomorrow. Or the day after, if tomorrow went anything like today. In the meantime, she would distance herself from Ryan. Keep it to phone calls and texts. No dinners. No heated glances. No sex.

How was she to know "in the meantime" would turn into two weeks?

There was always so much to do. The twelve-hour days didn't stop, and the last thing Elissa wanted was to bungle any of her accounts. She ate, slept, and breathed her work. Part of her knew she had to in order to keep up with the load. Part of her was doing it to avoid some hard truths.

Ryan called or texted nearly every day, and he was the only bright spot in her life right now. He was *there*, in a way no one other than Jules had ever been.

A funny meme. A dirty joke. A soft voice listening to her work woes and sharing his own. The best part of her day.

But whenever he tried to ask her to do something, go somewhere, or up the spice of their phone calls, she backed off. He invited her to go to a party his cousin was throwing. She said she was too tired. Not a lie, but she could've shown up for a bit.

He mentioned the Renaissance Festival. She had to work the weekend.

He suggested a movie. She had plans with her family.

Elissa refused to say the words, to demand time for this whole situation to settle. It was her fault. She should've told Karina that Friday after Ryan helped take Leo to the hospital. She should've told Mr. Samuels as soon as he assigned her Karina's clients. But she didn't, and now she was doing everything she could to compartmentalize, which meant keeping at least a little physical and emotional distance between them.

The weeks passed in a blur. She sat at her kitchen table, staring into nothingness. Her brain hurt. She was exhausted.

And all she could think about was Ryan. She missed him so damn much.

Elissa cleared the table and went through the stack of mail that had been piling up. At the bottom was Ryan's business plan. She'd been meaning to fill in the missing market research data, but she had no bandwidth to manage one more thing.

Wait, she may not have the bandwidth, but she had a friend who did this kind of thing for a living. She could email him, see what tips and tricks he might have.

She composed the message, giving as many details as she could, and scheduled the email for Tuesday. No need to send a non-urgent email on Monday.

The good news was the DeMarco Property Management taxes were prepared and the files had been digitized. Bailey was double-checking them before Mr. Samuels signed off, but the physical files were ready to be returned. She called DPM.

"DeMarco Properties. Ryan speaking. How may I help you?"

Calm washed over her, and a frisson of desire shimmied down her spine. She'd talked to him yesterday, and yet his voice still had this effect on her.

"Hi, it's Elissa."

She could hear the smile replace the cool professionalism in his voice.

"Hey! I wasn't expecting you to call me here. What's up?"

"This is business, unfortunately. I have two file boxes with your name on them."

"My favorite kind of file boxes. When do you want to drop them off? And can I convince you to do it at the end of the day so I can take you out to dinner after?"

Guilt struck a dart in her heart. She owed him an explanation for why she'd been so unavailable. But Karina would be in next week. A few more days and she wouldn't have to tell him anything. A blip in their relationship that time and attention of the sexy kind would mend.

"I wish I could, but things are hectic here. Does Thursday mid-morning work?"

"Yeah." He sounded disappointed. Of course, he sounded disappointed. A few more days and she could stop disappointing him. Stop disappointing everyone. "Looking forward to it."

When Elissa walked into DeMarco Property Management on Thursday, Ryan's face lit up like a kid's on Christmas morning. Like they hadn't been apart for almost three weeks. Relief flooded through her. She hadn't screwed up with Ryan, at least.

"Well, good afternoon, Ms. Wright. Welcome back to DeMarco Property Management. Can I help you with the files?"

No one should have the right to look this hot. His hair curled gently across his forehead and staring into his warm brown eyes was like coming home to a roaring fire and a cup of tea.

"I would greatly appreciate your assistance, Mr. DeMarco."

He stood and looked over the cubicle behind him. "Yo, Trin, watch the front for me for a few minutes?"

A hand appeared with perfectly manicured nails in a lovely shade of bright pink and waved. Ryan grabbed her cart, and they walked to the file room. He unlocked the room and wheeled the cart inside. Standing inside the door, he made a show of pulling the keys out of the lock and sliding them into his pocket.

"Well, that's a shame. You distracted me so well last time," Elissa said with a little pout.

The words were out before her better self could stop them, and she wished she could take them back. Flirting at the office was a bad idea now that she knew what Ryan DeMarco was like in bed. His pupils dilated as he grabbed her waist and pulled her in, kicking the door. His lips were on hers as soon as the door snicked shut. Tasting her, devouring her, worshipping her. She pushed aside her better self and melted into him, her tongue sliding between his lips. A low moan escaped him, and he pressed her into the door.

Of its own accord, her leg wrapped around his thigh. The kitten heel of her pumps pressed into the muscle, driving his hard-on into her belly. Oh, fuck, she had too many clothes on. He had too many clothes on. There were just...too many clothes.

Her fingers scrabbled against the crisp cotton of his shirt, tugging it out of his pants. She slid her hands against his smooth skin.

"God, what you do to me, Elissa."

He grabbed her wrist and brought her hand to his cock. She squeezed it through his pants, and he trailed kisses along her jawline and down her neck. With expert finesse, he undid two buttons before she realized what he was up to. His finger slid under her bra and found her nipple. He teased her, and she squeezed his cock harder. He drove into her hand before taking her mouth once more.

Laughter in the hall splashed cold water over her ardor. They weren't alone. Not by a long shot. Fuck!

She went still in his arms and broke the kiss, thunking her head lightly against the door.

"Stop."

Though the word was barely intelligible, he did. Immediately. She dropped her hands to her sides and breathed deeply.

"We can't," she said. "This is...it's beyond inappropriate."

He sighed and withdrew his finger from under her bra and slowly rebuttoned her shirt. He brushed a light kiss against her forehead.

"You're right. I'm sorry. I miss you. It's been so long, too long." Ryan tucked his shirt in, but his pants were still tented.

He ran a hand down his face.

"It takes two. I shouldn't have teased you."

The guilt struck deep in her belly. She should know better. Hell, she did know better. And yet, this man drove all reason from her mind. All she longed to do was lose herself in his sparkling brown eyes, in the feel of his skin beneath her fingers, in the sound of her name on his lips. She had it bad. Bad enough she'd made out with a guy. At work. Twice!

"Tell me I can come over this weekend." He stroked her cheek.

"If you keep touching me like that, we're going to do something beyond inappropriate."

"Promises, promises."

But he stopped. Thank god. She missed him too, but this was neither the time nor the place.

"With Karina back on Monday, I need the weekend to prep everything so I can bring her up to date on all the accounts."

"Dammit."

He stepped away and ran his hand through his hair, tousling it even more than usual. It was sexy. Too sexy. She looked at his shoes. The most unsexy part of him. Except they were motorcycle boots, not dress shoes. And motorcycle boots were, by definition, sexy.

Fuck me.

"I now owe the swear jar at least five dollars. Can we put a pin in this?"

"Yes, but only if you promise two things."

She rolled her eyes but smiled as their gazes locked. His eyes twinkled with impish delight.

"Fine. What are they?"

"First, you leave the office no later than six on Friday."

She could do that. "Agreed. And?"

"And you call me on Saturday. I want to talk to you."

"About?"

"Anything. Nothing." His finger grazed her cheek again. "I just want to hear your voice for longer than five minutes."

"Okay. I will leave the office by six on Friday and call you on Saturday. Now, let's put these files away."

"No, I'll do it. You get going, do what you have to so I can finally have you all to myself."

He kissed her nose and slid to the side. The tent in his pants was gone. Part of her was relieved. And the other part wanted it back. Now.

Elissa straightened her skirt, retucked her shirt, and smoothed her hand over her hair.

"Is my makeup completely ruined?"

"Maybe a quick trip to the bathroom before you head out."

Oh God. Her expression must have told him exactly what she was thinking.

"Oh, oh no. I don't think it's bad, but I was paying exactly zero attention to your makeup. Other things were on my mind."

"Okay. I'll talk to you in a couple days."

"You better, or I'm telling Jules."

"Jules is my friend."

"Yes, and she would be the first to tell you to slow down. Take five minutes for yourself."

He was right. In fact, Jules had said something to that effect last night.

"No fair."

"If you won't listen to me, at least listen to the woman who has known you for twenty years, gorgeous."

"Fine. If you insist."

"I do. Now go."

Elissa cracked the door. No one was in the hall. She glanced back. Ryan was filing, but he looked up and grinned. He angled his head toward the door, and she dashed to the ladies' room. Her makeup was…fine. Nothing anyone standing further than three feet would notice. She spent two minutes touching up.

Trinity wiggled her fingers as Elissa passed the front desk. "Need anything else?"

Crap! She resisted the urge to slap her own forehead.

"Actually, yeah. Karina returns on Monday. She wants an appointment for the following week to go over the returns and recommendations for next year. Totally forgot to ask Ryan."

"Mm-hmm." She smiled knowingly. Hell, what *did* she know? Had Ryan been blabbing? He didn't seem the type. Trinity flipped through the calendar on Ryan's desk. "Looks like Uncle Sandro, Aunt Giselle, and my mom will all have availability in two weeks, at one thirty. Will that work?"

"It should. Pencil us in, and if anything changes, we'll call."

"Great. See you soon."

Elissa turned to go.

"Hey, Elissa?" A bright pink finger beckoned her closer.

"Yeah?" She took a few steps toward the desk.

"Be careful," Trinity whispered, her voice barely carrying the foot or two between them. "He's more vulnerable than he seems, okay?"

Elissa froze. Crap, she knew. Or at least strongly suspected. She could continue to deny or appease the familial bond. Once more, guilt tore through her. This was a bad idea, but it was also the best thing to ever happen to her.

She answered in a voice just as quiet. "I will."

Before Trinity could say anything more, Elissa wheeled around and left. This was future-Elissa's problem. Today's Elissa needed to get back to work. Future-Elissa had enough on her plate.

CHAPTER 38
point taken

Two days later, Ryan could still smell her powdery perfume, taste her sweet mouth, hear her soft moans. It was driving him up a wall. He kept his phone within arm's reach all day Saturday. But no call from Elissa.

He'd been worried until the kiss on Thursday. She kept turning down dates. He told himself she was dealing with a lot, but a part of him, the part he thought he'd healed over the past five years, kept muttering she was one more person who put him second.

"Do you think if you keep staring at it, it'll miraculously ring?" Iz asked as they cooked dinner.

"No," he grumbled.

Iz cocked a perfectly manicured eyebrow at him and waved the spoon.

"Maybe," Ryan amended.

"That girl is busy right now. They heaped a shit ton of extra work on her. The best thing you can do is give her space. She'll be back."

Iz was right, as usual. And Ryan was wrong, also as usual. But dammit, he wanted to hear her voice. Wanted to see her face. Wanted to feel her pulled tight against him. Wanted—

It didn't fucking matter what he wanted. Not right now. What mattered was what Elissa needed. And right now, she needed him off her case. She would call when she could. She'd promised, and Elissa Wright kept her promises. He'd bet anything on that.

But maybe she needed what he needed. A little alone time. A little one-on-one. Sex. Fuck, he needed sex. With her. It had been too long.

Iz plated some huevos rancheros, and Ryan dug in. Teo was at his sister's in Glendale for the weekend—some kid's fifth birthday, if Ryan remembered correctly.

"So, how's the job?" Iz broke the silence.

"Sucks. Putting a smile on every day is hard enough, but meaning it is impossible."

"But it gets you closer to your goal." Iz waved their fork at him. "I know you know this, my dude, but there are half a million people in this city who would gladly trade places with you."

"I know, I do. Doesn't mean I have to like my job."

"Lots of people hate their jobs."

Ryan sighed. True, lots of people hated their jobs. He never imagined he'd be one of them. His privilege was showing.

"And I guess it will be a 'character building' experience for me. God, at least tell me the writer gets more creative later."

"You're a jerk." There was no rancor in Iz's voice, and a small smile played on their lips.

"I know, but I'm a lovable jerk."

"You're lucky you are."

"Yeah I am. You're one of the best things in my life."

"Only *one* of? Has the lovely Elissa replaced me in your teeny, tiny heart?"

"Shut up."

Iz shoveled a forkful in their mouth, but their knowing eyes locked onto his. Ryan refused to play this game anymore. He allowed the silence to grow, knowing Iz had a lower tolerance for the quiet than he did.

"I like her for you. I think you two bring out the best in each other," they said, almost once Ryan gave up.

"I like her too. But I miss her."

"That's a good thing, you know. Missing someone."

"How so?"

"If you miss someone, it means they matter. It means you notice when they're not with you. Do you miss me when I'm gone?"

"Most of the time."

"Only most? I'm hurt. Devastated!" Iz smiled to take the sting out of their words. "What about your parents?"

"Never. I miss Nonna."

"Me, too. She was awesome! Best hugs ever. Alex?"

"Sometimes. We never had the strongest relationship, but we had some good times, and he never made me feel forgotten."

"How often do you miss Elissa?"

Every fucking day. It hit him right in the gut as his brain answered Iz's question. If she wasn't by his side, he missed her. Every second of every day. But he wasn't ready to admit it to Iz. Of course, he didn't need to admit it to Iz. His best friend already knew. It was painted on their face, just like their red lipstick.

"Point taken." He was in love with Elissa. Simply, utterly, wildly in love with her.

"You should tell her."

"I did. And she still had to work."

"Not the missing her. The other thing."

"What—" Some days, he hated having a friend like Iz. Someone who knew him well enough to know exactly what he was feeling before he did. But today wasn't one of those days. "Never mind."

"Give it another month, max. Tax season will be over, and she'll have more time. I see you two together. She's almost there, too, dude."

Doubtful, but still his heart hoped. As long as it didn't drag his brain along for the ride, he was willing to let it.

His phone rang, and Elissa's name popped up on the screen.

"Nice talk. Gotta take this."

"Tell me again how—"

He flipped Iz the bird and slammed the door to his bedroom shut.

"Hi, Elissa. I was starting to worry."

"Sorry. Oh god, I'm sorry. I lost track of time and—"

"It's okay. I know you're busy. I'm glad you called. So what were you doing that you lost track of time?"

"Trying to organize things for Karina. I was so busy doing the stuff, I forgot to put it into any particular order. I can't imagine briefing her on Monday with how messy the files were."

"Did you get it done?"

"Yeah I did."

His libido skyrocketed. "Does that mean you can come over tonight?"

"I would be a danger to myself and others if I try to drive tonight. And I still need to put together a PowerPoint for her."

"I could come over there."

She sighed over the line, and his heart plummeted. He knew, more or less, what she would say before she said it.

"I promised Jules I'd go to bed early."

Part of him wanted to hate Jules. But she was right, and most of him appreciated they both had Elissa's best interests in mind. One of these days, hopefully very, very soon, her best interests would include a half dozen orgasms delivered by him.

"Jules is right."

"What was that? I don't think I heard you."

"You heard me. You can even tell her I said so."

She giggled over the line, and he flashed back to the first and last time he'd stayed the night, cuddling and talking and laughing long after they both should have fallen asleep.

"I miss you, Elissa."

"I miss you, too. I promise, as soon as tax season is over, I'm all yours."

"All mine. I like the sound of that. I'm gonna hold you to it."

"I'd be disappointed if you didn't."

She yawned over the line. He should let her sleep.

"Goodnight, Elissa. Talk to you tomorrow?"

"It's not even seven."

"Do you need me to put Iz on the phone? You know what they'd say, and it will be three against one."

"No fair ganging up on me. I can make my own decisions."

"Yes, you can. But the best decision is that you get some rest. And Jules is scary. I don't want her coming after me with the bat you keep by the front door. If you don't listen to her for your own good, do it for me."

An exaggerated sigh wafted over the line. "Fine, I'll do it for you. But I expect to be rewarded the next time I see you."

"That's my good girl. I think I have just the incentive."

"What?"

"Nope. It'll be a surprise."

"You're a tease. Goodnight, Ryan."

The line went dead before he could admit the secret Iz had figured out.

I love you.

CHAPTER 39
one gigantic nerd

On Sunday, Elissa did PowerPoint. All freaking day.

Her eyes hurt, her back hurt, and her head hurt by dinner on Sunday, but the PowerPoint brief for Karina was complete, fancy slide transitions and everything. Her boss was champing at the bit after being gone for weeks. And Elissa wanted nothing more than to hand over the responsibility so she could spend time with Ryan without the guilt weighing on her.

The presentation was a beautiful thing. The only application she liked better than PowerPoint was Excel.

"Nerd." Jules's voice pulled her into the present.

"What?"

"You're staring at the presentation like it's the second coming of Jesus. You, lady, are one gigantic nerd."

Her friend handed her a glass filled with pink wine, her favorite.

"But you love me anyway." She sipped the wine, slightly sweet and utterly refreshing after spending her entire day off hunched over the computer.

"I love you *because* of it."

Jules had a beer. She did not like pink wine unless it had bubbles. Jules would drink almost anything if it had bubbles.

"Awww. That's the sweetest thing you've ever said."

"Don't get used to it. Does this mean I'm finally gonna see you for more than ten minutes at a time?"

"God, I hope so. I mean, I appreciate the opportunity, but the amount of work has been overwhelming."

"Did you ask for help?"

Jules knew her well, but she could answer this honestly.

"Yes."

"Did you ask for *enough* help? Because I doubt Karina worked this hard last year."

"I don't know. First year, and we were a person short, so probably not."

"Baby steps. I'm proud of you. Got some leftovers from last night. Roast chicken and veggies."

"Oh, yes, please. Feed me."

Jules did, and Elissa took a bubble bath and went to bed at eight thirty. She slept surprisingly well given she had a big meeting in the morning, and rose, if not exactly bright-eyed and bushy-tailed, at least reasonably well rested.

Karina was already sitting at her desk when Elissa arrived a few minutes before eight. A wide smile greeted her.

"Elissa, thank you. Gary told me you handled everything like a champ."

"I hope so. It's good to have you back. Whenever you're ready, I can update you on where we are on all the clients."

"Ten work for you? Gives me a chance to ease in, return some emails, and all that."

"Sounds great. I'll see you in a couple hours."

Elissa steeled herself. She saved the DeMarco account for last, and she would tell Karina about her relationship with Ryan. Let her know Mr. Samuels oversaw all her work, and she had Bailey spot check her and look over her calculations. Yes, she should have recused herself. Yes, she understood she could no longer work on the DeMarco account.

At least it would be out there, removing the weight from her shoulders. At least she could date Ryan out in the open. At least this would be over.

Ten rolled around and she popped her head into Karina's office. Her boss was on the phone, looking like she was having the worst conversation ever. She waved Elissa in and gestured toward a chair.

"Yes, thank you. I will speak with my brother and we'll call later."

She hung up and pressed her fingers to her temples.

"I can come back," Elissa said.

"Today isn't going to work. Let's plan Wednesday."

"Anything I can help with?"

Karina smiled. "Just knowing we put our best junior accountant on these accounts has been extremely helpful."

Guilt stabbed hot into her gut and twisted. Suddenly, Elissa regretted the oatmeal she'd had for breakfast.

"I'm glad I could help."

"My mom is not settling in well to her care facility. I need to talk with my brother and get back to them by the end of the day. And despite having my email forwarded and everyone handling everything so well, I still have a ton of responses. And tomorrow…who the heck knows what's going to rear its ugly head tomorrow. I'm fighting hydras."

"I'll send over a summary with the appointments I've already made for next week, and we'll go over everything in what I'm sure will be excruciating detail on Wednesday."

"Thanks, Elissa. You're a rare bird, and I'm so glad we snagged you first."

As she left Karina's office, she doubted her boss would feel the same once she told her about Ryan. It wasn't a red flag, but it wasn't good. At least yellow, possibly orange. Hormones sucked.

She did not sleep so great the next two nights, tossing and turning as Karina's praise ran through her head. She felt guilty enough that when Ryan texted, she responded with short sentences and emojis, afraid she'd give away something she shouldn't. Even though they'd been talking normally for the past few weeks.

Wednesday rolled around, and Elissa went over the presentation again. Yep, she had about two hours left before her career got its first red mark. God, she'd always hated red ink.

She poured an extra cup of coffee and headed into Karina's office at nine.

The first forty-five minutes went perfectly. When she reached the DeMarco slides, her palms started sweating, and she swore the temperature increased ten degrees in the first thirty seconds. Her voice trembled from time to time.

"Do you need a break, Elissa?"

"No." Good, bad, or ugly, she needed this over. "Maybe a sip of water. I'm not used to talking for so long."

She grabbed her water bottle and sipped, then sipped a little more.

You've got this.

Elissa finished the presentation with her initial recommendations and the date of their appointment with the DeMarco Properties board.

"Excellent. I couldn't have done better. I knew you were the right woman for the job."

Here goes nothing.

"About that…"

She told Karina. Not everything. But that she'd gone on a blind date with Ryan in January, that they kept running into each other, and she'd gone on a few more. That she should have told Mr. Samuels when he assigned her to the DeMarco account.

"But everyone was so busy, and, honestly, I was a little embarrassed. I didn't mean for this to happen, and I got someone to spot check me. I swear I handled the account the same as all the others."

Karina's face had gone blank while Elissa explained. As the silence grew, she leaned back in her desk chair and steepled her fingers in front of her mouth. Elissa twisted the hem of her cardigan as her stomach sank and her heart raced.

What had she expected? That Karina would tell her it was fine, everything was unicorns and rainbows and lollipops?

Yeah, if she was honest with herself, that's almost exactly what she'd expected. Elissa Wright could do no wrong. It was a given in her family, at school, at work. She rarely made a mistake, was careful not to make mistakes. And when she did, they were easy to fix. But this one—the best mistake of her life— would not be an easy fix.

"Okay," Karina said after an eternity, "let me think through the options. I will need to loop in the partners and HR. You were put in a strange position, and I'm disappointed your first instinct wasn't honesty when Gary spoke to you. Now we have to navigate a delicate balance so we don't have to do all the work over and need an extension. Take the rest of the day and think about some outcomes. And reread the ethics handbook. I will be doing the same."

"Yes, of course." Elissa stood. "I am sorry. The longer I didn't say anything, the harder it became. I should have done better, and I understand if this means severe consequences."

"Keep your phone close, I'll call this afternoon."

Elissa nodded, clamping her lips shut and praying she wouldn't cry, then she left Karina's office. She rushed to her own and grabbed her bag. She stopped by reception.

"Hey, I'm not feeling well, so I'm heading home. Karina knows," she told the receptionist.

"Okay, Elissa. Hope you feel better."

"Thanks."

She made it to Bertha without crying. Even more surprisingly, she made it to her parents' house. She hadn't meant to drive to her parents' house, but autopilot must have kicked in. The garage door was open—right, spring break for Leo and her mom. But what was Ami's car doing in the driveway?

She parked next to Ami and walked up the gravel path. After a couple of knocks, she opened the door. Yelling spilled out into the overly warm spring day. Elissa slipped in and closed the door behind her.

"It's a shitty thing to invite your adult kid out to lunch only to yell at them for their adult decisions. We settled this a month ago! I'm not going back to school. Not this summer, not this fall." Ami's voice echoed from the kitchen. "We're done here, Mom."

A cabinet slammed shut and Ami stomped into the hall. Her brows rose when she noticed Elissa, but she didn't stop. Elissa pressed against the wall in the narrow hall, and Ami brushed by, waves of rage radiating off her. Elissa wouldn't touch her sister with a feather right now and expect to still have fingers.

"Don't you walk away! This conversation is far from over." Their mom followed Ami into the hall, but didn't seem to notice Elissa.

"I'm not a child, you don't get to tell me what to do!" Ami shot over her shoulder.

"You're *my* child."

Ami paused with her hand on the handle of the front door. She glanced at Elissa, tears trembling on her lashes.

"Please, Lissa, I-I can't do this anymore."

She opened the door and slipped into the sunlight and heat of a desert spring.

"Amicaria!" Mom shouted, but it was too late. The door was shut, and Ami was halfway down the front walk.

Her mom slumped against the wall, and her head thunked heavily as she leaned back.

"Elissa, go talk some sense into her. She won't listen to me."

Elissa studied her mom for a moment, then joined her, mirroring her posture on the opposite wall.

"I can't. You pushed her too hard. She won't listen right now, no matter who is doing the talking."

"Don't you start with me. I know my own daughter. Go be

the voice of reason."

Elissa took a deep breath. This was one of the hardest things she ever had to do. But she'd learned her lesson. Speaking up early is better than not speaking up at all.

"No."

Dana Wright turned her glare on her oldest daughter and her lips tightened. "Elissa, please…"

"I said no, and you need to listen. The harder you push Ami, the harder she pushes back. If—and I think at this point it's a huge if—she ever wants to finish college, she will one hundred percent need to come to that all on her own. If you keep pushing, she never will."

"You do not know Ami better than me. I know what my kid needs."

"You know what *one* of your kids needs." Elissa dug her nails into her palms, hoping the pain would stop the flood of words from flowing. It did no good. "You always know what Leo needs, and you're well versed in giving it to him. But Ami and me, not so much."

"That's not—"

Elissa ignored her mother and plowed on. As much as it hurt her to say it, as much as it would hurt her mother to hear it, it needed to be said.

"I get it, Mom. Leo needed extra help. Ami and I were fine, mostly. Easy. But when you were taking Leo to the hospital, I was the one consoling Ami. I read her stories to keep her distracted, played games in the waiting room while you talked to the doctors. No one did the same for me."

"Lissa…" Her mom's voice broke.

"I don't blame you, I don't. But I do resent it, a little. And I'm tired of being the peacemaker between you two. She's an adult. So are you—the adultier adult. Talk to her like one."

"I-I can't. I look at her, at you, and all I see are the beautiful little girls who needed me. I don't know how to be the mom of adults who don't."

Disappointment and anger swept through her. Elissa loved her family. She loved her mother so, so much. But she couldn't keep doing this any more than Ami could. It wasn't healthy.

"Then you need to make your peace with that. I gotta go."

Elissa pushed off the wall and strode toward the front door. She kept expecting her mom to follow, but she didn't. Instead, quiet sobs filled the hall as she left, shutting the door carefully behind her. She paused outside and let the sunshine dry the tears streaming down her cheeks.

It would be okay. Just some hard truths for all three Wright women today. They'd figure out their stuff. Probably. Maybe. *Oh, please God, let us figure it out.*

She approached Bertha, only to see her sister in her own car with the window open, leaning her head on the headrest. Tears and snot streamed down her face. At least Ami wasn't a pretty crier. That would have been too unfair.

"Gonna hold this over me too, Miss Perfect?" Acid dripped from Ami's voice, spilling out of the car and pooling unpleasantly in Elissa's gut.

"You're mad at Mom, not me. I don't care what you do with your life, Ami, as long as you're happy. You're so not happy right now. And I'm not perfect."

Far from it. Today more than proved it.

"Oh, you mean occasionally losing your temper and saying 'gosh, golly, darn it to heck'? Fuck you! You have no idea what I went through."

Years of resentment, of not living her own life, roiled inside her. Before she could raise her well-honed mental filters in place, she unloaded.

"And you have no idea of what I went through! I read you stories when Leo was in the hospital, told you everything would be okay. And last month, Leo called me, not you! How often did you take Mom for her treatments? Who do they call when they need things? Not you!"

"Yeah, they don't need me. That's a fucking great feeling, Liss. Way to rub it in."

"The next time they call, you can be the dutiful daughter. I love you, all of you, but I can't breathe anymore."

She turned away and fumbled with Bertha's keys, trying to open the fifteen-year-old piece of crap.

"Lissa, what—"

"Tell them I ran off with the hot guy on the motorcycle! I'm done."

The car door finally unlocked, and she climbed in, ignoring the heat radiating from the steering wheel from being out in the sun for longer than five minutes. Elissa slammed the door shut and started the engine.

Well, she tried. Bertha's engine refused to turn over. Son of a bitch!

Elissa put her head down on the steering wheel and cried, the heat from the hard plastic barely bothering her. It wasn't fair. She was owed a dramatic storm-out for all the times Ami had pulled this crap on her. Instead, her moment was ruined. She grabbed some tissues from the box she kept on the passenger seat and cleaned herself up. Her sister still watched from her car, mouth agape. Great, now Ami would have this story to hold over her, too.

Out of pure desperation, she tried cranking the engine again. It caught with a sputter, and she gave old Bertha some gas. It didn't kill the engine, so she put it in reverse and backed down the driveway. Elissa flipped off her sister, put Bertha into first gear, and gunned the engine. Her old junker lurched along the street.

She drove around and around, not sure what to do next. No, that wasn't right. She knew exactly what she wanted to do. Who she wanted to see. She was just too chickenshit. If there was one person who'd be sympathetic, it was Ryan. His family didn't understand him, either.

Fuck it.

A few minutes later, she pulled into the parking lot of DeMarco Property Management, then stormed into the office. Of the three people who looked up in surprise as she burst through the doors, she only had eyes for one.

Ryan stood behind the reception desk, a stack of files in hand. The smile that crossed his face and lit up his beautiful brown eyes was the best thing she'd seen in a week.

CHAPTER 40
do you want to get out of here?

Ryan's heart leaped as Elissa burst in, disheveled as if she'd taken on a dust devil and lost. She had an extra button undone, showing off her cleavage, not that he was complaining. Her unruly hair made him want to muss it even more. He hadn't seen her since her last visit to the office, and she was the most beautiful thing to walk into his life. Today and every day.

Red-rimmed eyes stared wildly around the office until they found him.

"Elissa, what's wrong?" He dropped the files on his desk.

Trinity and Alex were silent, their mouths open in surprise and their gazes like laser pointers on his back. But he didn't care one rat fuck about what they thought or who they might tell. The only person who mattered right now was standing in front of him with a tear-streaked face, looking nothing like herself. Why had she come here? Oh God, was her mom's cancer back?

"Do you want to get out of here?" Her voice was rough, but she kept her eyes on him. Those beautiful, lake-blue eyes shimmered with unshed tears. He was a complete goner. "I-I need to get out of here."

Elissa needed him, needed an escape, needed freedom. Fuck, and he needed her, needed escape and freedom, too. A wicked smile lit his face, and he loosened his tie. He balled it up and let it fall on top of the files he'd been holding a minute ago. She was offering him freedom, and he was taking it, taking her.

It was his dream come true.

"Let's go!"

He grabbed his helmet from where it sat under the desk. In a few quick steps, he stood in front of her. She wobbled back and forth on her feet, and he wrapped an arm around her shoulder, spinning her around gently. Elissa leaned into his side and allowed him to steer her to the door.

"What am I going to tell your father?" Trinity called.

"I don't care. Tell my father whatever you want," he said over his shoulder.

"I'll handle it," Alex said.

The door shut between them, finalizing the conversation. Whatever the consequences of this action, he would have it no other way. His girl needed him, and he wasn't going to put some ridiculous job above her. Hell, he'd been thinking of quitting since he took the position.

Ryan led Elissa to his motorcycle, sitting under the shaded parking area. With every step, his mind lightened. This was the right call. Everything about this woman screamed it deep in his soul. He was hers, and god willing, she'd be his.

It was fucking hot for mid-March, so he rolled up his sleeves and handed her the helmet.

"Put it on."

"What about you?" She took it from him with a crease between her brows.

"You'll be with me. I'm not taking any risks. We'll stop at my place for an extra."

Elissa put on the helmet and mounted the motorcycle behind him. She wrapped her arms around him and pressed her body into his. He tried not to think about how it felt. He'd need those brain cells to drive them safely to his apartment. As they drove out of the parking lot, his brother stood outside the door, watching them. The smallest of smiles crossed Alex's face.

Ryan pulled into a parking spot at his apartment complex.

As soon as he killed the engine, her grip loosened, and she slid off the bike. She took off the helmet and handed it over.

"Do you want to talk about it?" Ryan grabbed her hand, pulling her close. She buried her face into his shirt and shook her head. "Okay. We won't talk about it. Lemme grab a couple things and we'll get the fuck out of town. Does that sound good?"

She nodded and stepped back. He didn't let go of her hand, though, and tugged her along after him. He'd make this quick.

First settling her on the couch with a glass of ice water, Ryan went to his room and changed into riding gear. Digging in his closet, he found the spare helmet, a spare leather jacket, and a set of saddlebags, already packed with a simple toiletry kit and a change of clothes. Ryan grabbed an extra toothbrush from his bathroom and tossed it in.

He strode into the living room and handed Elissa the jacket. Ryan resisted the urge to ask her why again, afraid of breaking the spell. He liked this side of her, wild and ready to fly.

"Where to, gorgeous?" he asked instead.

"Just away. Anywhere but here."

"Gotcha. Been there. Done that. Have about a dozen T-shirts. Think I know the perfect place."

He pulled out his phone and called his cousin.

"Ryan! How are you?"

"Good, man. You?"

"Can't complain. Had a profitable winter, and this spring has been fantastic."

"Excellent. Listen, I know this is last minute, but something came up, and my girl and I need a break. Got a room available?"

"Yeah, you lucky bastard, as long as you're gone by Saturday. Got a cancellation a couple hours ago."

"Perfect, we'll take it! Thanks, I owe you one. We're on our way."

"Anytime. See you soon."

Ryan turned to Elissa. "My cousin runs a bed-and-breakfast

in Bisbee. Is that far enough for you?"

"Yes?" She sounded like she was trying to convince herself.

"It's less than two hours away and we gotta leave on Friday. What could happen in two days?"

"Let me call work."

He rolled his eyes. "Fine, but call work, text your family so they know you're okay, then turn the fucking thing off."

"Deal."

He could have sworn her fingers trembled as she called. A look of relief crossed her face.

Voicemail, she mouthed.

"Hi, Karina, I'm gonna take the next couple of days off. I'll be in on Monday." Her words were soft and even.

She tapped for a few minutes while he texted Iz.

"Is it off?" he asked.

She showed him the blank screen. He took the phone from her and tucked it, along with his, in the saddlebags.

"Are you going to be okay holding on for two hours, or should we get your car?"

Elissa sniffed. "Bertha's not going to make it two hours. We're in no rush. How do I let you know when I need a break?"

"Tap my shoulder three times, and I'll find a safe place to pull over."

"Okay."

She slipped on the too-big jacket and walked out the door. Ryan followed and locked the door. Elissa settled onto the motorcycle behind him and wrapped her arms around him once again. A shiver traveled up his spine. She would be this close for two hours, and he'd be unable to do anything about it.

It was two hours of torture and bliss, the only relief coming about halfway through, when Elissa tapped his shoulder three times. They took a short break, but his nerves were on fire. The only thing he could think of was getting her out of those clothes as soon as humanly possible. While she stretched her legs, he counted to ten over and over so he could focus. In order for him to see her naked again, they first had to arrive at the B and B safely.

They pulled into the parking lot. Elissa smiled as she pulled off the helmet, her cheeks flushed. Her body seemed looser, less tense, and her eyes were no longer puffy.

"You good?"

She took a deep breath and let it out slowly. "So much better now, here, with you."

He kissed her cheek and slung the saddlebags over his shoulder, then led the way into the building. A young man about the same age as Ryan sat behind an old-fashioned wooden desk. He looked up with a smile as they entered.

"Ryan! Long time, man." He came around and pulled Ryan in for a back-thumping hug.

"Durante. Good to see you, too."

A year was too long. He usually made it a point to come down to Bisbee a few times a year to see Durante and his family. It was a nice break from Tucson, especially since this part of his family, his Nonna's family, wasn't nearly as self-important as his grandfather's.

"Hi, I'm Durante, Ryan's—what did we decide we were?"

"Second cousins, I think. I don't know."

"It's nice to meet you," Elissa said, shaking his hand.

"Same. It's not often Ryan introduces his girlfriends. Oof." Durante rubbed the spot where Ryan had stuck his elbow in the idiot's ribs. "Keep it up, asshole, and I won't give you the keys to the jacuzzi suite."

"The suite? Really?"

"All yours. It's reserved for the weekend, but it's yours for the next two nights. Breakfast is usually from seven to ten, but if you want something before or after, help yourself. You know where the kitchen is. Just clean up after yourself."

"Awesome, man. Thanks."

Durante handed over the key. "I'd say don't do anything I wouldn't do, but we both know that's bad advice."

Ryan laughed. It was true. As much as Ryan had seemed to find trouble on his own in their teens, Durante had trouble falling on him like rain without even having to look for it.

He grasped Elissa's hand in his, cradling it as though he could crush the delicate bones under her skin. With him in the lead, they walked through the B and B and out into a courtyard. He led her past palms in pots and a tiled fountain burbling happily in the middle. On the far side of the courtyard was the other part of the house, white stucco with a terra-cotta tiled roof. Ryan unlocked the French doors with the key and held his breath.

CHAPTER 41
i don't want to sleep

They stepped into a serene oasis. If Elissa had a dream bedroom, this would be it. The cool blue walls offset the dark wood ceiling and wrought-iron chandelier. White linens did the same for the heavy, four-poster bed. A small seating area tucked into the corner invited her to sit and relax. Since she was playing hooky, she slid off the borrowed jacket and did.

Ryan joined her, a wide grin on his handsome face. He dropped the saddlebags on the ground and met her gaze. Whatever he saw there made him take her hand.

"What we do here is entirely up to you. You can curl up for a nap, or raid the library and read a book, or we can explore Downtown Bisbee. We can just snuggle tonight, no pressure whatsoever."

On the drive down, pressed against Ryan's body in forced intimacy, she'd had time to think. To overthink.

What had she done? She'd messed up one hundred percent. She'd yelled at her sister, fought with her mother. Ditched work. Her heart raced, her stomach roiled, and all her plans for the future caught like a wildfire in the middle of June.

"Hey, where'd you go?" Ryan brought her hand to his lips and placed a gentle kiss on the back. Their gazes met.

There, in the warm, comforting depths of his eyes, she found what she was looking for. Acceptance. Patience. Maybe even love, pure and unconditional. Ryan didn't care if she'd messed up. If she didn't have a job after today. If she yelled at the entire goddamned world. He was here with her now because she asked. Because she needed him.

Perhaps she should tell him how she felt. No, even better. She'd show him.

Elissa kicked off her shoes and rose out of her chair, the rug soft under her bare feet. She took two small steps to him and straddled him in his chair. It creaked under their combined weight. Framing his face in her hands, she bent down to kiss him, pressing her lips against his. It was a brief taste, but she wanted him to stop talking, stop being the good guy.

He moaned when she broke the kiss. Elissa leaned in and murmured in his ear.

"Are you saying sex is optional?"

"You're killing me." He leaned his head against the chair.

"I don't want to nap." She kissed his temple with a soft laugh. "I don't want to read." A kiss to his jaw. "I don't want to explore the town." A kiss on the corner of his mouth. "And I definitely do not want to 'just snuggle.'"

His control broke. His arms became steel bands as they wrapped around her, holding her close. His lips captured hers once more. He stood in a smooth motion and carried her to the bed, easing her onto it like she was made of something fragile. Still standing, Ryan unbuttoned her blouse, taking his time and allowing his fingers to caress the newly bared skin. Tremors of desire blazed through her body, and a heavy warmth settled low in her core.

He leaned over her, letting his mouth follow the path of his fingertips. Elissa arched her back, wanting more. His teeth nibbled at the sensitive skin above her belly button, and an incomprehensible noise emerged from her mouth. Ryan stood straight and worked on his own buttons.

"Did you like that?" His voice roughened with his need. One button.

Elissa nodded and canted her elbows to sit up. Two buttons. "I have a plan. Would you like to hear it?" Three buttons. "Yes," she whispered. Four buttons.

Elissa bit her lip as he exposed more of his chest, lightly sprinkled with dark hair. She yearned to run her hands over his firm muscles, trace the planes of his body, kiss every damn inch of him.

The last button. He shrugged the fabric off his shoulders.

"First, I'm going to kiss you, long and slow." He brushed a thumb against her lips before trailing it down to the valley between her breasts. "Then I will finish removing your shirt and toss your bra over there."

She shivered again as he pointed to the corner of the room with a wolfish smile on his face.

"After I pay homage to your beautiful breasts, I will trace a path down here with my tongue."

Ryan's fingers danced across the skin of her belly, weaving a path from the flesh under her bra to the top of her pants. He slipped a finger under the waistband and stroked the skin he found there. She nearly jumped off the bed. Every nerve ending was sweetly sensitive, every touch a day's worth of pleasure.

He licked his lips as he unbuttoned and unzipped her pants but left it at that. Ryan paused for so long, she felt compelled to ask, "Then what?"

A low, throaty chuckle greeted those words. "And then I will taste you and make you come."

She whimpered, and his smile widened. He sat down at the end of the bed, untied his boots, and kicked them toward the wall, his socks following quickly. Ryan stretched himself next to her, propping his head on a hand with some help from the many pillows piled on the bed. His gaze roamed down her body and the heat grew within her.

"Do you want to know what comes last?" His finger twined into her hair, giving a curl a tug.

Elissa couldn't find her voice, so she nodded.

"Words, please."

"What comes last?" Her voice was breathy, and her words trembled in the air between them.

He leaned close, his warmth tantalizing and teasing her. If she only would reach out, she could touch him, run her hands over him, but the anticipation had her almost paralyzed with need.

"I will bury myself in your body. It's been far too long."

She finally allowed herself to touch him, and his muscles twitched beneath her fingers. Elissa smiled as everything clicked into place. She could have this, have him, and still be Elissa. Only more.

"Yes," she said.

"Yes? Yes to what?"

"To all of it. But I have one request."

"Anything."

"I don't want to think."

"If I'm doing it right, that will not be a problem."

He covered her mouth with his and made her forget everything he told her. Each action was a new sensation, a new response. Ryan slipped her shirt off and undid her bra, tossing it right where he said he would. He cupped her breasts in his hands and brushed her nipples with his thumbs. His muscles coiled under her touch as she trailed her hands along his back. He tweaked her nipples, and the pleasure nearly crossed the line into pain. Elissa gripped his biceps hard.

He sucked gently until her grip lessened. Continuing his journey, he trailed kisses down her belly and licked a lazy line between light nips at the sensitive skin under her belly button. When he reached the edge of her panties, he looked up the length of her body, meeting her gaze.

"Are you ready?" he asked.

"No questions, no thinking," she managed to croak.

"Sorry, won't happen again."

He tugged on her pants and she lifted her ass. Ryan removed her underwear and pants in a fluid motion, dropping them off the side of the bed. He trailed a line down with his tongue, but she stopped him with a word.

"No."

Ryan stopped immediately, and his eyes met hers, a question in them.

"I want you naked, too." She grinned as wolfishly as he had earlier.

He worked his boxers and pants down over his hips, freeing his erection. She couldn't help staring as he pulled off his clothes and dropped them on the floor.

"Satisfied?"

"Not yet."

He kneeled in front of her and continued where he'd left off. Her nerves were on fire once again, every stroke of his tongue bringing her closer and closer to climax. When his tongue found her clit, she bucked against his mouth, and when he slid a finger inside her, she shattered. A kaleidoscope of colors greeted her behind her closed eyes as her muscles convulsed around his finger. Moments later, his tongue stilled, and she was finally able to form words.

"Your turn," she mumbled.

He smiled at her and rose off the floor to find the saddlebags. He pulled out a condom and smoothed it over his hard cock. Ryan climbed into the bed and between Elissa's legs. She spread them wider, and he positioned the tip of himself at her entrance.

She wrapped her legs around his waist and lifted her hips, urging him on. He buried himself inside her, filling her. With a groan, he slid his cock almost all the way out before quickly burying it deep inside again. He grabbed her leg and lifted it to his shoulder. The angle changed everything. Every stroke hit the right spot, spiraling her back up until she once again stood on the precipice of her climax.

Ryan dropped his hand between them and rubbed her clit as his rhythm stuttered. The tempo increased and his control broke. With a last stroke, they flew off the cliff together. Their moans merged into a single note and time seemed to stand still for a breathless moment.

He gently lowered her leg, then collapsed on his elbows with a satisfied grin.

"How was that? Any thinking going on in there?"

"Zero. You fucked it out of me."

"I do believe you owe the swear jar, Ms. Wright."

"Fuck the swear jar."

"Now that I can get behind."

He captured her lips with his, a fierce possessiveness to the kiss, before he rolled off her. His breathing was heavy, as was hers. She snuggled up to him, laying her head on his chest, listening as his heart slowed, and the air moved in and out of his lungs.

CHAPTER 42
BLTs in the bath

Nothing felt as right as Elissa in his arms. He'd lost control as soon as her legs had wrapped around him and owed her at least two more orgasms. She was perfect.

He'd wanted this woman from the moment she'd walked into the Sandpiper. Each interaction with her had only heightened his desire. Even now, as tired as he was, as satisfied as he was, he still wanted her.

What frightened him, however, was how much he loved her. He'd do anything for Elissa. Hell, he'd walked out of work in the middle of the day because she needed him. Him. Not his money, not his connections, not his family. Elissa had needed him. No one needed him. The thought sent his heart racing. What if he wasn't enough?

"What are you thinking?" Elissa placed a cool hand on his chest. "Your heart…"

He couldn't tell her. Could he? No, no way. If she didn't feel the same, it would destroy him. At least if he didn't admit it, he could pretend for a while longer. He kissed the top of her head.

"I gotta clean up. Don't move."

She stretched, arching her back, displaying her gorgeous tits and almost derailing his last brain cell.

"I don't think I could even if I wanted to."

Before he could give in to the urge to kiss her again, he hurried to the bathroom. There were two bottles of water, and he brought her one.

"Here, drink."

Lazily, she sat up and took the bottle from him. "Okay, Mr. Bossy."

He watched carefully as she sipped. "I have plans that require you to be well hydrated."

His stomach gurgled, and Elissa giggled.

"And it seems your stomach has other plans."

"Stupid stomach." He kissed her softly, undemandingly. She hummed beneath him, but her own stomach growled. It was his turn to laugh.

Elissa moaned and rested her head against his shoulder. "God, that's embarrassing."

"Okay, new plan. You get into a relaxing jacuzzi bath, and I'll go raid the kitchen. Bet I can find the fixing for BLTs. Want one?"

"BLTs in the bath? Sure, I'm in."

He started the bath, then dressed as Elissa slid into the water. He was tempted to join her, and his cock twitched, ready for another round.

"Not yet," he muttered.

"What's that?" Her head lolled on the edge of the tub, her eyes glassy with pleasure.

"I'll be right back. Do not fall asleep in the tub."

"You're no fun."

He slipped out into the moonlit courtyard and headed straight for the kitchen. He was right, there was leftover bacon, some thick sourdough, and lettuce and tomato. Fifteen minutes later, he returned with a plate stacked with BLTs and a couple of bananas. Elissa's head turned toward him sleepily, and the bathwater lapped her chest above her breasts. He could see the rosy tips, and all thoughts of putting his mouth on anything other than her fled.

"What?" She smiled, as though she could read his thoughts.

"I want you."

"Again?"

"Yes, again." *Always*, he didn't say.

"What about the BLTs in the bath?"

He put the plate down on the table. "Do you *want* to eat a BLT in the bath?"

She shook her head.

"What do you want, Elissa?"

She bit her lower lip and stood in the tub. "You."

In a few steps, he stood in front of her, his hand threading through the damp curls at her nape.

"I can live with that."

And he closed his mouth over hers, pulling her close. The water from her body soaked through his shirt, but he didn't care. All he cared about was holding her, kissing her, loving her.

She broke away. "You're all wet."

"So are you."

"Oh, you have no idea."

He helped her out of the tub and wrapped her in a towel. "Let's make sure you're wet in all the right ways."

"Yes, please."

Ryan led her to the bed and sat her down. He kissed her again, languidly, tasting her. He chased a drop of water down her jaw with his tongue. She shivered beneath him in the most delicious way. The drop disappeared between the valley of her breasts. With a dexterous flick of his fingers, he loosened the towel. It fell around her, putting her curves, her breasts, her body on full display.

She reached for the towel, but he caught her hand.

"No. Let me look."

He stepped away as a flush crept up her chest to her neck to land on her cheeks, highlighting her lovely little freckles. His cock, already at half-staff, hardened as he looked.

"Have I told you today how beautiful you are?" he asked.

She shook her head.

"That's a damned shame. I swear it'll never happen again. You are singularly the most beautiful woman I've ever met."

"I am not."

"Are you trying to call me a liar?"

"No—"

"Beauty is in the eye of the beholder. And what I behold is beautiful to me."

"Are you sure you're just a bartender-slash-office-manager-slash-podcaster and not a poet?"

He pulled his T-shirt over his head. "Touch yourself, beautiful, and maybe I'll answer your question."

Her flush deepened, but one hand lifted from the bed and cupped her breast. His breath caught in his throat as her thumb grazed her nipple.

"Like this?"

"Uh-huh," was all he could manage.

"Are you going to make me do this by myself, or are you going to play fair?"

He swallowed thickly and undid the button on his slacks. Her tongue darted out and licked her bottom lip as he did.

"Go lower, Elissa," he ground out.

Her eyes widened, but she trailed her fingers down her chest and over her stomach. They paused above the thatch of hair between her legs.

"I want to see it first." She bit her lip and lust flared in her eyes.

He smirked and unzipped his pants. He'd gone commando to fetch the food, and his cock sprung out as he pushed his pants down. She rewarded him by dropping her fingers to her clit. A quiet moan escaped as she rubbed a little circle.

"That's it, Elissa, good girl." He pumped his cock once, twice. He wouldn't last long.

She braced her other arm behind her and dropped her head

back, lust personified. That, he wanted to look up and see that.

Ryan moved to the nightstand, where he'd tossed a few condoms before making the sandwiches, and snagged one. She watched him through half-open eyes. He held up the condom.

"Wanna go for a ride?"

She laughed, a low, throaty thing that made his cock twitch and his heart swell. He could listen to her laugh forever. Dear god, for-fucking-ever.

Elissa nodded and he sat next to her, placing the condom in her hand. He lay back as she tore it open. Tenderly, she rolled it over his hardened length, and his hips rose of their own accord. She threw a leg over, straddling him and holding herself above his cock. Her eyes twinkled with mischief.

"Please, Elissa." He thrust his hips up.

"I like it when you beg." She circled the base with her hand, and slowly lowered herself, taking him in inch by inch, no matter how much he urged her to go quicker. No matter how his cock reached for her.

Finally, after a couple torturous moments, he was fully seated.

"Lean back, and we'll see who begs next," he growled, raising his hips.

She hissed in a breath and let out a moan. "That's so good."

Then she did as he said, bracing her hands on his thighs. His fingers found her clit and circled as his hips rose, thrusting into her. She met him, thrust for thrust, grinding down. Her fingers dug into the muscles of his thighs. He'd wear the bruises proudly.

Her voice pitched up, and her walls clamped down on him. She rode him wildly, proudly, beautifully as she broke with pleasure. It was his undoing. A last thrust, and he joined her in bliss, the world going fuzzy and golden.

Elissa collapsed on top of him, and he rolled them, slipping from her folds. He brushed her hair from her face and kissed her tenderly. She ran her fingers through his chest hair and teased his nipples.

He chuckled. "Enough of that, unless you're ready for another round."

"Mmm, not yet."

"Yet?"

Her stomach gurgled. "Hungry."

"Your wish is my command. But don't you dare get dressed. I'll be right back."

He took care of business in the bathroom, washed his hands, and grabbed the sandwiches. Elissa slipped into the bathroom to wash up and joined him in bed. It was still too long to be separated from her.

They ate BLTs in bed, washed them down with water, and Elissa grabbed a banana.

"What's up with this?" She waved it around.

"Potassium for endurance."

"Good to know." She put it on the nightstand.

Ryan squirmed down under the covers and held out his arm. "C'mere."

Elissa fit herself in the space he left her, resting her head on his chest as his arm wrapped around her. Yes, this was exactly how his life was supposed to be. His stupid job could go to hell, his trust fund could rot, and his podcast could fail, yet as long as Elissa was in his arms, life was good.

"You're awfully quiet. What's going on?" She trailed a finger along his arm. He caught it in his hand before she found his ticklish spots.

"Just thinking I'd rather hold you in my arms than go back to my job on Monday."

"What about your trust fund?"

"Lots of people don't have trust funds and do fine."

She snorted. "True. I might not *have* a job to go back to on Monday."

"You ready to talk about what happened?"

"Not really."

"I'm here whenever you're ready."

"Maybe tomorrow."

He kissed her forehead. "Okay. Get some rest."

Ryan held Elissa as her breaths slowed and her fingers stilled. When he was certain she was asleep, he kissed her forehead again.

"I love you, Elissa Wright," he whispered into her silky brown hair.

Then he allowed himself to join her in dreamland.

CHAPTER 43
answer bitch

The steady thudding of Ryan's heart lulled Elissa into a meditative state somewhere between awake and asleep. She'd never been so well fucked. Her limbs were loose, and for once, her brain was happy to revel in the tiredness of her body.

Then he whispered his confession.

She froze, praying he didn't notice she was still awake. But he settled in, and his body went lax. He was asleep and expected no answer from her, thank god.

He loved her. Holy hell, he loved *her*.

Victor was the last man to tell her he loved her. And that had ended...poorly. As expected. Because she hadn't loved him enough to put her family second.

What would Ryan demand of her? He always seemed to come in second in his own family. How would he feel if he constantly came in second to hers, too?

Her heart raced in her chest. He loved her, despite all the evidence she put her family first. Despite her tendency to overthink. Despite how she'd basically deserted him for the past few weeks, only turning up when she needed something from him.

But she hadn't needed something *from* him. She'd just needed him. They could've hung out at his place, gone for a walk, taken a moment from his busy day to reassure her that she would be fine. That she wouldn't lose her job because of their relationship. That she wasn't a horrible person because she'd fought with her sister and her mother.

Did she love Ryan? She'd thought she loved Victor. When he left, it had been a betrayal, but she hadn't been heartbroken. Not because of him, anyway. She had been more worried about her mother than about Victor abandoning her. She'd been more annoyed about moving in with her parents than she'd missed Victor.

So, she hadn't loved Victor, at least not enough.

What about Ryan? She'd been hurt and spiraling after her horrible day, and the first place she ran was to him. The only other person she'd ever taken her problems to was Jules. Elissa kept everything to herself. Her problems weren't nearly as bad as other people's. She'd grown up healthy, unlike Leo. She'd stayed out of trouble and finished college, unlike Ami. She hadn't been diagnosed with cancer, like her mom. They hadn't been rich, but they never had to go without, either. Anytime she had a problem, she was reminded it was a first-world problem. She was incredibly privileged, which meant she kept her problems to herself, solved them herself.

And then Ryan came into her life. He had money *and* problems, sharing both with his friends, with her, and he never seemed to think her problems weren't worth attention. He saw her, got her, in ways few others ever had. And she loved that about him.

She loved him.

Her racing heart stopped for a breathtaking moment.

She loved Ryan.

Oh, oh, this was worse. This was worse than thinking about what he'd said. She felt something real about him, something true, from her head to her toes, in her blood and in her bones.

Oh god, oh god, oh god.

Elissa glanced at the clock on the bedside table—ten o'clock. Jules should be off work soon. If anyone could help her stop spiraling, it was Jules.

She slid out of bed and found Ryan's shirt from earlier. It smelled like him—lemons and motor oil. Her heart rate dipped as she slipped it on. No way was she going to talk to Jules naked after a night of mind-blowing sex. She tiptoed to the saddlebags, rooted around, and found her phone.

Knowing she'd ruin the oasis Ryan had created for the two of them, Elissa turned it on.

When the three-year-old device finally loaded, she was greeted with a flurry of text messages and voicemails. At least a dozen were from Ami, and a dozen more were from her dad and her brother. There were two from Karina as well.

The top text on her screen caused her immediate concern.

Dad: Please come home

She unlocked the phone and scrolled down through the texts. The most recent text from Ami took away her breath.

A: There's been an accident. Mom in
hospital. Answer bitch

Shit, shit, shit. She glanced around the room, taking in the evidence of their passion. Of course. She'd finally found something just for her, and now the rest of her life went to shit. Her job was in jeopardy, and her mom was hurt. If she'd been there, if she hadn't let herself fall for the hottie on the motorcycle, none of this would have happened.

Somewhere along the way, she must have pissed off the fates, the gods, karma, something. She didn't deserve Ryan, didn't deserve his kindness or his understanding. She'd dropped the ball, and now her mother was suffering for it.

The words wavered under her tears. She'd have to read more later. Right now, she had to leave. Her family needed her more than Ryan did. More than she needed him. And after all, if this kind of bad luck followed her around like a sad puppy, he didn't need to face the oncoming shitstorm.

For the first time, Elissa was really, truly, utterly in love. And if this was the universe's reward for finally figuring her shit out, she didn't want to see what would happen if she told Ryan. He could be the next to end up in the hospital.

She dashed away the tears. There would be plenty of time for tears, regret, and recriminations. It was almost two hours to Tucson.

Oh god, she was going to have to wake Ryan and have him drive her all the way to Tucson. And then tell him to leave her alone.

No. She couldn't face him yet. Maybe not ever. Bisbee wasn't big, but it was the county seat. She could call a cab or see if any rideshares were available.

She opened her phone, found the app, and put in the details, setting the pickup time for twenty minutes. And someone accepted the gig.

Stuffing her emotions into the furthest corner of her mind, Elissa dressed quickly and looked in the bathroom mirror. Her makeup was on its last legs and her hair was a mess. She ran her fingers through her curls and removed the worst of the disaster on her face.

For a moment, she was tempted to wake Ryan and tell him what was going on. Beyond tempted. He'd hold her, come with her, tell her everything would be okay. And she would fail him, too. He deserved better, a clean cut rather than months of disappointment.

She found a pad of paper and a pen on the desk and wrote a note. She picked up her shoes and tiptoed to the door. As she reached for the handle, a voice stopped her.

"That's it? You weren't even going to say goodbye?"

The bedside lamp turned on. Ryan had the covers over his lap, sitting with his back to the headboard.

"I left a note."

"I deserve more than a note."

"But my mom…she's been in an accident."

"Oh, Jesus, Elissa, I'm sorry. Here, let me—" He tossed the covers aside, and she caught a glimpse of his firm ass before she turned away. The ass she'd been digging her nails into not long ago. He found his underwear and tugged it on.

"No, no, it's fine. You stay here, sleep. I've already ordered a rideshare. I'll…I'll be fine."

"Oh, so you need me when you want to stop thinking, stop feeling the bad stuff, but the moment you truly need someone in your life, someone to take care of you when you're hurting, you're gone."

"No, that's not—I don't want to bother you. You deserve better than someone who drops you the moment her family calls."

"Elissa…I have family too, and I'd be out of here in a heartbeat if one of them was in an accident. I get it. I do. Let me help."

How could he help? This was her fault. Her fault for confronting her mom. Her fault for running away. Her fault for dragging him along. He needed to stay away from her before her bad luck rubbed off. Before he learned how truly needy she was. She straightened her spine, telling herself it was for his own good.

"I don't need your help. I don't need you. Go back to sleep. I'll text you when I know more."

"You know, you don't have to be perfect to deserve love."

The certainty in his voice, the kindness, almost—almost—broke her resolve. "Maybe not, but you deserve better than me. You deserve to be someone's top priority, and I can't guarantee that. My family…it's only the five of us. You have so many, but if I lose my mom… I can't do this and take care of them. Goodbye, Ryan."

"Elissa—"

She didn't give him a chance to convince her to stay and

shut the door behind her with a click. Hurrying across the courtyard, she half expected him to come running after her, clad only in his underwear or no.

But he didn't.

Her heart lurched in her chest, and the voice in the back of her head said she was being a grade-A bonehead. She ignored both and walked barefoot across the courtyard and into the small lobby. She put her shoes on and the rideshare pulled up. It matched the picture, and the driver was a middle-aged Latina. Safe as houses.

The driver rolled down the window. "Everything okay, chica?"

"Yes—no. I'm fine, but my mom's in the hospital in Tucson."

"Okay, I'll get you there."

She settled into the back seat, refusing to watch the B and B shrink into the distance. Instead, she pulled out her phone to read all the messages. Ami's grew more unhinged, her dad's were simple, but she could hear the coolness that came over him in emergencies, and Leo's were plain emojis. Long strings of them, and she was too tired to parse out what the hell they meant. She sent a text to Ami, figuring her dad needed to focus on whatever was going on with Mom.

E: On my way.

She looked at the two from Karina.

K: Yes, take the weekend. The HR manager
is out today and tomorrow, so we'll talk
Friday and discuss with you on Monday.

The second was more personal.

K: Your father called. Get in touch with
him ASAP, there's been an emergency.
Stay safe, Elissa.

At least she hadn't ruined her personal relationship with Karina.

Elissa leaned her head against the window, watching the shadowy shrubs and trees pass in the headlights on the curvy state highway. Part of her heart lay ahead, part behind. She'd made her choice, and now she'd have to live with it.

"Hey, chica, we're here."

The rideshare driver's voice woke Elissa. She must've dozed off as they hit I-10. She rubbed her eyes and wiped the drool from the corner of her mouth.

"Thank you," she said, pulling out her phone. Only a bit past one in the morning. The driver had made great time, and Elissa added a generous tip.

"Hope your mom is okay."

Elissa got out. "Me too."

She watched the red taillights pull away and called her sister as she walked into the hospital. Ami answered on the first ring.

"Where the fuck have you been?"

"It…it doesn't matter. I'm at the hospital. Where are you?"

"Emergency waiting room. I see you."

Elissa hung up and looked around. Her sister waved frantically, and Elissa hurried over. Her brother was curled up in a chair, looking so small for a boy so tall. Her dad sat on the other side of Leo, his head in hands braced on his knees. She'd never seen her family so forlorn.

"Hi," she said, standing in front of them.

Her dad wiped away the tears brimming in his eyes.

"Hi, kiddo." He stood and encircled her with his arms.

"I'm sorry, Dad." Her voice quavered. Guilt settled in her heart, dark, heavy, and intimately familiar after the past few weeks.

He released her. "You're here now. That's what counts."

Elissa wasn't too sure but didn't have time to think as Leo uncoiled himself from his chair and hugged her tight, resting his head on top of hers.

"I'm glad you're here, Lissa. We were starting to worry about you, too."

"I'm fine. I just picked the worst day to go tech-free."

"No shit."

"Swear jar," their dad said automatically, then gave a rueful smile. "Later."

"How's Mom?" Elissa asked.

"She should be fine. She's in the recovery room, and they'll let us see her once she's settled in her room."

"Can I talk to you? Over here?" Ami didn't wait for Elissa's answer. She grabbed her arm and dragged Elissa out of listening range of Leo and their dad. "I don't know whether to hug you or hit you."

Elissa flung her hands out in a helpless gesture. "Both?"

And in an instant, her sister's arms wrapped around her. Ami's breathing was heavy, like she was trying to hold in sobs. Elissa didn't. She held her sister tight and allowed the tears to come, the tears she'd been holding back since she turned on her damn phone. After a few minutes, the crying stopped, as if they'd mutually agreed to cease. Elissa pulled away, releasing her sister.

She regretted it the next second, when Ami punched her shoulder.

"Ow. Bitch," she said.

"You deserved it, Lissa. You didn't answer your phone, and I had to take care of everything. Where have you been?"

"Tell me what happened first. Then I'll tell you where I've been."

"Fine." Ami dropped into a chair. "Mom got into an accident on her way to meet up with friends. They couldn't reach Dad—interviews for a new lab manager and his phone was off. They couldn't reach you, so the hospital called me. Dragged Dad out of his lab, brought him here, and picked up Leo from his friend's house. I kept calling and calling, and we worried something had happened to you, too. I've never been so angry and so relieved at the same time when you finally texted back. Your turn."

"Not yet. What's happening with Mom?"

"Her leg broke real good. I think the doc said a compound fracture. She also had a broken arm, but it was a normal break. They took her for surgery around nine. They came out about two hours ago to say it went well and took Dad to visit when she woke up. Just before you got here, he came back. They should be moving her soon but won't let the rest of us visit until she has her own room. That's it. That's all I've got. Your turn."

Elissa sighed. It was time to admit her failings. God, the guilt was eating at her.

"I ran away. I didn't want to be the good girl anymore, so I ran to my motorcycle-riding...I don't know what he is. My knight in shining armor? And he took me away from it all, like a prince in a fairy tale."

"About fucking time!"

It wasn't the reaction she'd expected. Anger, frustration, sadness, but not this tacit acceptance of her failure as a daughter and as a sister.

"What?"

"Listen, I'm not saying it was the best day of my life. It could've turned out to be the very worst, but what you said this morning? How I needed to step up? Well, I did, and it sucked. Now I know how you've felt all the times you've had to do the same. If you were fucking your brains out, then good for you. You deserve it after all the crap we've put you through."

Ami drew her in for another hug. Elissa's hair dampened from her sister's tears.

"Now, can you please take over? I'm so done being strong

for those two. How the fuck did you ever manage it, Lissa?" Ami broke the embrace and punched her sister's shoulder again, but softer than before.

"I pushed my feelings down deep and pretended they didn't exist."

"You know that's not healthy, right?"

"That fact is starting to dawn on me." They chuckled together, and Elissa wiped her eyes. "I've got your back, brat."

They returned to the rest of their family, arm in arm. Ami snagged a box of tissues off a table. Elissa settled herself into a chair between her father and Leo and grabbed a couple of tissues from the box Ami had purloined.

They waited but not long.

A tall woman wearing blue scrubs exited a door marked "Hospital Personnel Only" and walked straight to them. Elissa licked her lips and held her breath.

"That's one of the nurses. She came out with the doc after the surgery," Ami said.

"Dana is being taken to room 402. Mr. Wright, why don't you come with me and I'll update you on the way. The rest of you can join us in about half an hour, okay? Let your mom settle in," the nurse said.

She smiled, only a brief uptick in the sides of her mouth, and the tension surrounding her family softened.

"Thank you." Peter Wright kissed Ami on the head, patted Elissa on the shoulder, and ruffled Leo's hair. "See you in a bit."

As he walked away with the nurse, the Wright siblings collapsed into their chairs. Elissa passed around the box of tissues to dry the tears of relief.

"Lissa, I'm hungry," Leo said after a few minutes.

"Nice to meet—" Ami grinned mischievously.

"No dad jokes!" Elissa said. "Let's just feed the poor boy."

"Yeah, there's a vending machine around here somewhere."

Ami pulled their brother up and dragged him down the hall.

Elissa followed, the weight on her shoulders suddenly lessened. Her mom would be okay. She'd spent the past year worrying about cancer, but in the end, it was a stupid car accident that almost took her mom away. Something no one could predict.

Just like no one could've predicted Elissa would fall in love with Ryan DeMarco.

Oh god, she'd left him there. Didn't even tell him what she felt. Didn't let him help her. What had she been thinking? She hadn't been, obviously. And now there was no way to make it up to him.

But that was a problem for future Elissa. Now, she had a brother to feed and a mother to see.

CHAPTER 44
indelibly inscribed

R yan didn't know how long he'd been sitting in the chair, staring at the door. The air still smelled of sex and Elissa's soft powdery scent, and the covers on the bed were mussed.

He wanted a drink. Maybe ten. Maybe a whole fucking bottle of Jim Beam.

Had he imagined it all? Elissa running to him, the ride here as she clung to him, driving him nearly wild with desire, spending the evening exploring her body, making her come over and over.

No way he imagined her soft moans, his name dripping from her lips with desire. Her want, her need.

Need.

He'd believed she needed him. But she hadn't, and the only reason he knew was because he'd caught her trying to sneak out. He gripped the arm of the chair until his knuckles were white and the wood creaked ominously.

Anger replaced the shock. He'd done nothing to deserve being treated like some one-night stand, some hookup, some fuck buddy. Not when he loved her. Not when he'd bet his trust fund, and his life, that she at least cared about him. Elissa Wright wasn't the type of woman to hook up with just any man.

He had to see this fucking note. She could have more to say that she couldn't bring herself to admit out loud.

Ryan tore through the room until he noticed a scrap of

paper on the small desk, his name in her perfect penmanship. With trembling fingers, he opened it.

If it were possible for a heart to stop beating yet a human keep living, Ryan's would have. It sure as fuck felt like it. For an eternal moment, he stared at the note in his hand, his brain refusing to compute the four simple words.

I can't do this.

Do what? Sleep with him? Run away from her responsibilities? Stick around?

Love him?

Oh god, she must've heard him last night. He should've kept it to himself, buried it so far deep even he would forget. Waited until she was ready. Now he'd fucked up the one bright spot in his life. He'd pushed, though he hadn't meant to, and now she was gone.

It didn't matter if Elissa Wright was the woman he loved, the woman he was meant to be with, if she didn't believe it yet. She'd run, leaving him nothing but a broken heart.

From the moment she walked into the Sandpiper, she filled his waking moments. His dreams, too. The thought of her made his heart race, even now, as it stumbled along brokenly. The mere sight of her brought him peace. In her presence, all things were possible.

Ryan DeMarco was still in love. It would take more than this to stop him from loving Elissa. It was entirely possible he'd never stop loving her.

Fuck. And he'd let her order a rideshare and drive away. What had he been thinking?

He searched his saddlebags and found his phone, swearing under his breath as the damn face recognition didn't recognize his face. As soon as he unlocked it, he called. Straight to voicemail.

Fine.

Ryan surged to his feet, found his discarded clothes, and

dressed hurriedly. Then he tried again.

He hung up before the voicemail message finished. He had the smallest modicum of pride left. He would not beg. She'd made her choice, and he would let her go. For now. What else could he do? He didn't even know which hospital.

Run after her. Throw yourself at her feet. His subconscious was not getting the message. It would. Given enough time, he'd move on.

Don't wanna.

What he wanted to do right now was get the fuck out of here. Elissa wasn't coming back, and he couldn't stand being surrounded by her scent and the memories of the sounds she'd made as she broke apart around him. If he left now, he could shower at home and still make it to work today. Play off yesterday as food poisoning. An emergency at his apartment. Temporary insanity.

Did he care enough to?

Yeah, if not for his father's good opinion, at least to keep someone else from having to do his job as well as their own. Plus, what else was he going to do? Sit in his dark apartment and wonder what he did wrong? Call her over and over, when she'd made her feelings clear?

That wasn't his style.

It could be. She might be worth it.

Leaving a tip for housekeeping, Ryan texted his cousin that he had to leave early. He placed the saddlebags on his motorcycle and started his baby. Shit, Baby needed gas.

Ryan sped through the desert, down nearly empty highways, a man with a death wish. He stopped for gas and was off again, weaving through the light traffic.

He made it to his apartment before even the palest band of light appeared on the eastern horizon. He popped into the kitchen and flicked on the coffeepot before heading to the shower. Ryan spent fifteen minutes trying to scrub away Elissa's scent. It didn't fucking work. Somehow, the smell of her, the texture of her, the taste of her, had become indelibly inscribed onto his brain.

Ryan downed two cups of coffee, soaking up the caffeine with some toast. It was going to be a helluva day. He wove through Tucson rush hour, arriving exactly on time by some miracle.

Elissa's car was still in the parking lot.

Worry shot through him before he could quash it. Wasn't his problem. Couldn't be his problem. She'd left him.

He hurried to the front door, pulling the keys from his pocket.

"Where are you going?"

Ryan's heart raced and he nearly dropped his keys at the unexpected voice. Alex leaned against the door, wearing a suit with his arms crossed. If it were anyone else, he would call the expression on his brother's face a glower. But this was Alex's resting bitch face. As skilled a businessperson as he was, as personable as he could be, it was a mask. They might not be close, but Ryan knew how much it cost Alex to always wear the happy-go-lucky businessman face.

"Work?"

"And you still think you work here after the shit you pulled yesterday?"

Dude had a point.

"What do you say, boss? Do I still have a job after the shit I pulled?"

Wait, was that a smile on his brother's face? No, he must be imagining things. There is no way Alex would be smiling right now. Not when he got to deliver the riot act to his little brother.

"Well, since you got a bad case of food poisoning from your lunch and had to go home to get it out of your system, no one is expecting you at the office today. Which you would have found out if you'd bothered to check your voicemail."

Ryan pulled out his phone. Yep, there was a message from Alex. He read the first few lines of the transcription.

Sorry you're indisposed. Talked to Dad and we
agree you should take tomorrow off...

"Why?" Ryan asked.

"Your girlfriend needed you, and you've played nice for a couple of months. Figured I'd give you the benefit of the doubt."

"She's not my girlfriend."

"You dropped everything for her. Put your job and your trust fund at risk, just because she showed up at your workplace and asked you to get out of there. I mean, Trinity practically swooned with envy."

Ryan ran a hand over his jawline. He hadn't given any of that a single thought. Elissa needed him, and he went. It was simple.

"You have it bad, bro." Alex pushed away from the glass door and clapped a hand on Ryan's shoulder. "Go home. Whatever it is, you obviously need some rest. Come back tomorrow, and we can talk some more."

"What have you done with my brother? You're being *nice*."

"I'm always nice."

"Not to me." Ryan shoved his hands into his pockets.

"Fair. Consider this a couple decades' worth of being nice to you." Alex squeezed his shoulder gently. "You've been putting in the work, and I see how miserable this job makes you. Take the day off. We'll be fine. Go see your girl."

"She's not my girl," Ryan muttered. "She left in the middle of the night, would've left without a word if I hadn't woken up."

"That doesn't sound like Elissa."

Jealousy tore through him. What did his brother know about Elissa fucking Wright? His hands clenched at his sides. Alex looked him up and down, his eyes softening, and his lips twisted into a wry grin.

"Well, well, who would've guessed Ryan DeMarco had a heart to break? You're in love with her. Holy shit, man, I thought it was a fling. I was a bit jealous at first. From the moment you walked into the conference room the first time, I knew I had exactly a zero percent chance of ever—"

"Unless you want a fat lip, I suggest you *don't* finish that sentence."

Alex held up his hands and backed away until he was leaning on the door again. "Okay, okay, chill. So what the hell happened?"

"God, I wish I knew the whole story." Ryan's grip tightened on his helmet, and he struggled to keep his voice even. "All I know is she came in yesterday, needed to get the fuck out of here, so I took her to Bisbee. She got a call late last night—her mom was in an accident—and left."

"Of course she left, doofus. Wouldn't you?"

"Yeah, but she wouldn't let me help. She came to me yesterday, needed me yesterday, but…I dunno, when things got real, she was out of there faster than Nonna's spoon smacked our hands when we went for a cookie without permission."

Alex chuckled. No one got away with stealing Nonna's cookies.

"What do you mean, when shit got real?"

Ryan stared at his boots as the flush settled in his cheeks. "I…uh…may have told her how I feel."

"Oh, that you love her? Before or after she found out about her mom?"

"Before, but she wasn't supposed to hear."

"Dude. Duuude."

Ryan snuck a glance. Alex's eyes twinkled with amusement and he had that look, the one where he was trying really hard not to laugh his fucking ass off.

"Don't you fucking laugh."

"I would never."

"Liar."

"Okay, she obviously had a rough day. You tell her you love her, but she's not supposed to know, then she finds out her mom was in an accident. And you expect her to handle things rationally?"

Goddamn his brother for his logical conclusions. Taking all of Ryan's anger and morphing it into empathy and a little chagrin.

"Fine, you're right," Ryan muttered.

"What? Say that again."

"Fuck off."

"You should call her."

"I tried, but she didn't answer." Ryan sighed and scuffed his foot across the cement sidewalk. A rock skittered into the gravel lining the walkway, filling the silence between the brothers.

"I am no expert. Hell, my love life has only been marginally better than yours in the longevity department. But keep trying. Leave an actual fucking voicemail. Let her know you're thinking of her, you're waiting for her, you're there. It's all you can do."

"So, does this adulting shit magically appear one day, or…"

Surprise of surprises, Alex closed the distance between them with a few long strides and pulled him in for a back-thumping hug. The DeMarco men weren't exactly known for being all touchy-feely.

"I don't know, Ryan. I think we're all making it up as we go along. But I haven't ever seen you care so deeply for anyone not related to you. If she's the one, it'll work out. Give her a chance. I think she's good for you, and honestly, I think you're good for her. I like Elissa—"

Ryan shoved him away with a warning grunt.

"Not like that, dumbass. I like her because she brings out the best in you. And you wear down her sharper edges. Make her human, instead of a human calculator. Have you ever noticed how she smiles whenever you walk into a room?"

Ryan shook his head.

"Look next time," Alex said. "Trust me, you'll know exactly how she feels about you."

"I still don't understand why you're being nice to me."

"Because you're my brother, and despite our rocky history, I love you."

"Aw, you big marshmallow."

Alex slugged him in the shoulder but not hard. "Shut up, asshat. You've done okay with yourself, and you don't deserve even half the shit Mom and Dad put you through. I'm sorry I didn't stand up for you sooner. I can talk to Dad about getting you out of your stupid-ass deal. If I remember correctly, I owe you a favor for going on that blind date."

Best fucking favor ever! Ryan probably owed his brother, if he were being honest, but he was keeping that to himself for now.

"A deal's a deal, and it might serve me best in the long term, even if I hate the idea right now. But it can wait."

"Yeah, it can. Get some rest, see what you can do about your pretty accountant. I've got your back."

Ryan walked away but paused a few steps down the sidewalk. "Thanks, Alex."

A jaunty whistle was the only answer he received.

CHAPTER 45
mom, i screwed up

E lissa sat next to her mother, watching her sleep. Getting her settled and morning rounds had kept her from being able to truly rest. But the nurse had ensured the morphine was good to go and as soon as the hospital personnel left her alone, she drifted off.

At Elissa's insistence, Ami had driven Dad and Leo home to rest. Or at least a shower. When they returned, it would be her turn. She'd have Ami drop her off at DeMarco Properties to collect Bertha. Or get her towed, whatever. She really did need a new car.

"Mom, I screwed up." The words tumbled out of her. "I played hooky to be with a guy. He said he loved me. I freaked out and left. I don't think I can ever make it up to him."

Elissa dashed the tears out of her eyes. "I've been waiting for the shoe to drop. Accepted to USC, but you lost your job. No room for a music teacher when budgets were slashed. Got my CPA, and had a triple whammy—you got sick, Victor left, and Ami got in big trouble. Now, you're better and I finally fall for a guy, and you get in an accident. What am I doing that's so wrong?"

She broke, all the past losses overwhelming her soul, and dropped her head on the edge of the hospital bed. Every damn time something good happened, every time she put herself first, something bad would happen to her family. She wouldn't allow it anymore. No more taking for herself.

She had to let Ryan go. Focus only on her family until they were all okay. Then, maybe, she could have something just for her.

"I won't do it again, Mom. From now on, you all are my only priority."

"God, I hope not."

Elissa's head snapped up. Her father stood in the doorway, a travel mug of coffee in one hand and a bag of donuts in the other. He walked across the room and placed both items on a small table.

"Come here, Elissa." He held his arms wide open.

She threw herself into them, allowing their quiet strength to soothe her. When she finally quieted, he released her and handed a box of tissues to her. Elissa wiped her eyes and blew her nose before sitting again.

"Have a donut." He passed the bag as he joined her.

She grabbed whatever was on top. It tasted like sawdust, but seemed to make her dad feel better.

"Where's Leo?"

"Sleeping like a teenager up all night. Dead to the world."

"Good. He needed it."

"I always wondered what was going through your head. You keep things bottled up." He took a bite out of a powdered donut, getting a dusting of white on his dark slacks. "Your best moments often happened around some of our family's worst. But, Lissa, one didn't cause the other. The universe isn't out to get you."

"Every time something good happens, something bad follows. What would you call that?"

"That? That's life. But did you consider you're looking at it in the wrong direction?"

She shook her head. No, it was always good, then bad.

"Yes, most of the bad stuff came after the good stuff," her father said. "But we found out your mom's contract wouldn't be renewed before you went off to college, giving us time to adjust. You went to the U to begin with, which has an excellent accounting program, if I do say so myself, instead of switching halfway through. And yeah, your knucklehead boyfriend left you in the lurch, but that meant you were here when Ami needed you to bail her out."

"You knew?" Ami had talked to their parents about what happened. Had hell frozen over?

"Ami told us sometime later. She thought you ratted her out and was surprised you hadn't."

"She's an adult." Whatever else Ami was, she made her own choices and had solid reasons for them. Reasons neither Elissa nor her parents understood sometimes, but reasons. "I figured she'd tell you when she was ready. It wasn't my place to say."

"I never thanked you for that," her sister said from the door. She walked across the room and gave Elissa a quick hug.

"You paid me back, took the misdemeanor, and worked off the fine and community service. I was kind of proud of you."

"Did I ever tell you why I hit that asshole?" Ami snagged a donut from the bag their dad still held.

"I'm sure he had it coming, but no, not the exact reason."

"I caught him sneaking something into my girlfriend's glass." She waved the donut around wildly. "It got spilled in the 'altercation,' so I couldn't prove anything. And he flopped like a wuss. I didn't even hit him hard. I think he found a perverse joy in getting a lesbian in trouble."

"Aren't you bi?" Elissa's donut started to taste like something now. She took a bite and let the carbs do their dopamine work.

"I wasn't going to explain my sexuality to some asshat. As far as he knew, I was a lesbian. And I'd do it again but hit him harder." Her sister bit into her own donut, getting frosting on the corner of her mouth.

"Okay, now I'm even more proud of you." Elissa grabbed another tissue to wipe the stupid tears falling down her stupid face.

"So if you hadn't been there to pay my bail, Sabrina would've. She wasn't out yet, and her family would have found out. They're super conservative, and she would've been in big, big trouble. Instead, she was able to graduate and get the hell out of that house."

"And Victor leaving—" her dad said.

"Was a blessing. You were way too interesting for Mr. Snoozefest," Ami said.

"But Mom getting sick…" Elissa couldn't bring herself to finish the thought.

"A coincidence, Elissa." Her dad wrapped his arm around her shoulders. "You've taken your responsibilities as the oldest seriously. Too seriously. Not everything is your fault, and not everything is going to hell in a handbasket if you take some joy for yourself."

"But—"

"Enough. Being in town when this happened wouldn't have changed anything, except Ami wouldn't have had to step up. She's not the screwup we think she is."

"Thanks." Ami's voice was deadpan, but a small smile crooked up the side of her mouth.

"You can only fool us for so long, Amicaria."

"Daaad." Ami rolled her eyes at her full name.

"They're right, Liss." Her mom's voice was weak and scratchy from the intubation during surgery, but her eyes were bright. "You've done plenty. More than enough, if I'm honest."

"Let me get you some water." Elissa took a step toward the plastic pitcher, but her dad pulled her back.

"No, let *me* get her some water. Go sit."

Elissa sat, taking her mom's hand, the one with the IV, in her own. Her other arm was broken and in a cast. Her leg was in traction. She sipped at the water Dad gave her.

"You've been our blessing," her mom said.

"Hey!" Ami protested, but she was smiling.

"All of our children are blessings in their own ways, but we never had to worry about you, Elissa. You were right where you were supposed to be every time, helping with Ami or Leo, or picking up the slack." Her dad paused and shared a look with her mom.

"It wasn't fair to you." Her mom squeezed her hand. "You always acted so grown up, and I forgot sometimes you weren't. And now, well, I sometimes forget you are. Both of you. I'm sorry."

"I…I never minded, you know. I like being helpful," Elissa said.

"Bossy, you mean." Ami still wore a wry grin.

"Maybe a little." She nudged her sister's shoulder.

"But I think it's time we all learn to let go, at least a little. Give you both room to breathe." Dad pulled Ami in for a hug. "And I think the young man you ditched us for is an excellent place to start."

"Yes, you should go home, shower, and sleep, then go bang his brains out."

"Ami!" Shock had their dad's ears turning pink.

"'Bang' is not a swear word." Ami crossed her arms, a mischievous glint in her eyes. "I could've said—"

"I can't. I, uh, kinda broke up with him," Elissa said, desperate to stop the next word out of Ami's mouth.

"Why on God's green earth would you do that?" Mom asked. "That is the…."

Her heart rate monitor beeped a little faster, and Dad shot Elissa a glare before returning his attention to his wife.

"Relax, Dana. No yelling today, okay? Drink some water and let go. Elissa's got this."

Mom rolled her eyes but drank the water anyway.

"I… Well… God, I am a class-A loser. A guy whispers he loves me, thinking I'm asleep, and I freaked the fuck out."

Everyone's brows rose as Elissa swore, but for once no one brought up the damn swear jar. Good. She wasn't playing that game anymore. As soon as she had a moment, she was using all the money in her swear jar at the apartment and taking Jules out for margaritas. Or buying Ryan some "I'm sorry" flowers. Or liquor. Whatever.

"What did you do?" Ami asked.

"I told him he deserved to be someone's first priority, then ran away," Elissa mumbled as she stared at her shoes.

"You're a dumbass." Ami threw her hands up in disgust.

"I know."

"Ami, your sister is not a dumbass," their mom said. Three mouths dropped open in shock. Dana Wright *never* swore. Not once in Elissa's entire life, no matter how frustrated she got, no matter how dire the situation. "She is a grown woman who made a mistake. And what do we do when we make a mistake?"

In unison, the sisters replied. "Apologize and do what we can to make it right."

"So I think Elissa knows exactly what she needs to do." Dad sipped his coffee.

"I do. I will. But not when I smell like hospital and haven't eaten since Ryan brought me a BLT in the tub last night."

Their parents suddenly became interested in whatever the beeping machine was doing.

"Mom and Dad do not need to know your kinks, Liss." Ami grabbed her sister's hand and tugged her up and out the door. When they were out in the hall, she lowered her voice. "But I wouldn't mind hearing about this one."

Elissa shoved her away. "Shut up."

"You were right about one thing—you stink. Let's fetch Bertha, then you need to eat, shower, sleep. Don't come back until you've made things right with Mr. Wrong."

Arm in arm, the sisters walked out into the too-warm Arizona spring sun.

CHAPTER 46
showing up

A soft knock woke Ryan. He rubbed his eyes and glanced at his phone. Hell, he'd slept most of the day, passing out on the couch after a shower and some reheated leftovers. Some documentary ran on the TV, autoplay having decided he needed to watch dolphins getting busy.

Another knock sounded, slightly louder. He lumbered off the couch and stumbled to the door. His heart leaped as he opened it, and he stopped breathing for one eternity of a second.

Elissa stood on the landing, clutching a large envelope in her hands. Dark circles ringed her eyes, and she was dressed in ripped jeans and a faded T-shirt, but he would swear she never looked better.

He cleared his throat. "How's your mom?"

Elissa threw herself at him, and he caught her, holding her close and rubbing her back as she cried. Any doubts about her, about them, melted away.

"I'm sorry. I didn't mean it," she said through sobs. "I need you, Ryan, so badly it scares me."

"I know you didn't mean it. I know you're scared. I am, too."

"You are?"

"Fucking terrified. Here, come in and sit down."

He stepped back, keeping an arm around her shoulders, and guided her to the couch. She tossed the envelope on the coffee table as he settled into the corner. He pulled her onto his lap and handed her the box of tissues Iz kept on the end table.

She wiped her face clean. "Does that mean you forgive me?"

Ryan kissed her forehead. "Yes, you are forgiven a thousand times over. You thought by being the perfect daughter, the perfect sister, the perfect accountant, you could prevent bad things happening to your family."

"It sounds stupid when you say it like that."

"It's not stupid." Chuckling, he tucked a strand of hair behind her ear. "It's human. It's a good look on you, Elissa. But you still haven't answered my question. How's your mom?"

"She's going to be fine. Some broken bones, but nothing life threatening."

"Thank God." And he hugged her tighter. She relaxed into his embrace.

"I brought a peace offering." Elissa leaned away and grabbed the envelope, slightly wrinkled where she'd been clutching it like a life preserver.

"You didn't have to—"

"Yeah, I did. I emailed a friend from college who's an expert in market research. He filled in a lot of the blanks on your business plan. You can do this without your family now."

"Elissa...thank you. You didn't have to do anything to make it up to me but thank you. The only people who've ever had my back were my Nonna and Iz." He put the envelope on the table. He'd tear into it later, but this was more important. "And now you."

"I screwed up. Shouldn't you be yelling at me instead of being so nice?"

"I am always nice."

She scoffed, a cute little snort he could eat up all day long.

"Fine, maybe not, but I want the kind of relationship where you show up for someone. This is me, showing up. I freaked you out, then your mom got hurt. I was angry, but I don't know how I'd react in the same circumstances. Alex told me to give you some breathing room, and I figured he wasn't wrong."

"Your brother is pretty smart."

"Sometimes. Mostly he's a pain in the ass, but he'd say the same about me."

"It's been my experience everyone thinks their siblings are pains in the ass. I'm sorry for freaking out."

"I should have told you how I felt, right out in the open. Not whispered it like some dirty little secret. It's okay if you're not there yet—"

She shushed him with a finger over his lips.

"I'm there," she said huskily. "That's why I was so scared. I love you, Ryan."

It took a moment for his brain to catch up. He sat frozen until his body reacted. His lips crashed into hers, and he kissed her for all he was worth. He cupped the back of her head, threading his fingers through her curls as he devoured her. He licked the salt of her tears from her lips, and she opened for him with a quiet moan.

He swallowed it like ambrosia, like the finest tequila.

"I love when you make those sounds." He broke away to trail kisses down her neck. "I love the way you respond to my touch."

Ryan trailed a hand down her arm, and goosebumps followed in his wake. She arched into him. He met her gaze, watching those lake-blue eyes darken with desire.

"I love your laugh. I love your brain. I love how fiercely you love your family. There is not a single thing I don't love about you, Elissa, and it's going to take more than fear to drive me away. Okay?"

"If I agree, will you kiss me again?"

So he kissed her again. And again.

His hand slid under her shirt and traced the edge of her bra. She ground against him, rubbing against his hardening cock in his sweats. He tugged her shirt over her head and kissed over the soft swell of her breasts, tracing the lacy edge of the cups with his tongue. The sounds she made had him desperate with desire. Her head fell back and—

Knock, knock, knock

He'd know that knock anywhere. Loud enough to gain someone's attention, all business. Fuck.

"It's my dad," he muttered.

"Can we ignore him?" Elissa rubbed against him again, and he was so tempted. So, so tempted.

"I'm supposed to be sick. Food poisoning."

"Oh, poor baby." She smiled and trailed a finger over his lips, then slid off his lap. "I'll go hide. Bathroom?"

Elissa slipped her shirt on and turned away. Ryan grasped her arm.

"No. You should stick around for this."

"I-I don't want to get you in trouble."

Knock, knock, knock.

"It's fine. I'm tired of pretending to be something I'm not. You might be the perfect daughter, but I am far from the perfect son, and pretending I could ever be is killing me."

Before she could answer, he strode to the door and yanked it open.

"Hi, Dad. We were just talking about you. Won't you come in?"

Thrusting a plastic container at Ryan, Alessandro walked in, still dressed for work. "Your mother wanted me to drop off this soup after work—"

He spotted Elissa, and the slightly irritated expression he'd worn morphed into outrage. His brows drew down and his cheeks reddened.

"What the hell is going on here? You're supposed to be sick."

"I've been dating your accountant."

Elissa wiggled her fingers at his father, but didn't make eye contact, staring at a point over his father's shoulder.

"Hello, Mr. DeMarco."

"You lied to your brother and took the day off to screw—"

"Watch the next words out of your mouth." Ryan's voice was cold and calm. His dad's gaze zeroed in on him. "I will not have you disrespect the woman I love."

"What the fuck do you know about love? You've fucked every woman who would have you. She's after your money, like all the rest." His piercing gaze found Elissa. "He'll never see a cent."

"I don't care about his trust fund," she said from next to Ryan, threading her fingers through his. He had been so focused on his father, he hadn't noticed her approach. "I care about him."

The contrast between his father and Elissa was remarkable. He was mostly muscle softening a bit with age. The world revolved around him, and he acted accordingly. Elissa was barefoot in her jeans and—oops—inside-out T-shirt, tiny but fierce in her defense of Ryan, shaking the envelope at his father. Ryan himself had never stood up to his father this way.

"I will be informing your employer—"

"No need. I told Karina yesterday, and she is waiting for the HR director to return tomorrow. I'm sure appropriate disciplinary action will be taken."

"You're a smart woman. You think you love him now, what about in ten years, when he's still clueless, still foolish, still lazy?"

Elissa released Ryan's hand and focused on Alessandro like an asteroid ready to end civilization as he knew it, face set in a stubborn frown. She poked him.

She actually poked his father.

The man looked so taken aback someone had dared laid a finger on him that Ryan had to hold in a bark of laughter.

"You don't know your son at all," she said.

"And after what, two months, you do?"

She glanced at Ryan, her stubborn frown softening, and she

winked.

"Better than you. He knows exactly what he wants to do with his life, you just don't think it's worthwhile. But I've run the numbers, and he can make it work financially, with or without his trust fund. Even if he can't, he's miserable in your office. He'll be better off as a bartender, or almost anything else."

Disgust crossed his father's face. "You're a—"

That was enough. Another word and he'd sucker punch his own father.

"We're done here, Dad," Ryan said. "If nothing I do will ever be good enough, if who I date will never be good enough, I don't want the money anymore. The only thing DeMarco money has bought is my education and the tools I need to do what I want. I don't need it anymore, and I don't need you controlling my life. Consider this my resignation. I'll have it in writing first thing and will work until you find a replacement, but I'm done. Deal's off."

"We are *not* done!"

Elissa put the hand clenching the envelope flat on his father's chest and slowly, inexorably, pushed. "Yes, you are done. Come back when you have calmed down. And read the goddamned business plan."

His dad took a step back.

"Goodnight, Dad."

Muttering to himself, Alessandro snatched the envelope from Elissa and slammed the door on his way out.

"That won't be the last time we have to deal with his bullshit." Ryan threw the deadbolt.

"Family. Can't live with them, can't live without them. I'll print you another copy of the plan—it truly is a thing of beauty now."

She wrapped her arms around his waist and rested her head against his chest.

"I don't think I've ever seen anyone stand up to my father

like that."

She shrugged, which was cute. "You deserve better."

"I have better."

He lifted her chin with a finger and kissed her, lingering on her soft lips, relishing her gentle scent. She hummed as he broke away.

"Don't stop."

Ryan walked her backward until her back hit the door. "You like that?"

"Yes. More please."

"Well, since you asked so nicely."

And he kissed her again. Deeper this time, claiming her, letting her claim him. He never wanted to stop.

He left her mouth and trailed his lips over her jaw and down her neck.

"When does…Iz get home?"

Her words were breathless, and her hands threaded through his hair, driving him wild. He chuckled.

"We've got time."

"Time for what?"

"Oh, you know what."

He picked her up by the waist and slung her over his shoulder. She squealed and pounded feebly on his back as he carried her to his bedroom.

They had all the time in the world for whatever they wanted to do. And he was going to love every moment with her.

EPILOGUE
two years later

"And that's a wrap on my first AMA episode of *A Drink in Time*. I can't believe it's been two years and twenty-five episodes!"

Elissa sat in the corner of the mostly soundproofed office in their apartment. The purple velvet chair she insisted on getting shortly after they moved in together last year was comfy and helped absorb even more sound. She loved watching Ryan record when she had a chance.

JMS Accounting kept her busy. She would be taking over for Karina next tax season, with the obvious exception of DeMarco Property Management by mutual agreement. The fallout from two years ago hadn't been nearly as bad as she feared—an apology to the boards of both companies and a warning in her personnel file.

"Thanks for listening to me ramble about the weird intersection of food, drink, and history. I hope you've learned something, I hope I made you laugh a time or two. And I have some good news."

He glanced over at Elissa and winked before returning to his script.

"With your support and the money I've saved up, I'm going full time. That's right, after a much needed break, you're gonna get twice the episodes. *A Drink in Time* is going bi-weekly as of May first. And who knows? Once I set some new systems in place, I could go weekly."

He'd worked so damned hard the past two years, pulling shifts at Nopalitos five or six nights a week and putting in at least half-time hours on this podcast. His father had kept to their deal, and Ryan hadn't seen a penny of his trust fund. It had been slow going, and now his dream was about to become reality. Elissa was so proud of him, of what he'd built.

She helped where she could, especially with the accounting. A little with helping to run various numbers to see which patronage platform would suit the best, making heads and tails of the various ways to monetize. Iz threw in marketing materials whenever they had a few moments. Even Alex contributed— mostly the expensive bottles of booze or pricey foods for some of the episodes.

"Though I am truly, deeply grateful for every single one of my listeners, there is one particular supporter without whom this podcast never would have seen the success it has. She crafted my business plan, held my hand as I figured out the marketing, and files my freaking taxes every year. Elissa doesn't like the limelight, but I am not going to miss this opportunity to give her a shout out."

The heat rose in her cheeks, and she studied her toes. Nobody was even watching, they were alone in the apartment. Iz, Alex, Jules, and a few of the DeMarco cousins were coming over in a couple of hours for a celebration. There was chili in the Crock-Pot, beer in the fridge, and Jules was bringing a cake.

"I have to tell you, whatever you believe in—fate, karma, God, Aphrodite, the general universe—it was smiling on me a little over two years ago when she walked into the Sandpiper looking for another man. Long story, maybe I'll share it the next AMA. And I'd be a fool if I didn't make it permanent. So, Elissa Wright, will you marry me?"

Wait, what?

Her head snapped up—Ryan set aside the headset and spun

around in his chair. He pulled a small box from his pocket and got down on one knee. Nestled in the black velvet was a simple white gold diamond solitaire. Next to it was a matching band with engraved butterflies.

"What do you say, Elissa, will you marry me? If the answer is no, I'm gonna have to re-record that last bit."

She threw herself at him, knocking him to the floor, and straddled his hips.

"Yes, I will absolutely marry you."

She kissed him. She loved how their kisses still drove them both wild. She loved how his body reacted to her. She loved how safe he made her feel, safe enough to take these risks together. She loved Ryan DeMarco, and she was not going to turn down the opportunity to spend the rest of her life with him.

He flipped them over and kissed her right back. He slipped the diamond ring on her finger.

"Good. Will you say it on the mic?"

She pushed him off and scrambled for the headset, then pushed record.

"I said yes!" She hit stop and dropped the headset. "Now, where were we?"

Elissa grabbed his shirt and pulled him close. He threaded his fingers through her hair and tilted up her chin, staring into her eyes. His soft brown eyes gleamed with forever.

"I think we were right about here."

Ryan kissed her again, soft and slow, and Elissa had everything she needed in her arms.

the end

For a collection of Ryan's and Elissa's core memories, join my newsletter at EmilyMichelAuthor.com/Newsletter

ACKNOWLEDGMENTS

Back in the winter of 2018/19, around the time I published my first book, I read a BuzzFeed listicle, as one does from time to time. This one was bad first dates. It had been a long time since I'd been on a first date (at the time of *The Right Mr. Wrong*'s publication, my husband and I are approaching our 25th anniversary), and the vicarious cringe was lovely.

And then one particular entry caught my imagination. Some dude wrote that he'd been on a blind date once upon a time. A woman showed up, ate and drank, never saying a single word to him, then left. Later, he found out—it had been the wrong person!

I wish I could properly cite it, but by the time I realized I had a story idea, I couldn't find the list and give credit. Enough details changed that I don't feel like I'm borrowing whole cloth from someone's life, merely took the idea of "what if you had a blind date with the wrong person?" and ran full out with it.

This story was drafted as I was prepping my last book in the Magic and Monsters Trilogy for publication back in the fall of 2019, making it the fourth book I ever wrote. I finished it up in time for the November writing challenge that year, which I had another, completely different idea for. As it's best practice for me to let manuscripts rest for a bit, I figured once December hit, I could pick up this rom-com and start editing.

And I tried. So, so hard. But it wasn't working, and I wasn't sure why. I switched manuscripts, the pandemic hit, and I became distracted by all the other shiny ideas. Fast forward five

(five!) years, and I had completed all the other series, and once again, this story wouldn't leave me the fuck alone. So I finished it. I finished it good.

All this time later, I was more in tune with my author voice and had found writing and editing tools that worked well for me.

Thanks to the OP, whoever you are. I'm sorry you had a crappy first date, but I'll be forever grateful you shared it with the world.

Thanks to Emilia Abraham for always talking about cake in her books. Chapter 31 is for you.

Thanks to my beta readers: Liz, Dan, and Kelly Scriven. Thanks as always to Editor Supreme, Gail Delaney. Lee Hyat designed my wonderful cover. I won it at an auction benefitting organizations helping in the aftermath of Hurricane Helene in Western North Carolina. Lee is good people and does some lovely work for contemporary fiction.

I ran a contest in my newsletter to rename the dad after I forgot to replace the placeholder name. Melissa was the winner, and she liked Peter.

Much thanks to my family for their support and love. Now that the kids are grown, we've become good at sharing various household tasks, like cooking and cleaning, giving me a bit more time to do my thing. Watching these two grow up into kind, funny adults has been my life's joy. And having my husband by my side has been a true gift.

And as always, my deep and endless gratitude for my readers. Y'all rock.

ALSO BY EMILY MICHEL

Magic & Monsters Series
A widowed witch doesn't need anyone to save her from the
monsters, but one hardened hunter can't let her face them
alone.
Witch Hazel & Wolfsbane
Devil's Claw & Moonstone
Brimstone & Silver

The Memory Duology
How far will Hell's top assassin go to save the angel he was sent
to kill?
A Memory of Wings
A Redemption of Wings

The Lorean Tales
A series of gender-flipped fairy tale retellings for adults.
Blood Magic and Brandy
(Snow White)
Dragons, Briars and Blades
(Sleeping Beauty)
Midnight and Silvered Glass
(Cinderella)

ABOUT THE AUTHOR

Emily Michel spends most days reading, writing, and editing. She has a patient, supportive husband and two grown kids. When not neck-deep in the indie publishing trenches, she pets her feline overlords and crochets. Just don't ask how many book sleeves are in the tote. Just…don't.

Socially awkward and extremely introverted, she nevertheless participates in social media. Check out @EmiMiWriter on TikTok, Instagram, BlueSky, and YouTube. If you want to be the first to know release dates, cover reveals, and sales, sign up for her newsletter at EmilyMichelAuthor.com. There are several short stories available for free when you sign up, and each monthly newsletter includes a cat picture. For overlords, they're incredibly cute.

www.ingramcontent.com/pod-product-compliance
Lightning Source LLC
Chambersburg PA
CBHW020404260626
47156CB00007B/2223